GATEWAY TO K.

By

FRYN HAWKWEAVER

For Aethelflaed

'Lady of the Mercians'

The descendant of Thrydwulf-son-of-Ceolwulf?
One would like to think so.

Forward.

Kubenial, gowned in a burgundy robe—decorated with strips of many-colored opals—was naked save for the soft, amber-tinged sandals upon his feet. Pearly hair tumbled down about his shoulders, and he gazed forlornly out of the window of his marble tower. Far off, Kraghir circled tirelessly, the eagle's high-pitched cries shrilling upon the delicate wind. Below the high clouds, the lush Isle of Etmoran flourished, a paradise filled with ghosts redeemed from the sins of Kazhelma. Crystal waters ran like threads of silver, down from the mountains to the sparkling seas, wild in their fury, timeless, brisk and unforgiving.

The God wandered across the unblemished floor of gold and sat at a rectangular table. Upon it lay a map of the lands and the world he presided over. He stood, glancing at the biological movements of life—infinitesimal fleas on a gargantuan field of grass. For a thousand millennia, he'd been without her: Shakniran, the divine Goddess of the stars. She had formed into a planetoid and shattered into a billion shards of light. Why? Kubenial had tempted the Goddess from her orbit around the suns, and Tahfevnaree—her father—had punished her for her disobedience.

God—Kubenial—hung his head and wept. Each tear fell like molasses dripping from a finger; where it landed, a new rift hole appeared, impinging on parallel worlds and universes. As the tears eventually dried, the holes would reseal and vanish.

His children, demigods, the Galrandir, had morphed into light and darkness. Halxerizan, the darkness, had forged a magical net to aid him in his fight against his brother. Auknar, of the light, had wrought an enchanted sword to challenge his sibling. Knowing that his father, Kubenial, would send him into the void if he undertook the slaying of Halxerizan, he used the temporal passages evoked by Kubenial's tears, drawing in beings to use the sword as a prophecy, immersing himself in their essence, knowing that those born outside of the reality of the world,

Kazhelma, could be used to that end and destroy his brother and have him taken beyond the void, so light could prevail. Auknar chose many from a multitude of worlds. Only one lived long enough to achieve the goal: Thrydwulf-son-of-Ceolwulf, an earthling…

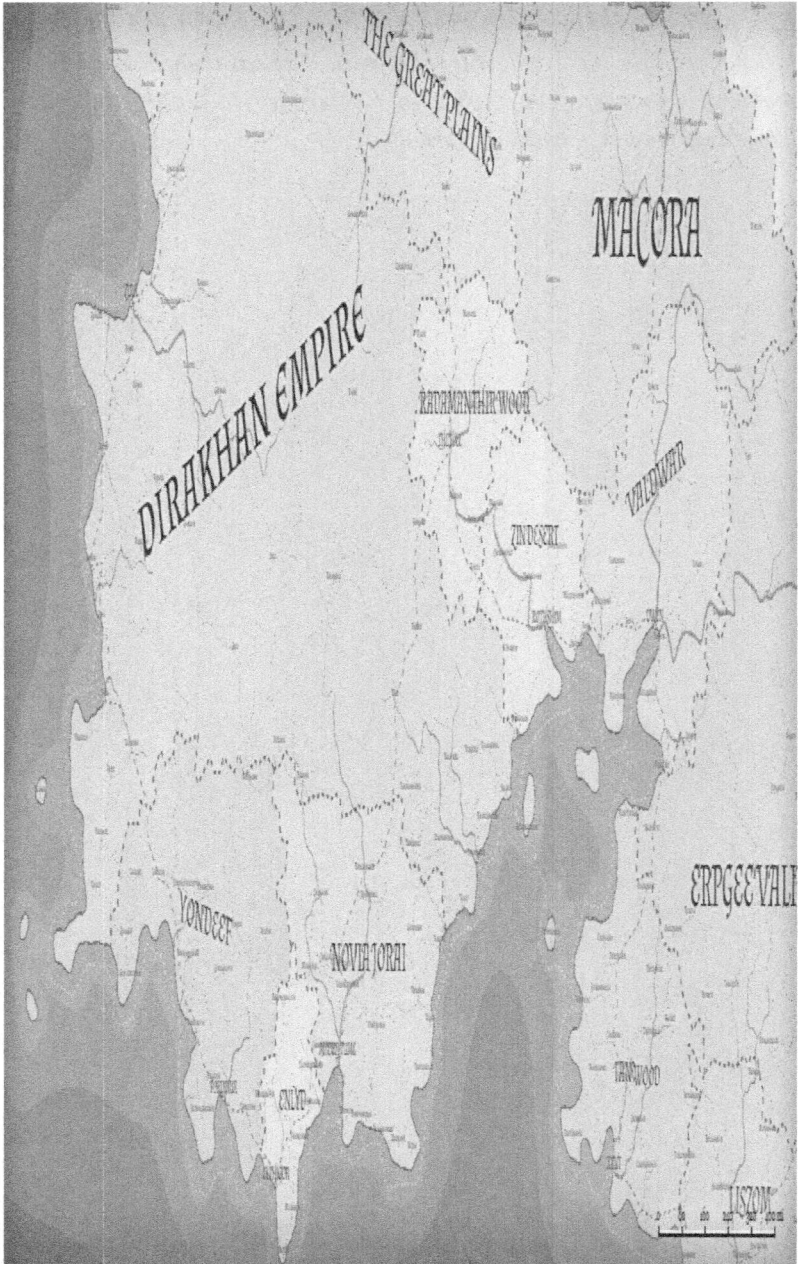

CHAPTERS

Chapter 1

THE WOLVES
(Britain, Southern England. 5th Century AD)

Thrydwulf scratched at the lice in his lank hair, blood stained his mud-encrusted fingernails.

"I heard the wolves again last night," he said.

Cynwise, his frail mother stirred stew in an iron cauldron, the savory aroma and curling smoke wafting across the hut.

"What did they scavenge this time?"

"The geese," he told her, buckling a belt around his green tunic.

"Bar the door shut, so fowl don't wander into the mouths of hungry wolves. You will eat before you leave." Turning, she pushed a bowl of piping hot sustenance into his grasp, spilling a smidgen of it down her orange dress. "Have you forgotten that it is a holy month?"

"The Gerst Monath," sighed the youth. "Hunwald has been lesson-preaching again."

"Then go to Caelin. It is not wise to disrespect a revered elder. Help them to labor in the last of the crop. He favors you," she said, rubbing at the slops on her garb.

"I'm the son of a *ceorl*," the youth objected. "*That* kind of work is for slaves. I'm not a farmer; I'm a pole lather."

Easily angered, the woman's eyes narrowed to a penetrating stare. Yet for all the tricks and traits that were *Cynwise-wife-of-Ceolwulf*, he forgave the widow. They were both sensitive and stubborn into the bargain.

"Do not test me, boy," she scolded.

Cynwise buckled, collapsing like a sack of broken bones.

Dropping the steaming bowl, Thrydwulf careened across the space between them, reaching down, taking her emaciated shoulders into his callused hands. She coughed violently, coating her garment with phlegm and blood. The youth wiped it away with a damp rag, tenderly stroking her raven plaits. Half-dragging her flea-ridden body across the shelter, he laid the woman down upon the sickbed of moss and deer hides.

"Of course, you are the son of a freeman," she said softly.

Thrydwulf gazed down into her eyes of peacock blue.

"Your blood is Germanic," she told him. "From the tribes of the north, by the sea."

Light shone through the pig bladder, veiling the small window. Heaving, Cynwise turned her gaze away; then the widow reached out, gripping the Saxon knot of his hair.

"Your grandfather aided Rome," she whispered with a stale breath. "He bled with Aetius at the Catalunian Plains. You are the son of warriors!" With that utterance, the strength drained from Cynwise, and she let her grip fall. "Warriors," she insisted. "Not farmers."

Life had tallied forty-two winters since that first breath in the weaver's hut. Swaddled in goatskin and linen, she had screamed pitifully against the cold. Now, every joint plagued her with arthritic torment. Five years had passed since Ceolwulf's body had been laid into the clay. Cynwise felt incomplete without him. She succumbed to sleep, a feeble imitation of the hardy figure that had clawed amongst the oats and barley the year before.

Thrydwulf palmed the beads of sweat from her brow. "Do not fear," he said, benevolently. "I will gather the harvest." He rose to his leather shoes, leaving Cynwise gently snoring in the hut.

***

Daegmund and Dhelweard raced across the meadow, scattering the cattle as they ran. Each bark was a frosted breath that shook the December air. Thrydwulf called the hounds by name, and they came to heel beside him. Pacing over the hard turf, crushing knapweed and clover underfoot, he gripped a long-hafted spear, using the weapon to aid his gait across the terrain. At the gap in the hedgerow, farther down the meadow, Aeva had arrived. The dogs caught her scent. Their muzzles raised high; they sniffed with enthusiasm at the crisp morning

3

air. And Thrydwulf, sensing that Woden himself could not have curbed their curiosity, bade them to fly. Off they ran, scampering towards the figure approaching from the mud road.

"They're exhausted!" Aeva said with a quibble. She crouched beside Daegmund and coddled the hound. "*Struggles* can appear with age," Thrydwulf told the maiden, reiterating an old man's words he had heard in the village. He fought to constrain his sexual excitement.

The young woman smelled of the forest, of nineteen cruel-wintered, sun-beaten years. Three autumns older than him. The fringe of her mousy brown hair beetled beyond the peak of her hooded shawl. Her tunic of blue linen was clasped at the shoulders with bronze fylfot broaches. Aeva, briefly, slid a hand inside her underdress, scratching the itch at her breast, tugging down the fabric to expose her skin and bosom. Thrydwulf's manhood stiffened, and she broke into a grin.

"Tonight, we'll see how accomplished you are with that stick of yours," she teased. Thrydwulf plunged the iron head of his spear into the dirt, spinning on her with a sardonic smile. "Why wait until dark?" he quipped back.

Aeva giggled, pointing at the aroused youth with her finger. "You'll plow no deep furrow with *that* measly thing," she taunted.

Suddenly, she shivered, breathless and aroused. As the youth lunged at her tunic, Aeva screamed and cavorted away. "You must help them bring in the last of the crops!" she spat over her shoulder. "If not for Cynwise or my father, then do it for me!"

The hounds yapped relentlessly at Thrydwulf 's heels as he raced after her, across the wet meadow.

The four collided in a heap upon the icy ground. Daegmund yelped, pouncing away as Thrydwulf playfully yanked his tail. In a moment, he was kneeling astride the maiden, pinning her blue sleeves against the frost.

"You were saying?" he said, between labored breaths. "About the stick?"

"Not here," she beseeched him; the maiden was wet and exhilarated. "What if my father comes looking for us?"

"We have time!" he pleaded.

Like an ill omen, a distant voice called out; its austere tone floated menacingly upon the wind.

"Get off me, you *dwæs!* He will punish me severely, but *you,* he will cut from crotch to throat!"

In panic, the lovers found their feet, and not a moment too soon. Back on the crest of the hill stood Hunwald, a bull of a man; he gazed at them, holding Thrydwulf's spear between his hands.

"Go to him. He is waiting," she admonished. Thrydwulf looked up and waved at the distant figure.

"Later, then," he gulped. "Once the celebrations have begun. It's been seven moons since we last laid together." He strode off. The hounds chanced their paws to follow, but Aeva barked a command. They turned, trotting in her wake. "And keep up! " She bade them, her voice full of irritation.

"Swiftly, boy!" Hunwald bellowed, "Caelin's men are sweating their acorns off. Have been since daybreak." He plunged the iron spearhead into the dirt. "I don't know why you brought *this*..." He gestured at the weapon, jabbing it with his finger. "Today of all days." He grunted in amusement, wrapping a brawny arm around the youth's shoulder, its great bulk as ponderous as a piglet boar heaved in from the hunt.

5

From crotch to throat!

The words replayed in the youth's head, his eyes darting from side to side, imagining the grisly possibility.

"You're shivering, boy, " Hunwald remarked. "Are you catching a chill?"

"I think I am," Thrydwulf uttered with a lie. "About the spear…"

"The wolves. Last night," the storyteller chimed in. "You heard them too? You did well not to unleash the hounds. They'd be no match for a pack of hungry wolves. Aeva tells me you lost some geese?"

"Four," the young man confessed.

"Four!" Hunwald's eyebrows knitted in contemplation. "Come," he groaned. "Let's not dwell on the matter. Caelin is already peeved."

***

Fields of arable crops, all green and tinctured gold, swept across the rolling landscape. Poplar trees, enormous in size, dotted the far-flung slopes. It was here that the last quarter acre of barley was being harvested, generating a pleasant, earthy odor, and slaves strained every nerve, working away with scythes in a rhythmic motion, whilst Caelin supervised others raking back the yellowed grass, tethering it into manageable bundles.

"Look how they are wedded to their labor," uttered Thrydwulf, bemused. "Caelin barks orders like a determined ox!"

The giant let out a booming roar of laughter. "And walks like a castrated one." Realizing what had slipped from his tongue, his demeanor became serious. "But don't tell him I

6

said it was so." Suddenly, Hunwald beamed from ear to ear. "The work should be done come sundown... methinks."

The sun cast extended shadows that crept across the terrain like cloaks of mourning; yet still the bondsmen had not ceased in their endeavors, even as the rain clouds mustered, leaving them freezing and soaked to the skin. By late afternoon, the crop was harvested, and Caelin grinned with blackened teeth.

"The eve celebration will be worth its salt," he told them. He surveyed the field from the hazel hedge to the adjacent boundaries. Satisfied, the weight on his mind lifted, and a crooked smirk formed upon his wrinkled face. "Just the wagonage now!" he bellowed at the exhausted serfs.

Two hours later, the laden drays began to move. "Don't just stand there, boy," snapped Hunwald. "The task of stowage is to be undertaken. Then it's to the hall for horns of mead aplenty."

At long last, Thrydwulf and Hunwald paced behind the rearmost of the rolling carts, making their way towards the village.

As sunset dipped below the woodland, splashing the sky with a shade of puce and honey, they laid the last of the crops into storage.

***

"'Tis as if the next village is ablaze," Aeva said wistfully. Hunwald agreed. He perched at his daughter's side, reeking of the day's labor.

"Tell me of Cynwise," he said, gently. "The sickness plagues her?"

Aeva took hold of her father's hand, squeezing it. "I dare not tell Thrydwulf, but I fear she will not survive another

7

winter." As she dropped her head, Hunwald lifted her chin with two thick fingers.

"You can do no more, child," he counseled. As she began to rock with tears, the giant pulled her into an embrace. "It's been twenty-eight years since I rowed here with Horsa and Hengest from the Motherland."

He recalled the beaching boats, their tall sails billowing in the freezing wind; the memory wafted away like a plume of smoke.

"Let us enjoy the feast," said Hunwald. "By the gods, we have earned it."

The glow of the flickering fire bathed the interior of the Main Hall. The riddle-saying echoed within its confines. Children daringly poked long twigs of wych elm and hawthorn into the crackling flames at the center of the lodge. Black-skinned piglets had been roasted and served as acrid smoke choked the fusty air. Ale flowed freely, and the merrymaking was contagious.

Wictred the Minstrel had his lyre thrust into his hands. Worse for wear, he climbed unsteadily upon his haunches, strummed a discordant phrase, and staggered, tumbling over a sleeping mutt. He lay there in an inebriated stupor as laughter levitated to the thatched rafters. The hours crawled by. The fire shrank, and the mood was one of drunken contentedness. Youngsters slept on the hides where they dropped, and the room stank of smoke and unwashed bodies. Some of the men were sprawled upon the tables, snoring to the annoyance of their nagging spouses.

From the nearby woodland, the raspy waoak of a short-eared owl began to haunt the night wind.

Hunwald stood, rapping his knuckles upon a table, demanding the attention of those whose faculties had not yet completely deserted them. Dramatically, he raised his arms, casting capricious shadows upon the wattled walls. In a theatrical pose, the giant tossed his gaze to the wooden girders, his mouth babbling an archaic German prayer. Suddenly, his eye fell upon one of the discarded corn dollies dumped beside a sleeping girl. This lit the spark. "Oh, great Earth Mother!" he began. "The Roman, Tacitus, reminds us of the sacred Frisian Islands! Of the ox-drawn cart! The painted image! Where one priest alone could bear witness to casting aside the iron weaponry, and the cladding of festive gowns! Of you, Nerthus! Of the bathing rite and the sacrificing of slaves!" Caelin— Saxon Lord and serf owner—tossed Hunwald an icy glance. "But those times may soon belong to our past!" he added abruptly, attempting to smother the unfortunate blunder. He spoke of the dragon Nidhogg that lived at the root of the World Tree, of Ratatosk, its squirrel messenger charged with delivering insults to the eagle at its crown, of Niflheim, deepest of the nine worlds of its utter darkness and freezing mists. Finally, he spoke of Ragnarok, the last great battle at the end of days. All at once, beyond the sanctuary of the hall, like beasts being summoned by a sinister prayer, the howling of wolves split the night asunder. The storyteller froze mid-tale as Thrydwulf and Aeva spilled in through the doorway. "They're attacking the cattle!" Aeva shrieked hysterically. Like a listless dragon waking from a sleep of sorcery, the congregation began to stir.

"To the weapons!" roared Caelin.

He lunged to his feet, clawing the pattern-welded blade from its tethering upon the wall. Hunwald threw back his russet cloak, seizing a long spear from the corner of the hall.

"Damn it, man!" cried Caelin. "Come on!" Brushing past the giant, he strode out into the night.

A woman ran to Hunwald's side, gripping him with white knuckles. "Where is our son?" she asked. Imploringly, she peered at Thrydwulf. "We thought Oeric was with *you*," he said in panic. Aeva watched the tears well up in her mother's eyes and slide like glaciers of ice across her cheeks. Thrydwulf bowed his head in shame. He wanted to reach out and tug the woman to his chest. "We didn't know," was all he could muster. "I will find him," said Hunwald. "The wolves are too far off to have taken the boy."

Even as he uttered the words, he doubted their validity.

His green eyes darted to the figure wrapped in pelts, restless before the fire. "Cynwise needs you."

The woman nodded obediently and wandered away to fill a clay pot with water.

"I need to help," Aeva said angrily. The big man glowered down, briefly, only to ensconce his dark thoughts beneath a shroud of concealment. "You will stay here with the other women."

Knowing her objections would be futile, the maiden turned and stormed away.

Hunwald clamped Thrydwulf's shoulder with an iron hand. "Fetch your spear. You may need it now."

Not so hard!
The blond boy grinned with victory and poked the girl once more with the makeshift sword. In reflex, she snatched at the blade of polished hickory, yanking it from his grasp. Then she thwacked the youngster vigorously across the rump. Hurts, does it not? She cast the sword away into the mud with a defiant frown.

10

Aeva remembered the moment and wept. She saw the red-burning torches, splaying out as the men ran toward the deep shadow of the woodland. Above the trees, a nimbus moon splashed the floating clouds. The muffled din of the hunting dogs carried on the wind, and once more the maiden sobbed in her helplessness.

The wolves had torn one of the cattle limb from limb. The smell was unnervingly sweet and pungent. Blood saturated the green swathe where it lay. "There is another one over here!" Caelin yelled. He pushed his flaming torch into the air, bathing the carnage with crimson light. "But no sign of the boy!" he conceded.

At the edge of the woodland, spots of reddish gold twinkled upon the blackness. The sporadic cries of Oeric's name echoed through the ancient trees. A sudden thought came to Hunwald as he ran: even if the boy was injured, he could not respond because of his affliction.

Thrydwulf appeared, suddenly, out of the darkness. Drenched in sweat, he gulped at the air like an exhausted plow-horse. "I found this!" He stuttered. He held up a smooth sword of gnawed hickory. Hunwald snatched the object from Thrydwulf's grasp. "Where?" Hunwald demanded.

The youth pointed back towards the woodland. "Not far from Cula's Ford. I told Caelin's men; they're on the trail."

The distant specks of glimmering torchlight vanished in the blackness. Without a word, Hunwald sprang away.

Thrydwulf coughed and gazed at Caelin with imploring eyes. "The boy is alive," Caelin said.

Thrydwulf was not convinced.

The old man swiped his burning torch through the air in an arc. "Look about you. The pack is fed. They'll have little need for human flesh tonight."

11

"You cannot know that for sure," Thrydwulf argued, forgetting his place, but he was undaunted.

"What if they crossed his path before they reached the meadow here?"

Caelin glared at the youth. "We wouldn't be deprived of our livestock. Come. If any can find him, it will be the dogs."

Oeric scampered through woodland, elusive, whilst the baying wolves circled the timberline. Whether the pack had caught wind of his scent, he could only guess. Flight or certain death were the only options.

Every flexed muscle burned with exertion, each whipping bush a blade that slashed a stinging wound upon the flesh; only the silent moon bore witness.

His green tunic snagged at every opportunity as if plucked by imperceptible hands. The more ground he covered, the closer the howling seemed to be. The frigid air rasped in his lungs. He stumbled and fell, instinctively tugging at his belt, reaching for the toy sword Thrydwulf had turned so deftly on the village lathe. It was gone. The wolves were closer. He clambered to his shoes and fled—already half-drenched— across the cold stream. Up the steeper bank, the boy hastened, past the gaunt alder trees, eyes wide, staring like a hunted fox. For a credulous moment, he tarried to look, and in that heartbeat of squandered time, his attuned ears detected the splash of paws upon water; they were following in his wake. He sensed their urgency, and this in turn fed his own.

Onward! ONWARD!!

A roe deer, discovering itself embroiled in the drama, flitted like a ghost through the hawthorn glade, its fawn coat caressed by the moon as it groped amongst the trees. A woodlark, or a hawfinch, he would never know which, truanted its perch, flapping furiously away above the leaves. Then, before him on the earth, there was a hole. He crawled in with the cold dirt rolling down his neck. In a heartbeat, the wolves were at the entrance, snapping at his heels, fighting among themselves for possession of the prize. Oeric screamed and dragged himself on. Suddenly, he experienced a peculiar crackle of energy; writhing in panic, he tumbled headlong into a deeper blackness.

***

"I cannot fathom it," said Immin. He shrugged, displaying his palms. The thick grey cloak, garbed about his shoulders, dangled to the woodland floor. "We could find no remains. The pack must have dragged the boy away." He sighed. "We are too weary to track any further."

Caelin waved the flame of his torch over the bodies of the dead wolves. "Hunwald will not accept this."

"I feel for Hunwald, but if we are to find this child, we will do better to search at daybreak. Worker of bone and horn am I. Fox, bat, or owl, I am not. You are Head Man, Caelin, you should advise wisely here."

"You are new to this village, Immin of horn and bone. One should take heed, advising a man like Hunwald in *these* circumstances. We came hither from the old land, he and I. We were among the first of our tribes to root this soil. You scarcely would have recognized him back then," said Caelin. "But you speak true. Our efforts will be in vain tonight. Tell the men and round up the others. We'll begin again at dawn."

"Caelin!"

13

The giant swept out of the trees with Thrydwulf in his wake. "Your men are making their way back to the village. Did you give the order? Have you lost your wits?"

Hunwald paced up, towering menacingly over the older man. As Caelin stared at the face of granite, he fought to keep an uncomfortable feeling in check. "They cannot go on," he said. We must wait till morning."

"He is my son!" Hunwald raged.

"We've found no sign of the boy," Caelin countered. "We will begin again at first light."

Without warning, the giant flung his spear into the mud. Dragging his sword from its scabbard, he began butchering the dead carcasses of the wolves.

***

Thrydwulf had draped Cynwise in a magenta cloak of twill, almost carrying the frail woman through the darkness, across the open stretch of churned mud, back to the sanctuary of their dwelling. He gathered the remaining geese, throwing them into the makeshift pen, covering the birds with planking.

Cynwise lay once more upon the wretched pile of furs in the corner of the hut. The smoldering embers glowed upon the burnt ash; blowing them to life, he constructed a pyramid of birch kindling, adding to it to fill the hut with heat.

The air outdoors had thickened with flakes of drifting snow. If the flurry settled, the search for Oeric would be futile. That ideation fueled his brooding; each imagining was a tiny bird that flitted within the cage of his skull. His memory strayed to Freda, the bitch hound that had torn the fingers of his hand.

14

As a child, he had lifted Daegmund whilst the pup had been suckling at its mother's teat. In a fury, his father, Ceolwulf, had snatched the brood bitch from its young, hauled it by the scruff of the neck out into the bushes, returning alone. Days later, wracked with guilt, Ceolwulf gave Thrydwulf a gift of two of the pups.

He dwelt then on Aeva, weeping with her mother at the gathering hall; how he had longed to push his way back through the folk to get to her, to hold her, to comfort her.

And now Caelin had declared freedom from bondage for any of his slaves if they found the boy alive. It was a noble gesture. But if snow were to blanket the landscape at daybreak, he may as well have asked them to snare the moon with a fishing net of gossamer. And he had never witnessed Hunwald in such a rage. The sight had terrified him. Yet he understood the mentality of the outburst. He turned his attention to the woman stretched out in the corner of the room. He thrust the linen cloth into the clay pot of water, wrung it, and crossed to mop her brow.

"If we don't find Oeric tonight, I fear we never shall," he whispered, kneeling beside her.

With a jerk, she seized Thrydwulf's hand, vomiting a mouthful of blood into the damp rag.

"Hush," she croaked. "Listen well. Seek Hunwald's son. If he is alive, bring him home. Word will spread to the outer villages. Courageous deeds will follow a man. I have seen it before. Be sure to hold Hunwald in your debt. If he forgets, remind him of it. Every time he takes his grandchildren into his hands, let him know that *you* were the one who saved his bloodline."

Thrydwulf knelt, stock-still, gazing down, pondering the words she had spoken. She lashed out with an open hand, striking him full in the face. Yet still, he did not flinch. At this

15

attestation of his love, her blue eyes welled with tears, and she began to caress the cheek she had so callously assaulted.

"Must we suffer this torment every time you're asked to do my bidding?"

"It has begun to snow," he uttered. "I will stay close to the hut tonight."

She gripped his wrist tightly and dug in her nails.

"All the more reason not to wait for it to settle and cover the tracks. Now go!" Cynwise fell back against the furs, shivering and wheezing. He tucked her within the hides and found his feet, knowing the woman who had given him birth had spoken in truth. Crossing the hut, Thrydwulf pushed the door ajar.

The drifting snow was gathering. He pinned on a cloak of blue. From the corner of the room, he snatched up his ash spear and an oak torch dipped in pitch. He thrust the timber into the flickering flames, and it ignited, drenching the room in soft hues of orange-red. The hut reeked of sickness, and he could taste the acrid smoke in the air. In the deeper shadows, Cynwise labored in her breathing. He pushed the door open and slipped out into the night.

Satisfied the hounds had not stirred, he sprinted toward the woodlands in the direction of Cula's Ford.

Cynwise peered through the smoky light of fiery gold. The dogs would not raise the alarm; she had drugged the animals. She had lied to her child to save him from the grief of witnessing her death. The ultimate sacrifice. She felt the chill in her bones.

The cold. Always the cold.

Without warning, her head voyaged. She was hoisted in swaddling clothes, a childhood memory, its clarity just as substantial in its reality as any of the objects strewn upon the straw about her hut. A spasm of pain ripped through her chest like a claw of iron nails. Twisting onto her side in terror, she reached for Ceolwulf. There, now, was just the vacant space where once they had writhed in the pleasure of their lovemaking. She convulsed, her uterus prolapsing. Warm urine gushed down between her legs, its odor filling her nostrils—one more added indignity. Amid the life and death struggle, Cynwise called her mother's name, spattering blood upon the wooden planking. Was she really dying? The agony convinced her that she was. Only the gods would truly know.

The nervous fowl clucked and cackled in the hutch across the room, sensing trepidation. Cynwise tried to rise, but the effort broke her will like a straw stalk battling upon the wind. It was then she realized her greatest fear was not the cold that had plagued her all her days, but construing this moment now. The greatest dread of all. To die alone. She did not hear the door creak open, the delicate footfalls gliding with a purpose across the hut, the emotional figure slumping down beside her pallet of fur skins. "I am here," Aeva whispered through her tears.

Two hours beyond midnight, from the brink of the wood, Thrydwulf scanned the dwellings lower down the valley. Lights twinkled there like minute stars cast upon a cloak of ebony. If Caelin's serfs *had* detected him, beetling away from the village enclosure, it was not clear. The bondsmen would be eager to begin with the hunt, the chains of servitude being there for the severing.

Time was a thin thread, and Thrydwulf was already weary from prior happenings of an eventful day. The essence of Aeva's womanhood was still pungent on his fingers. The notion of her nakedness melted from his mind as the wind-churned snow thawed about his fiery brand. Clutching the hood of his blue cloak, he dragged it over his ears.

'Hard as stone beyond the fall of leaf... Life-preserver... Foe of Fire... Dragon's breath when iron's forged... Nerthus' tears...The Salmon's girdle.'
As Hunwald grimaced, the scar at the corner of his mouth stretched into a purple blush.
'For the love of Woden!' he snorted in frustration. 'A soldier's hōre could solve the riddle!'
'Don't be so strict with the boy!' snapped Hilda, yanking a braid of grey-blond hair.
She stood behind the seated giant, grooming his thinning locks with an elaborately carved comb. Oeric grabbed a bucket of water from the corner of the hut, heaving it to his father's feet. Much to Hunwald's annoyance, the boy poured the cold water over his toes.
'There is your answer,' said Thrydwulf, observing from the doorway. 'The answer to your riddle is water.'
As he began to laugh, Oeric grinned mischievously, only to scarper past into the morning mist. 'Lose yourself, brat!' Hunwald bellowed after him. 'And do not return till dusk!'

Thrydwulf played the scene over in his mind as he weaved through the undergrowth, scouring for signs of the mute boy's passing. He located the grass track that led to Cula's Ford and pursued the path as it wound its way past many a beech and slender birch. In the clearing, the moon's pale luminescence groped at the shedded leaves, its silver light accentuating the falling snow as it drifted in the darkness. On the high branch of an oak, a short-eared owl observed the flickering of Thrydwulf's torch. Its *waowk* cry ripped the silence apart, startling the youth. Thrydwulf responded with an instinctive imitation of the bird.

From the oak tree, the owl stared down, its piercing yellow eyes studying with renewed curiosity. Eventually, it shrank in the gloom, disappearing into the night. The youth pushed on.

At long last, reaching the margin of the wood, he strode out into the falling snow, acknowledging the wisdom of having brought the heavy blue cloak for protection. Sticking to the bank of the meandering ford, wandering north, he came upon more than a dozen pairs of human spoor mashed upon the mud. He pushed his torch heavenward; the flame was waning, yet it bathed the mutilated bodies of the butchered wolves with an eerie glow. The gory scene fueled his sense of vulnerability. Other predators would soon be scavenging. The water lapped at the blood and gore—*the residue of Hunwald's brutal act of madness*—and bore it severally away further downstream.

Like a thunderbolt, something struck him, and he shifted his attention to the bank across Cula's Ford. The dogs had come from *that* direction, full of agitation, hours before, but Hunwald's lunacy had caused the fleeting thought to be propelled deep into his subconscious.

It rose from its wallowing like the Sun God, Wotan, rising from the lake of fire.

The blizzard blew into his face, and he waded with renewed motivation through the icy stream.

Caelin's desperate bondsmen had scoured the area; he felt sure they had missed something of importance—a gut feeling. He brushed the flickering brand frantically in the gloom. As Thrydwulf turned toward the moonlit clearing yonder, his eye almost blundered. There, below the butt of his spear, was a footprint on the soaking dirt, above that was one more, and yet another. He scaled the incline to a ridge; the glade above was ringed with twisting trees, awash with silver light and shadow. He fell to his knees before a black gap in the hillside. Trampled leaves were smothered around the entrance. A hawthorn trunk loomed above like a sentry, its sinewy roots protruding down through the entrance, like a hairy insect's legs clogged with dirt. The ground was torn up. Thrydwulf judged that Oeric had crawled into the hole for sanctuary.

There was a murmuring from deep inside, and a voice in a strange language, indecipherable.

Yet he girded himself, bent low, and thrust the yellow flame inside.

The bolt hole appeared to narrow. Sliding the spear through the wet earth, he dragged himself along.

The tunnel wound like a snake into the hill. Thirty feet, he wriggled. Claustrophobia caused his heart to palpitate in his chest. With one thrust of a clenched fist, his world crackled with static energy, and instantly the naked yellow flame of his torch glowed as if it were suddenly fueled by a sorcerer's incantation. It revealed a vast cavern. Amorphous stalagmites grew from the floor like totems of sculptured ivory, whilst stalactites dripped into verdant pools rippling upon the green limestone. Twenty feet down, directly below lay the pathetic figure of Oeric. Thrydwulf suspected that the pool of water where the boy lay sprawled had probably broken his fall.

Or his back!

Dread bubbled to the surface, and he shouted the mute boy's name. No movement or sound was returned. Every ounce of logic implored him to race back to the village to fetch the men. Confused, he panicked, dropping his spear into the darkness; he cursed the mishap as it clattered, echoing upon the limestone to the right of the water below. The flickering torch had lost its momentary illumination in that strange environment and was all but spent. He thought to move quicker, to reach the younger boy. The rash decision was another mistake. He lost his footing, careening down the rock face, sliding over the green sediment like a sled across a lake of ice. He gripped instinctively to the only source of light within the cavern, the expiring torch, and raising it high, he hit the cold pool with a splash.

The sudden jolt surged through his body, robbing him of breath—but for the water, his ankles would have snapped like twigs. He was chest-deep, with Oeric's body next to him, buoyant upon the mineral-enriched water. Without warning, he ducked the boy's head below the surface and shook him violently. Oeric gagged and spluttered. Shivering, he clung to his redeemer, like a drowning mariner to a floating log. Thrydwulf wrapped his arm around the boy, comforting him. With what was left of the flickering brand, he offered it up at the smooth green rock face. There appeared to be no way back, not that he could tell from where he stood. All at once, he shuddered as the last light of the torch succumbed. Unwittingly, Thrydwulf's palm contacted Oeric's mouth. It was wide open, screaming silently in the pitch blackness.

That night in the land of Britain, behind the falling snow, came a storm. It scattered the livestock and thrashed the woodland. Some of the ancient hawthorns upon the hill were uprooted by the wind; the narrow entrance collapsed and was filled with mud and clay. Some days later, the body of Cynwise was wrapped in leather and laid to rest beside her husband, Ceolwulf, on sacred ground. The search for the missing boys continued but was ultimately abandoned. By the end of winter that same year, despaired and broken, the last of the searchers, Hunwald and his daughter Aeva, relinquished all hope.

21

Chapter 2

THRYDWULF'S CAPTURE
(Kazhelma, Quilaxia, Radamanthir Wood.
3rd Millennium)

Thrydwulf and Oeric clawed their way over the green limestone through the darkness, their splashing and panting echoing in the space around them. Neither boy was willing to accept the prospect that this place could serve as a tomb for their bones. For an hour, they crawled and clambered until

Thrydwulf pushed Oeric up onto a ledge. There, suddenly in the distance, was an orifice of light spilling into the blackness. Thrydwulf hurled up his spear and pulled himself onto the overhang of limestone, following the blond mute who went stumbling on.

They crawled out into the sunlight. Oeric stood, fatigued, yet gaped at the surrounding woodland, unable to grasp the extraordinary setting. The trees—whitebeam, or a related species — were in full bloom. Anomalous. Yet, though they maintained their coppery bark, the flowers, which should have exhibited clusters of creamy white, were, in fact, a soft indigo blue, the leaves a flushed salmon pink. The air was scented, and flocks of exotic birds perched or flapped amid the lofted branches. Yet stranger still were the two yellow-green suns burning in the azure sky. Oeric curved a finger, brushing his forehead. "We are dreaming," he sign-languaged. His eyes brimming with tears, he spun his hands. "Or dead."

Thrydwulf sneezed, taking in the peculiar environment. "Not dead," he declared, nonplussed.

"But not home," Oeric signed.

"Not home," Thrydwulf agreed.

The cave from which they had appeared was a grinning mouth, the engirdling hill, a quilt of lush green, speckled with—what seemed like—yellowed bunches of wormwood and yarrow flowers. Thrydwulf stabbed the point of his spear into the earth and strode toward the nearest tree trunk. Whipping the dagger from its belt frog, he noticed the bronze chape was missing. All the same, he carved a simple rune ↑ upon the bark to mark the spot. He could not determine where they were, but he began to gesticulate clumsily with his fingers. "Maybe *this* is some whim of the Gods, unintended for mortal eyes." He re-sheathed the blade, strode across the deep ferns, and reclaimed the ash spear.

"The village must lie yonder the hill," Thrydwulf said. "If we hurry, we will make the midday feast." He was consumed with doubt, though he did not say so.

They scaled the steep grassy bank, breathing hard atop its crown, scanning the valley below. The village had disappeared, replaced by a kaleidoscope of multicolored trees, their leaves all lime green and delicate sapphire, blushed vermilion and milky white. It could, almost, have been the imagination of Hunwald's poetic mythmaking. Yet this ideality rooted them to the spot, where they now stood, knee-deep in a carpet of hanging...*bluebells?*

Oeric began to tremble, and Thrydwulf dropped his spear, hugging the mute boy. "We must go down into the wood," he acknowledged.

Oeric's eyes were like a timid Connie's, gripped by fear in torchlight. "Back to the cave!" he implored with a gesture.

"We shall, but first, we must make a climbing frame to reach the ledge where we fell. We'll gather straight branches and plant fibers to bind them, with dried moss for the torches to light the way back, and rock flint for fire. We have much to do."

The mute hurried after Thrydwulf, as he strode away down the incline towards the forest of trees.

The wood was alive with chirps and chattering that reverberated through the colorful canopy high above. Sunlight pierced through the branches of the unusual boughs, flickering like shafts of iridescent corn, flooding the strange glade with a hue the shade of sphene stone. For over an hour they labored. Thrydwulf had begun by shaping the sinewy limbs of fallen branches—those that were straight and thick enough to utilize.

24

A related species of lime tree provided strips of bark—twisted together as hemp—to tie the rungs of the frame poles, whilst the blond mute scoured the adjacent glade for ignitable foliage—this world be used to light the way back to their world.

Oeric swept through the bushes. Under one arm, he carried an array of dead twigs, dry bracken fronds, and bits of bark; in his right hand, he carried the half-eaten carcass of a rotting animal closely resembling a wild cat. The thing stank to high heaven, but there were still enough fat deposits in the cadaver to smear upon the torches they would need in the limestone catacombs.

The mute's hands and face were covered with scratches from his flight from the village, yet not once had he complained. He laid down the bits he had gathered and sat in the long grass amid the strange daffodils, watching Thrydwulf toiling doggedly at his task. As another hour passed, both were at their wits' end, twitching at every sound in the neighboring undergrowth. Thrydwulf cursed for leaving his ash spear stabbed amid the strange bluebells on the hill. Oeric climbed to his feet, standing in Thrydwulf's line of vision. "The blame is mine," he gestured. "I will fetch it."

Thrydwulf offered the mute an obliging smile. "We can find it on the way back." Oeric beamed as the problem hatched wings and flapped away into the wildwood.

"Aeva and you shall soon be wed," he finger-signed. Thrydwulf's eyebrows rose. "She told you?"

Oeric's fingers danced. "The whole village knows. Ricbert will smithy a sword as a morning gift. The bride offers the groom a sword as a hand geld. The Groom obliges samely. Rings are exchanged and oaths are uttered in a hallowed place. Says Father."

"I know the ritual," Thrydwulf said, more tersely than intended. "I have no sword or ring to give," he declared, returning to the task at hand. Oeric tugged at the older boy's cloak. "It is already done," he motioned. "Your mother offered the sword months ago." Thrydwulf scratched the annoying nits plaguing his hair. "She had no right," he chided. "That sword belonged to my father."

Oeric shrugged. "Now it belongs to mine," he gesticulated.

No sarcasm was intended, but the knowledge still rankled. "I cannot concentrate. Let me work," he said, peevishly. The blond mute slapped his thigh to gain Thrydwulf's attention. "So, you will have no interest in the whispers I have heard." He slumped down into the long grass and grinned like one of the ceremonial masks hanging from the pole in Caelin's hut.

"Maybe I should leave you here and tell those in the village I could not find you," Thrydwulf teased with a scowl. The mute sprang to his feet; his face pinched with apprehension; his fingers began dancing on the palm of his hand.

What the dance told of stunned Thrydwulf to the core. Had he read the boy right? He smarted at the mute to repeat the sign language.

"I heard my mother and my sister talking," Oeric motioned with his hands. "I could not sleep. I pretended I was. They were whispering, but I heard their words. Aeva told Mother she thinks she is with child."

Thrydwulf turned away, poleaxed. He brooded on Aeva, upon his mother's shame. On Hunwald's rage!

He dreamed, briefly, of non-return, but bringing back Oeric alive would surely absolve him of the offense, as far as Hunwald was concerned. Cynwise was right: he could wield the deed like a weapon in the giant's face if necessary.

26

High above in the crowns of the distant wood, a flock of bright-colored birds gave flight, scattering erratically upon the wind. The clarion of a remote horn blared in the distance. *A horn!* That similar sound he had heard before—men and dogs hunting a wild pig or an elusive stag. Thrydwulf froze, grappling with his thoughts as if they were fish cascading over a waterfall. *The spear!* There wasn't enough time. He clutched the Scaramax dagger tightly, only then realizing that Oeric had fled in panic. He spied a trail weaving through the long grass and leapt away, praying the hunters had not yet detected their scent.

Three times more, the horn blew, its demented shrills joined only by the hollering of foreign voices.

Thrydwulf bolted through the trees, too terror-stricken to face even the Semblance of those who were now in close pursuit. The swish of an arrow hissed past his temple, only to be swallowed by the undergrowth. Fear gripped him tightly. A second shaft thumped into the bole of the tree where he passed. A third—a black-feathered shaft—gut shot him at an acute angle. An explosion of air erupted from his lungs; his shrieks of pain engulfed the wildwood. Thrydwulf scrambled to his feet in terror, tears flooding his sight; he limped onward towards the twisted body of Hunwald's son, who was peppered with arrows.

Time seemed to wheel in slow degrees. Blood seeped into his clothes. Was he dying? In shock, he watched as the hunter, astride Oeric's limp body, gripped the mute by the collar, only to slide a curious blade across his throat. Thrydwulf screamed the dead boy's name, dropping to his knees, he rolled onto his side. Drenched in sweat, he was aware his wound had was throbbing, yet still, he could not wrench his gaze from Oeric's corpse. His thoughts breast-stroked across a lagoon of confusion.

'We were both wrong, Mother,' he murmured silently through his tears. *'I am neither pole lather nor warrior. I am a fool.'*

He reached feebly for Oeric across the glade. The shock tore him in two.

'We shall be together again before this day is done, Oeric.'

He wept through gritted teeth.

'We shall rattle the gates of Asgard, you and I.'

With that, he lay his head down upon the greensward. "Father!" he bellowed defiantly. "Meet us at the bridge!"

Chapter 3

GRYONAE

The riders cantered to the edge of the glade, their wrakens lathered with sweat.

These were Rissak's men: cruel, flat-featured, browned by the two suns burning above the world. They were clothed in cotton of oyster white, their breastplates—fashioned from black ironwood—were strapped about them, carved with a dragon motif, its claws splayed, its mouth agape. Helms adorned their jet-black ponytails, and they were Goatee-bearded.

29

The last man to arrive was garbed in loose-fitting trousers dyed a midnight blue. Soft leather buskins wove about his feet to the knees, while studded gauntlets were laced from his wrists to his elbows. A shock of blond-brown hair flowed about his powerful shoulders, with a serrated sword sheathed in a leather scabbard across his back. This was Gryonae of Novia Jorai, the emperor's ruthless champion. He had slain many men in the Arena of Blood, and the word Shadowgrip was whispered in the corridors of the palace. The women of Rissak's harems flirted shamelessly whenever the champion was summoned to the emperor's throne. He was considered a fine specimen of manhood.

Heat shimmered in the sun-cloyed glade. Butterflies of puce and ultramarine fluttered upon the wildflowers; a tinge of scent hung in the midday air, wafting from vibrant petals.

The bare-chested man dismounted his wraken and strode with an authoritative gait into the clearing. He eyed the hunter standing astride the mutilated corpse. Without warning, he struck out, the metal pyramidic studs drawing blood across the hunter's cheek. The assaulted man jumped back with a scowl. Gryonae crouched beside the body, running his strong fingers through the dead child's yellow hair.

He had let the veins of many men in the arena, drenched its sandy floor with entrails, but this ilk of barbarity would always be difficult to stomach by most of the civilized races on the planet—*save for the Dirakhan.*

Gryonae placed a finger on the boy's slit throat, smearing blood upon the forehead. He painted marks in the shape of two circles on the skin—an age-old ritual performed on the battle-slain Dirakhan, lest they wander doomed in search of the great eagle Kraghir, who would bear their souls to paradise.

"Fly well, little one," he uttered, stroking the eyelids shut.

30

For the slimmest juncture of time, his head was hung, as if in grief. But for the buzzing of the bees, the glade was stifled. He made no attempt to rise. Nor did he lift his head. Yet he spoke, suddenly, with a voice as cold as the slopes of a frozen glacier.

"Someone hand this hero a sword," he said. No one moved, but the wrakens, sensing the tension, shuffled timorously beneath their handlers.

"Should I ask again, I will leave this dung beetle some company."

One of the riders, afflicted from birth with a purple blemish—that daubed his pugged nose—drew a curved sword, and tossed it to the murderer's feet.

"Let us see how you fare against men," said Gryonae.

The hunter backed away.

"I did not know *it* was a brat," he stammered. "It ran. I shot!"

"And the mutilation," Gryonae responded. "Another misadventure?" Secretly, he coiled his fingers around the spent arrow shaft lying within reach in the long ryegrass.

"It needed to be put out of its misery," the hunter reasoned. He edged nearer to the sword, gambling that Gryonae had not read the play. A thin smile grazed the champion's lips; his eyes narrowed and shone.

"Pick up the weapon," he goaded, drinking in the man's fear. "It has been said about *you* that your mother was a brothel keeper's whore. Is that not so? It would explain why she gave birth to a wraken turd." He stressed the insult, probing for a response. Instantaneously, it sprouted wings. The hunter roared in anger and sprang toward the scimitar. Gripping it by the handle, he pounced at the kneeling figure of the champion.

"Die, you Novian dog!" He screamed across the sward between them. Gryonae shifted his weight to meet the attack. A deft tumbler, he rolled from the hunter's strike. The man landed face down in the long ryegrass; Gryonae swung the fierce barb in a looping arc, piercing the wretch through the ear with a sickening thud. He glared at the young captain, expecting a challenge from that quarter; the officer remained silent, turned his wraken, and trotted away.

"Get these bodies underground," Gryonae ordered.

"And put *that*...stinkard at the *dead one's* feet. I pray he trails the boy through the halls of Cadmanthia; his dog for all eternity."

With the toe of his buskin, he flipped the curved sword into the air, a dextral proficiency seen many times in the arena. Catching the weapon by its ivory hilt, he chucked it back to the rider with the flawed face.

"This one is still alive," said another member of the hunting party. "A gut wound." He ripped open the clothing to inspect the injured flesh. "Doesn't look good."

Gryonae peered down at the older youth. "Tend to the damage. Put him on the wagon. If he lives, maybe there will be work in the kitchens or with the wrakenmasters." He scanned the sinister glade. "We should leave this place," he told them with a frown.

'It's cursed by this crime. I feel it.'

"Make haste! Bury the corpses. We are far from the city, and we have a long ride ahead of us."

Thrydwulf flicked open his eyes. The arrow had been removed, but the injury was agonizing. The torn tissue had been smeared with a yellow pulp to prevent infection. A strange, serrated leaf,

32

mauve as a crocus petal, was pressed against the throbbing wound to stave the blood flow.

The wagon rolled lazily over several dead branches; the motion stoked a fire within his belly.

The young Saxon spat a curse, damning Woden to fry in one of Hunwald's mythical hells. He could smell the musk and dung from the dead animals slung to the front of the trundling wagon. Flies buzzed about the dead carcasses. Sick to the stomach, he vomited over the head of a huge-antlered animal—no more than a foot from his nose. Groaning, he twisted onto his back. Shafts of lime green poked down through the canopy, flooding his sight in a continuum of light and shade as they trundled beneath the branches of the colored wood. He raised a hand to shield his eyes, and a man's face loomed before him. Weaponless and too weak to respond, he ventured a feeble attempt to claw at the foreigner's throat. His arms were coaxed down, and he writhed in agony for the effort.

The stern face had a goatee beard, grey as slate. The stranger's thinning tresses—a shade of pewter, flecked with frost—were pulled tight into a long ponytail. His garments were a plain black tunic, laced from rib to chin, with loose cotton trousers dyed the shade of soft magenta.

Thrydwulf studied the perplexing stare of the man's stoat-like features.

"Be still, boy," the voice instructed.

The dialect—*Northern European*—he had heard before, uttered by travelers that had passed through his village back in his own world. Germanic in its origin, it was almost comforting.

"Where am I?" asked Thrydwulf.

33

The Greybeard bent close. "You are among the Dirakhan. Accept it. You are a prisoner here. You will never return home."

Thrydwulf knitted his eyebrows.

"I know your garbs," the man explained as if reading his thoughts.

Thrydwulf quizzed, "You are Druid-born?"

The stranger smiled with broken teeth. "No, but I know your people, Saxon."

"The trees. The leaves. I do not understand!" said Thrydwulf.

"Do not try—*yet*. Let not these heathens know we talk in a tongue only you or I profess to understand. On a whim, they would hang us as witches. I am Vargdenir. That is how I am known among them. It's not a birth name. I am Huntmaster to Rissak I. If Rissak is not the emperor of it, then it is not worth his subjugation. Be still now!" he snapped. "Speak no more until we are alone."

Vargdenir stood, gripping one of the oak rail braces on the wagon as the rider rode up. They began to converse in a tongue alien to Thrydwulf's ears.

"You did well to intervene and spare the boy, my friend," said Vargdenir. "Kubenial may not breathe your name with praise, but the goddess, Hyren, will light a candle in your honor. It was a noble gesture."

Gryonae gave a courteous nod and broke into a grin. "Come, Vargdenir. We are not like these people, you or I. Isn't it enough that we are held captive by them, let alone make the pretense of honoring their deities when we are alone?"

"The boy will live," Vargdenir said quietly. "I think he is sick of mind, but I shall take him under my service if it is allowed. You slew my best man, and he will need replacing."

34

"Rissak has more important things to attend to," said the rider. "We are here to hunt for a banquet, not to bring back urchins to place into servitude."

Vargdenir snorted a laugh. "Very well. We'll do our best for the foundling."

"It's a wife you need, my friend, not a waif or stray to foster," the rider said, beaming from ear to ear.

"I've had wives. Do you forget? You bedded two of them."

"But they were the bane of your life!"

Vargdenir shrugged. "That is why I still call you a friend, you dumb lummox." Gryonae laughed, and his face morphed into a serious pose. "But a word of warning," he breathed low. "Keep the conversations with your pet to your private chambers. It is known that Rissak employs language masters. I would grieve to learn you were hanged for teaching the boy tricks as a tongue master."

Vargdenir nodded, clenched his fist into a ball, and double-struck his right breast in the manner of State courtesy. "It shall be so."

Gryonae gazed through a break in the trees. "I think it's going to rain," he said, "Best dig out your canvas, Huntmaster. We make camp this night."

Vargdenir laughed. "You hold no position here."

"You think that scrawny wraken turd of a captain will decline my advice? I have informed him that today's events are to remain cloaked. His life depends on it."

"He will want to get these animals back to the kitchens. Get them skinned and gutted," said Vargdenir. "His men can do that tonight. They'll have naught else to do, save shelter from the rain. He may be young, but he is still proud."

"Point me out a mutt who isn't," said Gryonae. He heeled the ribs of his blue beast and galloped ahead to the front of the column. Moments later, the escort slowed, coming to a halt as the first drops of rain began to fall.

The hunting party had lashed their awnings to the trees. Beneath each one, a flame was burning. Icy droplets hammered down, soaking those ordered to gather extra wood to fuel the fires. A handful of men were allocated the task of gutting and preparing the animals hunted for Rissak's banquet. To appease the disgruntled group, the young captain allowed a few wild fowl to be roasted; the huntmaster volunteered to pluck and prepare the birds.

Vargdenir and Gryonae neighbored beneath a waxed, green canvas; Thrydwulf lay sprawled between them. Muttering, he turned in restless sleep, his thick blue cloak tugged about him, like a bat encased beneath protective wings.

The close of day had aged an hour since supper, the darkness ever clotting with a deep blue shadow as the driving rain moderated to a drizzle. Beneath the awning opposite, the young captain sat alone, lit by the glow of his fire, the entrance to his canvas womb tied open to allow the billowing smoke to escape into the night. The lone figure plucked a map from an oxblood saddlebag and unrolled a scroll, studying its details. The route had been traced by a reliable cartographer employed by the Master of Archives. It was a standard procedure for ranked officers to navigate the terrains of their empire.

"He's checking coordinates," said Gryonae, in idle chatter. "Or searching for the ravine to replenish the water. It's but a league or two yonder." He stoked the fire with a thin twig of hazelwood, pointing with the orange tip toward the west. "If the fool were but to ask."

36

"Pride and youth are ill-matched bedfellows," Vargdenir remarked philosophically. Vulgarly, he expelled phlegm into the hissing flames—the element spat back in the form of burning cinders, singeing the hem of Thrydwulf's cloak. The Huntmaster extinguished the embers, patting them out with his palm. The youth moaned in fitful slumber.

"Are they forest-born?" Gryonae asked. "This one and the urchin we buried. Kin perhaps? You know these regions well,"

"I do not remember much of my time spent in these woodlands. 'Twas long ago. But I have a fondness for them. *That* I will not deny." Vargdenir sensed the questions probed for answers of a deeper nature. "Do not be distracted by the gossip of fools," said Vargdenir. "I did not fire the arrow that slew the leopard. That was the doing of Emperor Radiantee's archer. I merely happened by. Much like the unfortunate wretch here. Though I *was* younger than he was. Nay. Radiantee's man, Frangur, took pity on me; that is how I came into service for the Dirakhan. No great mystery. We weren't *that* close. As for the origins of *this* one here, and the other poor mite. Local? I'm not sure, but things often have a way of unraveling. We shall see."

"You miss her still? Your woman, Sherab?" questioned Gryonae.

Vargdenir poked a stick in the fire, provoking the flames.

"You have not loved if that is a riddle that intrigues you," the older man replied.

"I had a father and a brother. Their faces vanish with the years. Ghosts in the memory," said Gryonae. In a mad rush of blood, he hollered into the rain. "Whoa!" The silhouetted figure of the map reader turned a helmed head towards them, peering across the darkness.

"What you seek lies to the northwest! The ravine?"

37

Vargdenir could hardly contain his laughter. "Why do you torment the poor fellow?"

"You have to keep these vermin on their toes," Gryonae retorted.

"Just checking the route!" The young captain called back; his words smothered by the weather.

The old man shook his head. "If you were not Rissak's Champion."

"I was born in Novia Jorai," said Gryonae, coldly. "My people are warrior-born. One day, they shall rise again.

"Keep those thoughts to yourself," Vargdenir admonished. "They would tie your body and toss it into one of the dog pits. I have seen the practice. It's not pleasant."

***

Thrydwulf sat with his back against the moving wagon. The slightest jolt was a dagger thrust, yet he gritted his teeth, ultimately succumbing to the fortuity of sleep. He drifted in and out of consciousness. At one point, his ears discerned the distant gurgling of flowing water. There was a cessation of motion as the wagon rolled to a halt. Voices uttered in an indecipherable tongue. He felt the wagon hie to the right and begin to wend its way slowly downward.

The green sky bled with streaks of turquoise. The long hours crawled by. Dusk melted beneath the reddening suns, and the wagon came to an abrupt halt. The man at the reins mumbled over his shoulder and Vargdenir rose to his boots. For a moment, he stood, surveying the landscape, only to kneel beside the youth and rune-worded into his ear.

38

"We have come to Quilaxia."

Thrydwulf heaved himself up and peered over the wagon rail.

The city spread in each direction as far as his eyes could determine. The towering walls, fifty feet or more, rose above the verdant sweeps of winding woodland. Huge buildings, domed and rectangular, peeped above the red sandstone battlements like curious children contemplating the neighboring mountains. Thrydwulf recalled Hunwald's descriptions of the colossal city of Rome. Yet this compared to those imaginings, accompanied by a dread that must have raced the hearts of all its enemies.

Thrydwulf sank into the wagon when the wrakens shunted forward. As the magnitude of the situation struck home, he ripped at the wound upon his stomach. It was as if his entrails were on fire.

"Give me death!" he cried.

With a curse, Vargdenir backhanded the boy across the jaw, as the bleat of a distant horn pierced the breeze.

Chapter 4

ESCAPE FROM ROTHSHIM
(Kazhelna, Zin Desert, Rothshim Prison
Mine. 3rd Millennium)

(Nine years later)

Tymarian dug away at the wall face, stretching his tired limbs against the intolerable ache.

The salt blocks were excavated and hauled to a processing chamber high up at the mouth of the mine. They were duly weighed, wrapped, stored, and documented. For nine years, the Novian warrior had been enslaved and forced to endure the honeycombed galleries of Rothshim—*Tunnels of the walking dead,* the sapient among men had given name to the location of torment. The industrious passages reeked of toil and death; the exhausted, old, and infirm were mercilessly dispatched, or on occasion, left on the scorching dunes for the sport of winged scavengers.

A diet of rice and water was a slave's only sustenance. But in this hellhole of lingering death, the sparse meal was a banquet.

Tymarian coughed in the salt-choked chamber, fumbling at a bone blade that was lashed and secreted beneath his blue rags. His black hair grew wild. His bushy beard was untamed and caked with salt dust. The Novian did not doubt the baseborn woman who had squeezed him into existence would have taken him for a stranger by his appearance now: six feet of toned muscle, sculpted beneath an array of grimy clothes. He moved with the lithe grace of a leopard, and when he spoke—though seldom now was the desire for conversation with the enslaved heathens of the prison mine—his voice echoed of the steppes, the rich dialect of his people far to the south-east in Novia Jorai.

Across the chamber, a co-condemned creature hacked at the soft sediment. There was no purpose in chaining the ill-fated souls—the empty seabed above the ancient mine unraveled for more than three hundred leagues in all directions. No man afoot could traverse the arid wilderness, not without knowledge of the fertile oases that dotted the vindictive oceans of sand.

A Dirakhan guard strolled past the entrance and barked at Tymarian to keep working. The captive obliged, exaggerating his effort.

The second prisoner in the chamber observed silently as the guard disappeared along the passage, the glow of his torch dying away as the tunnel snaked upward.

"When?" the creature growled, lowering the antler pick in its clenched claw. The Goblin was as tall as the Novian's shoulder, but Tymarian knew that to gauge its ability in warcraft by stature alone was a clumsy mistake. The flat-faced creature was *Grokonian,* an indigenous race from the country of Enlyd, a harsh, windswept plateau far to the west of Novia Jorai. The devil was a reaper of souls parading in a pauper's rag.

"Be patient!" Tymarian bit back, in the goblin tongue, his voice conveying the guttural pronunciation of Novia Jorai.

"I am beginning to sicken of that word," the Grokon rasped. "Why do we wait? The caravan will be bedded down. If it departs without us—"

"Then we are dead," Tymarian interjected angrily.

"They are returning to their posts. That is the twentieth dog that has passed."

"Twenty-second," Tymarian amended. "Three more are coming."

He peered menacingly into the creature's magenta eyes. No dread resided there; the wicked orbs stared back like burnished garnets.

"I bow to your judgment, Novian," it declared, raising its claw in a respectful gesture.

Tymarian saw through the deception.

At the entrance of the chamber, clad in the green faded robes of his office, a corrupt trustee appeared, carrying bowls of rice and water. The bearer placed the tray of nourishment upon the ground, whispered into the Novian's ear, and backed away warily, shrinking into the shadows.

Tymarian and the Grokon sat cross-legged in the center of the chamber, devouring the pittance of sustenance supplied in the bowls. The Novian flicked a brief glare at the last guard returning to his duty further down the mine.

The plan of escape had been a year in the making. Half rations, three months' worth, had been bartered for a length of human bone that had been shaped into a blade, and smuggled in from the surface by a trustee—*A man assigned to rid the tunnels of the dead prisoners.*

Tymarian and the creature dwelt silently as the time approached.

The caravan camped on the dry seabed above, contained eight hundred head of euganta, and was employed for the shipment of salt back to the city. Being the largest assembled retinue for a decade, a fugitive could hide himself amongst such an escort. Around this optimism, the desperate duo had wrapped a thing of feathers.

Tymarian passed the unwitting creature, and like a coiled snake, struck out, slashing the blade of bone across the Grokon's throat. Gasping for air, with blood gushing from the slit across its neck, *it* managed to flick a claw, tracing three red furrows down the side of Tymarian's neck. Without the element of surprise, the attack would have tilted in the varmint's favor. The Novian plunged frantically, and the Grokon died. Thick green gore leaked from its wounds,

43

seeping into the ground of the odd-shaped chamber. Tymarian dragged the corpse to the corner of the room. Stripping himself naked—but for the bone blade—he fled into the ovoid tunnel.

The passage wound upward, and Tymarian stuck to the shadows, his heart pounding, sweat oozing from his begrimed, stinking skin. He came to a gigantic cavern. At the top of the elevated walls, oil lamps winked within rusted iron sconces, bathing the void in a tone of soft lime. Black amorphous shapes danced upon the green walls, kidnapping the Novian's thoughts.

The two boys glanced at each other, excitedly seething beneath their calm exteriors.

'Gryonae, you must use the plant fiber and coat it with resin. It will bind the components together. Do the same as your brother.'

'I am ready, Father,' said Tymarian.

'Be patient,' said the man. 'The stag will not escape. But we are downwind, and he knows we are following. He keeps a safe distance between us.'

'How can he know?' Gryonae asked.

'He can smell us and will trust his instinct. So must you.'

Across the shadows loomed the tunnel entrance to the upper level. Seated to the left of the opening, two guards were at a table, gambling with dice, their coarse dialect resounding in the lime-bathed cavity.

Blood pinpricked from the scratches on Tymarian's neck, and he swallowed back the taste of dust and salt.

'Trust the instinct.' The words of his father echoed across the hourglass of time. *'Now!'*

He sprang from the gloom, covering the distance in seconds.

Tymarian, the boy, jabbed at the burly stag, spearing a deep gash into its graceful features. In alarm, the animal reared on its hind legs. The birch glade swirled with a thin mist, and for an instant, an eerie silence hung over the clearing. Locked in confrontation, the stag nasal grunted as the group circled, giving themselves room, should the powerful beast have a mind to charge. Foolishly, Gryonae trespassed within its peripheral vision, and the animal thrust its antlers, tearing a sickening gouge in the boy's flesh. Gryonae yelped as his brother vaulted. Staring deep into the stag's petrified eyes, Tymarian struck the killing blow.

As the man turned his head, the Novian prisoner slit his jugular with a single slash. Gripping his throat, the victim slumped from his chair. Tymarian screamed like a demon, shoulder-charging the younger man as he reached for the hilt of his sword. The winded guard crashed with a thud against the wall. In that moment of interplay, Tymarian clasped the stunned individual by the ponytail, peering into his green, terror-stricken eyes.

'Existence plays within a heartbeat. Trust in the instinct, the redeemer of life.'

Granting no quarter, the prisoner plunged the blade through the Dirakhan's temple. As the body went limp, Tymarian let it fall. As a final insult, he spat at the cadaver, stripping it of clothing and dressing hastily in the dead man's garments.

In that thimbleful of time, the scene played out. The carcasses were dragged into the shadows. In desperation, he

45

covered the bodies with salt from the floor, in a final endeavor to conceal the violation. Into the Semigloom, he flung the blade of bone. He lashed a curved steel sword and leather scabbard about his waist. Buttoning the loose burgundy shirt, he proceeded to wrap a headdress of black silk around his cranium, garbing it in the fashion of one of the slain dice players.

Tymarian knelt in the shadows, panting like a hunted animal, listening, trusting the instinct. Then he was up, weaving through the shadows once more.

He reached the entrance to the processing chamber, the largest in the network of excavated caverns. The area was crammed with an assortment of blocks of wrapped salt. The opening to the mine was ablaze with olive sunlight; his hopes took flight.

Nine years had elapsed since the last time he had glimpsed the mouth of Rothshim.

The slave trustee had told the truth. It was late afternoon, and the caravan that had arrived from the city of Quilaxia was being loaded. The chamber was like an ant colony; the opportunity could not have been better. To his left, a dozen trustees were loading slabs of salt— the wealth of the city. If he could but follow them through, and taste clean air before death, the attempt would be worth the sacrifice.

Tymarian, his heart still dancing, strode out into the sunlight and began to zigzag through the throng of activity.

The immense caravan was already moving. In the distance, the laden pack animals were pacing up the dunes, meandering

46

away towards the east. It seemed like an eternity as he wove his way through the jostling men and animals; at last, he spied a glimmer of hope.

The rider could not have been a year or two beyond twenty, still green to the ways of exploitation by higher-ranking officers. Tymarian patted the young man on the shoulder. "Do not loiter there. Help freight the animals."

"I'm packed," said the rider, turning to face the source of distraction. Patting the euganta's rump, Tymarian placed a foot into the stirrup, feigning to bestride the animal. With a fleeting glance, he surveyed his surroundings, checking for nosy traders or over-inquisitive soldiers.

Do or die.

He seized the unsuspecting rider by the ponytail, snapping his neck with a quick jerk.

The nervous beast snorted as Tymarian dragged the stooge away, leaving him to the curiosity of a stick-thin old man who was now kneeling over the body, examining the cadaver's wrist for a pulse.

"Easy," Tymarian breathed into the animal's ear. He stroked its shaggy mane with a touch that was foreign and unfamiliar. Putting a foot once more into the leather stirrup, he climbed into the saddle, heeled the beast in the ribs, and cautiously plodded away.

Tymarian reached the vanguard of the caravan. No one would question a sergeant from the mines, returning from a stint of wardenship. His intention now was to reach the city, steal the crown, and liberate his people. *That* absurdity, or it could have been the sudden comprehension of his own emancipation, whatever it was, caused a reaction: he leaned over the wraken's neck vomited onto the shifting sand.

"You are not Dirakhan by birth," said Zarmel. His keen blue eyes belied the wrinkled mask of age.

Wisps of grey hair had been twisted into a bootlace beard below his jaw, and a turban of Tyrian purple swathed his shorn skull. Cross-legged before the raging fire, he tossed Tymarian a goatskin of spiced wine and a chunk of smoked meat. Chewy, but a delicacy in comparison to the diet of rice he had been forced to endure at Rothshim; he ate ravenously. One swig from the leather bag went straight to the warlord's head. He corked the stopper and flung the wineskin back to the ferret-faced man.

"Novian perhaps?" Zarmel persisted.

The warlord slave had not uttered more than a dozen words since the caravan had bedded down for the night, but the oldster was unrelenting. "If not Novian, Schwarlee? Or Twarlusa?"

Tymarian smirked at the Salt Shipper's gall. "Do not insult me. You know my ethnicity well."

Zarmel squinted through the flames, pulling his black cloak tighter about his skinny frame, as the temperature of the desert was now just above freezing.

"How did you come by the position of sergeant at Rothshim? I thought *that* vocation was only open to those of Dirakhan parentage?" The old man peeped askance through the fire; the seated statue of flesh that was Tymarian was gnawing at a remnant of tough meat.

"It's not wise to meddle in the affairs of others," the warlord said, coldly. "I have known men butchered for less."

"All men die," Zarmel confessed. He stared at the stranger's features in the firelight. "The boy you killed today," he said, impassively. "He was my woman's bastard."

Tymarian covertly inched his sword from the confines of its scabbard.

"But it doesn't matter. I held no regard for him. Your secret is safe with me." Zarmel lay down on the thick euganta hide, wrapping the fur around him. "You *could* slit my throat whilst I sleep, but would it be wise to leave another dead body on the trail? *I* will be missed. The boy...maybe not so much."

Tymarian felt the urge to strangle the hoary insect and hide the remains under the sand, but the old man was right; it would only be a matter of time before some other mischief-makers discover a riderless euganta roaming among the moving caravans.

"What's in it for you, salt shipper?" Tymarian asked, glaring across at the fur-wrapped figure.

"The euganta, of course!" spat the old man with a laugh. "When we reach the city, you will give me the beast as payment for my silence. Your business is your own. We travel at first light. The caravan does not wait for stragglers; *I* will not be a straggler. Get some rest. If you are not ready at dawn, I will take the beast anyway. Be warned."

The warlord slid the sword back into its scabbard.

From their cabin home in Surss, Zarmel's woman had been seized and whored among the Novian people; the bastard she had borne being the product of her violation.

"All I want is the euganta. To sell at one of the markets in the city," said Zarmel.

49

Tymarian did not sleep that night. As the glory of the morning suns fringed upon the black horizon, he jerked the thoughts of the old snide from his mind.

Chapter 5

JOURNEY TO THE CITY

The young rider Tymarian had slain had made adequate provisions for the journey **to** Rothshim and the return to the city. For nigh on a hundred arduous leagues, there had been nothing more than shifting sands upon which to cast their gaze. The fugitive of Rothshim had forgotten how a mirage could push a man to the edge of sanity. On occasion, he squinted over his shoulder at the robed figures that seemed to be trailing them; he would blink only to notice that the volatile dunes had swallowed them. At one point, they had been seated, banqueting at a long table crammed with culinary delights that made his mouth water. They had beckoned him to join the feast only to vanish into the air as he attempted to dismount.

The caravan slid like a winding serpent down onto a rocky plateau. The day was dimming, and dots of light from the campfires were increasing. The salt shippers and the vigilant cavalcade were preparing to bed down for the night. The pace of the caravan slowed and then ceased altogether.

Zarmel slipped adeptly from the euganta's back and clicked a harsh phonetic command at the cumbersome beast; it bent to its knees, succumbing to the old man's behest.
He took a long stick that was attached to his high saddle and pegged the euganta's rein deep into the desert sand. Tymarian dismounted, and the salt-shipper grinned as the beast snorted and brayed, seemingly distressed. Zarmel took its strap. "These animals do not live well together. It's not wise to force them into each other's company. They will fight to the death if forced two abreast without constraint. We have a fire to make. Be of some help, Novian. Start building it." Tymarian glared coldly as the old man wandered away. Nearby, a small group of men huddled about their watch fire. The Novian warlord sat bolt upright as one of the robed figures sprang to his feet, cursing in the broad Dirakhan tongue. In the gloom, a euganta was trotting away. The creature had broken its tether and was trying to reach the far-flung dunes.

"The animal is obviously hungry," schooled the old man, never raising his eyes. He delved into his jute sack, fishing out more dried dates.

"Your woman," Tymarian muttered. "What is she called?"
"She was named Edatha."
"You say *was*."

52

"The great eagle Kraghir has carried her ghost. She walks now with Kubenial."

"You have my sympathy."

When Zarmel snorted, Tymarian assumed it was because he'd seen straight through the token words of condolence.

"And you," said the old man through scant teeth, "you have a woman somewhere?"

'Ty! Not so brutish. You are not pulling a piglet from a sow's uterus!'

Allina mock-slapped the man across his bearded jaw, and he became less demanding in his urgency. They moved rhythmically once more in the pelvic motion of their passion. With his pleasure spent, the woman had cloaked her disappointment with a benevolent smile. 'Let go of this foolish notion. Your brother may well be dead. How will you know him? Or he, you for that matter.'

'I will know,' he said with a sigh.

Allina tenderly stroked his ebony hair, her green almond eyes moist with pity.

'Your father has ridden in Welkrina's chariot and crossed the bridge between the two suns. He wanders in the forest of Fremsharin. Do not squander your life for the sake of an oath you cannot fulfill. When will you take me to the grove and utter the words a betrothed one needs to hear? I will not waste my years in idle expectation.'

'She has gone, Tymarian. She would not wait a day longer. Even as the dawn broke upon the evening sky, she was making ready to leave. She cursed that you were not here. When you did not come, she rode away at first light. You have broken her heart and spirit. She would not say her destination. I was bidden to say but this: she will come no more to Novia Jorai. A curse on love and all its deceits and whimsical fancies. You are dead to her. When you broke her, Tymarian, you broke a second heart, for I have loved you as a son. But a father must protect the blood child he

53

loves. Do not cast your shadow across this threshold again. Lord or no, I swear an oath I will rent blade to flesh and take a life.'

"No," said Tymarian. "There is no woman."

"Then you have been fortunate, boy, not to have experienced the grief of losing one."

"Perhaps," Tymarian uttered, tearing his mind from the painful memories.

Yet he understood this man's rage against the Novian hordes. Would not *he, Lord of Havoy*, have unsheathed a sword and stood alone against an army of butchers for the honor of a woman? Yet he had not ridden after her or even sent huntsmen to source knowledge of her. That weakness haunted him.

"How long were you a prisoner at Rothshim?" the old man asked bluntly. He uncorked the wineskin and raised it to his lips, but found it suddenly blocked by Tymarian's curved sword.

"Mention that hellhole again and I will leave your head rotting upon the desert. No matter who finds it. Do we understand each other?"

In utter defiance, Zarmel gripped the cold blade and gulped from the wineskin, his gaze locking horns with the Novian's eyes. "As I said before, your plight is meaningless to me. But be sure to treat the animal you ride with respect. If it dies before we reach the city, you will join it." The old man brushed the blade aside. "Now get some sleep."

An hour beyond the first blush of daylight, bleating horns shook the air, alerting the caravan in preparation for the passage onward. Zarmel watered and fed the animals, double-checking the rope knots that tied the salt blocks to his

54

creature's bulky frame. Vocal clicks brought the animal to its padded feet, and the old weasel mounted up.

Zarmel took great delight in Tymarian's inability to control the huge creature he was riding. Anxious, it shuffled away each time he made a conspiring effort to ascend its rump. "Do you possess *any* skills?" chafed the old man. The warlord launched his body up into the saddle; the mount pulled at its rein, tossing its head wildly from side to side. Zarmel tucked the end of his purple turban into place—noting how ridiculous the Novian appeared, now he had taken to tying his own head garment *bandana-style*. Was he really trying to avoid detection? Little wonder he had been thrown into the dungeons of Rothshim. Unable to resist a last indignant quip, he hollered, "Some men, it seems, are not destined to live a long life."
Tymarian tugged at his reins and cut across the oldster's path, causing Zarmel's beast to jerk to a halt, almost pitching the salt-shipper from his ladened mount; he cursed, righting himself in the saddle, scolding the stranger for the inconvenience. "*Dog!*" he screeched.

The caravan surged forward, worming its way down into the yawning plateau, heading for the lush, greener regions beyond. Zarmel squinted at the figure in the distance astride the cantering beast, its motion ejecting sand into the gathering wind. He shook his head. "Fool," he uttered.

The severe limitations of the deep desert eventually conceded, and Semi-arid conditions replaced them. Tufts of green grass, cacti, and date palms grew ever more in abundance. They had reached the thinly populated outer regions. Many of Rissak's cavalry took the opportunity to barter with salt for *legmi*—fruits from the local trees, fermented into a potent alcohol. Each fertile oasis became a memory as the leagues diminished.

55

Scattered herds of wild *camleb*—ridge-backed creatures with grey fleeces and twisting horns—roamed upon the rocky ledges, chomping at the vegetation, oblivious to the oscillating movement of men and beasts below, weaving through the valley. Even the foliage density had thickened.

The clouds gathered, and heavy rain lashed the landscape. Day and night shifted in an eternal conquest of light and dark. The nearer the procession journeyed towards the city, the less concerned the emperor's soldiers became, regarding the commodity they were transporting—The salt was now deep within Rissak's borders, and the threat of attack was unimaginable.

Dusk hued the sky a sanguine green. The two suns above the world proceeded to sink. Upon the horizon to the northwest, the peak of Mount Kutrania thrust its horn out into the spreading gloom, wounding the clouds with its prehistoric barb of volcanic rock. Beyond the mountain range, through the defended passes, stood the city. Tymarian, clad in his loose burgundy shirt, now stained and reeking from travel, grew ever more uneasy.

The outer settlements were a combination of crude wooden structures and market bazaars. The towns thrived with corruption as gangs of cutthroats vied for dominion. The caravan had passed by a dozen. In one township, bodies were hanging from the boughs of rugged trees. Zarmel pointed at the rotting corpses. "Examples," he explained. "Some merchants employ protection. Rissak's ex-soldiers, to a large degree. They have no fear of reprisal from the scum operating in these districts. Quite the contrary, the emperor approves."

Tymarian observed in quiet approval. He had ordered the execution of his own men when such crimes warranted it.

56

The lime sky rose in temperature as the day approached noon, the mountains stretching for leagues as they traversed towards the city.

Before the pass, at the foot of Mount Kutrania, the forest swept ascendingly, covering the foothills with a quilt of many-colored leaves. At the mouth of the pass, from a lofted rock ledge, a gigantic tusk horn began to blow, its eerie timbre spilling into the valley like the haunting death knell of some colossal beast. The caravan shed the constricted shape it had maintained for the last forty-two days and began to disperse through the greenwood. Gone now the oppressive tension and menace it had endured in the deep desert, yet as it slugged up the foothills, the retinue wove back into its worm-shape, entering the gap between Mount Kutrania and its dwarfed neighbor, Schukhular.

The pass splayed into a rocky chasm two hundred feet across. The din of the returning caravan echoed with excitement in the narrow pass. Plain wicker baskets were lowered, filled with dates, bread, wine, and other eatables—a practice a millennium old in its custom. Once depleted, the baskets were jostled back up the sheer flanks of rock to the guards above. The ceremony was brief, and the caravan was allowed to advance.

Some leagues further on, they came to a sandstone wall bearing a portcullis of iron shaped in the form of eagle wings: the gateway to the city from the south.

The clanking of chains and squeaking of un-oiled cogs resonated as the heavy gate was winched up.

Long hours passed as Tymarian and Zarmel waited for their turn. The warlord's heart drummed beneath his ribs as the old man rode to the soldiers at the gate. He watched like a hawk.

Long had he possessed the knack of reading the character of men, but insects like the salt shipper were a breed apart. Zarmel turned in his high saddle, thrusting a finger in his direction. Instinctively, Tymarian's hand reached for the hilt of his sword.

"Easy," murmured the salt shipper, plodding back. "One of the men is a cousin. Stay behind me."

Zarmel turned the overloaded mount once more and trotted under the iron gate into the shadows.

Tymarian listened as the creature's footfalls echoed softly on the sandstone. Breathing deep, he followed.

Grim faces scrutinized them as they passed, the agitation thick and tangible. The scene unfolded in slow motion as one of the guards pulled at the reins of Tymarian's mount. Stopping in his tracks, Zarmel shifted in his saddle. "Be careful now, Jusal. Remember, the animal is mine."

Even as Tymarian drew his scimitar, a dagger plunged into his thigh, searing the flesh like a branding iron. The warlord broke the perpetrator's nose with the heel of his boot. As the guard squalled in agony, Tymarian's mount reared, throwing him from the saddle. He was swamped, instantly, by four guards, who punched and stamped his sunburnt body into submission.

"What should we do with the cretin?" Asked Jusal.

"Whatever you see fit," Zarmel replied. "He *is* Novian? Sell him to the swordmasters at the arena. He murdered Edatha's son out in the desert. It'll be bad news to bear. She will take it hard."

Tymarian's eyes narrowed—didn't the old man say that his woman now walked with the Sky God Kubenial.

Zarmel smirked as the penny dropped. "She's not dead yet, Novian. She has the cancer. The great eagle Kraghir will soon

58

spread its wings and circle our dwelling." He pointed at the skittish euganta that had borne Tymarian for so many leagues.

"*This* pet will be returned to its master. She may find some comfort in it, at the end."

Tymarian spat, cursing Zarmel unto the hellfire of Grundunia.

"Just one last civility, Jusal," said the old man. "May I ask it?"

"Ask away, cousin," said Jusal.

"I cannot ride both animals. You know their temperament, should I try to tether them. Would your captain allow you to journey with me to the city? Of course, *he* and the others are welcome to the money they will earn from *this*...dolt." He pointed at Tymarian, viciously beaten by the soldier whose features he had so ruthlessly destroyed. The captain of the guard stroked his goatee beard, grey as stone, pondering the situation.

"Make sure you are back before nightfall. Argh! Go. Go! You will get me hung!"

Zarmel displayed a courteous touch of the brow. "He will be back. My word on it."

"The word of a maggot!" Tymarian shrieked through his agony. "When we meet again, worm! I will cut off your puny balls and lay them on the grave of your whore!"

He was struck by a fist, knocking him unconscious.

The two men would not meet again.

Warlord, Tymarian Kryack, fugitive of Rothshim, was bound, gagged, and dragged the last half league to the city. He was sold as a runaway slave to the swordmasters at the arena for two flagons of cheap red wine.

Chapter 6

A MESSENGER IN THE RAIN
(Kazhelma, South Palacoumia Forest. 3rd Millennium)

The tracks in the mud led into a dense wall of rich forest.

The pursuer squatted by the hoof spoors in the pouring rain. The beast had to weigh at least eight hundred pounds. The animal, a cortorvus—*hoofed, tusked, and sharp-toothed*—was dangerous when driven to the extreme. Stories told of the creature shapeshifting and outrunning a grown wraken, scaling trees, and vanishing into the mist. The hunter had acquainted himself long ago with the knowledge that such tales were absurd. The hog-like mammal was a forager by nature, mostly placid unless threatened. Prized for the delicacy of its liver, it had been hunted to the verge of extinction.

The young man stood, loosening a green canvas cloak. He dragged a black arrow from a quiver, notching the shaft to a bow of horn. His nut-brown locks were tugged into a knot at the right temple. A weak goatee beard was twisted and waxed stiff into a tight protrusion from the chin. Rainfall saturated his trousers, and his leather boots were clogged with mud and blades of green foliage. All that morning, he had tracked the elusive animal. Leveling the bow, he felt the adrenaline rush. He cast his eye down the shaft, rain dripping from his concentrating features as he strove to pinpoint the beast under his aim. Suddenly, the animal charged, snapping through the thickets. Steam hissed from its flared nostril, its black, beady eyes wild and determined. The hunter let fly the barbed shaft; it whistled an inch above the rampaging beast; the falling deluge was the cause of the archer's miscalculation. He notched a second shaft; spumes of doubt clouded his mind; the calm exterior belied the panic rising within.

Master the fear...Or be the victim of destruction.

The bowman flicked his agile fingers, and the second arrow flew. It struck with a sickening thud, but still the wounded animal came on, determined and irate. The hunter wiped the rain from his eyes and whipped out a third shaft. The cortorvus was almost upon him. He pulled back the bowstring and held his breath, steadying his aim on the target.

Master the fear… Or be the victim of destruction.

The bowstring twanged, and the pillar of death hissed through the rain, tearing into the animal's eye socket. It slid towards him on the mud, landing a yard from where he stood. Heaving a sigh, he sank to his knees, dropping the bow into the mire; he gazed back over his shoulder.

The old man was watching. Always he was watching.

A brown leather coif confined the oldster's white hair. He was clothed in bice green from tunic to leggings, save for a long waterproof cloak, dyed the red of human blood. "Make the first shot count!" he admonished, grimly. "Next time you may not be so fortunate." He gripped the wooden pole of an umbra—*a whimsical contraption of stretched wraken hide over a frame, which one employed as portable protection against the elements.*

"This apprenticeship is not a lifelong commitment on my part," he complained.

"The weather hindered me," the bowman retaliated.

The old man shrugged, offering a liver-spotted hand to the sky. "Then wear a hood," he said, as if the remedy were obvious.

Thrydwulf began gutting and quartering the animal. "It wouldn't hurt you to shoulder some of the meat," he groaned, as the innards slopped onto the drenched mud.

"I am the tutor. You are the student. Remember that. Do not damage the liver. And don't forget the bow." Vargdenir wheeled and wove away through the soaked undergrowth.

***

Thrydwulf removed the twists of bright copper that stabilized his braided hair, leaving it to dangle wildly about the shoulders of his black woolen tunic.

62

The young man was blessed with handsome features. The women of the Court flirted brazenly in his company. Even Rissak's court jester had made the folly of propositioning him one summer eve at the stables—he had dragged the deviant to a pig trough, forcing his deformed head into the stinking water. *"Drowned!" he had breathed, savagely.*

He gazed out at the gathering storm, his elbows leaning on the windowsill. The rain had not eased but was hammering now like a million miniature fists upon the tilted roof. If anything, the weather was worsening. Curiously, he observed the threads of jagged lightning—silver blinking for immeasurable moments upon the black sky.

"The Gods are angry tonight," he exclaimed, nonchalantly.

"Not as angry as I will be if you do not close those damn shutters." Vargdenir snapped. "You're letting the heat out, boy!"

In a round chair of basket weave, before the fire, he sat rolling a narcotic leaf; a pewter goblet brimming with spiced red wine sat on the table beside him.

"Thryd!" he barked. "The oil lamps will go out!"

The cabin was awash with light, all tangerine-blue and magenta-gold; the liquidity of those flickering colors somewhat heightened by the intoxication of alcohol, and the soporific weed the older man was chewing and smoking. The rain drove ever vengefully upon the roof, as plumes of acrid smoke wafted on the drafts of air within the womb of the cabin. For a long while the seated men were silent; in a state of mutual contentment, until Vargdenir felt the sudden pang of mischievousness creep into his thoughts.

"How long has it been since I saved your worthless hide from Rissak's dungeons?" he goaded.

"Nine years," Thrydwulf replied, familiar with the psychological contest.

"More like ten," the old man jabbed.

"If you say so," Thrydwulf conceded, making no attempt to rise to the old man's provocation. On the contrary, Thrydwulf cast out his own fishing line of cerebral warfare. "I seem to recall a certain emperor's champion levering the events that saved my life that day."

Vargdenir bit the bait like a hooked perch. "You think that without me, you'd have lived so long among these savages?"

"*You* managed it." Thrydwulf's words sank lazily, like a ball of clay in a bucket of contempt. But the astute huntmaster merely smiled as he exhaled, sarcasm dripping from his tongue like venom.

"I was a gifted hunter by the age of Eleven. And you were...?"

"Gut-shot. Tossed into a stinking wagon and forced into servitude." There was a calm fire behind Thrydwulf's words.

"But you live! Can you not at least be grateful for that?"

"Better to have died and followed those I have loved across the Bridge."

"'Tis the wine; it makes you maudlin," said Vargdenir, chewing more of the narcotic weed.

"Murder tends to do that," said Thrydwulf. The remark was scathing, but it flew over the old man's head like a phalanx of wild geese too distant for contemplation.

"Ah," the old man murmured. "The *boy*, Oeric. It was an unfortunate accident, no more than that. My man, Frug, could not have known it was a child he was slaying. How could he? And his cutting of the throat was an act of mercy. Gryonae knew it, but something did touch him that day. Something I have never known about the man. That and the fact that he

64

had tried to bed Frug's wife. She refused, but Gryonae is a man who will grip to a grudge. He merely used the opportunity to vent his rage upon the woman's husband. He slew Frug in cold blood. That is the fact of the matter."

"Then I kiss Gryonae's hand for it," Thrydwulf declared, trying to hide the bitterness in his words. Vargdenir spat out the chewed narcotic and poured himself more of the spiced wine. "Not if you'd known Frug. If things had been different, I doubt not you would have taken to him. The man possessed many qualities. Phwarr! But Gryonae is dear to me also. A dangerous man to misread." Suddenly, Vargdenir raised his pewter goblet into the air. "And an emperor's champion into the bargain. May he survive the arena long enough to attain his freedom. I, on the other hand, am destined to serve this position of hunt-master unto death. A toast!" he blurted and guzzled back the potent blend of red grapes.

"Tell me the story again," said Thrydwulf, "how you came to be here? Wherever *here* claims to be. I am now fluent in the language of these people, yet their stench in my nostrils cannot be hidden by bathing or the application of perfumes. I am repulsed by their very nature." The huntmaster laughed at that insult, and the cabin fell silent, but for the drumming of the rain upon the slanted roof. In the Germanic tongue of his birth, Vargdenir began to speak grandiosely.

"I was born, so I believe, in the year 413 AD to one of the Jute tribes...presuming that time rotation here is one akin to the seasonal lengths that govern our own world. I have calculated I'm sixty-five years in equivalence to the turning of the seasons here. Osric, I was called, if memory is not also subject to twisting fact and weaving fiction. I know that it *is*, but Osric is the name I recall."

Vargdenir rose, moved to the fire, and dipped a long wooden taper into the flames. Re-sparking the oil lamp on the table, he glanced at the figure sprawled in the chair. "Stack the fire, boy. If you please," he said. This request broke the spell, and the younger man obliged.

Thrydwulf drained his goblet, replenished the vessel, and slumped back down into the low round chair, the basket weave squeaking like a rat beneath the dead weight.

"You say there was a cave? A cavern of some description, where you entered this..." Vargdenir waved an all-encompassing gesture, "...other reality? I've hunted every foot of those woodlands. I do not doubt you, mind, after all, it is evident *you* are here. Call it what you will, but *we* are proof that they exist: Wormholes, doorways, fabric tears in nature between worlds. Heofen and Hel, Middengeard. It appears the storytellers of our people were not merely mythmakers. It would seem, Thryd, *we* are the first settlers here in Kazhelma."

"The cave of green stone is true," said Thrydwulf. "One day, I will find **it.** The way home."

The cooked haunch of meat from the beast he had bowshot earlier that day lay cold on the platter at his feet. The white congealed fat caking its charred skin now appeared to be a feast. He felt suddenly ravenous. He spat the leaves he was chewing into the glowing logs on the hearth. Beside him, Vargdenir was tearing hunks of bread from a black loaf, mopping up the dripping on his empty platter. "I have tried to find these doorways before," he said, through a mouthful of Pumpernickel. "It took me years. Accept your fate. "I was washed here by way of a river," he divulged. "Not much older than the blond boy Frug killed. Blindon, the place was called. West Wales. Our boat went over on the water. It landed me here."

66

Vargdenir's mind swam on a lake of reverie. "I miss the rivers where we fished. Our people would not favor the hot climes of this world," he said. At first blush, he seemed to be probing the deepest, shadowy corners of his ideation. "That would have been in the year 423. Yes, I recall it. The storm hit in a wink." Vargdenir swallowed back an emotive impulse. "The river broke its banks. My mother and a sister… younger than I…"

He pictured them groping at the reeds, their hands flailing in panic.

Once more, Thrydwulf sensed the old man's emotional turmoil.

"I prayed *Eartha* would spare them any suffering. I lost my footing, too, as the flowing water took me. I can't say how long I was in its swell, clawing for air, gasping in a struggle between life and death. I saw the changes of land in a series of snatched glimpses, the tree boughs swaying, their mauve leaves rustling in the wind. The river flowed on as I was sucked into a vortex. Surely, I would drown. 'Tis strange, our experiences within the clutches of death. The very essence that was '*I,*' Vargdenir the boy, observing my own doomed sinking flesh, through a boy's eyes. *My* eyes..."

The old huntmaster shook his head from side to side, confused; his brow creased, seeking to grasp a suitable sentence to interpret *that* divisional moment of body and soul. "Wide-eyed, *he* pawed for life in those watery depths like a drowning mutt. This was *his* death. *My* death. So, I thought. Speculation is all one can offer concerning the events that occurred between that moment of death and my waking by the edge of a brook of moss and stone. The water gurgled away over the boulders, as I recall. The storm had lifted. The sunlight was not as I'd known it. And the trees..." Once again, Vargdenir's mien was one of bemusement. "Somewhere along that journey, I was sucked down the vortex of light into one of those places between the worlds that we know exist, *you* and *I*. That is my history. If you do not want these barbarians—after they have flayed us alive for witchery—scouring that wildwood with dreams of new realms to conquer, you will never speak of it beyond these walls."

The room fell to an eerier hush at the gravitas of Vargdenir's emphasis on the matter.

"How did you survive? You were barely a nursling yourself," Thrydwulf said.

"Birds, fish, berries, other animals. They are abundant in that colored wood. I fashioned a bow. My own father's skills with the weapon were reputed among our village."

"All these years, "said Thrydwulf. "All my asking. Why now do you tell me?"

Coyly, Vargdenir said that the storm was lifting—*and he did not mean so metaphorically.* He plucked more of the pungent leaves from the leather pouch and rolled them into a ball, placing the spongy foliage under his tongue. "You needed me. That sparked my pity. You were destined for the kitchens. The Stables. Or worse. You have survived. I'll not have you squandering the skills I have taught you, searching for pathways back to a world you will never find."

Thrydwulf laughed. Not mockingly, but to show his adopted father that he had disregarded a fundamental point.

"Yet you have tutored me in the one feat of skill that will ignite those very yearnings: how to track the spoor and read the land."

The huntmaster sighed ruefully. "Therein lies a predicament."

No sooner had he spilled those words than his face turned grave; he cocked an ear a slight degree.

68

"Something approaches," he said, darkly, spitting the narcotic pulp into the flames. "Or someone," he added.

Thrydwulf rose—sobering partially—from the squeaking chair; he snatched the long-hafted axe from the wall. Vargdenir laid an arrow shaft across a bow of horn, moved cautiously to the window shutter, and inched it open, glancing momentarily at Thyrdwulf. The younger man had braced himself, gripping the axe, preparing to swing the block of death. Pinpricks of sweat formed upon his brow. There was an element of doubt behind the nut-brown eyes, but fear was a natural emotion before the action of battle. With his wild locks, Thrydwulf now seemed, in essence at least, akin to one of the Germanic warrior myth-gods of Vargdenir's youth.

"Easy," the old man whispered.

Thrydwulf gazed askance and nodded.

Vargdenir peered through the window slit into the rainy darkness. There was a figure at the threshold, lurking in the shadows. Cursing the weather, the unwelcome guest began to pound upon the cabin door. Startled, Thrydwulf blasphemed softly and stepped back. Vargdenir hollered. "You'll find no shelter here! Follow the path west, through the wood below. It leads to the village of Karfilia. Maybe there!" The old man's words, inhospitable as they were, did not budge the stranger from his purpose. On the contrary, the hammering at the door intensified.

"Open it," said the oldster, with a grim frown. Vargdenir drew back the bowstring, caging his breath, steadying his aim.

Thrydwulf slid the bolt, leaping back as the stranger lunged in out of the rain.

Water dripped from his black, waxed cloak. His trousers and knee-length boots were caked with mud and wet foliage.

The old man let out a sigh, lowering his aim as Gryonae pulled back the black hood.

"Curse this retreat," he snapped impatiently. "Why you chose to build this high up with no approach except a climb by foot is beyond my understanding."

"Maybe you should wait for less inclement weather, or a more favorable hour, the next time you ride by to insult a man at his own dwelling," Vargdenir fired back.

"This is not a social call," Gryonae replied. "Last night, I lodged in the village yonder?"

"Karfilia," Thrydwulf informed the visitor, placing the axe back upon its pegs.

"The place is a dung-pit," Gryonae said, brusquely.

Vargdenir sighed. "Thryd, take our friend's cloak. And get him seated before the fire. He'll lodge with us tonight."

Gryonae glared at the huntmaster with a grim expression, but it melted like wax licked by the flame, and he smiled benignly. "Forgive my rantings. 'Twas a hard ride. I took the liberty of stabling my mount with the animals down below. This wretched storm! To you, too, Master Thrydwulf, my apologies."

"No offense taken," Vargdenir assured the visitor. "Sit and get warm. What news from the city?"

Thrydwulf sat with his back against the wall of the cabin, the guest occupying one of the only two seats the huntmaster possessed. Gryonae gorged on a platter of roasted meat, overindulging himself with goblets of spiced red wine, much to Vargdenir's disaffection. However, he would never have admitted this to a guest, let alone to a friend.

"How long has it been since your woman passed?" asked Gryonae.

"Nine winters and a three-quarter year. And before you ask, yes, I miss her more than you will ever know," said Vargdenir, with an air of disdain.

"Aye. Sheruba was a good woman. Do you miss not having sons?"

"No, I have one now," said the huntmaster, flatly.

The declaration touched Thrydwulf, but he said nothing.

"There is talk at court that you spend far too much time alone here."

Vargdenir sipped at his goblet and placed it on the table beside him. "If you'd wish to see me in the throes of melancholia, you could have brought a tortured babe and laid it at my feet." The old man's sarcasm amused the champion. It was a cruel streak in them both—and probably the reason why they had survived together among the Dirakhan.

"What news from the city?" Vargdenir inquired a second time.

"Endambia is dying," Gryonae told him. "Wraken riding, I believe. Something must have spooked her mount. Broken ribs. Collapsed lung. She is black and blue all over. She will not last the week; the physicians have told Rissak. The men who brought him that news, he boiled in oil."

Thrydwulf imagined them writhing and squirming. He shivered, allowing the image to evaporate.

Vargdenir looked shocked. "Why did the emperor allow her to ride? And in such poor health?"

"She is a stubborn woman," said the champion. "She would not be dissuaded. "Rissak has ordered a pageant in her honor. I am to entertain him in the arena. Endambia is the last of his kin. When the old Princess dies, he will spill a river of blood."

71

"I presume, being a member of the court, I have been summoned?" Vargdenir asked.

"He could have sent any lackey to deliver that news. I chose to ride here, to warn you. Tiptoe on eggshells around him. In the days to come, there will be many deaths when the grief takes hold."

"Always the boon companion," said Vargdenir.

"You were no less to me in my youth," said the Champion.

The huntmaster smiled. "You were obstinate even then."

"I will be accompanying you?" Thrydwulf implored, full of excitement.

"In normal circumstances," Gryonae declared, "nothing would please me more than to have you riding with us. You are far from the boy I encountered that summer long ago. But you are not charged to go, Thryd. It will be wiser for you to remain here."

"It is settled," hailed the old man sternly. "You will stay. And that is not a request. Endambia is fond of you, but she will be in no condition to receive anybody. I will offer the liver of the animal you shot today; inform her you would be honored if she would accept it as a small token for her feast. I shall say you have much to do here, should she inquire after you."

"A gift!" said Gryonae in mock surprise. "That would go well for you, old friend."

"Tomorrow, you will salt and wrap the meat against rotting," Vargdenir told Thrydwulf. "I'd hate to hang for poisoning Rissak's most prized possession," he declared with a frown.

72

The huntmaster packed his pipe with a pinch of narcotic weed. Drawing deep, his mind flashed back to one of the marketplaces in Quilaxia.

He had met Sharee there, offering her coinage so she could flee the wretchedness of prostitution. For all her treachery, regarding Gryonae, he had liked the woman. He could never have declared the deed he had undertaken in helping her, judging that sending the woman away, in all probability, had saved her life. His only guilt was that the skullduggery concerned a man he deemed closer than a brother.

"Let's turn in," he groaned. "We'll depart early tomorrow for the city."

Chapter 7

BRIM THACKALTON
(Kazhelma, Central Palacoumia Forest. 3rd Millennium)

Green splinters of sunlight filtered through the cracks in the cabin; the sleepers' garments reeked of smoke from the night before. Vargdenir was the first to wake. He labored to his feet, ambled to the shutters, and thrust them open, scratching at his thin, unruly hair. Gryonae snored on the makeshift hides the old man had laid out for him, the black cloak pulled up under his chin. Vargdenir prodded the dreamers from their slumber, instructing Thrydwulf to bring a pail of water from the stream below.

"Check the animals whilst you are there. See that they are fed and watered—and saddle Rharhume. Make sure the saddle is hitched tight!" he barked after Thrydwulf had closed the cabin door.

"You brought a change of garments?" he asked the old man.

Gryonae sat up and wiped the sleep from his eyes. "Only those I am wearing," he yawned.

"At least wash. Or ride downwind. Have any of your stable wenches told you, you snore like a euganta on heat?" Vargdenir said, risibly.

"Only the ones *you* were wedded to," Gryonae countered with a grin.

The old man washed his hands and wrists, cupped his palms, splashed his eyes, and wiped his teeth— this was the full extent of his ablutions—undertaken only when summoned to court, formal occasions, or festivities. His chalk tresses, he pulled back and tied with a curl of bronze. The scraggly hair under his chin he twisted and re-stiffened with beeswax. Now, he wore leggings and a tunic of deepest royal blue, seamed with black thread. The cloak was fashioned the same as Gryonae's: hooded and waxed to weather the elements during travel. At last, he was cleanly garbed; the odor of Gryonae's reeking clothes did little to improve his mood. Vargdenir attempted to coax the Champion to engage in the cleansing ritual. Gryonae refused point-blankly, lashing the curved prestigious sword across the back of his tunic. He buckled the belt and bone handle knives around his waist and tied the leather tassels of his black cloak about his throat.

"We'll have breakfast as we ride," said Vargdenir.

"Agreed," the Champion replied.

The huntmaster closed the door of the log cabin, and they began making their way to the edge of the undergrowth. Through the gaunt, grey birches, they began the descent to the stable enclosure a hundred feet below. "I have an indulgence you may enjoy," said Vargdenir, as they inched their way down the steep incline. "A delicacy. Stuffed dates?"

"Stuffed dates," mimicked Gryonae, humorously. "They are sold in every marketplace throughout the city."

"Ah, but these are a specialty," Vargdenir assured him.

"Mind how you tread there," said Gryonae. "And how are they prepared?"

By the tone of Gryonae's voice, it was obvious he was not the slightest jot interested in the culinary ramblings but merely tolerating the huntmaster's informative whim.

"Pine kernels, small nuts, and a pinch of peppers. Rolled in salt and fried in honey. A gift fit for a king," Vargdenir stated proudly.

"Or a dying Princess," said the Champion. "Make of them a token for Endambia. Rissak will note it. It may cause him to rove his eye toward some other quarter. One he finds less favorable."

"My reasoning exactly," Vargdenir confessed. "But there is plenty for us to savor. There is Thrydwulf. He has saddled the wrakens."

Vargdenir fussed like a mother hen, rattling off a list of chores: Keep the cabin bolted. Keep axe and bow to hand and the fire burning. Stock the firewood. Feed and water the remaining wraken. Have an ear to the wind for wild predators. Fill the water bucket. Clean the cabin. Bar the shutters at night.

Gryonae roared with laughter. "'It is no wonder your women leave you. You bark at the man as if he were a weanling. Let him be. He is not going to be besieged by outlaws."

Thrydwulf blushed.

"Just do as I have say," uttered the old man. "I'll return as soon as I am able."

Thrydwulf charged him an oath to be vigilant, to which the old man swore.

"Do not fret," said Gryonae, mounting his wraken. "I will bring the scroat home once these formalities have been resolved."

Thrydwulf helped Vargdenir up into the padded leather saddle.

"You are sure you have packed everything?" the elder asked. "The cortorvus liver? Dates? Bread? Water? Wine? Blade? Opiate leaves?"

"Everything you asked for."

"Farewell, Thrydwulf," said Gryonae. "Keep in good spirits, till we meet again. And don't take too much notice of *this* old woman!" He indicated Vargdenir with a nod of his head and spurred the blue beast, trotting away towards the trail.

Vargdenir gazed down from the saddle. "My life was never blessed with children, but I am glad to call *you* my own. You would have made your tribe the envy of Germania. I am proud." He spun the wraken. The animal began to pace, and Thrydwulf could do naught else but watch, regretfully, as Vargdenir and Gryonae rode away.

The turbulent weather that had flooded and battered the forest into submission the night before was now a dissipating memory. League upon league fell away, and the light of the two suns filtered through trees. It was more yellow than lime this morning, and the two riders had shed their heavy cloaks, being stifled by the heat. They had dined in the saddle, Gryonae full of praise for the medullary morsels they had eaten back along the trail. The lush woodland thrived and rang with birdsong. A herd of garnaset—*timid creatures with a single conical horn of whirled white bone*—grazed, ever alert, among the undergrowth. The old man pulled his mount up to admire their grace. Drawing the attention of a fawn—too young for horn growth—it twitched its ear and stared blankly at him. The animal's inexperience cost it its life. Gryonae snatched one of the daggers from its sheath and launched it, taking the young garnaset through the throat. In a breath, the nervous herd took flight, vanishing deeper into the heartland of the forest.

"Well aimed," said Vargdenir, with the raising of an eyebrow.

"Well aimed? I kill men for coin and name. If this is more of your anvil hammer wit—"

"No!" the old man exclaimed with a sudden laugh. "It was an impressive toss of a blade."

"You have seasoning?" Gryonae asked.

"I have salt. I never take to the road without it." Vargdenir slid from the back of his mount, scrambled through the tall ferns, and retrieved the prize. Withdrawing the bone handle blade from the animal's throat, he tried to heave the carcass aloft. He took a step forward and tripped over a dead branch, tumbling into the unruly grass. Gryonae grinned in his saddle. "Well aimed!" he chaffed.

It was now the hour of the day's meridian. Clouds drifted across the empurpled sky. Vargdenir had stripped his tunic, storing it in his saddlebag, and was now garbed in a loose, grey

78

cotton shirt. He had not expected to be cooking for this journey, but he took to the opportunity with great enthusiasm.

The meat had been thrust into the fire flames to sear in the juices, set aside to cool, and carved at their leisure. They shared a wineskin of red grape; watered down, they drank it sparingly, and now they sat together in silence. A woodlark sang above in the trees. The bird seemed intent on returning to its perch, no matter how many times it was teased away by Vargdenir's morsels of black bread.

"The Endambia situation is a grave development. Her death will be the spark that ignites the flame," the old man declared. "'Tis a shame. I hold a deep respect for that woman. She was kind to me when Sheruba passed. But for Thrydwulf, I doubt I would have lasted this long. If anything should happen. If you should win your freedom in the arena, look after the boy."

"Consider it done."

"I fear for him," the huntmaster professed.

"I fear for us all," said Gryonae. He chewed at a slice of garnaset flesh, merely going through the motions of eating. The woodlark flitted down to the crust Vargdenir had discarded, bobbing in a graceful glissade of dance. As the champion looked on, Vargdenir studied the man, witnessing a rare moment of compassion. For one who had survived so long in the arena, he carried relatively few cicatrices of conflict. But the mental scars, he was in no doubt, had been far more damaging.

"The wound there?" he asked, nonchalantly. Gryonae blinked as he was tugged from his caper. Intuitively, he began to stroke the white flare of skin upon his bronzed shoulder.

"An arrow, perhaps?" the old man asked.

79

"No," Gryonae replied with some amusement. "A hunting accident when I was a child. I was gored by a Stag."

The old man flashed a grin. "But not what you tell the ladies, eh?"

"I don't *need* to tell them anything. Have you not heard? I am Shadowgrip. Just being in the presence of some women makes them moist."

Vargdenir laughed haughtily. "So, they are not overwhelmed by your wit or charm?"

"When one is blessed with a long lance, wit and charm can be tossed aside."

The old man roared with laughter, his merriment quaking the quiet woodland. A gust of wind breathed through the shimmering leaves, and he sighed. "Have you never thought of escaping? Making your way home?"

Gryonae's eyebrows knitted. "What, to Novia Jorai? *There*, I would merely be a man. Here, I am a prince among men. With women. Coin. Shelter. Nay. Perhaps if I had kin to return to, I would have tried long ago. I am loath to admit I have grown used to the Dirakhan. But if you were to make the journey with me… You and Thrydwulf, maybe we could pass the outer gates and reach the forests to the south. It is said the land of my people is a stark and unforgiving place, but that is not my recollection of it."

Vargdenir shook his head. "I'm too weary in limb and heart. If I were ten years younger."

"At least we can still dream," said Gryonae. With a wry smile.

"To each man his fate," Vargdenir told him. But even before the utterance had left his lips, he was rising upon his haunches, perplexed, peering towards the dense thickets. "I fear we are not alone," he said, urgently. Gryonae sprang like a cat, sword in hand.

"'Tis not an animal. Or it does not move like one," the old man said with concern.

Shadowgrip strained an ear. Faintly now, he detected the din of branches snapping; something was moving towards them in the golden-olive sunlight. At their rear, tethered to grey, wiry birches, their mounts had begun to nicker, nipping at their reins as the unknown danger approached.

"To the wrakens!" Vargdenir yelled. "We'll outrun it." With dogged determination, he clawed, dropped, and clasped again the sack of watery wine, throwing its leather loop across his shoulder.

Gryonae's heart hammered in his ribcage. "There is no time," he said, full of dread and wonder.

A huge hand, wide as a shield, swept aside the emerald leaves of the overhanging trees. The fist, attached to a veined forearm, was thick as a man's torso, its skin pigments a tree-bark brown. The unkempt hair, beard, and public thistledown were of a deep moss green, and upon the creature's shoulder sat a net crammed with broken bodies and an assortment of smashed, grisly heads. Even Gryonae had to authenticate his courage.

"I thought these oddities were merely figments of the imagination," Vargdenir uttered softly. He was clearly shaken.

The champion's jaw fell agape in disbelief. "What is this monstrosity?"

"A wood ogre," Vargdenir uttered, full of dread. The creature had inherited many epithetical names, but Vargdenir had no desire to discuss them in this muddle of a mare's nest. It lifted its hideous head, sniffing at the afternoon air, with one fist adhered to a club of knurled oak. Gryonae dared to shift

81

his weight. That simple function drew the Ogre's inquisitiveness, and the abomination flicked its gaze, peering at them both with eyes like pools of blood. Suddenly, it roared, sending the lashed wrakens into a frenzy.

"Give me your sword," said the huntmaster. "I will circle behind, strike a blow whilst you keep it occupied."

Gryonae scowled, his eyes fixed squarely upon the huge monstrosity. Baring his teeth, he roared back, defiantly across the forest lawn. "I will need the sword," he declared.

"You think you can defeat this abortion of nature alone?" Vargdenir bit back.

"Do not invade the killing ground. If I can draw it yonder," said Gryonae, "make for the wrakens and depart."

"We stand together!" The old man told him. They were brave words, but even as they spurted through his teeth, he felt his courage shrinking.

"I am the Dancer of Death," said Shadowgrip, "and you do not know the steps. If I should fall, say unto Rissak, that I regret not gracing his arena with my talents."

Gryonae colored the air with guttural curses, navigating from shade to sunlight with a single vault, taunting the ogre, mocking it, even though it was oblivious of understanding. He whipped one of the bone-handle daggers, snatching it by the blade, he hurled it at the behemoth. With a dexterity that defied its bulk, the ogre twitched its gnarled club, glancing the missile away into the drooping ferns. All at once, the monster began to growl. With pure contempt, it hawked and spat a puddle of black gelatinous phlegm onto the grass. Gryonae obliged, samely, winking as he did so. Both myth and man lingered in anticipation, poised upon the horns of their dilemma. From Gryonae's vantage point, the ogre's grisly bundle had been obscure, not so now, from where he was firmly entrenched. He blanched the color of a rain-washed bone.

The mutilated bodies had been decapitated and had fused together in a shocking mess. Bruised limbs, puce and black, poked through the hexagonal holes of the blood-soaked silver netting.

The creature had obviously raided a village from deep in the forest.

Spying children among the slaughtered, Gryonae blasphemed at the absence of a bow beneath his fingers. He longed to take an eye. He was startled as a myriad of distant voices rose upon the wind, painting the late afternoon with added wonder.

Vargdenir surmised the demon heard it too. Cocking its head, it peered over its broad shoulder.

Gryonae seized the moment and hurled a second blade, catching the unwitting ogre, piercing its cheek like a hornet sting. Straining its lungs in annoyance, it pinched the splinter of steel from its skin, discarding it like a plucked flea. Squandering no time, the abomination clutched its net of corpses, thrusting the bulk athwart its shoulder once more. Then it was gone, fleeing through the trees like an ungainly man might wade through a field of corn. Death was now trailing *it*, and the blade of revenge would be thirsty for blood.

As Gryonae searched for his knives amid the undergrowth, the pursuers from the plundered village scurried into view, studying the indentations in the earth as they came. The ogre's stride had been colossal. The measurement itself enough to inspire terror. But the butchery of loved ones was more than enough to tip the balance for revenge.

The old man had managed to calm the wrakens, but his efforts were undone as Rharhume and the animal beside it

83

began to nip and bite at each other, trying to break free from their restraints.

The woodsmen crowded the spot where the monster had lain down its gory catch. The remnants of innards had oozed onto the crushed ferns. A blue eye—*a woman's*—had been squeezed from its socket as the net had been hauled back up onto the giant's clavicle. A few of the beleaguered bunch wept. One retched, emptying his guts into the bright flowers. His woman and child were among the missing. Now there was only retribution to cling to.

Even that was shrinking.

Gryonae strode before the weary hunters, aware of his serrated sword sheathed across his back. The situation was volatile. The champion accepted that traumatized people needed objects upon which to vent their wrath. But the monstrosity had stolen away further into the vast, uncharted forest. He hoped he would not have to spill the blood of grieving men.

"You saw it?" asked one of the weary search party.

The burly man, grasping a barbed spear, stood, sucking the air greedily in the fading afternoon. With black curly locks and a bushy beard, he was arrayed in a plain three-quarter tunic and hose of leafy green; his keen eyes never relinquished their grip on Gryonae's own. "Forgive me," he said between gasps. "I am Brim...Brim Thackalton. I stay at the village of these folks when I have business in the city. They're good people. Courteous. Rare in these times. This man here..." He indicated the figure of a weeping woodman—The distraught individual sat slumped beside the aftermath of gore and blood.

"He is Elan Gummel. A friend. I am a weapons merchant... of sorts. I lodge with him sometimes. His woman and baby girl are missing. Maybe taken with the others?"

The old man had tempered the nervous mounts and was now impatient in the saddle upon Rharhume's back. "Leave them!" he bellowed through the trees. "There's nothing to be done!"

The merchant stared icily at the insensitive boor. Vargdenir was already dressed back into the blue tunic and was now fixing the black-hooded cloak about his shoulders.

"Forgive the man his manners," said Gryonae. "He has pressing business in the city. Were it not so demanding, you would find him more… agreeable. But I *will* say this. Return to the village. A merchant of weapons, you say. Be warned...the tools you carry cannot defeat this scourge. Your pursuit is a quest of vanity. I witnessed only a glimpse of their fate. Nothing born of a woman could have lived within that pile of ruined flesh." His eyebrows lifted toward the flumped figure weeping across the clearing. "Do you *really* think that poor fool could cope with burying the heads of his woman and child? Must I spell it out, man?! Do you not understand what I am saying? It will kill you all!"

There was a deeper reason for the merchant's pursuit of the monster— He sought the net! But he could never disclose that reason to Bone Maker, the scourge of Quilaxia. Brim Thackalton found himself liking the man immediately. For all his notoriety.

The merchant shook his head. "They won't be discouraged. If I've learned anything from these folk, it is that they're slow to anger, but once the tinder is lit—If you take my meaning."

"Then they are doomed," Gryonae told him. "And you along with them."

They locked stares once more, each assuming an impression of what kind of man the other might be. Suddenly,

85

they gripped arms, and Gryonae gave the merchant the glimmer of a smile. "I pray you prove me wrong."

Gryonae paced away through the brushwood, clawing up his cotton shirt and black-hooded cloak as he passed.

"The stories men tell of you are unfounded!" the merchant called through the trees. "They say you are uncouth and arrogant! They are mistaken! I will break the jaw of any man who says it is not so!"

Gryonae stopped in his tracks and turned. The stranger had known all along. The thought was unsettling; he had completely misread the fellow. For a moment, the merchant was distracted by the huge footprint in the earth.

The determined questers followed the ogre's trail into the wood, and Brim Thackalton stood alone. Without the need for words, he hoisted the barbed spear above his head and ghosted away through the thickets.

"Say what you will. I liked the man," Gryonae said, as they rode.

"All I'm saying is that he may have possessed the morals of a louse," Vargdenir was quick to counter.

The champion laughed. "You preach morality to an oaf that dispatches whoresons for the amusement of an insane brat."

"I wouldn't trust him," said Vargdenir defensively.

"How do you know? You never even shook his hand."

Brim Thackalton and the company had pursued the ogre into the heart of the forest, tracking it to a clearing and a crude dwelling of log and earth, large and ominous in the mauve twilight. Brim and the others had charged the hovel only to find it empty of anything living. The grim discovery froze all to the marrow. Grisly practices and the eating of human flesh were evident; a sweet, sickly odor tainted the nauseating den.

A long bench, bizarrely whittled, was spread asunder like a butcher's slab. The creature had been in the process of preparing the carcasses for the pot. Elan Gummel's cry—the catalyst that would rattle the numb intruders from their shock—had discovered the necklace of human heads. Tethered to it were those of his wife and child. It broke what sanity was left in the man. Brim Thackalton would pull Gummel away, and in a rage, set the foul construction to the torch, razing it to the forest floor.

Gathering water from a nearby stream, the ogre had spied the red glow in the evening sky and hastened back to its lair. It had snuck through the trees only to fall upon the unsuspecting villagers as they hid in wait.

The creature's revenge was swift and savage, slaughtering all to a man save three: Brim, Elan, and Grethal. With the determination of these three, the tide of battle spun on its axis; the creature was mortally wounded.

Elan Gummel, his madness complete, took the ogre's head, charging Brim and Grethal with the near-impossible task of dragging the trophy back to the village. Grethal refused point-blankly and was slain with a single sword thrust as he stooped, wearily in the blood-drenched clearing. Brim, himself wounded, aided as he could, dragging the hideous haul, wrapped in the monster's silver netting, through thicket and fern. When strength failed him, and he could labor no more, he was murdered in his sleep. Devoid of hope, the insane Gummel, with his back propped against the creature's butchered head, famished unto death.

Chapter 8

THE BEAR CLAW ALEHOUSE
(Kazhelma, Quilaxia City. 3rd Millennium)

In the city, the first locality Gryonae visited was a newly
opened brothel. Not to sample its sullied wares but to seek the
woman, Sharee. He had spent years systematically scouring the
vulgar stews. One day, he would find her, but not on this one.
He paced through the streets, casting a lengthy shadow as he
wandered under the high lanterns flickering throughout the
city. The nimbus moon—*a sickle of silver upon the black cloak*—
reminded him of the song Vargdenir had sung as they had left

the forest, riding toward the mountains. The words eluded him, but the tune was running around his brain.

As he turned down a blind alley, the old man's lamenting was snatched, ignorantly, from his reverie.

Two street women emerged from a darkened doorway soliciting for trade. Gryonae paused, asking them if they knew of a woman named Sharee? The loose sisters did not. Dismissively, he barged through them, pacing on, their taunts and curses echoing down the narrow alleyway after him. He turned on them with a mask of iron; wisely, they pilfered away back into the gloom.

The old man had been wrong. He had loved her—Sharee. She had been unfaithful, and he had battered the philanderer to death with fist and club. Sharee had fled in terror. Rumor of her plight in the brothels reached him a year later. There were reports of a child.

What if it were his?!

He came upon a group of guards implementing their nightly rounds. Festivities were underway, and patrols in the city had been doubled. He stepped from the shadows. One of the men, also sloe-eyed, but with a short beard and hair groomed in the traditional ponytail, paced across the cobblestones. It was obvious the man had been drinking; Gryonae could smell the overindulgence of ale on his breath.

"I thought we had cleared the streets of all you rabble," said the guard. "How many ill-bred laggards must we send scampering home to their wives? There is a curfew on, goddamn it!"

"Do you know that drinking on duty is a flogging offense? Likely now a capital one, knowing the mood the emperor has been in of late." Gryonae pulled back his hood. The guard blenched, sobering immediately, and stepped back. "Forgive me, Bone Maker... I..."

Gryonae studied the man with a stare from the grave. "The Bear Claw. Where is it?"

"You mean the alehouse? Follow the street down. Turn left at the bottom and left again. It's on the corner. You can't miss it."

Shadowgrip tugged the black hood over his head and turned on his haunches. "By the way," he added, over his shoulder. "The name, Sharee... Does it mean anything to you?"

Gryonae knuckled hard upon the tavern door. The shutter of wood, a foot square, slid back, and a lined face with pale blue eyes peered through the aperture.

"Go away," said a gruff voice. "We are closed." The partition was slammed shut.

Gryonae rapped again, and a moment later the disgruntled owner returned.

"Do you know the city is under curfew?" fumed the barkeeper.

"I'm seeking Vargdenir. The Huntmaster. He frequents this establishment. Is he here?"

"And you are?" the landlord hissed.

Gryonae dragged back his hood and leaned in close. "I am *that* which haunts your darkest dream. Now, open up, wraken turd, before I wriggle through this hole and strangle you. " Suddenly, the bolts were yanked loose, and the creaking door pulled ajar.

"If I had known it was Rissak's champion..."

Gryonae ignored the foul, skinny wretch of a man and pushed past into the alehouse.

Vargdenir was three sheets to the wind. He waved Gryonae over, dismissing the company of late revelers. For an hour, he had subjected them to fanciful tales of fallen heroes and otherworldly beings.

"They were called the Numikhai!" he hollered after the stragglers as they were herded out into the night. "Half man! Half wolf! By day, they sleep. But by moon... Beware the moon!" With a drunken gesture, Gryonae was offered one of the empty chairs. Don't hover over me like a vulture. Sit down. Ale for my friend!" Vargdenir croaked impatiently. "Landlord! Where are you, man?"

The lank-haired proprietor sidled up, mopping away the ale spillage from the table. Gryonae seated himself opposite the old man, who suddenly sensed an uneasiness about him.

"Bring me a jug of water, and stir in some honey," Gryonae instructed. Vargdenir tipped a nod and winked to the confounded proprietor; he stepped away to deal with the unusual request.

"I forgot. Tomorrow, you fight. What brings you here?"

Gryonae trawled the room with a sweeping glance, an old habit. Only a handful of customers remained, lost in their discussions. A jug of honeyed water was placed before the champion; the Landlord said nothing and wandered away.

"I come to warn you," muttered Gryonae, blinking in the candlelight. "Endambia has taken a turn for the worse. I have it on good authority. Rissak believes the gift you brought her was poisoned. The fool's mind is broken. You are no longer safe here."

Vargdenir cleared his head and pushed away the half-emptied tankard of ale. "The boy!" He blurted, suddenly; he made to rise. Gryonae reached across the table, clutching the older man's arm, coaxing him back down.

"Thrydwulf is not in danger—yet. *You*, on the other hand, are another matter. You must leave tonight. I will arrange for your departure. I'll have a mount saddled and waiting. Ride before word of these accusations reach the guards at the city gates."

"Come with me," Vargdenir pleaded. "We'll get the boy and ride to Novia Jorai."

Gryonae smiled ruefully, yet there was a glint in his nut-brown eyes. "This was to be my last bid to achieve freedom in the arena. I am a dead man that walks beneath two suns."

"Then come with us!" Vargdenir implored.

The last of the customers drifted out into the night. Save one. The man was built like an ox, a knife scar snaking across his broken nose. He met Vargdenir's gaze, raised an eyebrow, and peered down into the dregs of his tankard.

"I will seek counsel with Endambia," said Gryonae. "No excuse will be fitting, but I will conjure something to buy you time."

A rapping at the tavern door stilled their conversation. The surly proprietor strode across the tavern to the front door and slid open the peephole. Scar-Nose was behind him. Shoving the proprietor aside, he slid back the iron bolts; twenty men lunged in out of the night. These were the emperor's bodyguards, seasoned soldiers. They would die in the line of duty. Gryonae pushed his chair to one side. Reaching beneath his cloak, he grasped the hilt of his curved sword. This time Vargdenir stayed the Novian's hand.

"There are too many. The boy!" the old man hissed. "Speak to Endambia. She is our only hope."

"Huntsman, you are under arrest for treason!" barked Scar-Nose. He shed his cloak, revealing gold tassels on a black tunic, a rank of minor captaincy.

"By whose authority?" Gryonae snapped back.

"By order of the emperor himself." The guards rushed forward. "Now out of our way, arena rat," Scar-Nose growled.

Vargdenir was manhandled out into the shadows; the rain, drizzling earlier, was now lashing down.

"This is not an end to matters," Gryonae snarled. "Take me to the emperor."

"You, arena-dog, have not been summoned. Find your own way back, lest you mean to trail us through the streets like a lap dog."

Gryonae's knuckles whitened upon the hilt of his sword, but he subdued his wrath. "I will see you chained and flogged for this. That old man still holds sway with Endambia. She will have you digging out latrines for a year in the city barracks." Gryonae broke into a grin. "Shitmaster! It will befit an oaf like you."

The captain lashed his cloak against the rain. "That will not happen," he said with a sneer. "This night, she flies with Kraghir, the Great Eagle. Her soul now walks with Kubenial." As the door of the tavern slammed shut, Gryonae slumped down into his chair. Against all wisdom, he called for a flagon of ale. After a long hour, his thoughts wandered back to the woman Sharee.

Chapter 9

VARGDENIR'S FATE

Daybreak began to glow across the distant mountains, and
the rain was still drizzling from the night
before. Under house arrest, Vargdenir focused from the
window in the elevated tower, scanning the network of streets
below. Movement was everywhere in preparation for the main
festival. The news of Endambia's death filled him with
apprehension.

'Sit beside me, Huntmaster. Don't be shy.'

'Tis not a fitting thing to do, Lady.'

Endambia threw back her head and laughed playfully at the man's unease. She seized Vargdenir's hand, dragging him down upon the wooden bench beside her.

'Who will know?' she said. 'The guards are deaf. The servants are mute. Relax, lest you have me believing I repulse you in some way.' Endambia's long black hair was braided, her breasts full, her lips generous. Middle-aged, her pulchritude was unquestionable.

'Not even the flowers could compare,' he replied with a bashful breath.

'Quite the poet. I didn't realize you were so skilled with that tongue.' The woman's sexual ambiguity was obvious; it shone in her eyes, and she reveled in the man's awkwardness. Endambia smiled as Vargdenir blushed.

'Why have you called me here?' he asked her.

'Should there be a reason?' Suddenly, she lowered her chin, and the joy seemed to seep from her. 'Are we not friends?' she asked, her eyes suddenly sad.

'You are royalty. Such friendships are against the law.'

'I am above the law, you fool,' she quipped with a smile. In the colorful garden, the heady fragrances drifted among the flowers. His thoughts, suddenly dark and lustful, were to drown beneath a lagoon of guilt. They sat in silence, enjoying each other's company as the magenta suns were slowly sinking.

'I will always help you,' Endambia avowed. 'Should you ever ask.'

The lock turned in the door behind him, and Gaucuss—the Emperor's Assassin—entered.

"The emperor has summoned you," he told the huntmaster. "Come."

Vargdenir brushed his clothes as they paced through the Palace grounds, Gaucuss leading the way with a purposeful stride. Vargdenir noted the assassin's curved spine, the black silk garbs that fluttered in the light wind. His gait was almost a swagger; Vargdenir was not alone in his loathing of the man. His mere presence evoked the imaginings of a sealed fate. This, the huntmaster could not shake from his thoughts.

Gaucass entered the colonnade on the east wing of the palace; its sandstone walls were plastered with swirls and whitewash. Vargdenir peered through the fluted columns to the botanical gardens where he and Endambia had sat all those years before. The memory filled him with sadness, and the hope of her last promise scurried away to hide under a stone of profound hopelessness.

The autumn trees were shedding their pastel leaves of cream and tinctured blue, their stunning coloration still an enigma to him after thirty summers. Or had it been more? It did not matter. He would not relish another. By the pond, a mason was sculpting a block of red sandstone. The vivid features were Endambia's—or how she was being perceived to look at the brink of womanhood.

Gaucuss stepped into a maw of shadow, entering a claustrophobic stairwell of smooth granite. Round windows sucked in the sallow light from the morning beyond, the two men's footfalls echoing with dull thuds as they climbed.

"You think me guilty, Gaucuss?" the huntsman sought to know, his blue robes swishing with movement.

"You're a pawn in a game. As am I. You are unlucky. That is your crime."

"I am a dead man, then," Vargdenir said, resignedly. Gaucuss offered no reply. He strode out of the shadows into a wide anteroom, plush with ornate red carpets, woven with twirled threads of silver and gold. Light seeped in through the high windows, and the timber shutters were tied back against the peach-shaded walls. From burning candles, the scent of jasmine wafted in the air. These were being ignited in their gold sconces by a handful of maidservants, one of whom was yawning in her task.

At the entrance of the throne room, two soldiers stood guard. Unflinching. Eyes fixed to the front.

The Assassin stood arrogantly between them, knocking upon one of the wooden doors. Rissak's impatient, muffled voice echoed from the throne room. Gaucuss turned the iron rings and entered the womb of the deranged emperor's sanctuary.

Rissak, donning an ostentatious headdress of peacock feathers, was seated upon the ancient throne of his ancestors; composed of black wood, inlaid with intricate spirals of solid gold, it had been created by a pair of extremely talented hands. The elaborate object stood upon a dais of polished timber, embedded with patterned strips of turquoise. Mounted upon the armrests were the figureheads of snarling leopards, cast of platinum and burnished to a gleam. His long gown was oyster-hued and woven with helical threads of satin trim; his coal-black locks were combed in the traditional style beneath the iridescent plumage of feathers, his sloe eyes alert, shining with an arrogant madness.

Vargdenir felt the compulsion of a sick laugh. It was fear. He knew it, but he subdued it. Before the wooden dais, Gaucuss forcibly shoved the old man into a genuflection, kneeling beside him in turn, bowing his head in acknowledgment. Rissak gestured his indifference with the palm of his hand, and the subjects pushed themselves to their feet.

"Confess your crime, Huntsman. I will spare you the humiliation of the arena," said Rissak, devoid of emotion.

97

Sunlight spilled in through the slotted windows, illuminating those involved in the charade within the conical chamber.

"Why would one confess to a deed one played no part in?" the old man retorted.

"You deny poisoning our beloved Endambia?" Rissak threw the weight of his stare upon the luckless victim, but Vargdenir's pride returned. He projected his shoulders, and the moth of trepidation fluttered away.

"Your Majesty knows as well as I that the accusations are false. If my life is to be forfeit for the blunderings of your court physicians, let it be so. I will not concede to a false charge. If political purposes are at play, I was dead at the moment of their conception." The old man's shoulders slumped; he sighed and shook his head. "I'm tired. I will not grovel to you, boy."

Gaucuss clutched the handle of the poisoned blade upon his belt, but Rissak finger-signaled the assassin to stay his hand.

"Tis not difficult to see why Endambia admired you. She could have chosen a lesser man in whom to confide."

Rissak gripped the platinum leopard heads and leaned forward on the black throne. "What do you suggest, Huntmaster? Shall I summon every cook and quack in the royal palace? Get them to confess to the crime of which you claim your innocence? Maybe the rack or a little skin flaying would loosen the lying tongue."

Bereft of care, Vargdenir exhaled contempt through his nose. "When a man beats his dog, he punishes it for his own inadequacies. Some men recoil from their grief. Withdraw into themselves to hide from the pain. Though you sent a thousand innocent men to their deaths, it would achieve little more than defile the memory of a woman whom I have loved in friendship ere you were ever born, Dirakhan!"

98

'Hold him tighter! Lest you drop him.'

'Has Empress Eryon chosen a name? Take him before he wriggles his way out of my arms into the lily pond. I have no knack with children.'

'Give him to me, Huntmaster. My niece is coming. Look! She frets. Isn't he adorable? Of what sin could such gentleness be ever guilty? Oh, yes, the name. They have chosen 'Rissak. It means 'thorn of righteousness.'

"If not *you*," said Rissak, "then maybe the outlander, Thrydwulf… the man you have reared in your secrecy. Maybe he is the perpetrator of the deed. Or at least the cause of it."

The emperor sat back upon his velvet cushion, peering down his nose with scorn. "*Like* stick to *like*, do they not?"

Vargdenir felt the adrenaline rush surge through his body. In a spontaneous motion, he reached for the dagger at his side, but of course, even this ceremonial weapon had been confiscated. He felt something slide across his throat. Instantly, it panged, like a hundred hornet stings. He gasped in shock, hands clenching his throat, sticky blood seeping through his weathered fingers. He collapsed before the steps of the dais, his mind swirling in a kaleidoscope of life experiences. The image of a woman, chin-deep in water, clawing at long, resilient river reeds, came into his mind. Clinging to her was a blond girl. A swirling cloud of purple mist consumed his cognition. He had always imagined the warrior maidens thundering across fey viridian plains to bear his soul to the great hall of Valhalla. There were none. The purple mist swirled on an astral wind; two voices intruded upon his sense of ebbing into oblivion.

"Feed the body to the dogs," said one.

"And of the outlander, Thrydwulf?" asked the other.

"Bring back his head. He rots where he falls."

The ground before the old man's spectral feet swept open, revealing a grim mouth blazing with fire. The heat was scalding, the stench sickening. The remnant essence that was Vargdenir closed its eyes and tumbled into eternity.

Chapter 10

A MEETING OF BLOOD

The shadows were expanding across the courtyard in the grounds of the academy when word reached Gryonae of Vargdenir's disappearance. He had struggled to suppress his rage and grief, and the promise he had made the huntmaster, concerning Thrydwulf, stuck in his throat like an unswallowable fishbone. As the voice of the old man reverberated in his mind, Gryonae grinned through his tears. He lay in the gloom for the longest time. Rising from the bed, he pinned on his cloak and strode from the cell to clear his head.

He wandered the underground passageways of the amphitheater, passing the Gates of Death, the place where combatants were stripped of their armor and transported to the pits beyond the walls of the city. He turned right, ascending a stairwell hewn from stone. Up in the cold night wind, on a balcony, he inspected the arena where the games were held. The oval floor was a construction of wood, with elevated torches, bathing the newly laid sand with apricot light. Gryonae perched himself down upon one of the granite seats, evaluating the other competitors as they trained for the festivities.

Directly below, a swordmaster was goading three men to attack. A spritely fellow charged at the instructor but was dispatched, instantaneously, to make an example of.

"Never rush in!" he barked. "This slave was a fool. Always gauge the opponent. Look for weaknesses: Is he off balance? Does he have the suns in his eyes? Is he tall, leaving his legs exposed? Keep the elbows bent. Seek the flow; dominate the engagement." He stepped over the twisted corpse. "Now *you*," he said with a sneer, gauging the next fellow. "You think you can do better? Learn or die." The second adversary began to circle the swordmaster. He moved in close, hacking furiously, leaping back as the trainer countered with a sweep, cutting his assailant across the jawline. The man stumbled to his knees and was deftly knocked unconscious with the flat of the trainer's blade. He tested the weight of his curved sword; the ritual had been a lifelong habit. "Now you! They tell me you survived the salt mines. Not many do. Least not those born of Novian witches."

Gryonae leaned forward, suddenly intrigued.

The last of the three slaves stood, his hand resting upon the pommel of a sword driven into the floor at his feet. Gryonae studied the long, dark tresses, blown by the wind about the doomed combatant's naked shoulders.

"It's said your people are the creation of a mutt copulating with a sow," the swordmaster provoked. The lack of response was infuriating. "You are mute? Is that it? The salt mines of Rothshim can do that to a man. You have a pretty mouth. Shall I have the guards visit you tonight? Make use of it?" Gryonae was curious how much insult the man could take. When he eventually spoke, the champion pushed himself up onto his buskins.

"You wish to die here, swordmaster?" the slave bellowed. The threat rankled the instructor. "Bold words. For a bug!" he replied, inching closer. For your insolence, you will die slowly, Novian."

Ignoring the code of his own training, he lunged blindly, thrusting at the target.

Like a ghost, the Novian was gone. The swordmaster shifted his weight, instinctively blocking to the right as the slave's sword clanged against his own. Sweat beaded upon his brow. For the first time in years, he felt a twinge of fear, but as a swordsman of the Royal Academy, it would not have been evident.

Gryonae watched in fascination as the two men engaged each other. Each time the trainer flurried an attack, it was repelled. It was obvious to Gryonae, the dolt was tiring.

'Call the guards, then, you fool. Subdue him,' thought the champion.

The circle widened as the trainer backed away.

Twisted ankle, eh, Gryonae contemplated with a smirk.

The man has nerve.'.

103

"Guards!" the trainer roared. From out of the shadows, a dozen men rushed forward, putting the defiant slave at spearpoint.

"Kill him!"

Gryonae leaped down the steps to the wall of the arena. "Stay those weapons!" he cried out. The startled swordmaster spun his head, staring up into the darkness. "Who goes there!"

"Brezlin! Are you going to slay the only man capable of giving me some sport in this rat hole? If you keep killing the poor fellows, who will I fight?" The swordmaster lowered his blade and breathed a sigh of relief, convinced the intrusion had saved his life. "Shadowgrip!" he barked back. "You want him?"

"The emperor might. If he's not satisfied with the entertainment, he may take all our heads."

"So be it," Brezlin said, turning to the guards. "Take this dog back to the cells. Give him what he needs—within reason. No woman. I don't intend to breed these vermin."

The slave raised his sword and took the battle stance, as the spear points pressed in around him.

"You! Slave!" Gryonae called down. "Two things can happen here. Slaying at the end of those barbs, or a match with me before the emperor. You *may* win your freedom.

"And you are?" The slave called back.

"I am Rissak's champion."

"You are Shadowgrip?"

"Who wants to know?"

"I am from Novia Jorai. A warlord, once."

"Then we have more in common than you know." With that, Gryonae was gone, striding up the stone steps, making for the soft pallet where the warm harlot was sleeping.

"What will it be, Warlord?" Brezlin smirked, stressing and mocking the word.

"A duel with Shadowgrip, of course—you cancerous bowel!"

Tymarian let the sword slip from his grasp.

"Clear away this body," ordered the swordmaster. "Wake up *that*...sleeping dung heap and take *this* bird dropping back to its nest. Get him bathed and fed. But first, piss on him through the grates above his cell. Let him learn his place."

Tymarian was led across the sand, past the tall Gates of Death. The next time he would meet Rissak's champion, he knew he would not be taken back through them alive.

***

Tymarian eased himself against the stone wall of his cell as four streams of urine poured down through the iron slats above. Something else, stinking, dropped with a splat to the slabbed floor. He couldn't tell what it was, but he took an educated guess. "Here's your food and water, Novian." Laughter erupted in the chamber above. It dissipated rapidly and was replaced with an array of angry words.

"Rest now," said a voice. "These cockroaches will not bother you again."

Tymarian shifted into the feeble light filtering in through the overhead grate. "Shadowgrip! Is that you?" He breathed loudly. There was no reply. Tugging the piss-soaked blanket from the pallet, he wrapped the soiled garment about his shoulders. For an hour, he sat in the corner of the cell, shivering, unconvinced the defilers would not return. Later in the night, he rose on his haunches, navigated to the hay pallet, and collapsed.

105

'What are you doing, Father?' The boy observed as the stag was roped around its horns, laboriously hauled up and suspended from a lofted branch.

'We have to dress it,' the man answered. The brothers sat in silence as the animal was gutted and skinned. 'We'll break it down later, back at the settlement.'

One of the two sons, sable-haired and canny, heard the galloping of beasts. 'Riders are coming!'

The man turned his attention to the mauve leaves of the far-flung wood. Panic set a fire under him. They were riding blue wrakens; mounts of the Dirakhan. Urgently, he cut down the stag and grabbed the axe leaning against the knurled tree.

'Get behind me,' he told the boys.

Twenty-five men thundered across the open ground, drawn by the smoke from the fire. As the beasts rode up, one of the men slid agilely from his saddle. 'By whose authority do you hunt these regions? These lands belong to Ridiantee, Emperor of Quilaxia, and all the known world. They belong to the Dirakhan.'

'This is free land. Novia Jorai answers to no one.'

'Till now,' said the pony-tailed warrior. Ridiantee is extending the borders of his empire. War has been declared; you, my friend, are a prisoner.'

The Novian, about to object, thought better of it.

'These are my sons. Can you at least keep us together? I implore you!'

'I will try,' said the warrior, almost apologetically. 'But it cannot be guaranteed.'

Tymarian spent two days and nights alone in his cell. On the third day, buckets of freezing water were chucked through the iron slats, and he was fed a pauper's meal. On the fourth, training resumed. Brezlin had been replaced by a younger swordsman from the Royal Academy—one concerned with

106

the skills of entertaining the crowds in the arena rather than murdering the competitors before they could arrive there.

The manner of a man's death in front of the emperor was his own affair. A brutality well deserved if courage failed. Tymarian maneuvered through the sequence: Cut. Thrust. Block. Wheel. The monotony was mind-sapping. Rain hammered down the day before the games were due to begin; the young swordmaster was approached by one of the barrack servants and handed a scroll. Attentively, he read the contents under his umbra:

"Tymarian! It is official. You are to die at the hands of the emperor's champion. Back to work!"

Exhausted, the men were led back to their cells and would be allowed rest before the tournaments began.

The noon suns were high, flooding the blood-soaked sand with light, the shade of lime.

Tymarian lingered in the middle of the arena, clad in the ceremonial battle armor—hot and uncomfortable, but prepared. As the champion entered through the gate, the crowd erupted.

Gryonae breathed deeply, noting the physique of the man he had chosen to fight. He strode towards the royal balcony and raised his hand. "To us about to endure death's journey, I pray Kraghir flies our souls to the arms of Kubenial." Rissak customarily rolled his palm; the champion saluted and turned his attention back to the arena.

Tymarian scrutinized the confident gait of his opponent, and it sank home: one slip, and he—prisoner of Rothshim—would be ripped into the void.

107

Shadowgrip strode within ten feet, his bronzed torso scarred with the injuries of combat—how life-threatening they had been, Tymarian could only guess.

The Champion wore studded gauntlets and plain white leggings; his brown locks tied with a silk bandanna. The familiar belt of knives had been wrapped in gauze and placed beneath the pallet in his quarters. His only weapon—besides the deadly unarmed battle skills—was the long-serrated sword, sheathed in a scabbard across his back. The masses cheered as it was drawn and driven into the floor at his feet. When the champion spoke, it was in a language Tymarian had not heard for almost a dozen years.

"You are Novian?" the champion asked. Tymarian nodded, his black helm and visor concealing his features. "From Braytoria," he replied, in the guttural tongue of his people.

"I know it well," said Gryonae, with a rueful smile, stepping in closer. "Let's not give these dogs the contest they desire, eh? I will kill you quickly, spare you the humiliation of Rissak's sick pleasures. If you are wounded, he will send in the pygmies: Cruel in their torment. Famed for taking fingers as trophies."

The prisoner of Rothshim grinned broadly as the crowd became restless.

"You bear many scars," said Tymarian. "Others have come close, I see. You are not immortal, Shadowgrip."

Boos and jeers began to fill the arena.

"Scars," said the champion, stressing the word. He appeared genuinely amused. He pointed to the white slit on his toned belly. "This is the work of a disgruntled whore. This..." he lifted his arm, pointing to his shoulder, "A boyhood injury. A hunting mishap."

108

Tymarian untied the lashes at his throat, tossing his helm onto the bloodstained sand. He stared hard, his mind racing. "The animal…?" he said. "Was it a stag?"

"Say again?" said the champion, caught by surprise.

"Is the wound the goring of a stag!"

Shadowgrip was startled. Losing his composure, he seized the hilt of his sword. "Does Rissak now send a sorcerer against me!"

The crowd hurrahed, misconstruing the act.

"No!" Tymarian retorted, raising his hands. "Your father's name...was it Methorin?"

The champion stepped back, fearing he was in the presence of a man tutored in witchery.

"Do you not know me, Gryonae?" said the Novian adversary, bewildered and stunned at the sudden realization.

For a short while, the champion stared in disbelief, only to loft his sword.

"'It is I. Tymarian. Your brother!"

In one flowing motion, Gryonae lunged, piercing the sorcerer's belly.

The man from Rothshim dropped to his knees and crumpled in a heap upon the sand.

Chapter 11

GAUCUSS AHDOR-NEZ
(Kazhelma, North Palacoumia Forest. 3rd Millennium)

The length of rope hitched to the assassin's saddle was knotted to the rein of the wraken behind.

Gaucuss heeled the contrary animal, and it swiveled its head, nipping at his glove. Whipping it across the neck, it snorted loudly in the morning mist.

"Up you go, my beauty," he rasped. The wraken obeyed, contentiously, plodding over the treacherous shale, back to the road from which the beast had slid.

Five days from the city, the master assassin began to descend from the higher elevations of the mountain pass. The grey-green landscape was filled with twisted trees crowned with leaves the color of magenta. He shot a gaze under his fingers; his face indifferent as a flock of birds weaved in black amorphous swirls across the skyline; he rode on. Some leagues farther, he stopped to refill the water pouches in a rivulet running across the stones.

The clops of the shod wrakens echoed around him as they traveled through an outcropping of rock, a naturally formed tunnel, its smooth walls etched with drawings millennia old. He trotted through, out into the olive sunlight, and there, across an ancient rope bridge spanning a deep gorge, was the entrance to Palacoumia.

He knew the stories associated with the tales of its ancient forests. The myths of the giant ogres, supposedly glutting on human flesh. Sorcerers shape-shifting into wolves—or monstrosities of them. Then there were the witches, conserving their youth by drinking the blood of newborns. Wizards looting the souls of lost children, trapping them in a glass vial for all eternity. Gaucass suspected the tales were devised by the outlaws themselves, living deep within the confines of the greenwood.

Across the chasm, two colossal trees, bearing the weight of the bridge, had been intricately carved. Somber totem-esque faces peered out of the bark. If the purpose was to discourage those entering, the intention was effective. Gaucuss raised an eyebrow as a gust of wind rippled through the pastel salmon leaves. That split second ruffled his nerves. Silently cursing his

111

foolishness, he dismounted. Taking the reins of each animal, he led the wrakens across the bridge and entered the forbidding forest.

Shafts of bright green light poked down through the many-colored leaves, splashing upon the ferns below, painting shadows across the mosses and plants. The well-trodden path wove through the undergrowth. The deeper he ventured, the eerier the oppressive silence became. He kicked the wraken into a canter, dragging the skittish animal behind him in his wake. He galloped on until he came to a place where the route was divided into three.

"Whoa!" he hollered, stroking the wraken about the ears. The animal, lathered from its ordeal, turned its neck, its blue eyes wide and fretful.

"Soon, my beauty," Gaucuss assured the animal. He plucked one of the scroll maps from a saddle bag and unrolled the yellow parchment. The heading was *Palacoumia Forest*.

A thin black line was scrawled across the map, ending in a three-fingered claw, marked as *Lagantius' Talon*. He checked the direction to the right. It led to the lake. That was all the assassin needed to know. He struck the animal again with the leather whip, and the exhausted creature galloped on.

Gaucuss pushed the beasts to their limit. Eventually, through the dense thickets, he spied the silver lake rippling in the olive sunlight. He led the thirsty animals down to the water's edge; they drank greedily.

***

A canvas wikiup was erected against the elements; the sky-blue mounts were brushed and fed. A fire was built, and he sat before the flames munching on a morsel of black, nutty bread and sour cheese. He pulled tight his cloak as if to oppose the encroaching darkness, pondering the emperor's hunt-master. He had been easier to outwit than the assassin had anticipated. Vargdenir had never been a fool. Yet an eyeless cretin could have seen through the snare. Perhaps age had addled the old man's brain? Maybe the younger outlander would prove to be more challenging. Gaucuss pinned his hopes upon it.

The fire died down. Back among the trees, the roped wrakens snorted restlessly in the gloomy quietude.

In the wikiup, Gaucuss rolled in fitful slumber.

The dogs' fangs were dripping with blood, gnawing at the stumps where Gaucuss' feet should have been. He twisted, and the severed head beside him opened its eyes, and the mouth began to speak. '

Well met!' it rasped. 'We have been waiting for you.'

Gaucuss drew back in shock.

The grey landscape was treeless, the heat oppressive, and for the first time, he noticed the inky sky was devoid of stars. Fire spewed intermittently from a variety of fissures in the rock floor, casting formless shadows in the fey orange light. A torso of butchered flesh slivered through the settled ash, melding itself—with nauseating squelches—to the scorched head. Burnt, twisted limbs did similarly. The crippled figure gathered to its blistered feet. Stepping aside, it gestured with a deformed arm.

'They are coming, Gaucuss,' said the hideous figure of Vargdenir. 'They will not be denied.'

As the souls of the damned swept forward, Gaucuss woke, bolting upright, grasping the crumpled blankets in the damp wikiup.

***

113

The uncanny silence that had permeated Palacoumia for twenty leagues or more lifted, and birdsong rang through the forest. Monkeys—macaques—chattered among the branches, quizzically following the man and the two wrakens until their interest waned; they vanished long before Gaucuss realized they had gone.

The assassin came to the edge of a clearing—the remnants of a deserted village. Trees had toppled, crushing several of the raised wooden huts that were scattered around the perimeter. As he moved through the site, he concluded its abandonment had probably been recent. Broken pots and discarded bowls were strewn close to circles of scorched grass, the patterns extending wide where the fires had spread. But why had the inhabitants left and not simply rebuild? If this had been an attack, there was no evidence, no bodies or blood with which to gauge an assault by raiders.

Randomly, he rode, locating the mud trail leading away from the village to the south. Taking the scroll from his saddlebag, he unrolled it. According to the Emperor's cartographer, this location had been given the title Worlufia. '*The Silent Place.*' It was aptly named. Gaucuss found mild amusement in the irony. The scrawled line on the map indicated thirty leagues more to Karfilia, the village nearest the secluded lodgings of Rissak's dead huntmaster. He re-scrolled the parchment, replacing it in the saddlebag. Determined, he galloped away from Worlufia, pushing the ramshackle settlement and its mystery from his mind.

'I cannot bear to lose!'

'My dear Gaucuss, why else do you think you have been chosen to be schooled here? The empire needs those who are determined to conquer. You possess that quality,' said Prail.

'But I lost!'

'On the contrary. You neglected to duck. You must learn to focus. Jotard is strong, but your strength lies in your agility.'

'I got trounced,' Gaucuss contended.

'You got angry,' Prail told the student. 'Learn to control it. There are pathways from this school of learning to higher positions of duty for the emperor. Succeed here, and who knows? Court official. Emperor's scribe. Ambassador!'

'Or the Quwarshin,' said Gaucuss, suddenly infused with wonder by the thought.

Prail sighed. 'Men in those positions are chosen because they have no links to family. They are ruthless. Some say deranged. I accept they are needed. It's said they're deprived of human contact for the first three years of training, left to fend for themselves in the mountains. They are tutored in ways of killing with potions and tracking across most terrains. Oblivious to emotion. No empathy. They are nothing more than savages.' Prail said, smiling lopsidedly. They are orphans, with no kin. You, on the other hand, have an uncle in Qual-Tar who finances your education here at the school.'

'You did not hear the news, Master Prail?' said Gaucuss. 'A letter arrived from Qual-Tar, three days ago. He died. The inheritance I was to receive has been commandeered.'

Prail turned his worried face to the window, pondering the Quwarshin: The emperor's secret order of assassins.

He felt, suddenly, that this would probably become the boy's destiny. As precocious and talented as he was, the school would soon ascertain the plans for his future.

'My condolences, concerning the death of your uncle,' said Prail, sincerely.

'I do not feel the loss,' Gaucuss confessed. 'There was no bond between us.'

Prail informed the student that those words were profound in their acknowledgment, adding that he would do well, no matter what vocation he was destined to undertake.

The heavy rain swept across the valley; flecks of light flickered in the village far below, like static phosphorus on a murky sea. *'Kafilia,'* thought the assassin. The last pimple on the asshole of the world.

Gaucuss gazed from the shelter of his wikiup, warming his hands against the blaze of the crackling fire.

'Thrydwulf.'

The word sounded alien on his tongue. He reached into the pocket of his blue leggings, taking out the copper coin that had been in his possession for nigh on fifteen years. The worn, decorative head was that of Emperor Maxalian, the grandfather of Rissak. He pondered on Sheetha, the blond girl he had rescued.

He had ridden into the camp of a group of fur trappers. Four men. He had discovered the girl naked and bleeding on a filth-ridden blanket in one of the tents, her hands tied behind her back, abused and raped. Gaining their confidence, he had promised to take them to uncharted hunting grounds that would furnish them with valuable pelts—if they would but sell him the girl. Even as they refused, mocking him, their wine was adroitly laced with arsenic. The first signs of poisoning had the men shivering, vomiting, and dead within twenty-four hours. He had wrapped the girl in a hide, taking her back to her village. She had given him the only possession she owned as a token of her gratitude. He had not intended to take it, but she had insisted. He wondered what had become of her. One day, he would ride back to the village. Maybe.

116

A rumble of thunder drew him from the reverie, and he poked the coin back into the pocket of his leggings. Tomorrow, he would ride down and begin inquiring after the outlander.

He pulled the blankets around him in the wikiup. Closing his eyes, he thought of Prail and what the teacher's opinion would have been concerning the elimination of the emperor's huntmaster.

Two hours after dawn, he broke camp and found the road leading to the village.

With the amount of rainfall the previous night, the road was wet and muddy; on occasion, he slid, blaming the mount beneath him for his own shortcomings. He cursed, thwacking the undernourished animal with the leather whip. It brayed and nipped the assassin on the knee. "Whoa! That's the spirit, my beauty! Now keep pace!"

Karfilia, Gaucuss ascertained, had been fortified, and he assumed being visible from the higher altitude of the forest, was a ploy and precaution against attack. It made perfect sense. An enemy could take stock of its defenses and seek a more gullible prey to ransack. He offered an invocation to Kubenial, praying that his trials would end more favorably than they'd begun.

At last, he reached the timbered walls. Drawing a short sword, he rode to the gates, pounding on them with the pommel of his sword, intrigued and humored at how the knocking echoed like the annoying din of a persistent woodpecker.

"What do you want?" Came a gruff voice.

Gaucuss lifted his stare to a bald wretch with a long, grey beard.

"I seek one called Vargdenir, or knowledge of him."

"Another stranger wanting to press his nose into honest folks' business!"

"And you are? Grandfather?" Gaucuss called up.

"It was you who came knocking at my door. Who are *you*?"

"*Who* I am is of no importance. *What* I am is another matter. A messenger for the emperor, on an important errand. It would serve you well to cooperate. Vargdenir, the huntmaster, he lives in these parts?"

"You're the second man to ask that question. The first claimed to be Rissak's champion, though he appeared to fit the position he boasted more admirably than you fit yours."

Gaucuss chuckled inwardly at the impertinence. "I," he stressed the word, "Am Gaucuss Ahdor-Nez, emissary of the house of Yulesard, and I come bearing a scroll with the emperor's seal, allowing me passage anywhere within the known world. Let me pass. Or do I return with a few hundred warriors and raze this cesspit to the ground?"

With that threat, a hooded figure loomed at the greybeard's side. Lifting a long, primitive bow, it pulled back the string of the weapon, peering down the shaft at the unwelcome traveler.

"Let me finish! *You!*" Gaucass bellowed, "I will roast over a spit to attain what I wish to know. The men I will have butchered, and the women and children placed into servitude! Now open the gates!"

"We can talk from here," the patriarch retorted, unwavering. "You seek Vargdenir, you say? *He* and the boy dwell some leagues to the southwest." He thrust out an arm, pointing back along the muddy path.

"Cross the two rivers. You got this far. Only a resourceful man could have done so alone. There you *may* find him. That is all I know."

"If I had more time, I would teach you a lesson in manners," Gaucuss bid him, menacingly.

"Manners! You insolent dog! Be gone, lest I send men out and have you strung up by your bobblers!"

"If I do not find Vargdenir and the boy, rest assured, Grandfather, I will return to wrap your head in leather for the sport of the children, back in the city. They can kick it around on Chesteria's Day."

The patriarch found a whit of mirth in the threat.

"My woman would have probably elected to carry the token back to the city for you. But you shall not enter."

Gaucuss tugged at the reins of his mount, and he and the two wrakens trotted off back along the miry path.

As the stranger rode away, the greybeard followed the archer down the ladder to the wet grass.

"Teon," he said, addressing the man. "Take three of your finest trackers. Outdistance this pilgrim. Warn Vargdenir he is coming."

"What if he *is* on an errand for Rissak? Is it wise to meddle in the affairs of the empire?" Teon asked.

"I've always found Vargdenir to be an honorable man. It's a rare virtue. Do you forget so easily how he came to us in our hour of need when the village was stricken with fever? Gryonae...this...champion, who came before. I have heard Vargdenir speak of the man with great fondness. But this oaf, who seeks him out. I don't trust him. He wallows in the arrogance of his duty. If our neighbor is in peril, we'll do what we can. We owe him that much," said Betgar. "Now go! The suns' light is wasting!"

119

Chapter 12

THE TRACKERS OF KARFILIA
(Kazhelma, South Palacoumia Forest. 3rd Millennium)

The four trackers gathered their equipment and made their way towards the mud road.

Teon, a brawny man in his late thirties, with black receding hair and a curly beard, trudged from the sodden trail and scrambled up the embankment. The three accomplices, clad in short green tunics, with brown trousers and braies, followed stealthily through the damp ferns.

The forest road out of Karfilia wound west until it came to a river, spanned by a bridge of wooden slats and rope. *'Cloformeran.' The men of old called it.* Teon and his companions, marching from the northwest, reached it first—a day before Rissak's messenger could ride hoof across it. They deliberated murdering the rider in the saddle as he rode across the bridge. Arrow shafts were favored—End the matter. No one would know. The river would take care of the body. They could make a feast of the animals and bear the wrakens back to Karfilia. Betgar would not be pleased, but the greybeard's time is coming to an end. Teon would see to it.

"Very well," he said. "We slay him on the bridge."

"And if Betgar disapproves?" one of the others piped up. Teon stared the younger man down. "Let me worry about Betgar. We have at least a day's start on this dog. Make camp, back there, by the clearing. And build a fire; I feel a chill in the bones."

***

Gaucuss dexterously scaled the arms of the tree to its crown. perching his legs over a thick bough. In the gloom far below, the rumbling ebb of the river was carried hauntingly on the wind. Gripping tightly with his thighs, he peered with a frown through the rustling leaves. A thumbnail of light flickered in the remoteness.

'Congratulations, old man,' thought the assassin to himself. *'Your men are imbeciles, but your ploy has merit. They intend to spring a trap. We shall see.'*

Gingerly, he descended from the vantage point, making his way back towards the wikiup.

Teon and his compatriots sat bunched before the fire. The chilly wind blew through the trees, and the heat was a godsend.

"I have heard of this champion of the emperor. I know the old huntmaster...and the younger outlander," said Lotan, the most junior of the four trackers. He was ever wary. A nocturnal critter scurried through the distant bushes, and he snatched a blade from the belt about his waist.

"Easy," rasped Teon. "It's just something scavenging."

"Do you remember when the outlander came to the village?" asked Efriack. "Did he not heal your daughter from the black sickness?"

Lotan squeezed the neck of his tunic. "Aye. He did at that," he admitted. "We owe that old rascal. That's why I volunteered."

"You mean why your woman volunteered! " Quipped Dern, with a broad grin.

"Well, at least I have a woman, dunghill," Lotan bit back. "What with that gnarled hand of yours... It must be like dipping your maggot into one of Teon's hunting gloves." Dern smirked, snorting through his nose as the other three trackers fell about laughing.

"All jesting aside, I would like to repay my debt to Vargdenir," Lotan told them, sincerely.

"I understand," said Teon. "Yet, it will not be possible. We have agreed to slay Rissak's messenger at the bridge. This is the plan. Then we will return to the village. Betgar's time is ending.

122

He is old. We can put this behind us and carry on—far from the Dirakhan and their troubles."

Efriack picked up a twig and poked it into the flames of the fire. Sheepishly, he spoke without lifting his head. "Betgar is held in high esteem by the elders in the village. They will not hold with him being tossed aside like a glove puppet."

"They rely on *us* for their survival," Teon said frostily. "They would die if not for our protection. It's time for change. Think long and hard. I will hold all those who oppose me accountable for their disloyalty."

"We are with you," Dern assured the rugged hunter.

Efriack said: "But rebellion... is there no other way?"

"Then it is settled," Dern horned in." We slay Betgar and take over Karfilia. The elders are not boneheads. They'll see the wisdom in it."

A bird screeched from a high branch, and Lotan shunted nervously upon the grass.

"An Elta," Teon confirmed.

Another squawk rented the air nearby. " That's a female. You can tell by the pitch. It's higher," Efriack said. "Hunting rodents. Probably."

It was silent but for the remote hum of the river.

"Wasn't there a boy?" asked Efriack.

"Thrydwulf," Lotan answered.

"A strange name," Dern pointed out.

"A strange boy," Teon added. "So Betgar declares."

Efriack tossed the stick he was toying with into the fire and peered across the flames. "How so?"

"Withdrawn. Sallow. Odd," Teon told them.

"A bit like Lotan, then," quipped Dern. The merriment circulated once more.

"I need to grow a tail," Lotan confessed. He rose, stepping away into the night.

"Don't be long," Teon called after him, pulling his tunic tighter about his shoulders. "We must make for the bridge and set the trap."

***

In the wikiup, Gaucuss sang softly. A glowing candle was placed on a slither of tree bark, an arm's- length away; he poured black powder into a paper-thin leather pouch and tied it to the shaft of an arrow.

'What is this?' the young student inquired.

'Saltpeter, sulfur, and charcoal,' explained the teacher. 'Two act as fuels, one is an oxidizer.'

The student stared at the mixture in amazement.
'What does it do?'

'Nothing. Unless ignited,' said the teacher.
'The candle; there in the sconce; bring it to me.'

The student obeyed and was commanded to place the candle on the table before them.

'Now, stand back and observe.' Taking a palmful of the black powder, the teacher sprinkled a line across the table, rubbing the excess from his hands. Taking a long, thin tab from his robe pocket, he dipped it in the candle flame and ignited the powder. The pupil watched in amazement as the mixture dissipated in a puff of smoke in the air.

'Impressive?' the teacher asked.

The student nodded. 'What is it used for?'

'If the portion is high enough, it will cause what we call an explosion. We are still exploring its potential. Could be useful to those among us here at the school of the Quwarshin.'

124

'A weapon, then,' the pupil stated, intuitively.
The teacher gazed hard at the burn pattern on the wooden table.
'We believe so,' he concluded.

The pink moon, with a hint of sapphire, gradually climbed above the world. In the unnerving blackness, Gaucuss checked the tethers of the wrakens. The animals were agitated, but this was always their nature. He fed and watered the beasts, unable to calm their restlessness. Taking the bow from its saddle peg, he positioned the weapon around his back. Emptying the leather quiver of arrows, he placed the six fabricated shafts back within the case. Looping it over his shoulder, he paced away towards the distant rumbling of the river, to the bridge of rope and wood; reaching the destination, he snuck across.

Lotan untied his leggings, pulling them around his ankles, squatting in the ferns. To his left, he heard a noise in the bushes; he could not estimate the distance. *Was* it merely a critter, hunting? He hoped so.

Why had he listened to Elean? He was no tracker. But the woman was right, they owed the hermit for the life of their child. Emptying the contents of his bowels, he stood, lacing his trousers about the middle. A stone's pitch away, the fire was ablaze; he fixed a glare upon the odd fellows situated around it. They were guffawing at some joke, no doubt at his expense. *'Chowderheads.'* He froze. A shape was moving through the trees. Not knowing whether to call the others, in a quandary, he snatched the blade from its belt. Crouching back down in the undergrowth, he was nauseated, appalled by the stench of his own defecation.

Gaucuss flicked an eye to where the lone villager had ducked down into the ferns; he would deal with *that* cretin accordingly.

The assassin drew back the string of his bow, sending a shaft into the distant fire. A surge of flames erupted, and the trio of hunters scrambled to their feet.

Teon gripped his neck as a sickening thud tore into his larynx. The ringleader toppled headfirst into the blaze.

"Away from the light!" shrieked Dern. "Keep low!" A buzz split the air, and a second explosion burst from the blaze, showering Dern and Efriack with fiery particles, singeing their garments. Efriack seized his bow. Kneeling in position, he fumbled to nock a fletched pole to the string. Bat-blind, he peered into the darkness.

"Get down!" cried Dern, crawling away on his belly.

A *pfft* of sound hissed above his mop of grey hair.

A second later, Efriack lay dead.

"Fool!" spat Dern. He kept low, staring, stony-faced into the sable shadows, striving to adjust his vision to the darkness. A thought induced a bitter laugh, and he snorted at the absurdity.

'Teon! You rancid goat bladder. Why didn't you place a watchman?' He scoured the distant trees searching for Lotan. 'Where are you, boy, when I need you?'

Again, there was a whizzing in the air, and the sparks from the fire flared out.

"Stand up, you grub!" Gaucuss cursed softly to himself. He let loose another arrow, tethered to a bag of black powder. It flashed, but the tracker lay still, unwilling to move.

"Not as slow-witted after all," the assassin hissed gently. *But dead, all the same.* "Boy!" he barked. "I *may* let you live!"

126

Dern crawled away, snaking through the undergrowth, heading for the ironwood, looming like stiff sentinels in the distance. "Damn you, Lotan," he snarled. "I'll take your woman. The child, too." He reached the trees and leaned back against one of the gnarled boles, cursing for not snatching his bow and quiver.

'So, it was the emperor's messenger.' Dern acknowledged to himself.

He recognized the voice that had shouted at the gates of Karfilia. He knew the man had to be more than an emissary. What message-bearer would even try to tackle four men alone in the wild? The next ideation was like a hammer blow; he almost reeled at the contemplation. The messenger had to be a member of the Quwarshin.

"Shit!" he uttered under his breath. "How far is the bridge?!"

Gaucuss shifted in the deep gloom, circling the farthest tracker, as the moon dipped among the twisted trees, painting their crowns with hues the shade of salmon and blue. With the horn-bow fixed across his back, he clasped a well-honed knife. Parting the tall grass, he spied the villager, kneeling, staring in the direction of the grisly remains, sizzling upon the fire.

Sensing the man's fear, he remembered.

'There are many sides to a man's nature,' said the teacher. 'They will fight or flee, but they will almost certainly weigh the situation before acting. It is at that moment that you must strike. There is much to learn here at the school, but some knowledge can only be reached through empirical endeavors. You must serve the emperor. Do his bidding. That is The Quwarshin's priority.'

'And if I fail?' the student was intrigued to know.

'That is not an option,' the teacher responded. 'You must learn or die.'

Dern listened keenly. Far off, the river grumbled. He stood. If he could reach the bridge, he might have a chance. Was Lotan dead? Foolish boy. Dern would not stay to find out.

In a blur, his hair was gripped. Before he could take a step, a serrated blade slid across his throat; he slumped to the ground. In the process of dying, he twitched and bled to death in the long grass.

Gaucuss Ahdor-Nez wiped the blood from his knife and slipped away beneath the trees.

Lotan crawled towards the rocks and peered down into the gorge. Hundreds of feet below, the river was a foaming, turbulent monster, but at last he discerned the taut bridge spanning the chasm.

The night seemed to squeeze the air from his lungs. If he were to return to Karfilia, he would need to fish the situation, somewhat like a man with a wand and a magic hook angling for invisible minnows.

'*Use the cover of darkness,*' whispered the voice on his right shoulder.

'*Wait for the dawn,*' came the utterance on his left. '*By the suns' light, you can assess the position with more clarity.*'

'*The others are dead, fool!*' whispered the mouthpiece on the right. '*Do not delay. Run!*'

Lotan tethered his tunic jacket tightly in place and took flight.

Images of Elean and the child swirled in his mind; in the moonlight, he gave the impression of a bipedal beast. But he vaulted, sprinting across the bridge, over the wide, weather-worn planks of wood. Reaching the other side, he dived into a tapestry of wild forest flowers. He lay stark still, his chest heaving, his heart pulverizing his thorax.

Gaucuss collapsed the wikiup, lashed up the bundle, and shouldered it to where the wrakens were tied. As he approached, the blue beasts snorted their dissatisfaction. The assassin tied the whip to the saddle of one of the animals. He gathered the arrows he had ditched earlier, loaded them back into the quiver, and looped it, along with his bow, over the saddle peg. "Easy," he uttered. The wraken nickered. "You smell him too, eh?" The beast nipped at his hand, and he smacked it violently upon the snout for its impertinence.

"Behave," he said. Undoing the reins of both animals, he tied one to the back of his tall saddle.

Lotan viewed the scene from the multicolored blooms; he was numb and weary. As the figure and the two beasts passed by, he breathed deeply, praying he had found sanctuary from the demon in human flesh. Suddenly, the rider's voice piped up. "Follow me!" it urged. "We need to talk."

An hour later, Ahdor-Nez was raising the wikiup once again. "Do not loiter," he said, subtly to the gangly tracker. "Gather some kindling."

"You were wise not to flee," Gaucuss said, coughing into his clenched fist. "Now, tell me about the boy. The outlander," he said, holding up his hands to the dancing flames.

"Thrydwulf is not a boy," Lotan replied.

"The man, then," said Ahdor-Nez, cloaking his annoyance.

"Vargdenir would rather die than give him up."

"I would expect no less from Rissak's huntmaster," Gaucuss said, his impatience growing.

129

He recollected the dogs tearing Vargdenir's dead body to shreds. To most men, that sight would have been horrific, but he was not most men.

"How did you know it was *I* who possessed knowledge of Vargdenir and his adopted son?"

"The wind has ears," the killer remarked ominously.

"There is a crime. On their part. I take it?"

"That is official business," Gaucuss responded. "But I say again, tell me of the younger outlander."

 Lotan bit his lip in contemplation. "He wears his hair in a strange fashion: Combed and plaited on the right-hand side. He is willowy. Bears a scar here." The woodsman pointed an inch above his hip. "Arrow shot, as I recall, by one of the emperor's huntsmen. There is a tale regarding him, but I was never told the entire story. He would not declare much either. And he admires the emperor's champion."

Ahdor-Nez pricked up his ears. "The champion knows the location where they dwell?"

"Betgar—that is the elder you chided at the gates of Karfilia—declares Vargdenir and the emperor's champion are allies."

Gaucuss chuckled inwardly, knowing that what was left of Vargdenir had probably been scraped off the sole of some unfortunate dullard's boot, back at one of the city's dog pens.

"Do you have any idea at all where they might be?" he quizzed.

"My guess is if you follow the forest road, you are sure to chance upon their dwelling."

"Is that so?" The assassin muttered. He heaved himself upon his haunches and strode across to one of the tied wrakens. From out of a leather saddlebag, he pulled a pigskin wine sack and two crude wooden cups. "Join me in a drink of *Kooshla Red?*" Stepping back, seating himself, and without waiting for an answer, Gaucuss filled the two cups, handing one to the unwitting tracker. You can tell me more as we ride," he said. He winked, pretending to swig the wine.

The morning sun stroked lime green fingers across the forest lawn. Gaucuss yawned as he crawled out of the wikiup. He climbed to his wraken-skin boots and stepped over Lotan's poisoned remains; the grey-faced corpse had twisted in agony.

'Some cretins do not retain the good sense they are born with,' he thought to himself, mockingly.

He dragged the body away into the grass, for no other reason than to hide the problem—he was about to breakfast and did not want his appetite marred. He dined on nutty bread and sour cheese, packed away the wikiup, singing softly as he got ready to ride.

Chapter 13

THE DWELLING
(Kazhelma, South Palacoumia Forest. 3rd Millennium)

Thrydwulf forced open the crooked shutters, airing the smoke-filled room. It had been years since he had dreamed of Aeva. If the baby had survived, it would be nine—or was it ten—autumns old now? The thought hung solemnly in his heart; he hoped Vargdenir would return soon; he was beginning to miss the old man's dependable nature.

The sky above the trees was pale mauve and full of rain clouds. He would have to clean out the hearth and rebuild the fire before the downpour began. He scratched at the old curse, the infestation in his hair, and decided that this morning, he would boil pots of water and bathe.

For nigh on an hour, he bucketed water up the wooded scarp, drawing it from the pebbly stream below. Systematically, he filled the iron cauldron, suspended above the burning flames in the hearth. From this, he filled a wooden bath, stripped off his green breeches and black shirt, and climbed into the tub. Sinking into the steaming water, he lay his head back. Reflecting on Aeva, his mind wandered across the years. He could never confess to his adoptive parent how he ached for that boisterous charm and passionate intimacy in which she had excelled. The guilt of Oeric's death clouded that fond ideation. Even after all these years, it haunted him: a trapped ghost ever doomed to scratch at the walls of his conscience.

"Forgive me," he murmured. He massaged the old arrow wound still plaguing him with its irritation. The pitter-patter of rain began to drum upon the slanted roof, and he closed his eyes.

'Are things different here because of the two suns?' Thrydwulf quizzed.
Vargdenir expelled a plume of opiated smoke and laid down his pipe. 'Hmm,' he said. 'What do **you** think?'
Thrydwulf shrugged. 'I think it is an intelligent question?'
'Then give me an example,' the old man countered.
Thrydwulf momentarily mused. 'The flourishing plants?' As Vargdenir hesitated, the young Saxon perceived that answer alone would

never be enough. 'Brighter days. Shorter nights. The twin shadows. How the moon passes between the two suns. How things corrode much quicker here on Kazhelma.' Thrydwulf sighed. 'I miss my village.'

'You miss the girl, Aeva,' Vargdenir said. 'Maybe it is time to find you a wench in Karfilia. Suzin would be a good match.'

Thrydwulf laughed. 'I'd rather bed down with one of the wrakens.'

'That can be arranged,' Vargdenir uttered with a grin. 'If you start getting...fidgety, know that I will fix up a pallet in the barn down below.' He picked at the congealed rabbit meat on the platter lying on the hexagonal table beside his chair, washing morsels down with spiced wine. Taking up the long curved-stemmed meerschaum pipe once more, he leaned forward, placing a thin wooden tab into the low crackling fire. Reigniting the object, he leaned back in the woven chair.

Thrydwulf said, 'Gryonae speaks with great fondness of Novia Jorai. Yet he does not speak of wishing to return to the Novia Jorai where he was born. He could ride off to that land from here. I cannot understand why he does not."

'Denfurnan was once a mighty city,' Vargdenir stated. 'Until it was sacked and laid waste by the Dirakhan.'

'What happened?' Thrydwulf asked.

'It is said the Dirakhan made their way across the Casindrian Ocean, in search of new lands to conquer. They burned their ships and built the city, Quilaxia, from sandstone. They are the oldest race on Kazhelma. Have you ever noticed the size of Gryonae's feet?' He chuckled, changing the subject.

'Only discreetly,' Thrydwulf said, with a shrug. 'I wouldn't mention it to him. You don't prod a rabid wolf with a sharp stick and hope not to be bitten.' 'Don't be a fool,' said the old man. 'You think he would bite the only trusted friend he has left in the world?'

'The Germanic tribes would have favored him, I guess,' Thrydwulf said. 'If they had been able to convince him to war with them against Rome.'

'In their past,' said Vargdenir, 'the Novian nation practiced religious cannibalistic rituals. Specifically, where children were concerned.'

'I didn't know,' Thrydwulf responded, shocked.

'They are a cruel people. Hard as an iron hammer,' said the old huntsman, rhetorically.

'There are stories of how Dirakhan prisoners were treated at the battle of Froushika Vale. They were cooked on great spits. They were eaten alive.'

Thrydwulf pushed away his platter of congealed meat. 'How can men reduce themselves to such...barbarous acts?'

'You'd be stunned to know how the most committed moralist can become when he is dying of thirst and starvation. At the base level, we are all animals. No more. No less. And these are dangerous days. If anything should happen to me, you will stick close to Gryonae.'

Thrydwulf paled at the old man's words. 'Do not fret,' Vargdenir added, noticing. 'I still intend to outlive you. Whatever occurs,' he said with a grin.

Thrydwulf coughed and spluttered, thrusting his head above the lukewarm water. The fire in the hearth was dying, the rainfall upon the slanted roof now a full drumming tattoo. He slipped out of the tub, stacking more wood onto the fading flames. Re-dressing in his green breeches and plain black shirt, he dragged the tub of soiled water to the door, emptying the contents onto the ferns.

Satisfied that the two wrakens had been fed and watered earlier, in the barn below, he barred the door against the dangers of the unpredictable forest.

Among his people, back in Engla land, books were relatively unknown. He recollected his father speaking of Rome and its erudite men, but he had forgotten their names long ago. Here, on Kazhelma, books—or codices—as

Vargdenir had always referred to them, were prevalent amongst the Dirakhan. The ornate sketches on the fiber paper had been a revelation upon his first encounter. Vargdenir possessed six volumes, bound in leather and inscribed with Dirakhanean runic symbols. It had taken years to digest the complexity of the language. But he had reveled in the subject matter. He lit the oil lamp on the table, strolled to the bookshelf, and pulled a volume down.

LOGIC BY DUFOSS OF FARLINDUNE

He flicked through the pages, pausing for no apparent reason at a chapter heading termed:

DEATH AND LIFE BEYOND BONE

and began to read.

Whether the gods of * Zune, (fire) ** Twilda,(water) ** * Grissan,(earth), or ****Si, (air) exist beyond the thoughts of the mind is a phenomenon that cannot be validated. Yet, one experiences in life many such examples that cannot be dismissed...

Thrydwulf became bored at the depth of the proposition. He closed the tome and placed it back upon the shelf. Outside, the puce-tinted clouds had dispersed, and the green illumination of Kazhelma's two suns spilled down through the diversely colored leaves. Reloading the fire with more timber, he paced back through the Semigloom to the aperture with the open shutters. He pondered upon Suzin from the village of Karfilia. She was buxom enough, but he found her undesirable, or so he thought. He frowned at the sudden sexual urge

136

swelling beneath his breeches and ushered the carnal rumination from his mind.

Through the twisted branches, atop the slanted climb, he spied a pair of birds, bobbing along the gnarled limb of a tree, their green-gold wings flapping in play. He envied their interaction. Realizing in that instant that the contemplation of his return home was a fool's pondering. He laughed bitterly, blaspheming the moment of madness. Tossing his gaze to the lower, far-flung pathway, he detected that something was on the move. Caught off guard, he jolted upright. Snatching the horn bow and quiver of arrows from the wall, he raced to the door to seek a more advantageous position at the edge of the wooded hillock.

The black-clad rider and the light blue wraken he had in tow, rounded the deep ferns, emerging from the shadows at the brink of the trickling stream. The stranger dismounted, leading his beast by the rein. Kneeling, he drank with a cupped hand, scouring the crest of the incline as he did so. He sensed the watcher. The instinct of self-preservation stroked across his soul with icy fingers; he bellowed with a challenge: "Who dwells up yonder?!"

"Who trespasses down below?!" Thrydwulf's voice barked back. "Who are you? What do you seek here? Know you are within bowshot, and that I seldom miss a target."

"I am on an errand for Rissak, emperor of all Kazhelma."

'Or at least, those lands the Dirakhan deem worthy of their rule,' he thought.

"I seek the emperor's huntmaster. He is required to appear at court, at Rissak's command," the Visitor bellowed with a lie. Thrydwulf lowered his bow and stepped from a thicket. "The

137

demand has already been met, carried forth by the emperor's champion. They departed for the city some weeks back."

"Would you be the huntmaster's son?" questioned the intruder.

"Adopted son. I am Thrydwulf. Vargdenir is the man you seek."

"I am Gaucuss Ahdor-Nez. Will you come down so we can talk and set things a-right? So, I can carry your counsel back to the city?"

Thrydwulf impulsively stroked the dagger handle on his belt, bit his lip, and scratched at the wisps of hair on his chin as he deliberated. "Nay!" he hollered with a scowl. "But you *may* come up. If you have a mind to."

"That I will," replied Rissak's Emissary." May I tie these animals somewhere?"

" There is a barn through the bushes. You can leash them there."

Thrydwulf placed one of the wicker chairs before the fire, inviting the stranger to sit and dry out.

Gaucuss shed his black leather doublet, throwing the garment over the back of the wicker seat. He slouched down, depositing his weight, raising an eyebrow as it squeaked like one of the many vermin plaguing the streets and alleyways of Quilaxia.

"So," said the assassin, "Gryonae has delivered the news, and he and the huntmaster are heading for the city." Gaucuss clapped his hands, rubbing his palms together, holding them up towards the fire. Undaunted, he surveyed the domain, noting the illegal books stacked on the shelf at the corner of the room. Beyond the walls of the sacred city, such artifacts were outlawed. He smiled inwardly at how ridiculous that seemed, especially regarding the situation he had been commanded to undertake. There was little else adorning the room—save the squeaky chairs, two small hexagonal tables, and crude sleeping pallets. It was adequate. He had always considered himself a minimalist. He approved of the size of the living space.

"Will you share in a bowl of stew and some wine?" Thrydwulf asked. The newcomer gazed askance with sloe-shaped eyes. An awkward silence hung briefly in the air between them; then, a broad grin began to creep across the stranger's sun-tanned features. "I accept," the assassin replied.

Thrydwulf took an S-shaped hook and hung a pot of cold stew over the fire. Gaucuss began to unravel the inky silk head covering, an act that disclosed a shaved head and an orange sickle-mooned tattoo just above his right temple.

Thrydwulf glimpsed the symbol, and his heart raced. *The Quwarshin!* Pretending not to notice, he stirred the stew with a long, wooden ladle.

"So, you recognize the motif of the Brotherhood," Gaucuss stated astutely. "It is a good sign of your master's teaching."

He pointed to the corner of the dwelling. "They can be useful, even to the uninitiated. The illegal books?"

Thrydwulf filled two wooden bowls with stew and handed one to the Dirakhan. Pouring wine into the wooden beakers, he repeated the gesture.

"From where came you to these lands? It is believed by some that you and your master are not from any region known to the Dirakhan?" Gaucuss said, brazenly.

For an instant, Thrydwulf was at a loss. It was obvious the emperor's agent knew. He stared down into the steaming, spicy bowl of food. As if an obliging message might emerge from it.

139

"The stew is delicious," said the man from the Brotherhood.

Freshly bathed, Thrydwulf could detect the odious smell of the traveler. He turned his nose away and began what he hoped would be to weave a web of believable deception.

"From Anzetoan? It is a small hinterland—"

"North of Krec," Gaucuss interrupted. He smirked. "Those mongrels ravage their own daughters. I know their tongue, and it has not a hint of the one you attempt to hide behind. *They* would have bowshot me and left me for dead already, as a carcass for the carrion. Lying is not your strong point, by the way."

Thrydwulf's hand impulsively slipped to his bone-handled knife. "That would not be wise," said the messenger. The cursory spell broke, and the young man found himself scratching once more at the hair on his chin. "And what does it matter from where I came?" Thrydwulf asked defensively. "The news was for Vargdenir...not me. He has gone to the city. As I have said."

The Emissary's brown, almond-shaped eyes studied the foreigner. "Be at ease," he said. "It is just the way of the Brotherhood. " He grabbed the carved wooden cup and sipped the spiced wine.

Gaucuss had no fear of the food or drink being poisoned. His arrival had been unexpected, privy only to the emperor. But he was to find himself intrigued by the strange, younger man. And if he were being honest, he was intrigued to say the least.

The Saxon sat in the wicker chair, feeling his dread expand. Gaucuss said. "I am bound by law as the emperor's envoy. I answer to him alone." He chuckled, saying deceitfully, "He

140

does not...he could not trouble himself with every whim or woe of every peasant or noble within the empire."

Thrydwulf opened his mouth to speak but was cut off before any word escaped.

"And before you ask, neither is The Brotherhood." Gaucuss raised his carved cup of wine. "I am just a lowly servant," he assured the younger man. "As are we all."

With that, Thrydwulf sighed, and the snare was pinched a little tighter.

"So, tell me your story," said the assassin.

Gaucuss supped his wine and leaned back in his chair, listening intently to every word the foreigner had to say in his Dirakhanean patois accent.

"I come from Engla land."

"There is such a place?" asked the assassin. "Within the Empire? I have not heard of it. Beyond which borders?"

"Beyond your world," Thrydwulf said, astounding the stranger. "There are gateways. Openings in the fabric of time… so Vargdenir calls them. He, too, is from there." Thrydwulf caught himself as if he were being twisted to divulge his own mother's deepest, unspoken secrets. Gaucuss leaned forward in the Semi-shadows. "Perhaps you could not know this, but Vargdenir and I are old friends. He may have mentioned Ahdor-Nez to you at some point?"

"He has never done so," Thrydwulf replied with a frown.

"Isn't that just like him?"

"Yes," answered Thrydwulf, almost self-bewilderingly. It was subtle, and the snare had him at the point of choking.

"Trust me," Gaucuss admonished. "He'd forget his own pips if they weren't in a bag."

That metaphor caused the Saxon to laugh nervously.

"As you were saying," Gaucuss probed. "Engla land?"

Thrydwulf took another slug of wine, and all his defenses seemed to wash away. "There was a boy. He perished. A girl I loved. A child. My mother was dying. I did not want to leave her." Tears welled up in the Saxon's eyes, and Gaucuss—rare for him—was touched by pity. But not so much that he forgot the task at hand. "Go on," he said.

"Oeric was my woman's brother. Slain by a maggot called Frug. Gryonae. You know of the emperor's champion?"

Gaucuss nodded.

"He killed the pig. Vargdenir raised me here, though I have been to the emperor's court on many occasions." Thrydwulf's mind wandered back to his mother, Cynwise, shivering beneath the fur hides in the corner of their dank hut, long ago. Grief strived to overcome him, but Thrydwulf swallowed it back, as Gaucuss reached out, affectionately patting his shoulder.

"Be at ease," he uttered. "Vargdenir will return soon," he appended with a lie. "There are certain...elixirs that can curb such sorrows. One is tied to the saddlebag on my wraken. It has a knack of alleviating stress." Gaucuss pushed himself up from the squeaking chair. "I will fetch it."

Thrydwulf wiped his eyes. "There is no need," he said.

"But I insist. Vargdenir would have it so. We'll share a drop. My joints ache from this whole endeavor."

Thrydwulf heard the door shut quietly. As the emperor's envoy left the dwelling, the spell of Thrydwulf's foolhardiness began to unravel.

'Everybody lies, to some extent. To solve a predicament. For gain. To conceal. It reveals how shrewdly we can exploit the world to our advantage. What the flame does not burn, the untrue vow can devastate.'

142

'But surely, great kings...or even nobles, do not need to lie?' Thrydwulf had said.

'Oh, but they must!' Vargdenir had answered gravely. *'To perpetuate their survival.'*

Gaucuss returned, carrying a small bottle.

"What do you have there?" asked Thrydwulf.

"An ancient recipe from a mountain tribe, the Wabee." Even though Gaucuss rambled on concerning the mixture's ingredients, Thrydwulf declined. The stranger pulled the bottle cork and seemingly took a slug. "Very well," he said. "Tell me more about Engla land."

Thrydwulf placed his beaker to his lips and sipped—the reaction was instantaneous.

A fey blue flame began to dance and twirl upon the wall of Vargdenir's cabin. A grotesque form appeared and grew claws; Thrydwulf cowered in his chair, reaching to protect his throat, as the aberration stepped from the woodwork into their dimension, lunging with an open talon of curved fingernails. The deformed succubus, hideous and horrifying, metamorphosed, and Thrydwulf fitted from his chair to a heap on the floor—the wooden planks splintering his skin. Helpless, he screamed.

"Do not fight it," a voice uttered at the edge of his sanity. "It is futile. Rissak wants your head, but I will not allow the abomination a souvenir. I'll weave a tale for him, regarding that. May your gods have mercy on your soul, wherever those deities reside. Sleep. Let them guide you." Gaucuss dragged the young man's body down to the barn and laid it, almost dutifully, beside the water trough. The tied wrakens were nervous as he jostled among them. Finding a hessian sack by a post on the mud, he snatched the material up and veiled the corpse about the head and shoulders. With the assignment fulfilled, the assassin made ready to ride. He would

Gaucuss drew the copper coin from his pocket, rubbing the worn head of Emperor Maxalian between his fingers and thumb. Sheetha—the amber-haired girl he had rescued—would be twenty-five years old now—almost. She, in all the world, would delight in their reunion—surely.

This fueled the fantasy. He'd dwell on it as he rode back to the school of the Quwarshin, east of Rissak's city. Maybe he could redesign a more advantageous future.

Chapter 14

BROTHERS
(Kazhelma, Quilaxia City. 3rd Millennium)

Tymarian sat up, gulping the air like a landbound fish.

Exhausted, he clawed at the tight gauze wrapped about his midriff. "Do not tamper with it," advised a voice in the gloom. "That would not be wise." Tymarian assumed the cut would have been saturated with wine to prevent infection. Fat and honey applied. "Now," came one more proclamation, "Speak true. Or you will die. Take *that* as an oath."

Ignoring the threat, the man, who had spent years of adversity in the salt mines of Rothshim, eased himself down upon the straw pallet and shut his eyes.

Gryonae caressed the cicatrix he'd carried since childhood. The stag had gored deep. As he thought of the notorious emperor, Radiantee, a cold rage surfaced.

'This is free land. Novia Jorai answers to no one,' his father had flouted.

The Dirakhan rider with the ponytail had threatened otherwise.

'These are my sons; can you at least keep us together? I implore you!'

'I will try,' the rider had said.

The scrawny officer had lied. Tymarian had been the first to be ripped from his father's arms and sold into slavery to a surly euganta trader in one of the marketplaces in B'Herma. Gryonae relived the moment his parent had been cut to pieces, being left to the mercy of carrion birds, their wings gyrating in the emerald skies. He shifted his stare to the corner of the cell, to the sleeping figure sprawled upon the straw pallet. He recognized himself in the tortured soul: the strong jaw, the defiant brow, the strength of character. Even the mannerisms reflected the father who had instigated his birth. How hadn't he seen it in the arena?!

'If you are my brother,' he thought, *'there will be much to consider.'*

"Do you remember the birch glade? "Asked Tymarian, suddenly. He winced in pain, pushing himself up onto his elbow. Leaning against the sandstone wall, he grinned at the impassive face of Shadowgrip.

"I remember the mist," Gryonae replied. "And that whoreson of a stag." He sneered.

146

Tymarian delved at his wound with the fingers of a doting governess. "What happened to Father?"

Gryonae shrugged, "He died," he said, soberly. There was no apparent distress in the revelation. But each brother remained alone in his silence for the longest moment.

"I fear that we meet again," said Tymarian, "only to die, once more, at the hands of these dung beetles. I should have perished in Rothshim. It is a miracle I survived."

"So, it is true," said Gryonae. "You did escape that bowel hole. Kubenial must hold you in his favor. Take solace—at least—in that miracle."

Tymarian spat. "Kubenial is a Dirakhanian deity," he said, stormily. "No god ever walked those death mines whilst I was there. Nigh on ten years, I endured. *My* only gods were water and rice. The hope of freedom was all-consuming. Do not talk to me of religion. Save it for the old men who live in Rissak's prodigal temples."

The faint glimmer of a smile mushroomed across Gryonae's lips.

"What's so amusing?" Tymarian asked, his voice cold and rasping.

"You remind me of my father, " Gryonae responded.

"That cannot be," the dark-haired man shot back.

Shadowgrip's eyes screwed in bemusement.

"Because," Tymarian said with a grin, "he told me *you* were not born...not even a difficult birth... but…though it may be strange... that you were hatched!"

Gryonae roared with laughter. Leaping to his feet, he marched across the red sandstone, lifting his brother into his muscular arms.

147

"It's not enough that you soil the arena with my innards," Tymarian wheezed. "Now you aim to crush the life out of me! Have you no shame?"

Gryonae dropped the man like a sack of spoiled potatoes. "There you go," he quipped.

Tymarian groaned. "Obliged," he said. "Next time, just hit me with a club."

Shadowgrip paced to the wooden door, peeping through the iron bars at the square hole.

The corridor beyond was lit by flickering torches. More than a hundred paces down, two prison warders sat at a table, quarreling over a game of bone-dice.

"Please tell me you have a plan?" Tymarian asked.

"A simple one," said Gryonae. "We steal a couple of healthy wrakens. Flee the city. Raise an army. Ride to Novia Jorai. Then ride back to Quilaxia and boil what's left of the royal family in oil."

The wounded brother responded with the same dark humor.

"So, we'll need money, supplies, weapons, mounts—just for us. We equip a non-existent army. Defeat an insane brat-emperor—and his unconquerable hordes—and free the world of two thousand years of tyranny. Did I get that right?"

Gryonae gave an unhinged smile. "It's close enough."

"Maybe we can seek The Galrandir," whispered Tymarian, mockingly. Then he frowned, "It's been years since I have spoken that name."

Gryonae rose from the chair. "The land. Its people. They are fables. Guard!" he bellowed.

Beyond the cell, the echo of footfalls shuffled in the gloom. The framework creaked as the heavy door swung open.

"This man has lost his mind. If he doesn't conform, whip him. If he talks too much, gag him."

"If he dies?" the jailer interrupted, raising his eyebrows.

"If he dies," Gryonae said menacingly, "The names of you and your playfellow, down the corridor, will be added to the trophies of dead men I carry notched upon my belt. Nod if you grasp my meaning."

The guard bowed, subserviently. "It shall be as you wish, Shadowgrip."

Gryonae flicked a coin at the individual's frayed boots. "Tell the surgeon I want *this one's* wound redressed. I want him properly fed and watered. Up on his feet. And clothe him... in a dead man's garbs if need be." He swiveled to face Tymarian, secretly winking. "You'll be sure to tell me more of your exploits in Rothshim. I find the story... compelling."

That night, Tymarian dreamed of Allina. It was one filled with explosive sexual intensity, possessing many scenarios, some nacreous and unhinged. In his sleep, he reached out as the bare-breasted woman, her long hazel hair twirling in an intangible wind, gripped the mane of an aroused black stallion and vaulted onto its back. He bellowed her name, but she could not hear him above the fey storm. The seductress galloped away. The sudden loss and emptiness were devastating. He stood naked. The dark tunnel of the salt mine began to uncoil before his eyes. He began to run, but the unfurling blackness was swifter. The ghosts of those who had died in the mines of Rothshim tugged at his bloodied feet. Like a jester, long-suffering, he traipsed on. The tempest swirled salt about the foredoomed tunnel. In the distance, a deep guttural groan erupted. The bulky stag charged by, and he flung himself against the saline wall. In its wake came Gryonae, sword in hand, an expression of rage plastered to his sunburnt face.

Shaken from the torment, the sleeper's green eyes opened lazily.

"It is time, brother," uttered a voice in the darkness beside him. The hilt of a sword was shoved into his grasp. Instinctively, he wrapped his fingers about the smooth, stitched leather. "Can you walk?" the voice asked.

"Just don't expect me to jig in honor of Welkrina," he mumbled. He was hauled to his feet.

The brothers made their way down the red sandstone passage. The table beneath the torches was upended. Dice, clay cups, a smashed bottle, and its contents lay scattered on the slabbed floor. Two bodies were slumped in the shadows, butchered beyond recognition. The sleek passageway scaled in slow degrees, and they came to a blank wall. The torch flames in the high sconce fluttered; whiffs of smoke traced the corner to the ceiling. They ascended the stairwell to the level above. Natural light washed through the open shutters. The walls, elaborate in comparison to the ones below, were textured and painted a duck egg blue; they proceeded right. At the far end of the corridor, a lone sentry stood guard, an erect spear in hand, his ebony locks yanked into the conventional ponytail. Tymarian's brow furrowed.

"I know him personally," the champion said. "From good stock. His father spoke out openly against the emperor."

"Why does Rissak let him live?"

"He doesn't know the details. The boy was born a bastard. Give me that sword." He slid the bone-handled dagger back with the others strapped across his chest. Snatching the weapon from Tymarian, he re-sheathed it in the scabbard on his back. "Go in front. Leave the talking to me."

"Yanir!" barked the Novian as they approached. The young guard grinned, leaning his spear against the frame of the open doorway. "Shadowgrip," he answered, bemused and delighted. "Your prisoner is unshackled."

Gryonae pounced, head-butting the man, crushing his nose, taking a minute to strangle him barehandedly. "In an hour, our ploy will be discovered."

"You secured everything in one week?" asked Tymarian, surprised at the sheer callousness he had just witnessed. "Can your sources be trusted? What if we're betrayed?"

Shadowgrip examined the cadaver at his feet. "Dead men don't talk. And we are being aided by Quelk and the Hinera. We are wasting time."

Beyond the door, upon each side stood a tall parapet of arenaceous rock. A hundred feet further was a military courtyard. "There should be two wrakens loaded with supplies," said Gryonae.

"We just ride out of the city?"

"We'll crawl if we have to. From here on, you're just chattel."

"And if I'm questioned?"

Gryonae raised his shoulders, spreading his fingers. "You're mute." Gryonae twisted the iron knob; the door creaked as he wrenched it open.

"Our mounts?" Tymarian quizzed, peering around his brother.

"How should I know? Wrakens all look the same to me."

"How are the Hinera able to accomplish such tasks? Look! There are three animals and supplies!"

"I'm Rissak's arena champion, not his court strategist."

Around the corner, to their right, a figure appeared, carrying a saddle and some sacks.

151

"We'll let him work." Gryonae eased the door shut. "Not just a pretty face, eh?" he added with a grin.

Tymarian snorted. "Not even a pretty face."

Finally, they heard the nicker of a vexed wraken being ridden away. Grasping the moment, they strode out, unhitching the reins, and mounted the tetchy animals.

Gryonae led the way, Tymarian at the rear, mantled like a peacock in the guise of a poor bazaar trader.

***

The pea-green suns had vanished, and nighttime clothed the city in an inky mauve shroud.

Princess Endambia's state funeral had been set for the 14th day of that month. The city was congested; the populace packed into the inns and available lodgings like sardines. The brothers realized this could be to their advantage. The sky-blue-coated beasts trotted to the door of the Cullcut Inn. The sign indicated the establishment had vacancies; Gryonae cast his eye over the ramshackle building; the dilapidation explained why. He slid from the saddle, lashing the reins of the exhausted wrakens to the makeshift hitching rail. Tymarian swung his leg over his mount, thumping to the dusty street with a groan.

"Are you sure we can afford this place?" The words were drowning in sarcasm.

Gryonae, ignoring the complaint, climbed the rickety steps and hammered on the door. Through the grimy glass, the brothers spied a candle floating in the darkness. The Inn door was unlocked, and the odious proprietor stooped before them.

"You have rooms?" Gryonae asked. The innkeeper raised the brass ring candle holder.

The fellow before him was clad in a black hooded cloak, midnight blue trousers, and leather buskins laced to the knee. The sword across his back and the bone-handled knives athwart his chest were now hidden—the studded gauntlets were another matter.

"You can pay?" the Innkeeper grunted.

Tymarian pushed forward. His maroon pleated shirt and bright red speckle-patterned keffiyeh were almost comical.

The Innkeeper chuckled." You're obviously with the pranksters hired for the old Princess's celebration. May the gods rest her soul. There are no discounts."

Gryonae clasped his brother's arm, subduing him. "We are tumblers," he announced. "And we can pay."

"Three copper bits a night. No meal. That's it," the innkeeper told them.

"We want one room, for one night."

" Very well," said the proprietor.

Tymarian grumbled. "We'll grab our stuff."

"In advance," the crippled Innkeeper was swift to interject. "And take those animals to the barn out back. I take no responsibility for them being left on the street and stolen."

Gryonae bundled his brother down the wooden steps. "Now, do as the man says. I'll take in our belongings."

"Before we make for Novia Jorai, I have an errand to attend to in Palacoumia," said Gryonae. He was settled in a chair beside the bed. Tymarian lay stretched upon the rickety pallet. A long candle dripped into a brass candlestick holder on the table beside them; its blue-white flame was casting shadows in the flea-bitten room.

"Are you insane?" Tymarian chided, watching the silhouettes dance across the walls and ceiling. "Why there?"

"I had a friend; he disappeared. I believe Rissak had him killed. But there was also a boy whom the friend fostered. I made a promise I would...take him under my wing...so to speak."

"Shadowgrip making covenants with mortal men. Folly to the extreme." Tymarian's green eyes wrinkled in astonishment. "The boy resides there?"

"Thrydwulf is his name. Vargdenir, the friend I speak of, had a dwelling deep within the forest. Rest assured, he is there. We need to reach him before Rissak does."

"He joins the party?" Tymarian chimed in disbelief.

"He joins the party," echoed Gryonae.

"Brother," Tymarian yawned. "Get me beyond the city gates to taste freedom one last time, and I will follow you down into the halls of Grundunia itself. But right now, I need to rest."

"So be it," said Gryonae. "Shift over, brother. I can't sleep all night in this chair."

***

They jostled through the marketplace, gripping the reins of the wrakens they had in tow. Every bartered sale was a conspiracy to prevent the brothers from their endeavor—So they believed. Occasionally, they stopped to purchase extra rations. Gryonae now sported a soft blue conical cap, pulled tight about his ears, striving to hide his notorious features. The crowd began to thin as they approached the southernmost gate of the city.

The plethora of citizens entering Quilaxia was as contrasting as winter stone and summer flowers. Many were entering, only a few were departing, and none without an Imperial Seal.

"You have a pass? " Whispered Tymarian.

"Of course not," Gryonae replied categorically.

"I should have guessed."

"Don't guess." Shadowgrip retorted. "Just follow my lead."

"I need to see a permit," said one of the soldiers at the gate.

"*This* is my permit," Gryonae informed the man. He unlaced his studded gauntlet and slid back the dark leather, revealing a ruby-red pentagrammic tattoo, the mark of Rissak's champion.

"I need it in writing," the guard added ruefully.

Gryonae strode to where Tymarian was holding the two irascible wrakens by their straps. "Mount up," he snapped. "We'll ride straight through. They won't expect it."

"An arrow in the back," said Tymarian, "as opposed to a sword thrust in the throat. It's preferable."

As they climbed to their saddles, Gryonae clutched the reins of his mount. "Now, brother,"
he said, resolutely. "Ride like the wind!"

Chapter 15

CAELINFORD 10 YEARS LATER
(Britain, Southern England. 5th Century AD)

In her thatched dwelling, Aeva stirred the bean stew, adding onion and parsnip. She swallowed the dregs of beer, peering at the primitive abode fifty feet away. Her woolen robes, mint green, stank of smoke and sweat—a metaphor for the cruel years slipping by so rapidly. Algar raced, screaming from the neighboring hut, as Leax, his only playmate, gave chase.

"Algar!" screeched the woman. "Come in! This is done!"

A pang of sadness stroked a wintry thumb across her spine. Those closest to her—family and friends—were gone: Hunwald, Hilda, Oeric, Thrydwulf, Cynwise, Ceolwulf, Immin the bone-shaper. Even the hounds, Daegmund and Dhelweard, had abandoned her. Without the child, she would have crawled into the inescapable barrow long ago.

"Just a little while," the boy pleaded, panting in the doorway. The air rang with laughter as Leax tumbled headfirst into the planks of Aeva's hut. Algar sprang away with Leax in dogged pursuit. The woman bellowed after him, "The sun will be going down!"

The rug rats cavorted through the ancient forest, wind rushing through the towering oaks, lobed leaves quivering in the late afternoon. It began to rain, to patter upon the red ferns about their feet. "We have to get back," Leax insisted. 'We'll get a beating." Their tunics and leggings were saturated.

"We're here now," Algar assured the companion. They paused at the edge of the trees, and he thrust out an arm. "Cula's Ford," he panted.

"I know where we are," Leax bothered to answer. " But why are we here?"

The youth's drenched woolen clothing hung awkwardly, like half a sack of mashed corn. "This is where my father vanished," Algar said bitterly. Leax placed a hand on his friend's shoulder.

"You're trying to pick a fight. I will not rise to the bait. We're in enough trouble; they're not coming back. Accept it."

The golden sun was crawling, descending the firmament like a wounded snail. The rain—as if nature itself was weary of its own exhaustion—began to peter out.

"We'd better go," he continued.

157

"Not even a bone left," said Algar.

"Scavengers don't leave much," Leax murmured philosophically.

No matter how many beatings Aeva dished out, the boy would never obey. His stubbornness was more typical of Hunwald, her pater, than Thrydwulf, father of the child. Now he was gone. Aeva's parents had goaded her to marry for the sake of their grandson—She had sworn to herself never to contemplate such an arrangement. Perhaps here, too, was her own bullheadedness. Aeva walloped the boy, stripped him of his clothes, and put him down to sleep. The guilt had been instantaneous; it always was.

She watched the boy from the comfort of the sizzling flames, the pungent smoke floating about the hut. "Forgive me," she whispered glumly. In her mind's eye, Thrydulf danced a merry jig. She chuckled dreamily at the image as he tripped over Caelin's tangled staff. Aeva planted another log onto the fire, tussling with her emotions. Pacing to the pallet in the corner of the hut, crawling under the fur hides, she yawned, closing her taupe brown eyes.

The autumn morning bloomed, bitterly cold. It was Blotmonath, the month of blood sacrifice. The domesticated animals, too old or incapacitated, would be offered in sacrifice to the gods, in the hope of a mild winter for the desperate community. The snow was beginning to come early, and the rains were followed by blizzards. The Saxon village had long harvested in anticipation, with timbers prepared and stacked in the appropriate places ready for burning. All that remained was the livestock. By the end of the second day, the tasks had been accomplished. Aeva invited her neighbors, Feran, Sunn, and Leax, for an evening meal.

The remnants of a piglet were added to the bowls of vegetable stew. Goblets were filled with honey mead, and two loaves of wheat-rye bread were laid out ready for supper. Only ten and twelve years old respectively, already considered adults, Leax and Algar sat apart from their parents, wolfing down their provender, sniggering at some quip.

Aeva rolled her eyes. "I wish those two would stay away from Cula's Ford. That place is ill-fated."

"It is time for you to marry," said Feran, downing his brew. He slid the empty goblet toward his host. Casually, Aeva refilled it and pushed it back.

"Mind your business," Sunn chided. "Forgive him. What do men know?"

Aeva patted the woman's fawn-colored sleeve. "He's wrong," she replied. "And I shall not."

"Cula's Ford is not cursed," Feran told them. "It's just a place. He nodded toward Algar. "Unfortunately, it is a place where the boy's father went missing, but a Ford no less. Find yourself a warrior. One who will warm your bed and founder more sons."

Sunn gaped in disbelief. "Hark!" she blurted. "Spoken like one who couldn't tell a teat from a bunghole." The woman laughed as Feran shook his head in submission. "An ox," Sunn said. "But I wouldn't be without him."

"That," quipped Feran, "is because I know where your teats and bunghole *are!*" He grabbed lewdly at Sunn's gown, elaborating the point, sending a glare to the urchins. "Why do you two keep exploring that place? Oeric and Thrydwulf won't return. They are dead."

With that revelation, the hut fell silent. "I'm sorry," said Feran, "But it is true."

"We don't need reminding of it," Sunn said bluntly. The woman squeezed Aeva's hand. "It's hard enough for her to bear. Without your foolish song and dance."

"If she doesn't come to terms with it, she will never move on."

There was at least some veracity in the Saxon's words. He scratched at his brow. "Bah!" he added. Somewhat disobliged, he gazed into the flames of the fire.

Aeva's eyes brimmed with tears. She conquered the emotion with a swallow. "He is the father of my child. If he never returns, so be it. I will never marry."

"Then let us toast these boneheads," cracked Feran, defeatedly. "Wherever they are."

"They are here." The maiden clenched a fist and pounded her breast. "Always," she said willfully.

"Why must they always blather on about it?" Algar mumbled.

Leax leaned in close. "They're drunk. Show it to me."

Algar opened his palm. In his hand sat a worn bronze object, scribed on each surface with a raven's wing.

"What is it?" Leax grilled.

"I don't know."

"Where did you get it?"

"Cula's Ford."

"When?"

"Harvest time. Last year."

Algar was startled as the abstruse treasure was snatched from his mitt.

"This is a scabbard chape," said Feran, rolling the curiosity in his palm. You found it by the Ford?"

Algar snatched the item back, gripping it tight, like a starving beggar to a coin.

As Aeva rose from the bench, he shoved it behind his back in a spirited attempt to conceal it. "What have you got there, boy?" She brushed Feran aside, placing her hands on her hips. Defiant as he was, Algar knew he was no match for her. Reaching, he unwrapped his fingers. The bronze artifact slipped onto the carpeted floor of rushes. As Aeva bent to retrieve the metal, Sunn hopped up beside her. "What is it?" She poked Feran in the belly.

"A chape," he told her. He scanned the piece of bronze, shrugging.

Aeva examined the object and blanched. "Where did you get this?"

"Cula's Ford," Algar replied. He looked at his mother, unsure of her intent.

"Is it important? "Sunn asked.

"Of course!" Aeva barked. She retreated to the bench, slumping down, laying the object on the table; she looked haunted. Sunn, irritated, felt her passions rising. "What?" There was silence. "What?!" she shouted. Aeva was powerless to tear her attention away from the chunk of bronze. "It's Thrydwulf's," she said, wonderstruck. "Do you remember where you found this?"

She held her son's gaze, and he nodded.

"On one of the banks, where the water runs deep, where Hunwald butchered the wolves."

"Tomorrow," she vexed, "you will show me."

"We will come too," said Sunn, guaranteeing her solidarity.

Feran brushed back his lank brown hair. "Is that wise?"

When neither woman answered, he spread his hands. "The weather is setting in. Why not wait till summer? The whole village will help."

"We will come," Sunn promised once more. She smirked at her clumsy husband, shoving him out into the chill night air. "In the name of Woden," he sputtered. "It's been ten winters. What could one more hurt?"

Sunn grabbed Leax as she passed, wrenching him to his leather shoes. "He's just drunk, Avae," she said, apologizing. "We'll see you in the morning."

Aeva waved without turning.

"He was my father," Algar whispered in the Semi-gloom.

Aeva sighed, removing the clasp on her leaf-green shawl. "I miss him more than you could know."

"I thought you and Grandfather searched every spot of that Ford."

"So did I," she replied. She pondered on Hunwald and her own efforts at finding Thrydwulf. A pang of grief clawed through her. "Now get to bed. It's late."

***

Dawn blushed all grey and gold, ushering the sky from its crow-black slumber. Aeva, Sunn, and the two bairns followed the path through the trees; the earthy odor of the woodland, stimulating in its nature, assailed the senses as they moved briskly onward. Sunn carried her spouse's spear. Danger was always a possibility. Shafts of silver sunlight poked through the shedding leaves of yellowy brown. Away yonder, a woodpecker hammered on one of the archaic trees, preparing a hole to store acorns against the encroaching winter.

162

"I couldn't wake Feran. The earsling!" Sunn uttered. "He was snoring like a rutting stag."

Aeva noted the boys had scuttered ahead, leapfrogging, piggybacking, fencing with makeshift slithers of oak. Soon, they put pay to the woodland, treading out over the tinted spines of autumnal grass. At the brink of Cula's Ford, they stood; the icy water cascaded across the jutting rocks. Algar lifted his sleeve.

"Further down. The bank is wider. That's where the wolves were slaughtered."

The butchered carcasses had long since been ravaged by scavengers. Not a bone remained. Grey mud swept back against the fading turf, like a slate-colored skull crowned with a sward of yellowed receding hair. Algar led the way over the slippery boulders in a futile attempt to keep dry. He slid, thigh-deep, into the freezing water as the others waded past. Aeva seized the boy, dragging him along by the scruff of the neck. Complaining, he broke free, traversing the opposite bank of the Ford with the group in tow. Soaking and shivering, Algar and Leax were the first to scale the leaf-choked incline. Sunn, with the aid of Feran's spear, poled herself up beside them.

Aeva tripped, muddying her burgundy garb about the knees. "Scitte!" she cursed. Climbing to her wet leather shoes, breathing hard, she lashed out, clumping Algar's ear.

"That's for straying from the village and not doing what you're told."

Leax grinned and abruptly gawked as his mother's eye fell upon him. "Don't you dare, she warned. "Where did you find the chape?"

"Over there," Algar piped up.

"You combed all along these rises," said Sunn. "Your father many times."

163

"But if we missed *this*," Aeva held up the piece of bronze, "There may be other signs."

"More riddles," Feran grunted, appearing below them. With ease, he scaled the slippery slope. Groggy, due to the amount of mead he had consumed the night before, the latecomer was extremely peeved. "You. Woman." He pulled Sunn to him. "Will never take my spear again without permission." Feran sized the weapon from her grasp. Embarrassed, Sunn pushed him aside, brushing off the flame-orange leaves, sprinkling down from the molting hawthorn trees.

"That's why I didn't wake you. You're not worth the trouble," she spat like a viper.

Feran broke the news. "We've been summoned to the main hall."

Aeva undid her clasp, shaking the autumn debris from her green shawl. "What for?"

"Guess." Feran retorted, grabbing Sunn's arm. "We must go," he bid her.

"You told Seaver we were here?" she asked in disbelief. The warrior's expression betrayed the treachery.

"Damn you to Hell," she fumed.

Feran bared his teeth. "What could I say?" he snarled. "You were seen leaving the village. Boy!" He bellowed. Leax sprang to his father's side. "Take this." He pitched his javelin to his only son. "Follow us." Wheeling to Aeva, he bade her, "If you still possess even the slightest pinch of common sense, you will do the same."

Feran dragged his wife down the steep gradient; Leax trundled after them, wading into the freezing water, making for the primeval oaks and the village settlement beyond.

Aeva hid the bronze chape in the pocket of her garb. Clasping Algar's frozen hand in her own, she smiled remorsefully. "For once, Feran may be right. We should go."

"Will Lord Seaver be angry?" Algar asked.

"Only at me," Aeva told him.

"Are we keeping father's chape?"

"If we can. But that's not a promise."

They wove back, under the trees, past the creaking trunks of oak; the leaves, coppery-green, shivered eerily on the wind. In silence, heading homeward, Aeva's anxiety began to grow talons.

The mead hall stood like a lonely warden, resolute, austere against the shuddering of autumn. Horn gabled, the thatched roof rolled down upon its sturdy timbers, clothing the frame with a straw fleece of bronze. Smoke drifted from a single opening at the center of the edifice. Evening blanketed the Saxon homesteads as the sun slowly began to pass away over the gentle hills.

Aeva, Sunn, Feran, and the two boys entered Seaver's hall of festivity and governance.

Four great logs, intricately carved, braced the wooden structure. A fire blazed in a long-dug pit, and at the far end of the chamber sat the imposing figure of Lord Seaver and his somber thegns. The man oozed power, but he was prone to short spasms—jerks and twitches—that for the merest of moments supped the aristocratic persona pitilessly away. At the end of such an episode, he would cough, perhaps with embarrassment, only to fix his subjects with a questioning stare.

Seaver was Caelin's son. That position of authority, tied to him, was like a horde of Valkyries to a bloody battlefield of wandering souls. "Bring them forward," he commanded.

Aeva, with her party, stood before the Lord's highchair. "Remove them," Seaver said, pointing at Algar and Leax. "They were not summoned." He frowned, noting Feran—one of his lesser warriors, proud yet self-serving—and the two women, their chins raised, illustrious yet fully resistant. Good stock.

Seaver wrinkled about the eyes and snorted a chuckle. "How long must you hold to this foolishness?"

"My Lord?" Aeva responded, feigning surprise.

"Our fathers were old friends. The time of grieving is past. Hunwald would want you to take a husband. I can hear him screaming it from the depths of Valhalla."

A ripple of laughter rose from Seaver's thegns. He fixed the men with a stony glare; it blew away like mist before a storm. "Where is the object Feran spoke of?"

She flicked the warrior a sideward glance. Feran returned an apologetic smile. Optionless, Aeva drew the bronze chape from her gown and stepped forward, placing it into Seaver's callused palm.

"You know for certain this belonged to Thrydwulf-son-of-Ceolwulf?"

"It was wrought for my father. He gifted it to Thrydwulf. You can see the raven wings. I know the design." To the astonishment of all, Lord Seaver stood, flinging the metal token into the crackling flames of the fire pit. Aeva clenched her fists in disbelief.

Sunn seized her closest friend by the sleeve. "Know your place," she whispered.

"Wise words," Seaver professed, slumping back down on the crude wooden cathedra. Aeva rocked on her haunches but did not give the Saxon lord the gratification of her tears. He was not surprised, after all, this was Hunwald's seed.

"As I have said. The time for grief has passed. It is not in our tradition to force a woman into marriage, but I do it out of respect for your father. The man was worthy."

A fellow with long black hair and a beard rose from one of the benches. He was handsome, yet lame from a battle wound procured two winters before. He carried scars on his neck and cheek. By his attire, Aeva assumed, he was a noble. But clothes—as she had always known—could belie a man's virtue.

"This is Kim, our neighbor," said Seaver. "Favored by Caelin-son-of-Oswin. I have told him your story. He desires your hand in marriage. And you *shall* give it."

The black-haired Saxon limped before Seaver's chair and bowed. Spinning, he turned to face Aeva.
"Forgive my presumption, Lady." Politely, he arched his back with another bow. "It would curb my mother's incessant tongue were you to accept." He took her slender fingers and planted a kiss on the rear of her hand.

She withdrew, piously.

"My heart belongs to another," she uttered. "It always will."

"Nonsense!" bayed Seaver. "She accepts. Make the arrangements."

Beyond the wattle daub fences, within the confines of her primitive dwelling, Aeva sat at her bench, softly weeping. In the corner of the room, Algar was snoozing beneath the skins his grandfather had tanned long before his birth. The woman wiped her eyes, addressing the sleeping youth. "I have no choice, child," she whispered. She took the bronze chape she

167

had managed to save from the flames in Seaver's hall. Crossing to the deer hides, she knelt, wrapping the melted object in Algar's hand.

Chapter 16

IN SEARCH OF THE OUTLANDER
(Kazhelma, North Palacoumia Forest. 3rd Millennium)

"Of course, I can't read the future," Gryonae argued.

"I'm not trying to hit the moon with an arrow," said Tymarian. "What if he's dead? We should ride straight to Jorai; skirt around the forests to the east."

"We ride through Palacoumia! If you wish to travel to Jorai alone, be my guest."

"It's taken too long to find you, brother. I'll not lose you again," Tymarian sighed. "We'll find the boy."

"My thanks," said Shadowgrip, gratefully. "Though Thrydwulf could hardly be called a boy any longer. He'll be twenty-five years old, or thereabouts, by Vargdenir's reckoning."

Tymarian grumbled, "He better be worth the trouble."

Gryonae laughed heartily. "He always held my favor. Though his tale is one of intense drama. Well-nigh cloak-and-dagger. Vargdenir's too. It's a curious tale."

Shadowgrip and the quondam warlord had fled from the city gates. Onward, a long route, in a tameless squall, around the mountain range of Schukhular, avoiding its lesser neighbor, Mt Kutrania. Evading the patrols, the brothers had ridden southwestward over the tall grasslands; restless in their evening slumbers; ever watchful beneath the green suns blistering above Kazhelma. On the fifteenth day of the month—the people of Quilaxia called Shyvor—they trotted down from the hills. The wrakens clopped through a bubbling stream. A hundred feet farther on, an oval tunnel loomed, carved into the solid rock. Mysterious runes, etched on the jaggy walls, glorified the emperors of the Dirakhan.

"This is a grim place," Tymarian broached as they traveled through. Gryonae, though he'd been here many times before, was inclined to agree; he buttoned his cloak against the sobering remark. They galloped on and soon, there before the brothers, lay the dilapidated bridge spanning the river.

"Do you see those?" Gryonae lifted a gauntlet, pointing at the distant trees. "They were carved by unknown artisans long

170

ago. It's believed their purpose is to terrify feeble folk. Rarely do the Dirakhan enter Palacoumia anymore."

The hewn effigies were grotesque like doomed souls forced to endure the tortures of a vindictive god. Gryonae dismounted. "Be careful as you cross. The bridge is treacherous."

Palacoumia was a location of folklore; Tymarian had heard the stories. And though the warmth of the two suns radiated through the multicolored leaves, his maroon shirt seemed inadequate for the fey, creeping cold. Delving into his saddlebag for the cape, identical to Gryonae's, he yanked it free, eased it over his shoulders, and fastened it at the throat. "These are army issue," he grumbled.

In their coal black cloaks, astride their cerulean mounts, they could have passed for cavalrymen of Rissak's guard. Whether this would be advantageous or complete foolishness, considering they were bound for the wild steppes of Novia Jorai, only time would tell.

"Has anyone ever told you, brother?" said Shadowgrip.

"What would they tell me?"

"That you grouch like a man who works for peanuts, only to be told he is about to be paid in monkeys."

Tymarian found the remark comical.

A flock of beige-feathered birds took flight. As they winged toward the north, the two fugitives were peppered with droppings, Tymarian catching most of the excretion. Gryonae belly laughed as his brother trotted by. "Wait!" he hollered. "You don't know the way!"

After a day lost among the trees, they found their way back to the forest path. The leagues fell away behind them, and they came to three forks on the trail. Tymarian heaved at his reins. "The way is not marked," he explained.

"You expect it to be signposted?" said Gryonae with a frown. "This is Lagatius' Talon. Keep to the right. It leads to a lake. We can rest there tonight."

They refilled the water sacks, building a fire. Unrolling their canvas bedspreads, they sat cross-legged on the foliage, dining on bland vegetables and bread, sharing a leather bottle of spiced wine. Gryonae studied his companion across the flames. The man was mid-thirties. Muscular, astute in nature, amusing. His thick black ringlets curled to his shoulders. He was far removed from the spindly-limbed figure the champion remembered from his youth. Shadowgrip trusted no one, yet given the circumstances, he decreed he had no choice.

"Tell me of the salt mines. The scars there, upon the neck."

Intuitively, Tymarian stroked the three ivory blemishes below his beard. "The creature was a Grokon," he said. Ripping a hunk of bread from a loaf, he dressed it with a slither of stale cheese and scoffed it down.

"Those wretches are unpredictable," Gryonae mumbled.

"And lethal," added Tymarian.

"What do you recall of our plight? As prisoners, all those years ago?" Gryonae asked.

"We were captured below the Thoo Hills. Taken through Tendia Wood, back into the North. We were parted. For many leagues, I was forced to run behind their mounts, at the end of a taut rope. There is an outpost east of Schukhular. They sold me to a deaf innkeeper. For five years, I stayed with the family. They were good to me, but the yearning for home was too strong. I stole a wraken. As incredible as it seems, I *did* reach Novia Jorai." Tymarian chuckled. "I lived in Havoy for six years."

172

"That dung hole!" said Gryonae.

"I know. I killed a Chief. Urt was his name. A foul man. Despised. For my trouble, I earned the position of warlord. The enemy drove deep into our lands. At one campaign, I was captured. Imprisoned. Handed over to a nomadic tribe, loyal to the Dirakhan. Then shipped off to Rothshim. The rest you know. But what of you, brother? How does your tale run?"

"Do you remember? They separated us at Lanitir?" asked Gryonae.

Tymarian scratched his cheek. "The village, west of the river?" he said. "Yes. I recall."

"You were snatched from father's arms. He protested, striking two of the dogs down. For his boldness, he was slain."

Gryonae had dispatched so many mortals in the arena due to these circumstances. He had long forgotten the number of the dead.

"The dogs towed *me*, likewise, with bound ropes. In the city, I was rescued by the Hinera." Gryonae gave a sour laugh. "Some have called them a resistance group. Others…*a* difficult gang of street thugs. I took refuge with them till I was arrested and imprisoned. I killed a jailor. One of the swordmasters pleaded my case. Rinue, he was called. An honorable man. Swore he would negotiate my freedom. A year later, he was executed for treason."

Tymarian sighed with disappointment. "Father was right. We Novians are cursed by the gods."

"I reached the status of arena champion. After *these* present games, I may have attained my freedom."

"I apologize, brother," said Tymarian.

"For what?"

"For robbing you of the chance."

"Don't be a fool," said Gryonae. "Rissak would never have sanctioned the agreement."

"Why not?" asked Tymarian.

"Because…" Gryonae answered, feeling his bile rise, "he is Mad. Insane. Yarra!"

Tymarian leaned back in his saddle, unsure of how to address his sibling's rage.

Shadowgrip breathed deeply to negate his anger. "Likely as not, we will be taken back to the city to be flayed alive and fed to the dogs as an example."

Tymarian blasphemed, turning the night air an indigo blue. "Then let us swear an oath not to be taken alive."

"The only reason I intend to enter those city gates again," Shadowgrip snarled, "is to sever a rat's head from its shoulders and devour its brains. *It* and all those eager to protect it."

"Tell me. "Said the ebony-haired Novian with a grin. "Have you ever sought the advice of a headshrinker for such…notions?"

The morning greenwood rang with singing birds. The extinguished fire left a pile of silver ash upon the ferns. The brothers had wrapped themselves in their canvas rolls during the night, oblivious to the nocturnal critters that had strayed close only to spring away due to the men's loud snoring.

Tymarian was the first to wake. He fed and watered the wrakens, washed his face in the cold lake, and kicked Gryonae from his slumber. They breakfasted on oats and curd milk, sweetened with wild blackberries; lashed their belongings to their mounts, and set off again.

***

"Look there!" Tymarian pointed through the trees.

174

Two nervous wrakens were lashed amongst the undergrowth. An erect wikiup stood nearby. The brothers tied their beasts and circled the secluded bivouac. A trifling area of forest floor had been scraped away. In a circle of stones, charred wood remained. The warlord placed a hand on the black twigs and branches. "A day. Perhaps," said Tymarian, wiping his hands with soggy ferns. "What do you suggest?"

Gryonae was already clawing through the paraphernalia within the canvas structure. "We steal what we need and flee!" He bid from the wikiup.

From his place, astride a slick tree branch, a figure clothed in a black doublet with a coal-colored turban watched the thieves gallop by with his goods. Rushing to avenge the robbery, the Quwarshin assassin slipped, tumbling and crashing to the rigid roots below.

He did not live long. Where he lay, he rotted, never to escape the forbidding forests of Palacoumia.

***

The leagues withered away. They reached the clearing where Shadowgrip and Vargdenir had encountered Brim Thackalton months before. Gryonae uttered nothing of the exploit but galloped by, grim-faced and withdrawn.

Four hours past noon, a light mist hung in the air. The willow-green suns slipped on the purple flowers; they had arrived at Vardenir's secluded cabin.

The brothers tied their wrakens out of sight. Crouching in the ferns. They surveyed the decrepit barn through the trees. "You check the stable," said Gryonae. "The lodging is upslope. Quite a climb." Gryonae shook his head. " Don't ask."

175

Tymarian drew his sword and crept across the stream, melting into the dense thickets.

With both hands, the champion slipped two blades from their sheaths, praying he would not discover Thrydwulf's rotting corpse upon the cabin floor. The thought shook him to the marrow.

Tymarian burst into the barn. Crossing the patchy grass and heaps of wraken dung, he knelt upon the mud, close to a wooden trough of stank-ridden water.

"The lodge is empty," Gryonae revealed as he entered the shelter.

"Whoever lay here was covered by this sack," said Tymarian. "It's been vomited into." He scrunched up the hessian bag, tossing it into the shadows. "There were two or three men. The spoors are hard to read. There is no blood. No sign of struggle. What now, brother? Do we spend our days unraveling riddles? Or do we head home, build an army, and rid the world of these whoremongers once and for all?"

Shadowgrip sheathed his knives. "There is one last hope."

"More puzzles," the warlord sighed.

One look at his kinsman's face, and it was obvious the man was exhausted.

Gryonae said: "Indulge me. There's a village. Westward, a few leagues. We can search there."

"And if he's not found?" the warlord asked, wearily.

The champion, grieved to admit defeat, proclaimed: "I will consider the oath fulfilled."

Tymarian studied the scene one last time, grimaced, and shrugged. "To the village, it is."

Through the night, they journeyed across one of the many wooden bridges spanning the winding river. Hooded—their

176

black cloaks buttoned against the rain—they cantered across the sploshing mud, spying at last, the timbered gates of Karfilia.

Betgar, the white-bearded chief of the village, stood in the downpour, squinting beneath his umbra. The men on the parapet were bellowing down to the strangers at the gate. Impatient, he bawled at the hapless souls. "What do they want?"

The guard said something to the woodsman at his side, and both men grinned.

"What does he think they want?" said Vimton to his comrade. "Shelter from the weather, for one thing." He called back down to the old man. "They want to enter!"

Betgar raised his umbra. "Who are they?"

"One says his name is Gryonae. He and Vargdenir were old friends?"

Something struck Betgar, unbalancing the old man. Something he may be misconstruing: The man said, 'Were!'

"Let them pass. See to their needs. And have Suzin bring them to my hut. Come on, damn it! I'm drowning!"

Suzin washed Thrydwulf's naked body, redressing the cotton sheet about his neck.

For weeks, she had been administering wild fruits and cups of uncontaminated rainwater. His condition was no longer critical. When Teon and his trackers failed to return, Betgar had dispatched two more men. They had discovered their slain brethren, buried the corpses in the forest and pushed on to Vargdenir's homestead. Finding Thrydwulf alone and dying, they ferried the young man back to Karfilia, saving his life.

"No more of this water," Thrydwulf griped, pushing the cup away. "Bring some ale."

177

Suzin rolled her eyes and turned to leave. "And some meat. Please!" he spat after her.

Weak as Thrydwulf was, he raised himself to his elbows, shoved himself up, and leaned against the planks of the hut. The door creaked open, and Gryonae entered.

Thrydwulf gaped in wonder. Rissak's champion was a ghost of his former self: Disheveled. Undernourished.

"You're back!" The Saxon could hardly contain himself. "I need to dress. Suzin must fetch my shirt and breeches." The door groaned again. Thrydwulf's heart vaulted as he slid naked to his feet. "Varg!" he hollered, almost hysterical. The feeling was transitory; his happiness shrank like a withering vine. Where the old stepparent should have stood was a stranger with a black beard, his chiseled face gaunt. He smiled, but it did little to ease Thrydwulf's distress. "I am called Tymarian. We've traveled a long road to find you, Thrydwulf. You and Gryonae need to speak."

***

The rain had passed into the north, and Tymarian sat alone, outside one of the huts. He was downing potent ale from a curved drinking horn, wallowing in self-pity. He was thinking of Thrydwulf's tears when he had learned of Vargdenir. The weeping had practically ripped him in two. He understood the loss. Tossing the dregs of beer from his ivory horn into the grass, he went in search of Betgar.

"You should come to Novia Jorai. This forest will be crawling with Dirakhan. The emperor will take my brother's escape as a personal insult. It would not be wise to remain," Tymarian advised.

178

"I couldn't endure an excursion seven hundred leagues into the south," Betgar replied. "In truth, these fragile bones could barely make it to the edges of Palacoumia...let alone the Thoo Hills and beyond."

"Mark me well," said Tymarian, his mood still a crow-wing black. "Rissak's hordes will decimate these forests. Think of your folk!"

Betgar had sought, always, to protect his people in the secluded village, but years of philanthropic duty had gradually reduced the old man to an egocentric pretender.

"I have a granddaughter," he said, pondering.

Candles flickered on the table between them, and a keg of intoxicating beer supplied their ivory-drinking horns.

"Suzin?" asked the former Warlord.

Betgar nodded glumly.

"Then do not leave her or any of your people to the mercy of these animals. Come with us. If we can reach Jorai..." He spread the fingers of his left hand as if this was an unspoken answer to a weighty concern.

"I'm not sure the people would follow such extreme counseling," Betgar told him. He pitched the dregs of his beer onto the hut floor, laying the empty vessel on the table. Gripping his white beard, he yanked it in agitation.

Tymarian's face, a semblance of carved granite, said, "You do know who is leading us?"

The village patriarch raised an eyebrow. "Prisoners on the run from the Emperor of Kazhelma?"

Tymarian snorted with amusement. "Point taken. But nay," he said, his eyes sparkling. "A hero known as Shadowgrip.

179

Slayer of three hundred adversaries in Rissak's arena of butchery."

Betgar scowled and spoke with bitter sarcasm, "Who better to raise an army of bone-skinners to change the world, eh?"

Thrydwulf remained reticent for three days, morose, unwilling to leave Suzin's hut. No matter how stiffly the maiden badgered, he would not comply. On the fourth morning of Gryonae's arrival, he dressed and left the solitude of the hut.

The first thing he noticed was how busy the community had become. Carts were crammed with belongings. Ox carts—or beasts he considered comparable to cattle—were chained and yoked. Everything imaginable was stowed and ready for travel. On one of the long-pointed posts ringing the sequestered village, a blue-winged warbler of sorts, far from its preferred habitat of shrubland and thicket, trilled joyfully from its perch.

Birdwatching was a hobby that had long encapsulated his imagination. The moment lifted his spirits a slight degree.

He turned, and Gryonae was there. Without a word, the warrior stepped in, pulling Thrydwulf into an embrace. "I'm glad you have returned to us, little brother," he said. "It's hard to bear. You're not alone in your grief. But we have a long road ahead, and there is much to do. If you are up to it, you can help lash the livestock to the carts?" The arena champion gave an obligatory smile, yet it was obvious he was racked with guilt and grief.

Thrydwulf nodded and buttoned his shirt. "I will help."

Chapter 17

THE NEW KING
(Kazhelma, South Palacoumia Forest. 3rd Millennium)

The rabble now numbered three to four thousand men.

The menfolk paced along carrying spears, blades, or wood-cutting tools as weapons. Most of the women, children, and elderly men had boarded the carts, wherever they could find a suitable place to roost.

Gryonae and Tymarian led the procession on their mounts; Betgar, Suzin, and Thrydwulf were close behind in the first cart, drawn by two ponderous kaalers towards the Thoo Hills. Each day, the throng was growing. Hunting parties were established to feed the expanding numbers: wayfarers, groups of homeless vagabonds, and entire villages had been absorbed into the vagabond army. Fear of the Dirakhan and their objectives—via the rumor begun by the brothers themselves at Karfilia—was mushrooming, sweeping like a brush fire into the south. Shadowgrip and the warlord considered their opening gambit a success.

The journey was hard going, but Thrydwulf pulled a woolen blanket around his collarbone and lay down and settled the best he could.

He dreamed of a smoky hut, a wood and wire cage of cackling geese. In the corner of the shelter, a pile of fur hides occupied the darkness. The familiar drama was unraveling. He crawled to the moribund figure. 'Mother...?' he whispered. The woman's emaciated jaw dropped open, but the mouth was now incapable of forming words. The eyes—ever imploring—closed, and Cynwise stopped breathing.

Thrydwulf sat up. "I have to get home," he said. "My mother!" Not a soul noticed the Saxon's commotion. Most were lost in grave concerns of their own. Aeva engulfed his ideation. Was she still living? Did their child survive? So many questions were left unanswered.

Thrydwulf-son-of-Ceolwulf.

That in itself was farcical. He had despised his bully of a father. In the eyes of others, it must have appeared that he had worshiped the man. Only Aeva knew the truth.

182

Suzin spun on her rump, passing him a hunk of grain bread and a cold rib of kaaler meat. He thanked the maiden, wolfing down the food, wetting his lips with the ale supplied to complement the edibles.

"How far have we traveled?" he asked.

"Two hundred leagues, maybe a little more," Betgar answered. "Our numbers are multiplying daily. It's staggering. At this rate, Gryonae will have an army before he gains the Thoo Hills."

The Saxon smirked. "There are more infants, women, and bedridden old men than warriors," he was swift to propose. "I don't wish to appear a defeatist, but if he thinks he's going to lay waste the might of the Dirakhan with this...route? Huh! We may as well have razed Palacoumia to a pile of ashes... and us along with it."

Suzin stared at the disgruntled Saxon. "Tell me of Vargdenir," she said, endeavoring to shift his mood.

Betgar spoke up. "A good man. Noble. One you could trust."

Thrydwulf sighed. "Why must you always do that?"

The old man tugged at the long reins; the wheels of the cart stopped rolling. "Do what?" he asked.

"Answer for her!"

"An old habit," Betgar blabbered in his defense. "The suns will be going down soon. Seems we are to camp here tonight. Get yourselves busy. We need wood for a fire."

Many flames twinkled beneath the trees. At one, cross-legged on canvas sheeting, sat the brothers, Betgar, his granddaughter, and the shivering Saxon. Dining on a pot of wild game and horns of spiced red wine, the mood was somewhat maudlin, and the moon was full.

183

"Do you miss your homeland?" Betgar asked, scratching his bald pate.

Thrydwulf raised his head to speak. Realizing the question was meant for the brothers, he swallowed his horn of red wine and lowered his gaze.

Gryonae and Tymarian took up the tale of their ordeal, the death of their father, the mother they had scarcely known, dying at childbirth while bringing a dead sister into the world. They spoke of the women they had loved, Tymarian of Allina, the almond-eyed beauty whom he had foolishly let slip away, and Gryonae spoke of the tragedy of Sharee, and the mysterious child that may or may not have been his.

Betgar spoke of his wife and daughter, Theena and Stora. They had ventured into the forest with clay pots to fetch water. Hours later, the vessels had been discovered, smashed to pieces at the edge of the stream. The hunters could find no spoor to track. The women had simply vanished. Suzin sniffled, and Thrydwulf put his arm around the maiden, aiming to soften the hurt. Lastly, Thrydwulf spoke of Aeva, and of the child he also had never known. Betgar announced that it was the wine driving the group to sentimentality.

Tymarian laughed heartily. "I survived Rothshim. I will squeeze every hour from every day, from here till the end. Relishing the gift of life. Be it wrapped in a woman's breast or dancing at the point of a savage's sword. A toast to life!" He offered up his conical horn and drained the plonk dry. Wiping his beard with the sleeve of his maroon shirt, unashamedly, he burped.

"Excuse the warlord of Havoy," said Shadowgrip. "He is an oaf. But I will toast him." A rumble of uneasy laughter trickled through the group, and the killer lifted his arm, an act that seemed to lighten the mood.

Time tumbled on.

Then out of the shadows, a man strode up before Gryonae and knelt, as one might genuflect in the presence of a king.

"My Lord," he declared.

Tymarian, soused, grinned, shrugged his shoulders, and offered his palms. "The only lord here is me. What is it you want, woodsman? Speak up."

"I have news, " the man said.

Belying his intoxication, Gryonae wove to his buskins like a lithe ballerino. The stranger stood too, a snail's crawl in comparison.

"We are closer than thirty leagues to the edge of Palacoumia."

"Excellent," replied Gryonae.

The woodman nodded, idling.

"There is more?" asked the champion.

"We have prisoners," the woodsman told him.

"No need for prisoners. We can use the arms. Have the men join us."

"These are not men," said the woodsman.

For a moment, Gryonae was lost in thought.

"My Lord, these are Grokons. Imps?"

"I know what goblins are. Show me," Gryonae commanded.

The warrior nodded and strode off with the arena champion at his heels.

"Don't kill them all—yet!" wailed Tymarian. "They may be useful. You don't know their tongue!" He grappled to his boots and zig-zagged after them.

Nine of the grotesque captives had been bound by the wrists and were now seated on the ferns at spearpoint. Black-

185

skinned, shaven-headed, five feet tall. They were clad in peculiar armor, talkative amongst themselves, but more importantly, weaponless.

The siblings could tell immediately they were foot soldiers from Enlyd—the land a slew of leagues west of Novia Jorai. Their people were practically neighbors. Tymarian inaugurated a spokesman for the bunch. *Shtritch-Nal-Oule* was his name. Tymarian settled on Nal—It was the easiest part of the name to pronounce.

He spoke in the Grokon tongue, rasping and unfamiliar to the forest folk.

"Why so far from home, boys? Have you come to plunder among the hills?"

Nal's flat face was invisible in the darkness, but his bright yellow eyes shone like moons on a black sea.

"Our peoplez are at war, Novian. Your nation will fall. My kindred will glory in your deztruction."

"We can argue that score till the gods decide to come and wrestle upon the plains of Chanindoria. Who now is king in Novia Jorai?" Tymarian quizzed.

The Grokon was mystified. "Leetzune, of courze! You do not know who rulez your own country?"

"I was forced to part from her long ago. And not of my own accord. Now we return. My brother and I, Gryonae, he is called. Shadowgrip by some. Bone Maker by others."

Shtritch-Nal-Oule studied the intimidating figure, its hands resting upon the pommel of a sword plunged into the earth. "The Emperor'z Champion," he said, his voice scouring to the ears. "I know the name. There will be but a few amongzt the Grookarn who do not."

"Is *it* talking about me?" asked Gryonae. "I will make it shake in my presence."

186

"I doubt *that* brother," Tymarian responded. "This goblin would fight four of you and spit in your face at the moment of its death. Do not underestimate these creatures. You know who they are. They have a kingdom to be reckoned with. *It* says our countries are at war, but if we can convert them to allies?"

"What do you propose?" said Bone Maker.

"Set them free. Send them back to Enlyd. Convey that Shadowgrip has come to seize the crown in Novia Jorai. That he seeks an alliance with his neighbors. That he will crush the Dirakhan. Free the world of their tyranny. Once and for all."

"You think they'll listen?"

Tymarian shrugged his shoulders. "We can try."

A man known as Floder was the last to leave the temporary encampment. Stowing the Imps' odd equipage of weaponry into the cart, he stepped onto the wooden wheel spokes and climbed aboard the wagon. Lifting the reins, he slapped the kaalers' rumps, and the cart began to roll.

At the edge of the spindly trees, he spun, affording the eerie glade a final glance. He could see them now in their entirety. Nine bodies dangled at the ends of crudely rigged vines. They swung lifelessly in the breeze. Not so much as a warning to those who dared to trail, but more a consequence of the new King's impatience.

The last leagues died away, and the brothers left the confines of the legendary forest.

The scouts were about their business, constructing fires and digging latrines someway off among the thickets. During the journey, the women had taken to sewing old sheets and sacks together, attempting to create crude tents for folks to

187

take shelter from the elements. A lucky few were grateful for the endeavor.

Thrydwulf spectated from one of those erected tents, as Gryonae and Tymarian began the preparation of turning ordinary men into soldiers. Merciless in the venture, they backhanded the clumsy, scorned the weak-willed, and reprimanded the foolhardy.

"The Dirakhan will not spare the incompetent. They will relish it!" Gryonae was baying. "If you desire to return to Palacoumia, go! That won't save you. This base emperor, who would smear a woman's monthly discharge across his chamber floor for amusement, will not hesitate to saw the head from a newborn babe. Scurry back to your wood. He is coming. I have offended his honor. He intends to bury Kazhelma beneath landscapes of blood and entrails. I aim to stop him and take back our world, if I can."

This was typical of Shadowgrip. Thrydwulf had witnessed it before. But there was an urgency in his words now, and seeing his brutality caused a deep concern.

Tymarian was less aggressive in his instruction. At times, he employed banter, even mirth. Most favored this instruction. Less cruelty. But it was just as effective.

Thrydwulf was beginning to appreciate the man as the months wore on. Though he loved Gryonae—they shared a deep experience, not knowing the fate of their children for one—but he saw something in Tymarian's personality that reminded him of Hunwald. That could never be a bad thing.

Betgar was snoozing at the back of the tent as Suzin crawled in beside Thrydwulf.

"I'm terrified of that man," she declared, bobbing her strawberry-blonde locks at Gryonae.

188

"He scares me too," Thrydwulf confessed. "Anyone not frightened would have to be insane or an imbecile."

Suzin slapped his forearm playfully. "Or both!" the maiden appended. Her long tresses tumbled about the shoulders of her green tunic. Not a classic beauty, but she was buxom, and Thrydwulf, knowing she had seen him naked, was excited by *that* detail.

"Have you ever loved?" he asked her, bluntly. Embarrassed, her cheeks flushed.

"That is none of your business." She replied, stroking her hair. "Is it true, what grandfather says? You are not from Kazhelma? You or your father?"

Her blue eyes fixed him with an inquisitive stare.

"Vargdenir was not my father. Yet more of one to me than my own blood." Suzin sensed the rage lurking below the surface. She snorted, ignoring the subdued anger. "Come," she breathed, "Speak true. Where were you born?"

Thrydwulf bit back his annoyance and smiled idiotically.

"In the forest, under a mulberry bush."

Suzin glowered. "There are no such bushes in Palacoumia."

He lay down, cloaking himself in his woolen blanket. "They were seeded by Rome...even before the tribes arrived in Britain. One day, I will explain it all to you. Whether you have the wit to understand is another matter."

She slapped him again, the assault good-natured. Betgar rolled on his bedspread. "Hist!" he grumbled. "Get some rest. The journey to the hills will be a trial. For these old bones at least."

Thrydwulf silently imitated the headman of Karfilia, in not-so-flattering terms.

Suzin giggled, prompting her grandfather's irritation.

"Sleep or be gone!" he barked.

189

The sound of iron clanged remotely, filling the open plains with the echo of swordplay. Gryonae's irate commands boomed above the swordplay. Thrydwulf drank in the solace of the new king's presence. Weary and aching, he slept.

Chapter 18

RISSAK
(Kazhelma, Quilaxia City. 3rd Millennium)

The time of mourning was over. Endambia, the elderly princess, Rissak's last remaining kin, had been laid out on an ornate bed of cotton linen and silk. She lay atop an open sarcophagus, her title chiseled in the red sandstone, her long silvery hair plaited down to the waist.

The state funeral had been a hive of formal activity, but the crowds were back to their mundane lives; the royal

191

administrators were attending to their conventional duties. He had no empathy for those who bemoaned Endambia's passing. Sympathy itself was little more than an external process acted out when the need for its portrayal arose. He experienced nothing that touched him emotionally, apart from infernal rage if his desires or commands were unmet. The brutal games had dissolved into farce. Without the arena champion, the crowd had become restless, half of them leaving in disappointment.

The angry mob had chanted the familiar epithet. When the champion had not materialized, they had attempted to storm the arena. Fifty-two citizens had lost their lives, and the tournament was cut short. Even so, Rissak had stood, raised his hands, bidding them to be silent.

'Your champion has absconded! He killed three jailers! Other bodies are being discovered! Slain by his hand!' He had spoken into the ear of the priest standing beside his seat of polished obsidian. 'Tymarian! A vagabond from the butcher's own country! What should we do with this traitor?!' In an awkward moment, he lingered till the incredulous spectators began to chant.

'Death! Death! Death!'
'If he seeks to take refuge among the heathen hordes in Novia Jorai?! What shall we do?!'
The arena rang with thirty thousand exuberant voices.
'War! War! War!'
'It is time to show the world, once again, that the sleeping dragon has awoken! We are now at war!' he had trumpeted.

The echoes faded from his mind as he departed the chamber.

The corridors beyond were blue-painted walls of sandstone. Pictorial fabrics decorated the walkways, and numerous textiles glorified long-forgotten battle scenes from history. Small

192

tables, ostentatious in design, were placed along the walls, each one supporting a vase of smoldering incense, pluming the air, delighting the nostrils. Servants conducted chores, doubling their steps wherever the emperor passed. He pondered Endambia once more. The thought swam off, swifter than a shoal of fish before the jaws of a hunting predator. Over the ensuing months, he had begun to experience acute boredom, as opposed to the deep grief one might encounter after the death of a loved one. His mother and father had been struck down by a mysterious illness. Or, as only he knew, poisoned by the hand of his assassin, Gaucuss Ahdor-Nez. Where was the slayer now? Rissak presumed he was probably nothing more than a statistic. He would send word to the Quwarshin and seek a worthy replacement.

The staircases buzzed with the annoyance of bees that had found their way in from the royal gardens. Rissak swatted at the insects as he moved by, cursing their very nature, condemning them to the depths of Hell—Nephthrionigal, the Dirakhan called it.

Rissak stepped out into his illustrious bedchamber and crossed the smooth granite slabs. Near the open balcony stood a brass gong. He picked up the mallet and struck nonchalantly upon it. Less than a minute later, a servant appeared. He bowed, lowering his eyes.

"Empty the chamber pot. Bring me a dish of food. Send for a food taster and a cupbearer. And send for Yast-Dutan. I will dine first. That is all."

The servant nodded and went about his duty.

Rissak had been furnished a midday meal of boiled eggs, fish, dates, and wine, ordering the dish to be tasted and the rich wine sampled. Satisfied, he carried the token feast out onto the balcony, sitting at the oval table of burnished wood.

Far below, Quilaxia was like a termite colony, brimming with its customary, daily commotion. Across the breadth of the sprawling city, nuzzled amongst the myriads of twisting streets, perched *'Alhulbat Alkubraa'*, the Great Arena. Its fluted columns penetrated the skyline; its vandalized sandstone walls a red scab beneath the olive-green suns. An army of men had shed their blood for the gratification of the citizens of Quilaxia. Eighteen hundred and ninety-two years, it had persevered, almost as long as the empire itself. The names of the dead, carved into stone plaques above the mighty gates, read like a solemn commemoration of fallen heroes. Last upon it, defaced and ultimately removed, was Gryonae Kryack.

Shadowgrip. The Butcher of Quilaxia.

Down through the centuries, captured enemies had been forced to fight and die. That longstanding tradition had gone; selecting warriors from the king's bodyguard had returned—at least until the emergence of Gryonae Kryack. The man had achieved legendary status before Rissak's birth. He was close to approaching his freedom. That dream was dead. It had been half a millennium since one of Rissak's ancestors had stormed the walls of Denfurnan in Novia Jorai. The time had come again for the Dirakhan Empire to show its force. They would crush the world once more.

Yast-Dutan scaled the smooth steps to Rissak's room. This was where the emperor engaged in his deepest degradations. The bodies of young women Dutan had been commanded to dispose of, after many a night of drunken debauchery, would—so he believed—eventually leave his own shattered soul to the mercy of those demons dwelling in the underworld. Whether

194

it was redeemable, he could only guess. He got stung by a bee as he passed. This he counted as one more curse, attributing the misfortune to his innumerable sins. He climbed the last steps, his knees creaking. He lumbered over the square granite slabs to the balcony; the emperor was spectating on his subjects far below. A party of children, led by their teacher, was wandering towards the gates of a local school. One of the children broke away—a petite sable-haired girl. She gazed up at one of the patrolling guards—with a mischievous smile, she waved enthusiastically.

"They are irresistible at that age," Dutan remarked, as the child returned to the moving line of pupils.

"At any age," Rissak replied, darkly.

The statement had appalling connotations, but Dutan had long known the younger man's sick mind.

He had agonized over the rumors surrounding the deaths of Rissak's parents. His heart tussled with the idea that he should consider the whispers—his wisdom implored him that he should not.

"Have the patrols reported back with information?" Rissak asked.

From the deep pocket of his purple gown, Dutan produced a scroll. The seal was unbroken. He nodded formally and handed the document to Rissak.

"It claims the patrols tracked south. Hmm. Into Palacoumia itself. Slaves were taken and dispatched. That is unusual. Seems the deeper they entered, the thinner the numbers of resistance they encountered."

Dutan tired of the formalities. He sighed, mopping his brow. Crossing to the balcony wall, he placed his flat palms on the hot stone, gazing out over the city, muttering and beginning to ramble.

"Wait," said Rissak, ignoring the older man's lack of protocol. "There is more. They discovered empty settlements. Whole villages deserted. One of the slaves, it doesn't say whether they still live, told a tale worth mentioning. Shadowgrip and others are leading vast numbers of people into the South. So, it is as I expected. The brothers are heading for their homeland, building an army as they move. Impressive. But if the vermin intend to win over Novia Jorai, it will take more than two fleeing criminals."

Dutan, wrinkled about the eyes, nonplussed. "Brothers, you say?"

"Of course. You were not at the arena that day? Gryonae and Tymarian Kryack?"

"I didn't know the champion had a brother," the Vizier said in surprise.

"Walls have ears, and millions of pairs of eyes. That doesn't include the far-reaching capabilities of the Quwarshin." Rissak tore his attention away from Dutan, back to the scroll. "The plot thickens. Look here. They came upon nine bodies rotting in the trees. They were hanged. Not human but Grokon. I detest those goblin men. At least Shadowgrip committed a noble act when he strung up those mongrels. The Quwarshin received news from the West a year ago. Enlyd and Novia Jorai are at war."

"Those Grokon hordes answer to no one," said Dutan.

Rissak nodded in agreement. "Even the Dirakhan spilled a river of blood, subverting those maggots. An eon ago. But if they are at war with Novia Jorai, that will be helpful to our cause. I think it is time to reaffirm the might of the Dirakhan. Too comfortable has Kazhelma become. We shall unfurl the flags of gold and green suns, reassert Kubenial's right of religious supremacy."

196

"Let it be so, my Lord," said the Imperial Adviser. He straightened, bowing before the emperor. "It will take many months for the armies to prepare for war. There is only one man capable of the task. I believe that is General Poya," the Vizier propounded.

"Tell the General to get his house in order and begin the undertaking. It cannot take months."

"Do you require anything else, my Emperor?"

"I require Shadowgrip's head and sword. They will journey with me into the afterlife. What other companion would one want beside him in the catacombs of the dead?"

That night, Rissak got madly drunk. His whoops of joy carried through the high palace; women from his harems were abused verbally and sexually. After the depravities, three of the ill-treated maidens were dead. Rissak slept through the following day, as Yast-Dutan burnt the remains. Concealing the crime, he went to pray in the sacred temple of Kubenial.

Rissak rolled beneath his silk sheets. Confused and nauseous, he fumbled for his chamber pot. He was alone now. The blood-caked whip snared his glance and filled his head with debauched imagery. It did not take long for the thoughts to waft away like a cloud of smoke driven by the wind. The deceased girls would not be missed; the women of Rissak's harems were not allowed the mingling of siblings and parentage; they would easily be replaced. He slid on a pair of gold-patterned brocade slippers. Naked, he crossed the room, fumbled with the gong mallet, and assaulted the sphere of bronze.

"Empty this bed pot," he shrieked at the vassal, who had stepped briskly into the bedchamber. "Fetch a towel and a bowl of clean water. Bring a robe. And clean this room!"

Midmorning found Rissak in his library. The shelves were crammed with books and scrolls. At one of the cloistered tables, he sat with a pile of tomes. Momentarily, he clasped his hands—an old habit—and proceeded to open one of the books. The work was a heavy-bound volume. Dusty and fragile; the title, embellished with gold leaf, read:

ETFOR (EMPEROR OF KAZHELMA) THE BUILDER IN SAND

The book was ancient and could be traced back to Kullane, the first city of the empire, or so it was hypothesized by the scholars born much later. The Dirakhanian fleet had set sail across the Casindrian Ocean. More than a thousand laden ships, sailing east through enormous waves, some a hundred feet tall. Sea giants, the courageous mariners labeled them. Two hundred and thirty vessels were lost. Eftor had commanded his men to burn the boats. There would be no return. They battled east, establishing Quilaxia. The world, in due course, would be driven to its knees. After centuries, to the south, in Novia Jorai, the impregnable city of Denfurnan was besieged. The defenders, to a child, were slain, the city razed, leaving naught to claim, lest shards of broken rock could be counted as booty. It was said that on cloudless days, the ruins staged plays for shiftless ghosts, only to be scourged away by whistling breezes and summer rains.

The book was irreplaceable. If *it* were ever stolen, he would forsake a thousand sacks of gold for its return—or wipe out a nation. Which ever secured its safe return.

Even as the suns were sinking, he devoured the ancient runes of his fathers. He ordered the torches in the sconces to

198

be ignited. Still, he did not tire. If it were not for the arrival of Cyltii, his only real confidant and minstrel, he would have consumed another large segment of the work.

"My Emperor? Should you not be resting? The hour is late." Cyltii rasped.

Rissak closed the tome and peered at the unfortunate wretch. "Cyltii...my trusted friend. How are *you* on this agreeable night?"

The shrewd dwarf was from South Ranurma, an impoverished town bordering the frozen plains of the East Pole. He stood but four and a half feet in leather boots, hunchbacked and articulate. He had dressed in yellow Hoos and a black tunic, wearing his grey receding hair in the style of the Dirakhan. In his knurled hand, he carried an aguitzee: a five-stringed, leaf-shaped instrument with a wide fingerboard. "Do you want me to play something?" asked Cyltii.

Rissak yawned. "I think I shall retire. Come to my chamber. Perhaps a lullaby will send me to sleep."

"As you wish," the dwarf countered with a bow. Cyltii shuffled away, and Rissak, now bearing the book of Etfor under his arm, strode off, making his way to his bedchamber, his indigo robe sweeping across the tiled floor behind him.

"What is your choice of song tonight, my emperor? Something religious, regarding Kubenial? There is a lay concerning the death of a sprite called Triobafir's Song. The tale is long and sad. Or perhaps something that has its roots in Novia Jorai? The ballad of Noi-Sul-Jenir. It recounts the tale of the fall of the ghost city of Denfurnan. The story is a hymn, and it does not flatter your people. I could rearrange it to suit?"

"That would not befit you, Cyltii, my friend. Candor is your greatest virtue. Sing your song, and do not dress it in a floral gown."

The Dwarf pulled close his chair and tuned the aguitzee to an open minor chord. He strummed the instrument half a dozen times, checking it was correctly tuned. Satisfied, he raised his pearl-grey eyebrows.

The emperor breathed low and yawned. "Let it begin," he mumbled

"There are green hills that break upon the land. Thoo they are called, to the south, in Jorai. Grim ships from the western main. Cruel hordes, scourging, swarm Denfurnan on the southern plains..."

The Dwarf concluded the long lament. "Sleep well, boy," he whispered, with genuine affection.

There must be a heart in there somewhere...but where it resides...?'

Cyltii shook his head. "A wench is awaiting my song," the hunchback professed with a soft breath "Maybe tonight she will pet and favor me.' He leered, slinging the cord of his musical instrument across his slumped shoulder.

Chapter 19

PLEDGES
(Britain, Southern England. 5ᵗʰ Century AD)

The moon sat like a blob of gold upon the inky sky. The village was glad of the gathering; the long
winters were always a trial, and any communal festivity a godsend.

Two months had evaporated since Kim and Aeva's first encounter in the mead hall. She had grown to respect the lame warrior—whether there was a chance of genuinely loving another man besides Thrydwulf, was doubtful. Kim and his parents, Brant and Quenna, had come by cart and horseback to Caelin's Village.

The settlement designation still retained Caelin's title—even though his son Seaver now governed it.

They sat at one of the lesser tables in the mead hall, Aeva, Algar, Kim, Brant, Quenna, and Lord Seaver, discussing the marriage proposal. Kim responded keenly to all questions. Aeva, less so. Still dead set against any such arrangement.

"Aeva, daughter of Hunwald and Hilda. Your parents are dead. I shall speak in their place," said Seaver. "I agree to the terms of the Morgengifu and Handgeld. The price of ten silver coins will be paid to the bride. I will offer Kim any gift he desires—within reason. Hunwald's land will be held for Aeva and any of her family, should they ever need to return."

Kimball-Son-Of-Brant nodded in accordance.

Where are we going, Mother?" Said Algar.

She turned to her son, but it was Kim, the lame, handsome warrior, who spoke in her stead.

"After the festivities, we are to return to my village. We have large holdings there."

"But we have friends here," Algar replied.

Brant, a kindly grey-haired man adorned with fine colorful clothes, said comfortingly. "You will make new ones. That's a promise."

Algar was about to object when Seaver twitched in a wild episode and slammed his palms upon the table. "Enough! The agreement is settled. One week hence, you *shall* marry and return to Ciselhyrst. Now, let the celebrations begin."

The mead hall was awash with light. Seaver, now drunk, was snoring in his lofty chair. A vassal had gathered up the Lord's

202

fallen helm and had hung it on a hook next to a decorated shield upon the wall. Thegns, placed wooden logs onto the fire, feeding it life, cozying the hall against the cold, southern winds.

The rafters were filled with song and laughter. Sunn found Aeva in the commotion, practically dragging her to the closest table. They sat down, facing each other on a long, rickety bench. "Typical," Sunn uttered. "Of all the benches here," she whispered, "we get one that would walk like your new husband."

Aeva proffered a vague smile.

"Show some cheer," Sunn continued. "You're getting married, not hanged. He's an honest man—so Feran says."

Aeva's face bloomed, ever so slightly. "What would he know...he still pilfers eggs from my chicken coop."

"He returns them," Sunn said defensively.

Aeva pushed her friend's shoulder. "I know. I'm teasing you."

"He will miss you...Lonely Eyes." Sunn said. "We all will." Aeva felt her mood shadowing once more.

"You haven't called me by that name in years."

Sunn's long locks had been plaited for the occasion; there was a simple beauty in her strong Germanic features. "I will miss you, Aeva." Her brown eyes welled with tears.

"Show some cheer," said Aeva, turning the tables. "I'm leaving for Ciselhyrst, not for the old country!"

They hugged each other, neither knowing it would be for the last time.

"Find your feet," Sunn told her. "Look, your husband is waiting to dance." She hauled Aeva back into the throng, into the arms of Kim-Son-of-Brant.

"Treat her well," she said, choking back the tears. "If you don't, my husband *will* kill you. Nobleman or not."

203

Kim took Aeva to the center of the room. The music played, and they danced before the fire flames.

This was a ceremony before the coming marriage, and he, at least, intended to enjoy it. He leaned close to her ear. "Lady, I was in love the first time I saw you."

"We only just met," Aeva said, matter-of-factly. "At least I can count on the marriage not lasting."

"So, there is still hope for me?" Kim threw back his head and guffawed boisterously.

"Lame, *and* an oaf," Aeva said, spitefully. She regretted the cruel slight, instantly. "I did not mean that," she said.

"Apology accepted," he told her. "But it is true. The first time I spied Hunwald's daughter, I was smitten." Kim stroked her ringed plaits; he found it encouraging that she did not object.

"You dance well...for the lame." The affirmation was void of sarcasm.

"I'll take that as a compliment," he said. Kim pulled her close and whispered into her ear. "Now, come drink some beer with me. Let us talk. We have not had the chance."

He bowed to the sleeping figure of Lord Seaver, took Aeva's hand, and led her to the doors of the hall.

"Get this lady a thick shawl," Kim ordered one of the vassals. "Bring me a cloak and two horns of your best barley. We'll wait for it here."

They sat outside the hall, on a bench of oak, sipping the strong ale. The moon had crept across the heavens, and a cold mist had drifted in from the hills.

"My son would benefit if we could stay," Aeva told the thegn.

"I do not take you off to Ciselhyrst as a punishment. Seaver may not have mentioned it, but we *are* wealthy. The boy will be happy there. By all the gods, you and the boy are the last of your kin. Seaver is right. If not for yourself, do it for your son. I will take none other, Lady. There is none other I desire. If I cannot have your heart, I will take your hand. You will find me a worthy husband. Kind. Not cruel. At times, we may visit. You would like that."

She knew it was useless to fight on. "My son has a friend—"

"Leax. I know," Kim interrupted.

"Will you promise them we can visit when the opportunity arises?"

"My word on it," he said with a lie.

"Then I accept," the Saxon maiden told him.

Kim grinned from ear to ear. "It's getting cold. Let us return to the hall and enjoy the rest of the bride-ale."

Algar and Leax sat behind Lord Seaver's chair, their rawboned backs against the wall of the mead hall.

The chape Seaver had discarded into the fire was now a rippled circle of melted bronze.

"What are you doing with that?" Leax exploded with excitement. "Your mother will larrup you; you fool!"

"It belonged to my father. I'm taking it with me to Ciselhyrst. I'll keep it hidden."

"If Lord Seaver ever finds out. Put it away!"

"Who would ever know what it was? It's just a piece of melted bronze," Algar contended. He slipped it back into the pocket of his brown linen trousers.

"Do you think you'll ever return?" Leax was anxious to know.

"I'll be a guest. If such a thing is possible."

"My parents would take you in. Wouldn't they?"

"I'll pray to the gods," said Algar.

"So will I." The boys sat in silence for the longest moment.

"Vow that if you get the chance, you'll come to see a friend. For old times' sake," Leax whispered sadly.

"One day, we'll ride ponies all the way down to the white cliffs. You'll see," said the Leax. "With our mothers riding behind us."

Algar laughed. "I hope not. Two warriors and two old women with their bony arms wrapped around our waists. What a sight."

Leax frowned. "They are our mothers," he said.

"Exactly!" Algar chuckled.

"I pray it comes to pass," said Leax, ruefully.

"With the ponies, you mean?"

The older boy nodded, clasping the other's hand. "I'll ask Woden to grant it as a gift."

Seaver had awoken, draped in an assortment of robes, tinged with a multitude of colors. The fire was a bed of blackish grey, and the mead hall reeked of stale smoke. He wriggled free from the blanket of robes and stood, shakily, on his feet. Demanding a bucket of clean water, he thrust in his head. A second later, he withdrew his wet hair, twitching violently.

"Woosht!" he yammered. He hoisted the bucket to his lips, gulping furiously.

"My Lord," said one of Seaver's thegns. "The woman, Aeva, is at the door. She seeks your counsel?"

"Then let her enter," bid the Saxon Chieftain.

'What now?' Seaver thought. 'You've only been wed a day. For the love of Eostre! Will I ever be at peace?'

206

"You wish counsel," he said, amidst an ungainly spasm. He stank of body odor—though it did not faze them—and was now breakfasting on an equally pungent bowl of pike and bread. "Girl!" he blasted at the nearest maidservant. "Make sure you remove *all* the bones from the fish."

The Chieftain focused on the problem at hand. "Well, woman? Speak!"

"I know you blame me, Lord, for Caelin, but we did all we could. Your father's death was an incurable malady of the lungs. Even the gods did not meddle in his time of passing."

Seaver felt a storm rage within him that took all his effort to control.

"Of course, I do not blame *you* for his demise. On the contrary, it gained me power. What I cannot forgive is how *you* drove a man like Hunwald to the grave, with your wild quests and foolish meanderings."

"Such things are shouldered out of love!" she retorted.

"You think I know nothing of love?" he growled, rising to his arthritic feet.

Aeva stared hard at the inflicted chieftain, her face blank, close to tears. Seaver flung his bowl to the floorboards. "Hunwald needs honoring!" he roared. "Duty, on your part, would not go amiss!"

Seaver shivered, his anger spent; he flumped down upon his seat of office.

The outburst stung Aeva to the heart. The burden of the last ten years had hung about her shoulders like an anvil. She crumbled beneath its load, her weeping resonating through the mead hall.

"Begone!" Seaver snapped. "Ungrateful wench! Do not darken my door again. It would not bode well for you, daughter of Hunwald."

Aeva wiped her nose on the sleeve of her gown and pushed back her proud shoulders. "Know this," she said, impervious now to any threat of punishment. "You are not worthy to stand in my father's shadow, Lord of Caelinford."

Osmond, one of the Chieftain's thegns, strode up, wrapping a muscly arm about her neck.

"Nay!" yelled Seaver. "Let her go, Osmond. Kim would kill you for such an act. I do not want a war with my neighbor, a day after his marriage to one of my villagers."

The thegn loosened his grip, bowed, and stepped away.

"I pledge to thee, daughter of Hunwald. Should you enter Caelinford again, without first begging my pardon, *you* and *yours* will be taken into the north and sold into serfdom. Now…be gone!"

Aeva ran from that place, as familiar as it was to her as the fallen leaves of autumn, out into the wintry air. She fled past the daubed fences. Broken by Seaver's grim promise, she reached the warmth of the hut. Kim was laying logs into the fire. She flew awkwardly into his arms. "Let's leave for Ciselhyrst," she said quietly.

He looked into the woman's eyes, brown as a thrush's wing.

"Why?" He asked, dumbfounded.

"It's beginning to snow," was all she would say.

The next morning, they left the village of Caelinford for Ciselhyrst.

Chapter 20

THE HINERA
(Kazhelma, Quilaxia City. 3rd Millennium)

The tavern, usually raucous and uncontrollable, was quiet by comparison. The occasional clanking of tavern cups irritated one or two customers, but most were listening to the sweet overtones of an aguitzee. As the song ended, the crowd erupted. "Well sung, little man," cheered one of the spectators.

"How about something less maudlin. A *Bandarah*, perhaps!"

"There are ditties I have for those not so big between the ears," Cyltii retorted.

"One cannot be big in all places, eh, little man?" flouted the heckler.

The Dwarf smiled, self-satisfyingly, and laid the five-stringed device upon his lap. "Thought that was you, Haal. Surprisingly, you have a valid point. One can't be big in all places. Unfortunately, Shaveling, *you* are only big around the mouth—so your street women have told me."

There was a howl of laughter as he took the leaf-shaped instrument into his masterly hands. The dwarf stroked a few chords. "So put a cork in it. Take some advice. DANCE!"

He played the brisk air at lightning speed, his adept fingers flicking across the vibrating strings, filling the alehouse with gaiety. His gruff voice spat like words of fire. "Topple in the barroom, end up in jail, tell the captain o' the guard to flack off! Let *him* pay our bail!"

The crowd was in stitches, the sound spewing like a volcano from the delicate aguitzee. At the crescendo, the room burst into applause. Cyltii stood and bowed. Leaning his instrument in the corner of the tavern, he placed his stool in front of the expensive accessory as an added precaution.

The crowd went back to its exuberant chatter and frivolity.

"Haal! HAAL!" Cried Cyltii. "BEER!"

The accomplice stood, nodded, and waved the dwarf over to the table. "Sharee, my dear, you came," said the dwarf, jubilantly.

The woman was over a foot taller than he, golden-haired, with eyes of aquamarine. Her skin was tanned by the Kazhelma suns, yet her prime feature—at least according to Cyltii—was her ample breast. Nigh on every time he ogled these assets, he unconsciously licked his lips.

210

"You've heard the news, then?" He said, his voice distinct and gruff.

"Of Gryonae, you mean?" said Sharee.

At the mention of that name, the girl beside the woman pricked up her ears.

No more than sixteen years of age, her ovular eyes were a tree bark brown, matched in color by her long curly tresses.

"I'm thankful he no longer haunts the taverns of the city in search of me," the blond-haired woman stressed.

The dwarf looked squarely at her and blew a tired sigh. "*You,* he would kill. *Me* he would—"

"Hang by the feet and gut-spill," the young miss interjected. No emotion emanated from her fair face, and Cyltii wondered if the youth possessed any empathy at all for the world or those that inhabited it.

"It speaks!" He quipped.

"Of course I speak, little Cyltii," she said through a smile of ice. "My father is a man who could tear down mountains."

"Seems you have me there, Devorra. Yet, if he were here, it is unlikely he could tear down his britches, long enough to exercise A bowel movement, before losing his...erm...head?"

"Do not tease the girl," warned Sharee. "She *would* kill you, Cyltii."

"I wouldn't advise such a venture, wee Devorra. Harm one silver hair on this head and the emperor would flay every known member of The Hinera, crucifying them from here to the city gates. You should live so long, child. Now run along. Your mother and I have business to discuss."

Sharee indicated with a slight nod, and Devorra scraped her chair away from the beer-soaked table.

"I'll be outside," she mouthed to her mother.

211

"Pharr! That child rankles me," carped the dwarf as he watched her move through the busy establishment.

"Of course she does," said Sharee, with a deadpan guise. "Her father is a man who would shake Kubenial by the throat and dangle your emperor over his balcony by the feet."

"You have a cruel tongue, Sharee. We'll find a place for that, somewhere." He grinned fiendishly at the perverted wisecrack.

She said, "Tell me about Gryonae."

"You are free. He is a wanted man. A dead man. You did not hear the emperor's announcement in the arena?"

Sharee smirked and shook her head. "Just tell me."

"He murdered some jailers. The gods know who else. Freed a man who was a long-lost brother and fled the city."

"He still lives?" The harlot asked.

"The fool is as good as dead," laughed Cyltii. "There are rumors that he is making for Novia Jorai. The place where he was born. Sounds logical. Only an imbecile would return here."

"That would make sense," said Sharee. Her eyes squinted. "I never knew he had a brother. It's uncanny the way things turn."

"You and the girl?" said the dwarf. "The Hinera has your loyalty?" The woman said nothing, peering towards a fracas escalating at the bar.

"Bone Maker was once a member of that droll group you run with."

Sharee paled, and the dwarf gloated.

"You did not know? There is much the outlaw failed to reveal, Lady. But take heart. Lesser women would have succumbed long ago, knowing the Butcher of Quilaxia pursued them. But that was many years ago. Quelk still runs that band of cutthroats." the dwarf stated.

Sharee said nothing, and the Dwarf took her silence as an acknowledgment that he had struck a nerve. His head shook in amusement. "They'll never learn. They are lice upon the back of a wild beast. You'd do well to stick close to me." Cyltii tilted his head back, expecting to catch a glint in her eyes; instead, he discovered Haal looming before him with four tankards of frothy ale, beaming like a comical mask.

"They've gone, you dolt..." Cyltii seethed

Sharee and Devorra had returned to their squalid quarters to eat. An hour later, they were hurrying over the sandstone slabs, avoiding the groups of churlish soldiers patrolling the city. The high-poled lanterns swung in the wind, casting flame and shadow where they passed. The streets were relatively quiet now, except for a few hapless drunks and ladies of the night who were still roaming the gloomy avenues. They came to the alleyway located on Cirn Street and wove into a back alley. Like thieves, they stole across the dust and filth, slipping into the blacker shadows, hiding against the wall at the slightest sound. Gweps—*yellow-colored rodents with intertwining curly tails*—scurried amid the garbage—*stopping momentarily in their tracks*—only to move on swiftly through black shadows. Lastly, they neared a dilapidated door, propped behind a rusty iron gate. Sharee knocked thrice upon the palm wood door, then once, then thrice again. Finally, it was pulled ajar; words were exchanged, allowing admittance. They trailed the Dirakhan renegade through the candle-lit hallway, up a squeaky flight of stairs, arriving at the room where the Hinera discussed their covert proceedings.

Sharee had been there many times, but seldom in the company of her daughter—*As deadly an opponent as Devorra was to the servile citizens of Quilaxia, among the Hinera, she was counted a*

213

child: vulnerable and commanded to know her place—Sharee breathed deep, striving to quell the inner dread that always accompanied such assignations. The door creaked on its hinges, and the man named Quelk beckoned them in.

"Sharee. Devorra," he announced with a nod. Sharee had always found the tall individual polite, even charming on occasion, but she did not trust him—She would sooner place her faith in the emperor's dwarf—Should the need ever arise.

"Come. Sit." Quelk motioned to a ripped mauve divan. "You had words with Cyltii. How does the hunchback fair?"

Sharee and the girl perched upon the soiled furniture.

"As always: Ill-mannered and perverse. These are the last dealings I have with that sick cur," the fallen woman declared.

"Come," said Quelk, calmly. "Those who dwell too close to the desert should not drink water from canteens made of straw."

Devorra laughed inwardly.

The man had to be the world's worst riddle maker.

As if he were wading through her introspection his stare suddenly pierced her to the marrow, and she cast her eyes to the filthy floor.

"You've grown, child, since we last met. I hope all is well with you."

"As well as can be expected," Sharee answered for her daughter. "Considering the mess we are in."

"You chose the life, Sharee. You alone." The tall, thin Hinera renegade scratched his shaved grey hair about his ear, brushing his slender fingers over his bald pate. His emerald eyes were penetrating; their depth and meaning scribbled. "Now, what did the emperor's lackey impart...concerning Bone Maker? All else is irrelevant to the Hinera," he told her.

214

Quelk flicked Gwep hairs from the lap of his blue trousers.

"He has fled the city and makes for his homeland. He will not return. Only a madman would," Sharee divulged, poking sand grit from her blue pupil.

"My dear woman," Quelk uttered with a voice of silk. "One does not force a man like Bone Maker from a city, being so close to acquiring his freedom, and expect him not to hold up his hands in protest. I knew the rogue when he came as a youth out of the east. When the Hinera was but a handful of misfits squabbling for scraps and thieving from whores." He concurred with a nod. "No offense intended. We all must survive, no matter the circumstances we find ourselves in."

"None taken. We are all sisters under the skin," the streetwalker riposted. That tickled the leader of the Hinera. He smiled. "You have a cruel tongue, Lady."

"So Cyltii, your repulsive cripple keeps telling me."

She knows we play the dwarf against the emperor!

Quelk turned his attention to the almond-eyed daughter.

"What say you of such matters? Do you think your father will return to avenge his honor? "

"I pray to Kubenial that he does and that he scoops up every fly upon this turd of a city and casts it into the latrine of the gods."

Quelk chuckled. "Devorra, you are more like your father than you could ever know. He *may* return. We do not declare all our intentions. Only the hierarchy among the Hinera holds such knowledge. Rumors are sweeping in from the south. The Hinera has a long reach...almost as long as the Quwarshin."

Sharee panicked, feeling the attack wash over her.

"As I say," said Quelk, "he may well return. A sluggish king thrones the lands of Novia Jorai. Gryonae could seize the crown and build an army. Attempt to change the situation in

215

Novia Jorai. Do not fret, Sharee. The Hinera is loyal to its hirelings. We will protect you."

Devorra spoke wisely above her years. "How do you intend to achieve this? To make a play against a man who may bring down the Dirakhan?"

"Simple," the leader quipped." We send you to the east. He never needs to know your fate."

"If you leave, Mother," she said, "you leave alone. I will stay and aid him all I can." She blew out a puff of air. "Leave Bone Maker to me. I will persuade him to let us all live."

Quelk raised his brows, rolling his apple-green eyes.

"She may have a point, Sharee. Devorra is *his* child. He loved you once. Of that, I am sure. You may have misconstrued him wanting you dead. Is this girl really your main concern?"

"Of course!" Snapped Sharee. "So, what now?"

"We wait."

His remark was a smack of disbelief.

"That's it?" she said.

"That's it," Quelk replied. "We have arranged living quarters across the city, for now. I have argued that we should be thankful for your services." He tugged a leather pouch from the pocket of his blue trousers and handed it to the blonde streetwalker. "Use this wisely. Who can say if the next payment will be forthcoming? Go now. Live, for a while, free from deprivation. These matters are now beyond your concern. Hide whilst you can and leave Cyltii to me."

"Will you at least let us know your intentions?" Asked the teenager, her nut-brown eyes inquisitive.

Clever, clever child,' thought the renegade.'

"We don't need to know," Sharee broke in. "We must go."

216

Quelk, of the Hinera Underground, studied the hazel-haired girl with a mask of petrified stone. His eyes shone like frozen sapphires, for a dram of time, till the corner of his lips turned upward and his brow wrinkled. "The Hinera's intentions...Hmm. First, we dethrone the emperor. Then marshal those of the Quwarshin into the jails. Try them. Execute them. Burn down their schools and banish all those faithful to the old regime. Then, lastly, we scoop up every fly on this turd of a city and cast the dung into the latrine of the gods."

"Praise be to Kubenial," Devorra chanted in triumph. "Let the game begin."

Quelk detected the mollifying refrain of the dwarf's aguitzee, seeping in from the adjacent room. *"Raqu ha-mor, gwan ur difurtir,"* he began to sing. The ballad was in an ancient tongue that had derived from the east. Quelk shook his head. The hunchback may as well have been conversing with a wraken, for all the Hinera headman could perceive. He entered the adjoining lodging without knocking.

Cyltii laid his instrument upon the grubby sheets beside him as the dignitary entered.

"You promised her to me, did you not?" said the pocket-sized crookback. He rotated, comically upon the rickety pallet, and laid his head into his gnarled hands.

"Of all the sisters in the empire, you desire the woman of the most dangerous fugitive on Kazhelma. Have you lost your marbles, little man?" Said the Hinera commander.

"That was the agreement," Cyltii parried. "A soldier's whore, and still it is beyond your accomplishing."

"That was before you allowed Bone Maker to escape into the south. You were to finish this before he reached the gates of the city."

Cyltii sensed the man's anger was about to take flight, but the aguitzeer player had not survived six years at the disposal of an insane emperor without knowing how to adjust to a situation before it could topple him over the edge of an unassailable abyss. "I take your point," he said. "I take all the blame. There. You have it. Are you satisfied?"

Quelk was a reader of men. Of an arrogant dwarf that had the ear of a tyrant like Rissak, he would have to tiptoe among the eggshells.

'I could kill you now, dwarf.' He toyed with that thought. 'But that could be dangerous. What are you after, little man? You gave up on the woman too easily for her to be the purpose of your endeavor.'

He analyzed the hunchback's motive. The realization whipped him like a tree branch twirling in the eye of a storm.
'The Girl! Of course!'

"Take her," he quipped, as if he'd read aright the hunchback's devious mind. "But for what purpose? I'm intrigued. Do not lie that it is all based on a sexual nature. Taking Bone Maker's child is a million-fold worse than taking his woman. Harlot or not"

"You mean the girl," the dwarf rasped. "Firstly, let me thank you for thinking so abominably of me. Secondly, no, it is not for want of a sexual nature. The move is a political one."

"Explain?" Quelk could not mask his fascination.

"When Bone Maker returns, *you* will aid him in his struggle. The Dirakhan Empire is losing its grip. Rissak's generals have grown old and comfortable. His armies lost their savagery and lust for power centuries ago. A time of change is coming. And what better bartering tool than the child of the man who may possess the nerve to rule the whole of Kazhelma."

Quelk laughed. "Surely you cannot believe that The Butcher of Quilaxia will overthrow the world and let a cripple simply hobble off with his only spawned brat? This time it is absolute...you *have* lost your marbles."

"I will bear her away beyond the Great Plains. To the edges of the East Pole. Once we are satisfied with the new kingdoms—that he *will* grant us —I will return her. Quelk, my influential, deluded playfellow, do you *really* wish to spend the rest of your days tied to the Hinera? They will be a lost cause. Not even owning the nuisance status they already occupy in Quilaxia. We could be rich...beyond our wildest imaginings."

"But the girl will talk, you fool!" Quelk blurted in the dank room.

"Not without a tongue. For added assurance, I'll remove the hand she runes with. You will take care of the mother. She's just a pawn. Nothing more."

The dwarf studied the tall man as he stroked his newly shaven cheek. For a knave's moment, Cyltii thought his boat was sinking.

"So be it," said Quelk. "Sounds to me like a ruse."

Cyltii rose from the unwashed bedding. Reaching his lavish leather boots, he snatched his aguitzee. Brushing past the Dirakhan rebel, he paused in the hallway. "Do not false-talk me again, Quelk Insar," he threatened over his shoulder. "Else the only lost marbles will be the two green eyes Rissak rolls across the floors of his harem."

The Hinera gave an exaggerated bow, an act brimming with mockery.

"As you wish...King of the Eastern Plains."

When the dwarf had left, Quelk smiled in self-satisfaction. The Hinera executive pulled many strings. He wondered if Brim Thackalton had found the silver net. It was more than a stab in the dark. More than a needle in a haystack. More like a snow flea on a mountain! And he, himself, had aided Gryonae and the brother with their escape from the arena. Of course, the Hinera needed Rissak's empire to fall. How else would the organization be able to take control?

Quelk was proud of the successes and his manipulations of matters so far. The marionettes were dancing, and he, as the puppet-master, was pulling all the strings

Chapter 21

THE THOO HILLS
(Kazhelma, Novia Joria, Thoo Hills. 3rd Millennium)

The procession moved across the expansive grassland leaving serpentine ruts in the deep grass. The twisted groves were thickening, their fey blue crowns swaying in the southern winds.

"Do you remember the L'wur trees," said Tymarian. "They were naked then; the terrain yellow; snow patched."

221

"I was there, brother," Gryonae answered. "Have you forgotten?"

"No. I remember the trees is all I'm saying. Seems like a lifetime ago."

"Nay," Gryonae said, bitterly, "seems like yesterday."

"As you please," Tymarian sighed. Attempting to lighten the mood, he said, "What was the name of that fellow the Old Man used to latch onto every time he went to the market at the village? The wretch liked a drop of rotgut. They both did!"

Bone Maker laughed as he recollected. "That was Danar. I wonder what happened to the scrote."

"How many years would he be carrying now? I wonder if he's still alive." Tymarian tugged at his wraken's rein. The beast had become boisterous as a group of children ran screaming across its path.

Gryonae screwed up his face and pondered. "Probably as old as the empire, or the suns themselves?"

The siblings found the banter humorous. When the laughter faded, the warlord uttered with a twinge of melancholia: "I never liked hunting. I realize we must eat, but some find too much sport in the act. I always thought of myself more inclined to the preservation of nature, rather than being blind to its destruction."

"Probably why you became a warlord, eh?" mocked Shadowgrip.

"Survival, brother," Tymarian bit back. "I reckon even you understand that master."

"Father could have been right of course." Gryonae reached down, tousling the brown hair of a solemn-faced girl as she handed him a piece of fruit. He took a bite, crunching the mauve produce.

Like a priest anticipating a confession, Tymarian awaited the cutting taunt he felt sure would accompany the remark. "Go on," he said.

"Simply," mumbled the bronzed athlete, swallowing the mouthful of ursan, "that you should have been born a woman."

"Very droll," Tymarian groaned. He rose in his saddle and peered out beneath his palm.

Bone Maker's jovial manner traded for an agitated demeanor of stone. "What is it?"

"We are almost home," said Tymarian.

Thrydwulf wriggled frantically between Suzin's thighs; lustfully reaching the juncture of orgasm, he moaned, rolled off beside her in the tall grass, and wiped his brow.

"If I am begotten with child, we will have to take the vows," the maiden said scornfully.

"I cannot do that," he told her. "There is a place east of Quilaxia, Radamanthir Wood, Vargdenir called it. One day I shall ride back there; find my way to Aeva and the child—should Woden grant such a wish."

The remark cut Suzin to the bone, but she hid it well. "Woden?" she said, suddenly nonplussed.

"To whom do *you* pray?" he asked.

"With the hands placed together, you mean?"

He nodded.

"Gwithwaena. The Lady of the Forest," she replied.

"The god of my people is Woden," he told her. "This is my divinity."

"Then let us beg Woden and Gwithaena that I am not with child. Otherwise, *you* can tell my grandfather that you are not prepared to marry me. I will not stand beside you if that happens."

223

In this life, Thrydwulf found himself stepping one pace forward and six steps back.

"Scitte!" he cursed in the ancient tongue. "We'd best get back. They may not have noticed we've gone."

The two pulled on their clothes and waded through the tall spines heading towards the distant campfires.

Floder sat polishing the Grokon scimitar, gently humming. He knew that overworking the blade with such a method could damage the geometry of the steel—he wrestled the niggling contemplation from his mind. Long black greying locks dangled to his bony shoulders. A bald pate—a circumference upon his misshapen head—banked forward. Violet eyes capped an enormous nose. The man was ugly, renownedly so. He wiped the silver sword with a dry piece of twisted rag, sheathing the weapon back into its exotic scabbard. The pan at the edge of the fire was sizzling with bacon; the aroma should have driven Floder's pet to distraction, but due to the number of leagues they had marched that day, the animal seemed too exhausted to bother. The Executioner—a vocation newly appointed to him by Bone Maker—wrapped his twisted rag around the handle of the pan and deposited the skillet on the grass next to his out-rolled hide. He forked the rations onto a smooth wooden plate, poured a beaker of spiced wine, and savored the snack, homely as it was. He lay down upon the deer spread and closed his eyes.

The hangman breaststroked through a turquoise lake of stressful unconsciousness, shortly plunging headfirst back into a cold wind-blown world of reality.

The half-breed mut woofed at the darkness, growling as the approaching figure drew near. "Shut up, you dint!" Floder growled. The animal whined, wagging its tail uncontrollably.

Tymarian strode across the newly scythed area of sward. "Keep that dog quiet. Else I'll have the cooks prepare it for breakfast!"

The hangman could hear them now: The yaps of baying pets and hunting hounds—a disarrayed recital set against the ceaseless chirring of the crickets.

"Muzzle it," said Tymarian, "And spread the word. Any fool who does not handle his animal, will be forced to destroy it. I'll add it to the supply menu. Do you understand? We won't trumpet our arrival into Novia Jorai."

"It is done, Master." Floder tied a length of string around Droogle's snout, watching Tymarian vanish into the darkness. "See, dummy," he breathed low. "You'll end up in there." He dipped his head at the empty frying pan. "Now hush!" He tied a leather lead about the canine's neck, leashing it to a stake, and hammered the wood into the earth. "Stay. Arghhhh! STAY! I won't be long."

"I've sent scouts into the hills," Tymarian informed the troupe.

The deep night had chilled, and extra clothing had been donned by the tired travelers.

"A wise choice," Betgar announced. "So, you still intend to battle your way across the country,
fattening our numbers and seizing kingship. A bold plan, my friend."

"Novia Jorai is home to a proud people. Already she wars with Enlyd to the east," Bone Maker declared. "Leetzune may

225

be king, but he *will* surrender the crown to me. I shall take his head if he refuses."

"What of the Grokon hordes?" asked Tymarian. "We shall need a truce. We cannot lynch every unwilling Imp in the country of Enlyd. We cannot fight on two fronts."

"Good point, " said Betgar. "Would you heed an old man's advice?"

"Speak," said Tymarian. "No man is above counsel here. Least not yet."

"You have two options," Betgar went on. "You either defeat the Grokon armies or strive to obtain peace with their nation. Woo them under your banner, so to speak. You may defeat the Dirakhan yet—If you can achieve this."

Tymarian called to Han-Taglur, a stocky warrior, now part of the brothers' newfangled personal guard.

"If there are any among us capable of fashioning flags, find them. No matter how basic their flair for design. We require a plain background; any material will do. A black wraken rising, set beneath a silver helm, with four red moons, one in each corner. See to it." Tymarian shifted his attention back to the elderly chieftain. "Good advice," he stated with a shrug. "I concur. If the new king can hold his temper, a truce with Enlyd might pave the way."

He lifted a horn of wine. "To the new king!" he bellowed, toasting his brother.

Gryonae sheepishly parroted the gesture.

"From this night hence," said Gryonae, "I will attempt to listen to the sound guidance of you all." He bid them goodnight, downed his wine, stood, and trod his way across the sward towards the extravagant pavilion.

"He is no king," Tymarian loathed to admit, "but he *is* my brother. He will play his part. Or die. All our fates are bound

226

to this venture. For victory or failure. We may yet change the world for the better."

"Praise be to Woden," Thrydwulf shouted drunkenly.

Tymarian shook his head. "Get some sleep, little brother. I await word from those scouting in the hills."

One by one, the tight group disbanded, slipping away towards their makeshift tents. Soon, the warlord sat alone.

Loneliness. It could destroy a man easier than a poisoned rusty shank.

He pulled up the hood of his blue cloak and began to contemplate the unforgettable mines of Rothshim.

Daybreak flushed all green and puce. Songbirds sang amid the blue trees, and a few folks were replenishing the smoldering fires against the early morning frost. Still, the vanguard had not arrived back from the Thoo Hills. Tymarian yawned and yanked down his hood. Gathering timber from the nearby woodpile, he laid the lumber upon the orange embers, coaxing them back to life.

"My Lord!" bellowed Han-Taglur, sprinting through the trees. The black-bearded hulk stood panting before him. "The scouts return."

"Good," answered Tymarian. "Get them fed. I will wake Gryonae. Bring them."

Twenty dog-tired foresters sat in a circle around Bone Maker, Betgar, and Tymarian.

"Let the tale begin," said Gryonae, impatiently.

"We reached the pass," said Drivid—A man short in stature but capable and confident. "There was no challenge. No encounter. Not on the first day. Halfway through the canyon, we came upon a vagabond astride a hoary wraken. He claimed Novia Jorai was close to acquiring a ceasefire with its neighbor, Enlyd.

The war has cost more than thirty thousand lives on each side of the border. We gleaned what we could. Ate his animal and turned him loose. Beyond Thoo, there are patrols, but there are no assembled forces. What lies beyond is anybody's guess. I think we could march right in unassailed. Beyond the flatlands, who can say?"

"There are no villages? No settlements?" Asked Tymarian. "The steppes are normally riddled with them."

"We spied deserted ruins," Drivid replied. "Not much else."

"You men are to be incorporated into my personal guard," Gryonae told them. "You answer to us three. As you may or may not know. I am Gryonae. This is Tymarian, and this is Betgar. Drivid, you have risen to the rank of captain. You are from Betgar's village. That will work in your favor. This is another training day. Those who toil hard may live, those who slouch will die. Remember that. Get to work. *We* will attend shortly."

"Also," Tymarian added. "The halcyon days are over. We are now an army. Insubordination will not be tolerated and will be dealt with harshly, according to military law. Our law. Spread the word. You have one more day to decide your future. Those who wish to leave may take their wares and travel whatever road they choose. They will no longer be our responsibility. We will leave them starving at the side of the road if we encounter them further. Those who stay will be fed and cared for. But mark me well: The troublesome will be flogged. Deserters hanged. So, get your head around the words. That's it. Let's go!"

The brothers' host had swollen, astonishingly, to over fifteen thousand in number.

The drilling of the sloppy soldiers had been torturous, but essential if the men were to have even the slightest chance of reaching King Leetzune's walled encampment.

Through necessity, Thrydwulf joined the drilling. The smiths, relentless in their forging of weaponry, had manufactured a sword for the Saxon. Comparable to a scimitar, it was long and double-edged, razor-sharp, and fashioned with a guard that completely clothed the fist. He knew something of round wooden shields, but the new fabrications were thin metal, concave and oblong, though relatively light, considering their scope. The Saxon began to enjoy Bone Maker's instruction. Though fierce and demanding, Thrydwulf sensed the fabled champion was far more lenient than when he was drilling the lines of strangers ordered to imitate his instruction.

'Stick close to me in battle,' he had said. 'Should I fall, seek Tymarian, and never relinquish hope.'

They rolled into the pass between the hills; the path was well-traveled between the bluish-yellow leafed trees. Lower down the valley, a deep stream was flowing; the new army was ordered to replenish water sacks and barrels for the expedition deep into the unpredictable countryside.

Bone Maker's army was basically still afoot—a situation that would need remedying were they to lay siege to the ancient stronghold of the Dirakhan. Wherever they could, the hordes were stealing mounts from wayfarers. They would have to gather herds of wild wraken roaming the steppes—once roped, the animals could be trained—though they could be unpredictable. Those who were too temperamental would be duly slaughtered and added to the food rations.

The day was relatively warm as the Kaalers plodded their way through the motionless trees. Thrydwulf and Suzin sat up front of the cart with the Saxon at the reins; Betgar was flopped

229

down among their belongings with a bunch of ursan on his lap; he peeled and devoured the cerulean-colored fruit, enjoying the tidbits immensely. Thrydwulf chewed at a rib of cold meat, and Suzin, noting the contented gormandizing of both her companions, simpered mischievously.

"Grandfather," she uttered, without swiveling her head. "Thrydwulf has been asking about one of your tales."

The Saxon swallowed his morsel of burnt Kaaler flesh, gazing askance, a look of bewilderment plastered across his drawn features.

"He does?" Said Betgar. The chieftain set aside his bunch of fruit, spat pips over the side of the wagon, and brushed his palms. "Which one?"

Suzin inched away from the unsuspecting Saxon as she feigned deliberation. "The one about the Stench Monster?"

Thrydwulf took another bite of rib but expectorated the mouthful of meat into the flowers where they passed. He was unsure of the effect the conniving maiden was attempting to rouse, but he surmised by the term *Stench Monster,* the story would not be one of delight or fortitude.

"Must we do this now?" he whispered, irritated.

"Shh!" Suzin murmured. "You've eaten. You'll survive. As children, we couldn't get enough of Karfilia's storyteller. Grandfather," she persisted. "Where does the yarn begin?"

"Long before the ancient city of Denfurnan was founded by the races of Novia Jorai," Betgar initiated, "there existed in that region a castle belonging to a monstrous king… a foul creature—once fair—known among his people as Hiatwend. He came out of the east, some say, beyond the mountains and the deserts, beyond the thousand leagues of ice from a place unmapped and unknown. Unlike other men, he was tall as a flourishing yen—*the rugged trees*—that bloom in the mythical

230

forests of Benthane. Some claim he was a celestial behemoth of flesh and bone. After years of ruling his subjects with a fist of iron, he began to feel his mortality. His spine began to bend. His legs tremble. His joints stiffen and ache with age. He sent his noblemen out to the four corners of Kazhelma, seeking tinctures and tonics that could lengthen life. In his youth, he had heard tales of such anomalies. In the third year of their wanderings, they chanced upon a cunning necromancer, Rarkoth Azemudas. For his amusement, the acute mage swore an oath to aid the failing king. Even before the end of that cruel winter, Hiatwend was dead. Poisoned—the wisest locals maintained. But Azemundas had cast his spells...deceiving all that came to question his over-lording. Of course, there are no such potions that extend life, and Azemundas too succumbed to old age and senility. Nearing his end, his judgments became warped, his mind confusing spells and enchantments. Even his daily defecations became tainted. Below the castle, in the sewer, something was born of his fecal matter. Eckthung was the name he gave it. It Grew, and Grew, and Grew! None would venture nearby. They say the monstrosity haunts man still. Which is why when we do this..." Betgar raised his left leg and broke wind, "we can still smell the Stench Monster."

The uncouth oldster smiled absurdly, as Suzin fell about laughing, like a child half her age.

Thrydwulf merely shook his head.

Oeric would have appreciated the humor.

Eventually, the Saxon cleared the image of the blond youth from his mind.

Betgar had drifted off to sleep whilst Suzin had begun to complain of nausea again; she had left the moving cart twice to be sick. It was becoming more regular as the weeks went by.

He was a moon's stretch removed from the regimens of women, but his mother had divulged the knowledge that a woman would vomit when expecting a child. The thought of Suzin being pregnant terrified him. He dwelt on Aeva; that also clawed at his marrow like a raven at a half-eaten beetle.

Suzin clambered back up onto the moving cart. "I'm getting worse," she said, flustered, rocking and crossing her arms across her belly. They sat in silence, lost in their thoughts as the wagon trundled on.

Chapter 22

NOVIA JORAI
(Kazhelma, North Novia Jorai. 3rd Millennium)

Three hours later, as the lime dual suns were dipping, Tymarian came galloping towards the wagon.

The curious red keffiyeh hat had long been discarded. He was garbed, still, in the brown leather trousers, the begrimed maroon shirt, and black soil-caked boots, the hood of his cloak down about his shoulders. The jet-black hair had grown long, and his green sloe eyes never missed a trick. He reined in his wraken and trotted beside the trundling cart.

"The scouts will be combing the hills. Gryonae and those with mounts will be close behind. Soon we will enter the country where I was born. I have missed her."

"And you, lady," he said, his almond eyes lighting upon the worried maiden, "how are you faring?"

Suzin leapt from the cart and scurried off, dropping to her hands and knees, vomiting into the purple flowers. Tymarian looked over his shoulder at the spewing damsel.

"I seem to have left an impression," he quipped.

The warlord stared hard at the figure of Betgar lying cozily among the wares and baggage. Certain he was sleeping; Tymarian leaned down off his wraken and breathed into the stoical Saxon's ear. "Gryonae mentioned staying close to me, should he fall?"

Thrydwulf shook his head. "I'm no warrior, Ty. In my own world, I was beaten by my father for not scything in the fields when I was needed." He laughed bitterly. "The girl will probably give you more help than I can."

"Firstly, I have no inkling what scything is. Secondly, where the girl is concerned, I wouldn't stand with your back to Betgar should he draw a sword? If my guess is right, she is with child." The Warlord grinned from ear to ear. "You did not know? If the brat is not yours, all the better. If it is! Beware. Betgar is old, but behind him stand more than a hundred men. Take heed, little brother. I'll have Han-Taglur and Drivid keep an eye on you. I'll have them march behind the cart."

The Saxon was numb with Tymarian's conjecture. "Good," he said, tangling with his dark thoughts. "A giant and a dwarf to watch over me. What could be better?"

234

"Little brother, each day you sound more spiteful than Gryonae. I won't burden both fellows with your ingratitude; they wouldn't appreciate it—though they will die for you when the time comes."

"Why are you doing this for me? You owe me nothing? We are practically strangers."

Tymarian Kryack filled the noisy woodland with ironic laughter. "I don't do this for *you*, Thrydwulf-Son-Of-Ceolwulf. I do it for me!"

The Saxon looked puzzled. "How so?"

"My brother has assured me that if anything should befall you, under my command, he will tie me to a wraken and drag me across the desert straight back to the mines of Rothshim."

Now it was the Saxon who laughed—though the reply he proffered was one of a tormented man. "And you believe him?"

"He is Bone Maker. Who am I to doubt him?"

"You are his brother."

"Ah," echoed the warlord, trotting away on his mount. "Now you remind me of *me*."

"When do we rest?" Asked Thrydwulf.

"We don't," replied Tymarian. "The girl drives the cart. You are to meet me with your sword and shield in the glade yonder." He indicated with his thumb over his shoulder. "I have been ordered to turn you into a man. Be ready within the hour. The moon will soon be rising."

"Attack!" said Tymarian. "Or shall we ask the enemy to wait whilst you make ready?"

Without warning he sprang at the unsuspecting Saxon, screaming at the top of his lungs like an enraged maniac. Instinctively, Thrydwulf raised his concaved shield, thwarting the warlord's loosely aimed kick. Staggering backward, he drew his blade and charged, surprising Tymarian, who had to sidestep to block and fend off the assault. As the metal clanged, filling the air around them, the warlord glowered. "Don't be too keen; you'll leave yourself open for a counter thrust." Tymarian pounced to his right, thwacking the student across the buttocks with the flat of his sword. "You want to die on the field, *Son-of-Ceolwulf?* Defend yourself!" A flurry from the dueler's sword sent Thrydwulf rearward into the bushes; the Saxon came slashing back, his face plastered with a scowl.

"Excellent!" roared Tymarian, his forehead pinpricked with sweat. He lunged, catching the dazed Saxon across the round finger-guard of his sword. "Always expect the unexpected," he barked. "Fight till you drop. Is it the girl who consumes your mind?" He slashed at the long thin shield encircling Thrydwulf's shoulder to the knee. The outlander absorbed the blow and hacked at Tymarian with such ferocity that it astounded the Novian.

"Sorry!" Thrydwulf bawled. "I got a blood rush!"

"Never apologize to your enemy," said Tymarian. He had the point of his sword at his pupil's throat. He pressed harder, causing a trickle of blood to run and stain the collar of Thrydwulf's shirt.

"Enough," muttered Thrydwulf, swallowing hard.

"Do you understand yet, little brother?" Tymarian pierced his stare through cold, slitted eyes.

"You've made your point," said Thrydwulf, panting. He seized the shaft of the weapon, intending to remove the tip pressing against his jugular. His eyes narrowed as the pressure increased.

"Do you understand?" asked the voice once more, harsher and unyielding.

236

"I understand," uttered the shocked outlander.

Tymarian's features softened as he relinquished the pressure on the steel blade.

"Even should the sky fall, the suns explode, or the ground beneath your feet spread open, keep focused on your enemy. They may be tricks of the mind under stress. Falter, and the foe will strip you of life. No matter what base or religion men believe, life is the most valuable possession." The Warlord sheathed his brand and bid Thrydwulf do likewise.

Crowds had gathered, amazed at the outlander's efforts. The Saxon was greeted with whoops and hand claps. Thrydwulf turned to the spectators and bowed, like he had seen the warriors of his village do thousands of times, for Caelin, the head chief, back in his own world.

"The fires will soon be burning," said Tymarian. "The moon is near; time to eat."

He wrapped his arm around the Saxon's shoulder—A gesture so familiar, Thrydwulf began pondering on Hunwald. The yearning for home had been like strangling fingers growing tighter as the years breezed past; he wiped the blood from the nicked wound at his throat.

"You're learning," said Tymarian, noting the gesture. "Control the rage. Battle is a hard dance to master. But do not fret." He offered a wry smile. "Most men never make it past the first few steps."

***

(A few days later)

Thrydwulf now carried a handful of scars and nicks through training, but his body was filling out. He knew now without doubt that Suzin was pregnant. Her slightly swelling belly and

237

strange food cravings had become obvious to some. Thrydwulf had dealt with the encroaching problem by simply avoiding Betgar, throwing himself into the preparations for battle. Gryonae had become extreme; daily drumming it into all those capable of engagement that they would either fight in his army or be cast out and left to fend for themselves.

"Betgar will not be pleased," said the champion. "You'll offend his honor. Once he finds out. Lust is a costly mistress."

The Saxon sighed. Pulling a blade of grass, he chewed at the root.

The late afternoon suns were waning, and smoke from the surrounding campfires danced upon the blustering winds.

"Did Vargdenir ever tell you how we met?" Gryonae asked.

Thrydwulf said: "If he did. I don't recall." He spat the bitter grass root into the breeze. He felt guilty.

Would he ever find the limestone caverns and return to Aeva and the child?

"It was at a brothel," the champion said.

"I thought you were only sixteen years old?"

Gryonae gave a haughty laugh. "I wasn't seeking pleasure. I was running an errand for the Hinera. If Vargdenir hadn't rescued me only the gods know how deeply I'd have been entrenched." He never declared how entangled he still was with the renegade group.

"You'd be far from here," Thrydwulf said, gloomily.

"I'm heading home."

"But to what fate?"

"Fate can be an open wound," Gryonae told him. "To breathe the air of Novia Jorai, once more, would be a dream realized. The old country... I would die for her."

238

"You may have to," said the Saxon, bitterly. "But I understand," he said with a sigh. "I long to see my village again."

"Never relinquish hope," the warrior told him. "Without it, you are already dead."

Later that morning, the strange assembly was moving once more. Hundreds of circles of black-grey ash and a vast array of discarded materials dotted the landscape. The tall grass shimmered in the heat, and where the walking figures passed, it smelled of an earthy scent. The stunted trees, painted with many shades of bright-colored leaves, dwindled. Eventually, once more, they ceased altogether. In the distance, the hills sloped towards the rolling clouds. The wraken riders had driven their mounts further into the lowlands, keeping a constant vigil for the ragged army following in their wake. Those afoot had slogged on for thirty leagues, and the deep, spindly grass, once again, became a memory. Yet another valley splayed out like a spreading fan, all green and weather-beaten. They pushed on. At dusk, they came to a plateau, and the brothers informed them that it was named Fenlandas. In the distance, the rain clouds were mustering. Suddenly, Gryonae turned to Thrydwulf. Struggling to hide his emotion, he whispered, "We are here!"

Patting the blue hide of his wraken with both hands, Tymarian rose in his leather stirrups, "Behold!" They heard him bellow. "The land of Novia Jorai!"

Chapter 23

THE CITY OF WOOD
(Kazhelma, Novia Jorai, Medra Tume. 3rd Millennium)

King Leetzune paced the balcony in the palace of his wooden city. Spreading his hands, he leaned upon one of the wooden railings, gazing into the distance, towards the stone city of Denfurnan. It was now so sacred that none could enter without written approval. Its ancient, tumbled blocks had remained untouched by human hands for more than a

240

millennium. He had seized the throne of Novia Jorai by combat—not through his own efforts but by employing a brutal giant of a man known as Yargurgen, a nephew, born on the slopes of the Thoo Hills. Leetzune *was* fond of the man but doubted his loyalty. On more than one occasion, the sovereign's champion had wandered alone into the heart of the desolate city. Queen Urtarn had saved the man's life in those instances. Leetzune did not doubt that this night he would be asked to forgive the giant once again for his shortcomings. But other difficulties now filled the King's mind. The war with Enlyd had claimed so many lives in his army that he would soon have to capitulate—or, at the very least, lose the lands at the edge of his kingdom. Also, there was news of unknown hordes entering the realm of Novia Jorai. For what purpose? Had they come to invade? Leetzune scratched beneath his grey braided plats and returned to his royal bedchamber. Fully clothed, he slid under the sheets beside Queen Urtarn. He stroked the black silvery-flecked hair, kissed her cheek, and drifted into a slumber.

***

Early the next morning, a group of the King's advisors sat waiting in the council chamber. Numbering a score, they were there to debate the strategies regarding the events happening within the empire.

"Do we know who they are?" said Jaan. "Or what they want?"

"Our scouts claim they are nothing more than a growing rabble," said Dauline—a tall, skinny man with red thinning locks. "They come from the ancient woods. A handful of our men joined them for a while. They insist that the host is coming to claim the kingship of the crown. They are led by one known as Bone Maker. Killed many a devil in the arena at Quilaxia. One of our own. By all accounts."

"Their numbers are small," Jiet remarked.

"We should crush them before they reach the city," said one of the council.

"Before they put *it* to the torch!" added another.

"If we must fight on two fronts, we will do so," said Leetzune, entering the room.

All the councilors rose from their seated positions and bowed to the crown of Novia Jorai.

"My Lord," said Jaan. "Our armies buckle under the weight of our ongoing war with Enlyd. This could be the straw that breaks the wraken's back."

Leetzune unclipped his purple gown and tossed it onto one of the gilded chairs; he ordered the men to be reseated. "We have a choice?" he asked.

One of the astute members voiced an opinion. "We could seek a truce with Enlyd."

"Turn and run tail, you mean," the king bit back.

Jiet pulled a white handkerchief from his pocket and mopped the sweat from his bald head. "Maybe we can send an emissary to this…Bone Maker. Ally against these foul goblin folk," he said.

"He comes seeking the crown," said tall, skinny Dauline. "If his army is negligible, there is no real chance of his forces defeating you on the open plains."

"The alternative?" asked Leetzune, pacing the oak floor, his arms behind his back.

"We offer him battle one-on-one," Said Jiet.

The King looked up as the coin dropped. "Yargurgen, you mean?"

"Who in all the kingdom could face your giant and live?" echoed another councilor.

"Why waste more lives in bloody battle?" said Dauline, his skeletal frame twisting to stare at the other members of the council.

"If we can but parley," said Jiet.

"And if Yargurgen falls," Leetzune replied.

"Those are our choices, my lord."

Emag, at heart a jolly man, broke into a reserved smile. "If Yargurgen is slain, we will still have the element of surprise on our side," he explained.

"To do what?" Leetzune demanded.

"To kill as many as possible with an immediate maneuver."

The grey-haired king snorted. "How noble," he said, his voice drenched with sarcasm.

"Set things in motion."

***

Gryonae and Tymarian sat upon their sky-blue beasts. Behind them in ranks of twenty were mounted a hundred of the fiercest men the Novian brothers could muster from the ranks. They were now Gryonae's bodyguards. Short, stocky Drivid—Gryonae's chosen man, and Han-Taglur—Tymarian's black-bearded goliath, were to their left and right, respectively. A handful of makeshift flags fluttered in the wind. Each bore a black wraken, poised upon its hind legs, beneath a silver helm, with a red moon stitched at each corner.

"This will be the emissaries," said Tymarian, gazing under his hand.

Gryonae pushed out his chin and stretched his neck in preparation.

The brothers now wore green tunics and had wrapped their black cloaks around their shoulders.

Tymarian said, "They will ask us to accompany them to the city. Do we go? It could be a trap."

"If that is what they ask," said Gryonae, "*I* will go. *You* will remain here and await my orders. I *will* kill him if necessary. But we *must* take the city and be ready, should Rissak decide to launch an all-out war. That will ultimately be his desire. None will dare to oppose him in the empire. But the Dirakhan have grown idle. This cocky wretch who sits on the throne in Quilaxia may be their downfall. There will be no surrender this time, brother. We either win back the world or perish in the attempt."

The brothers gripped arms, soldier-fashion.

"We have to stop saying goodbye," said Tymarian. "It's becoming a hard wraken to ride."

"Remember your promise to me concerning the outlander," said Gryonae.

"I will do what I can."

"That is all I ask. Have faith, brother. The tides may yet turn in our favor."

Tymarian gave a wry smile.

"What?" asked Bone Maker.

"I have never seen the sea."

Tymarian turned his wraken and galloped away, back towards the encampment.

Fifteen men rode up the incline, the black wraken hooves thudding heavily upon the wet grass. They were clad in blue leather armor, with winged helms laced under the chin.

"Note the banners," said Kwill as they approached the unwelcome strangers.

"Something is amiss," said Bron, riding at his side.

"The depicted wrakens are black," Kwill told him.

"Yes. I see it now. An error, d'you suppose?"

"Nay," answered Kwill. "The man who leads them was born in Jorai. Or so we have been told."

"Maybe he taunts us," said Bron.

"Maybe," Kwill replied.

The King's messengers trotted up before the lone figure of Bone Maker.

He appeared to be a formidable individual. The heralds took notice when he slid the serrated sword from the sheath on his back and laid the weapon in his lap.

Kwill raised his hand and moved closer. "Hail-fellow-well-met! Why came you to the lands of Novia Jorai? On whose authority?"

"This is the country of my birth," Gryonae replied. "I need no permission."

"You are the one they call Bone Maker? The champion of the Dirakhan? You need no permission, you say? The king of Novia Jorai would beg to differ."

"I am the man the Dirakhan call Shadowgrip. Amongst many other things. At last, I have escaped their clutches and have come to take the crown of Leetzune. I will rebuild the city of stone and wipe the name of the Dirakhan from history. Once and for all."

"The city of wood may not give up her ghost so easily," Bron retorted.

"You are at war with the goblin men of Enlyd. If Leetzune surrenders to me the crown, I will aid him in either winning

245

that war or seeking a truce to join all forces to oppose the emperor in Quilaxia," Gryonae told them.

"The king could make *that* truce on his own behalf," said Kwill

"If he does, he will have me setting torches to the gates of his city, whilst he stews on the matter."

"Battle on the open plains. Is this a plan of your choosing? Or do you still hold the courage, as the emperor's champion, to battle for a kingdom in single combat? What does Shadowgrip say to that acknowledgment? "

"I will fight any man Leetzune sends forth," Gryonae bade him.

"There is such a man. Yargurgen. The king's nephew. He will face you."

"Then parley no more. Bring him to me. I am '*Bone Maker,*' and you could not reckon the times I have trodden the dance of death."

"Come, then, to the city." Said Kwill. "I have a scroll, with the king's seal, guaranteeing your safety."

"Should the men behind me be granted the same conduct? We few shall come."

"The pledge is assured," said Bron.

Gryonae sheathed his sword as Drivid trotted up beside him. They sat watching as the king's entourage rode back down the incline bound for the wide bridge spanning the lake.

"Do you think they noticed the flags?" asked the stocky woodsman.

"Most definitely," Gryonae replied. "But they do not know the purpose—yet."

"There *is* a purpose?" Drivid asked with a grin.

"There is always a purpose," Gryonae told him. "It will be the new emblem for the rebuilt city of stone. Should that task ever come to fruition. Tell the men to beware here. It could be a trap."

"I thought the fellows of Novia Jorai were a noble lot?" said the woodsman.

"Forget what you've heard. The mightiest warrior may cower faced with destruction."

Across the expansive bridge, the main doors to the capital were open; Gryonae and his bodyguard galloped over ten abreast, their crude attire as varied as colored shells upon a beach. The clattering of hooves rose steadily in the green sunshine. Finally, Bone Maker, the most dangerous man in the new-fangled army, cantered through the massive gates into Medra Tume: *'The City of Wood'*

In the main courtyard, at the center of the square, was a stack of stones. These were placed there when Medra Tume was first built: sacred tokens from the ancient city of Denfurnan.

The heralds led the way past the anomaly, through the narrow streets, presently closed to the citizens by order of Leetzune. The round grey cobbles led ever upward. Solemn faces peered from the dwellings; children waved, and soldiers lined the route on both sides; with their blue leather armor tightly strapped, they gripped long spears, appearing stern-faced in the eerie quietude.

The heralds guided Gryonae, Drivid, the giant, Han-Taglur, and the diverse group of riders to the gates of the king's inner citadel. The heralds led them under the portcullis, suddenly turning their mounts to face them. "This is the king's private sanctum." Said Kwill. "There are facilities here for you and your men. For those of you dealing directly with the king, you are to bathe. There are ponds beyond the orchards. Latrines over yonder. Do not defile this place. These gardens are sacred. The king will address you tomorrow. Be ready at his bidding."

As the heralds rode out through the portcullis, the men watched in silence; the iron gate slowly lowered.

"I feel like an insect in a web," said Han-Taglur, with a deep, expressive voice. In the eerie aftermath of that statement, the warriors climbed from their tall saddles.

The area was crammed with a mixture of ripe citrus trees. Gryonae's heart lifted as he observed some of the comrades being hoisted aloft from brawny shoulders, only to climb into the branches and shake the fruits from their stems. An hour later, most of those fellows had stripped themselves of their garments and were now relaxing on their backs in the coolness of the late afternoon. A few dozen had taken to the ponds to bathe. Always their weaponry within arm's reach. The practice drummed into them by Bone Maker at every appropriate opportunity. He now moved among them. Ordering them to dress and prepare.

Lastly, the suns went down, and a pearl moon came floating in the darkness, intensifying the sensation of peace. Gryonae lay on his spread, wrapped in his black cloak, thinking of his old friend Vargdenir, remembering the lines of a poem the outlander would recite during times of maudlin.

'Some men will never reach their stars, some are bound to their past, some are born into wealth and coin, like vagabones tied to a mast. Listen for the wind on the meadow, let summer and winter depart, reach for the dream of the green-headed gull, seek for the jewel in the heart.'

Throughout the city, bells rang at dawn to begin the day. Gryonae and his companions had been summoned to the great

248

hall. From the carved pillars of oak-like timber, lanterns hung, filling the cavernous chamber with gold-white light. On a raised dais, on a throne of rich, polished timber, sat Leetzune, surrounded by a handful of his trusted aides. On the second-floor balconies, archers lingered in the shadows, while several of the king's guards stood, strategically placed, along the perimeter of the walls.

Leetzune found his feet and strode to the edge of the dais. With hands on his hips, he stared down at the vagabonds before him. His cold stare fell upon the strapping figure with brown shoulder-length hair, and it was hard for the sovereign to conceal his irritation. "You must be Bone Maker," he said with an arrogant smile.

"Gryonae, my father named me. But Bone Maker...or Shadowgrip will do. Whichever suits my lord's preference."

"I am told you came for this." In a staggering display of absurdity, Leetzune lifted the silver crown from his head and dropped it to his feet. On the balcony above, archers appeared with arrows fixed to their composite bows. The king's sentinels raised their spears and took a fighting stance. Leetzune raised a hand to still them, but not before Gryonae's men had slid their swords from their leather sheaths. "Hold!" he bellowed.

The king lowered his arm, emitting a deep sigh. "Then it shall be done. The challenge is a dual to prevent the spilling of much blood. But there are terms. You were born here in Novia Jorai?"

"*That*, I would be proud to admit," Gryonae replied.

"Let one of the sacred stones be brought to this hall. One from the courtyard at the gates of the city. We will swear an oath upon that sacred stone to honor these terms." Leetzune spun momentarily to his council. "There will be no treachery in this matter," he commanded. He pivoted back to address the granite-faced stranger. "Do you agree?"

Gryonae nodded. "Let it be done."

"I call on Yargurgen to stand as champion for the city of Medra Tume. If he defeats whoever you decree as your champion, your hordes will leave this country, never to return. I will rule as I have these past years and sue for peace with the goblin men of Enlyd, on my terms. Should Yargurgen be slain, I will loan you the crown, temporarily. If you can achieve peace with the Imp king of Enlyd and persuade their nation to join you. Novia Jorai will also join your forces to fight against the emperor of the Dirakhan. If we are not all doomed to destruction in this… insane venture, the silver crown will be given back to its King and Queen. Hopefully, they will be allowed to live out their final days in peace with their people free. If it can achieve it."

"The terms are agreeable," Shadowgrip proclaimed.

"Lastly," the king added. "The emblems of the wrakens on the flags? They stay blue."

Gryonae grinned. He could meet that demand. It was less absurd than believing he could have rebuilt the ancient city of stone in a few months. As confirmation, he gave the merest hint of a bow.

Chapter 24

WEB WITH MANY SPIDERS
(Kazhelma, Quilaxia City. 3rd Millennium)

Two Hinera snoops tailed the dwarf through the marketplace. He paused at a stall, eyeing the bright garments; running his hands over the cloth, he created an argument with the vendor. The brown-skinned Dirakhan scratched his white beard and wagged his finger, objecting. Cyltii blasphemed and hobbled on.

251

"Take h-heed," stuttered the Snoop, into his accomplice's ear. "The Quwarshin m-may be close by."

"Probably, Frir," said the taller man. "But try not to speak till we leave the bazaar. Otherwise, we'll never get out of here."

"But Shem…I-I'm just s-saying!"

"I know," said Shem, frowning. "Keep up. He's traveling again."

The stunted minstrel turned his nose up; he'd passed a booth of large arachnids frying in a pot of wraken fat.

Frir and Shem pushed through the crowd in pursuit.

Wherever the dwarf was heading, the Hinera could only guess. They watched like hawks as two women met Cyltii. One, rangy with blonde tresses, leaned in close as they spoke beneath a sandstone bridge. The other female, chestnut-haired and shorter, studied the throng like each soul was an authentic danger. She scowled at the diminutive figure, keeping her distance.

"Quelk was right," said Shem. "The Hinera *will* benefit if they have the mother and the child as a trade exchange."

"So, w-we just kill the d-dwarf and take them to another safe h-house?"

"Yes," Shem cut in. "Somewhere out of the city, where we have complete control over them. The Hinera will see how the game with Rissak and Bone Maker plays out."

"But. But. I-If the dwarf is d-dead!" Frir stammered.

"He will be another inconvenience we no longer have to deal with!" said Shem, his irritation building.

"There they all g.g—"

"Go!" said the taller Snoop, completing the unfortunate fellow's sentence. "The dwarf wants the child as a bartering tool. He may offer them both to the emperor. We cannot let that happen. Rissak and the Quwarshin cannot gain the advantage."

The odd trio climbed the sandstone steps to the bridge road above the main street.

Shem scoured the individual faces of the public. If the Quwarshin were in attendance, they were invisible.

"We'll observe till we can make our move," he uttered.

A myriad of long white headdresses adorned the skulls of the men bustling through the streets. Many were dressed in long light-blue robes; most of the women wore patterned yellow gowns, and the children displayed a wide range of colors, decorated with the Dirakhan motif of fingered claws and green suns.

The dwarf and the two women slid into a back street, full of filth and shadow, steering towards another flight of sandstone steps. Shem and Frir decided to race the trio to the street above.

The Hinera winged a path like determined hawks through the adjacent alley, careening into the dregs of humanity as they punched their way through. The unsuspecting trio was suddenly cornered. Cyltii cowered as the Hinera drew their blades.

"Have no fear, ladies," Shem told them. "Quelk sent us. This hunchback aims to sell you to the emperor. You have heard the stories they tell about those harems?"

"So that was your intention!" Said the golden-haired, sun-tanned, Sharee. The harlot cussed at the hunchback with the words of an angry streetwalker. A profession she had known well.

"E-Exactly," stuttered Frir. He twisted his knife, indicating the woman's daughter. "She is p-pure?"

253

Shem sighed. "Of course she is pure. She'd be no use to a harem if she wasn't."

"Take me to Quelk Insar," the dwarf spat from the dusty shadows.

"I am to give the King of the Eastern Plains a message," Shem retorted.

Sheathing his hooked dagger, he stepped forward, gripped the obnoxious manikin by the scruff of the neck and the seat of his pants, and hoisted him straight off the top steps into mid-air; he landed with a sickening thud, and the discordant twang of aguitzeer strings, on the cobbles far below. "You are to accompany us," Shem declared to the shocked women. "The Quwarshin will discover the body. We cannot be here when they do. Cyltii was a pet, treasured by Rissak. It will anger him deeply. We must go. Quelk is waiting."

***

Down on the squalid back street, a crowd had gathered about Cyltii's remains. No citizen dared to address the broken body. The minstrel's leaf-shaped instrument lay close by, smashed and splintered. Four determined interlopers squeezed through the mob, ushering the nosy onlookers away from the scene. Beneath the unfamiliar headwear, they sported shaved scalps, tattooed with an orange sickle moon above the upper cheekbone.

The Quwarshin.

One of the four knelt over the dwarf, checking his pulse. Rissak's minstrel was dead. The man swore under his breath. He stroked his fingers through the corpse's grey hair. At the temple was the faded tattoo of an ochre moon. "Zroonda!" he

254

bellowed. "Fetch the guard. We need to get this body back to the citadel.

Rissak gazed from his high window. The wagon was being pulled by a lone euganta. The huge animal, docile from the heat, plodded up the steep ramp. Four wraken riders accompanied the cart, and the young emperor had an ill omen as he watched it veer right and vanish into one of the olive groves. Footfalls echoed behind him in the private chamber, and he spoke without facing the visitor. "You should send word to our patrols in Palacoumia. No need for them to return. They are to await General Poya and our armies, as they make for Novia Jorai. Your thoughts on the matter?"

"Grave news, Majesty," said Yast-Dutan, uneasy. "I fear you may need to be seated."

Rissak positioned himself upon a chair with a green cushion. Sipping water from a glass tumbler, he fixed the imperial adviser with a grim stare. "You were saying?"

The vizier swallowed hard. "Cyltii," he uttered. "His body was found near one of the marketplaces. Two men and two women were spotted fleeing the scene. Hinera...so the Quwarshin believe. Quelk Insar and his rebels are getting bold."

The unstable Rissak wiped his eye. The tender thoughts were fleeting. "You will send the Quwarshin to hunt them down—every one of the Hinera. Our armies will soon be ready to march on Novia Jorai. And Enlyd, and the other nations. If we are to survive, we must strike. Do you see, Yast-Dutan? Leave no Hinera or any sympathizer alive. Take me to Cyltii. I wish to bid him farewell."

It took sixteen arduous days and nights to round up the men and women connected to the insurgents. It was a

255

desperate bid to ensure there were no absconders—but such things can never be guaranteed. Those taken captive were herded into the ghettos of the city and systematically disposed of. The corpses were carted away under the cover of darkness and burned far beyond the walls of the city. Quelk and the two women were arrested on Cirn Street, attempting to reach the dilapidated building where the Hinera secretly operated. Quelk strove to charm his way out of the sticky dilemma. When all efforts failed, he unashamedly surrendered the woman and her daughter to the Quwarshin, disclosing their identities. The treacherous act hastened his death. Sharee and Devorra, the only two souls spared from the extermination, were brought before Rissak to determine their fate.

The young man, Rissak, was lithe and durable, a match for anyone with a blade. The swordmasters had pushed the cunning student to the pinnacle of human endeavor. Sharee and her daughter had spent two weeks in the dungeons reserved for the worst criminals of the empire. Foul-ridden and starved, they clung to what dignity they could muster, standing before the dreaded sovereign of the Dirakhan. But Sharee broke, her rank malodor offending her nostrils; she wept, recounting the years she had spent in prostitution, driven there by circumstance. The adolescent beside her was more robust. She was half-Novian and a thousand times more bitter.

The emperor removed his peacock headdress and tossed the oddity over the back of his ancient throne. He coughed. Scratched himself and cooled his face with an elaborate fan of precious stones and feathers.

"Why did you kill my minstrel?"

"We did not," Devorra informed him.

"You aided The Hinera in this act?"

256

"We are innocent. We played no part in *that* deed," said the teenager.

"You can speak freely. It does not matter. The Hinera are no more. They have been eliminated. You women are all that remain of those...undesirables."

Sharee wiped her nose on her soiled sleeve. "Why were we left alive?" she asked.

"I have my reasons," he told them.

Fear struck Devorra like a club. She chose her words carefully. "You think because I am Gryonae Kryack's daughter, he will bargain with you for our lives?"

"If he does intend to return to Quilaxia and take it by force, I will make it known to him that he stands to lose his offspring."

Sharee laughed through her tears. "He does not know her!"

"He will. Should he strive to make it past my armies and return from those backwoods of Novia Jorai."

"We are pawns, then?" said Sharee.

"You, lady, will be nothing more than a serving maid, held in that position to keep this wench in check." Rissak pointed at the daughter, "She will serve in my harem. Till the threat of Shadowgrip is no more. Or until I decide to rid you of such an undertaking. Whereupon you will be placed in personal servitude to me for the rest of your days."

Rissak waved forward the vizier; he had been standing in the shadows by one of the fluted pillars.

"Yast-Dutan. You have heard my words," said the emperor. "Carry out your duty."

Chapter 25

HALL OF SHADOWS
(Kazhelma, Novia Jorai, Medra Tume. 3rd Millennium)

The great hall was empty but for two ill-fated combatants.

Both wore simple loincloths. Both gripped swords, gazing at each other in the semigloom.

Gryonae held his long-jagged blade. *Bwanaril.*

Singer of death—the Smiths at Quilaxia had anointed it.

The other man clasped a long-hafted, double-edged weapon, jewel-encrusted, its cutting edge shimmering with a pale magenta light.

Gryonae considered the opponent. He was lighter than a bear—not by much. A horseshoe mustache. Bald. Half a foot taller. But something behind the eyes suggested that the colossus was simple-minded.

Shadowgrip had battled many such souls: Those thrown into the arena for the sport of an unwinnable wager. He had disposed of the poor wretches quickly, unwilling to gratify their masters with an exhibition of cruelty. He would do the same in this place. Claiming the magnificent sword as a trophy was an added incentive.

The secluded combat zone was a hall of shadows; half of the lanterns had been removed. From the balconies, all concerned parties gazed down. No man would surrender his arms.

Invisible in the darkness, Leetzune cried out. "We all know what's at stake. Yargurgen. Kill him!"

The giant hoisted the majestic sword and slashed at Gryonae's face. The attack was so nimble that it belied the weapon's weight—and the opponent's encumbering proportions!

Bone Maker blocked the strike with a loud clang of steel, jumping promptly out of range as the broadsword chopped toward his shoulder. He blanched at the speed. Suddenly, he flurried with Bwanaril, but the big man's competent brand swatted aside the endeavor, and a seed of doubt crept into Shadowgrip's mind. He stabbed at Yargurgen's belly. With a whoosh of air, the giant's broadsword blocked and parried, slicing Gryonae across the cheek. Without a word, he sprang to the right as blood gushed from the wound, spilling down his neck and across his chest. Suddenly, the huge cretin grinned inanely and charged. Gryonae crouched and sprang as the giant passed, his serrated blade cutting the opponent's thigh. Yargurgen yelped and grimaced. Slowly, they began to circle. The giant was panting. He leaned—for a tad of time—upon the curious sword, his uncertainty suddenly sprouting wings.

He had killed his fair share of men, and his tongue had been severed for entering the ancient city of stone without permission. All because of an uncle who cared little for a nephew's well-being. It was there, at Denfurnan, that he had discovered the remarkable weapon now balancing beneath his hands. He had stumbled upon the scrolls in a hidden chamber. Lighting a torch, a stone door had rumbled open. He had struggled to read the parchment oddities and could not decipher their meaning. 'The Galrandir' was scribbled under one heading—a race from a bygone age. Another parchment exhibited a drawing of the two-handed sword he was battling with. The blade had power. He felt sure of it. He would kill with it. He would kill for it. He would lie for it! But not for all the sacred stones in Denfurnan would he ever part with it.

Gryonae spun towards the light of a glimmering lantern. Leaning his back against one of the timber pillars, he sucked at the air. His adversary would be no match; he lacked endurance. But the big man's broadsword took some serious grappling.

"Drivid!" he shouted up into the gloom. "Are you still there!"

"Aye!" A voice responded.

"We are here!" roared Han-Taglur.

In a second of sheer lunacy, Gryonae laughed at the predicament.

He ducked. The broadsword hacked into the column where he had just perched; he vaulted into the shadows. The perilous

260

sword swished and cut the leather gauntlet on his arm; only the giant's lack of stamina kept Gryonae alive. The thudding of heavy boots echoed as Yargurgen limped from the gloom into the pearl lantern light. Five solid minutes more they battled. The big man's boot was splattered with crimson. With immense effort, he stood, only to slump, pathetically, against the timber pillar that had taken the brunt of his sword's onslaught. Bone Maker, his face and torso drenched with blood, swung *Bwanaril—singer of death.*

The place reeked of sweat. The giant's gem-studded brand danced in his grasp, the steel shining with a glow of fuchsia. Invisible hands seemed to guide the weapon until Gryonae lunged at the exhausted simpleton, piercing him through the heart.

Yargurgen sank to his knees, the long brand clattering on the plank floor. In a last defiant twist, the behemoth wrapped his bulk around Bone Maker's feet. The deed spawned a final gasp, eerie and tragic in the quiet aftermath.

The champion stepped from the embrace and sheathed *Bwanaril.* Kneeling, he cautiously lifted the dead man's double-edged sword. A mixture of flushing gemstones had been smithed into the cross-guard, but it was the poundage that astonished him. It could have been wielded, single-handedly, with relative ease.

Gryonae Kryack was momentarily bewitched.

The doors of the great hall were thrown wide open, and illumination from the corridor torches beyond plunged through. Leetzune was nowhere to be seen, but Dauline, the thin man from the King's council, strode forward. Bearing the silver crown upon a red velvet pillow, gilded with gold, he bowed his head, offering the object to the victor.

"The pledge will be honored," Dauline said.

261

"I claim this also."

"As you wish. The weapon was Yargurgen's. It means nothing to Leetzune."

Gryonae frowned. "You mean the King."

The skinny counselor smiled, but there was no warmth in it. "*You* are the king," he said. "At least for now."

"Send word, then, to Tymarian, my brother. The hordes that came with us from the forest of Palacoumia are to enter the city and mingle with the citizens. Organize festivities; they may yet get to bond. This will allow us to make plans concerning the goblin men of Enlyd."

"We have been at war with those devils for so long," said the gaunt councilor. "What do you intend?"

"I will make with them the same deal I offered Leetzune: An alliance. Or the extinction of their race."

Thrydwulf and Tymarian located the provisional ruler of Novia Jorai; he was barking orders at a small gang of carpenters, regarding a new project he was undertaking.

"I want buildings along the back! A cobbled road, wide enough for two carts!"

Tymarian noted his brother's scraggly beard had gone. There was a wound across the cheek, stitched with silk thread. The sight pained his heart. He swallowed it back, denying the emotion any words.

The Saxon blinked, saving the real question, concerning the hideous laceration, for another time. "What's the occasion?" he wanted to know.

Gryonae threw his muscular arms about both of their shoulders. "Schools. For the children. The country requires scholars. I know Vargdenir tutored Thrydwulf, but brother, you and I can barely write our names. If our people are to

262

survive, we need to compete. Most men can swing a length of steel, but can they write a saga?"

"You know what oral traditions are?" Tymarian interjected.

"Brother, I said I couldn't write, not that I was a half-wit."

Thrydwulf mused and nodded his head. "I agree with Gryonae. Progress is not always won at the tip of a sword."

"My point exactly," said Gryonae. "Which reminds me. I have a gift for you." He turned and began walking away.

Thrydwulf frowned and gazed at Tymarian.

The survivor of the salt mines shrugged, showed his palms, and spread his fingers.

"It's a souvenir for our little brother," Bone Maker declared over his shoulder.

"I know. You said. What is it?"

"A killing blade!" came the response.

Thrydwulf shook his head, scratching his braided locks. "So much for the teaching of babes," he muttered.

In one of the king's palatial dormitories, Suzin counted the row of draping tassels. The luxury was a blessing from the difficult traversing of Palacoumia and the expansive hills. She had been in the city for a month and had learned to cope with the mood swings and food cravings, but the constant tiredness and vomiting were a bind. With both hands, she stroked the contour of her belly. She prayed to Gwithwaena that it would be a boy, and that the outlander would change his mind and wed her. She cursed herself for allowing the stranger to take advantage of her. There was no choice but to see where the path would lead.

Gryonae had brought the anomaly to the room and stood it in the corner. He had not engaged with her much but informed her that the weapon was a gift for the outlander. A prize that should be treasured because a brave man had perished as a result of its acquisition.

Suzin glared at it. Jealous. Knowing it would probably mean more to him than the unborn child she carried Then she looked away, and the dark notions evaporated.

Betgar's granddaughter placed her palms together, as in prayer. "Lady," she whispered. "Bless this child. Bless the one who sowed it. Bless those who gave me life. Bless the old one, the last of my blood, my grandfather. We are in your hands, Gwithwaena. Lead us down a righteous path, that we may dwell in your house of bliss forever."

She was asleep when Thrydwulf, the worst for wine, stumbled into the dorm. "Where is it?" he muttered irritably.

The green suns were vanishing; the room was dim, so he plucked one of the long fire tapers from the mantlepiece, dipping the sliver into the coals on the stone hearth, and proceeded to kindle the lanterns. The chamber flooded with the light of warm amber tones.

There it was! All as Gryonae had promised: The exquisite gift.

A soft red sheen glimmered within the blade. He lifted it. Shocked. It felt less ponderous than a pillow. Thrydwulf touched the edge of the sword. Razor sharp. He lunged and parried as Tymarian had taught him. Experiencing a moment of utter invincibility, he winced as the brand danced from his clumsy hands, clanging duly on the red rug at his feet.

"What are you doing?" Suzin stormed.

"I was looking at the sword Gryonae gave me."

"Then do it in Gryonae's room. I'm tired. Do you even care that I'm having your child?"

She spat the words viciously, in the tongue of the forest.

Thrydwulf picked up the double-handed weapon. "So be it," he retorted.

264

Extinguishing the lanterns, he left the maiden alone in the darkness, hoping Gryonae would still be awake.

Chapter 26

THE SWORD OF GALRANDION STEEL

*T*he surrogate king had sent Thyrdwulf, Tymarian, Drivid, and Han-
Taglur to the city of stone. They were to seek
among the ruins of the three churches for relics, parchments, anything that
could make sense of the strange sword now in their midst.

Gryonae began to have a crazed notion that it was the weapon forged
by the Galrandir smiths of old. He had dreamed, witnessing its creation,
being hammered into existence by fey sturdy hands.

266

In the second week, the trusted men had returned, bringing a shabby yet intricate, metal and leather sheath. Accompanying the rare find were several brittle scrolls.

Leetzune and his Queen, Urtarn, had retired to a location far from the main populous of the city. Refusing to be bothered unless it was necessary.

Gryonae thought it best not to involve them—yet.

Loremasters were employed to help decipher the ancient parchments. To the astonishment of all, their conclusion filled the newcomers with a modicum of hope, yet there was a dread of anxiety that clung to each of them like a talon that would not relinquish its grip.

"Don't stand on ceremony, be seated," Gryonae said. "Loremasters Semonese and Vultry?"

The two experts, snowy-haired and wrapped in robes of pale green, bowed and sat in the adjacent chairs. The formalities of kingship were beginning to irk Shadowgrip. He was starting to loathe the office he had chosen for himself. But there could be no other position that would aid him in the annihilation of the race that had destroyed anything he had ever held dear.

He sat at the head of the long table. Chairs scraped on the wooden floor as his company of underlings followed suit. The sheath and scrolls had been placed in a sack upon the varnished wood. The objects were examined as they were passed around the group. Thrydwulf looked bemused as he shunted them along.

"I do not understand runes," stated Tymarian. Embarrassed, he pushed the artifacts away. Drivid and Han-Taglur considered the curiosities, like infants examining a proposition on geometry. Betgar, summoned from his daughter's bedside, peered studiously inside the sack. Gryonae snatched the hessian bag from his grasp and tossed the collection back to the Loremasters.

"Your findings? After examining the artifacts? As you will have gathered, we are poorly skilled in rune-reading."

"We presume the sheath is for the brand you bestowed upon your captain here. Thrydwulf?"

"And?" said Gryonae.

"The weapon is crafted from Galrandion steel," Semonese proclaimed. "The king's nephew must have chanced upon it whilst wandering the sacred city. He had already paid with his tongue for setting foot in the holy churches. There is also mention of a net of silver. Though what this *is* or *means* is not clear."

"As we know, our ancestors deemed the Galrandir a myth," Gryonae said. He curled his lip with a smile that failed to reach his eyes. "Is this even possible?" he ventured to ask.

"Yes. According to these runes," Vultry responded. The Loremaster delved into the sack and tugged out a scroll of yellowed parchment. "This speaks of how the steel was forged. But the metallurgy itself is beyond our understanding. It mentions mines and procedures we cannot fathom. Holding such an object could be fraught with danger. Handling it persistently..." He shrugged, splaying his fingers.

"What think you, Thrydwulf?" said Gryonae. "Do you have the courage to take this weapon into your care and defend the people of Novia Jorai? It could be dangerous. Yet it may play a vital role in the days that follow."

Thrydwulf stood, pushed back his chair, and bowed proudly. "It will be an honor," he replied. The sound of his words made an aberration of the Novian dialect.

268

"Loremasters," the newfangled king stated. "You will take the scrolls and hide them. If needed, I will have one of my captains call on you. You may go."

Shadowgrip, devoid of the silver crown of office, respectfully climbed to his leather buskins.

His companions obliged similarly.

"Be seated," he said as the Loremasters departed.

Gryonae's bodyguards from Palacoumia had been equipped with dark yellow gambeson outercoats as their protective armor. Egg-shaded breastplates of light steel and bone were fashioned for the new sovereign's cavalry, including Thrydwulf and Gryonae himself, with matching winged helms of silver steel. Betgar had begun frequenting Leetzune's distant, secluded palace; both men had discovered that they had much in common, despite their statuses as plebeian and king.

The Saxon had found himself torn between his responsibility for the woman bearing his child and Bone Maker's recent gift. The sword—though he would never have admitted to it—was winning the struggle for domination of his time—or of the little he could spare. His hair was now braided in two plaits, which dangled behind his shoulders. His eyes were keener; his brown, wispy beard fuller, and he bore yet another blade nick across his eyebrow.

"To other business," said Gryonae. "We have tidings from Leetzune's army in Enlyd. A plague devastates the goblin ranks. Leetzune's soldiers have retreated across the Ouig River.

"Do they know how things stand here in Medra Tume?" asked Tymarian.

"They are aware that Novia Jorai has a new king—temporarily," stated Gryonae.

"Even if we can draw Leetzune's fighting force back to these lands without casualties from the sickness," Betgar

269

declared, "without those Imp hordes aiding us, we will fail to topple the Dirakhan."

"We cannot wait," Tymarian urged.

"Aye. Agreed," Han-Taglur added. "I've been informed that Rissak's spies are already sweeping through the forests of Palacoumia."

Drivid said, "War is coming. With or without Enlyd."

Deep in thought, Gryonae stroked the red wound on his cheek. Gravely, he uttered: "Then mark this. Leetzune will call back his army from the river. Leave these goblin hordes to their fate. It will keep them from marching upon Novia Jorai. We'll leave a token force here in the city, march on the emperor. Leetzune will ride with us. If he is half the man I believe him to be, he will not decline. We'll sweep through Palacoumia." He raised himself from the chair, laying his palms flat upon the table, spreading his scar-knuckled fingers. He glanced at Thrydwulf with a face full of remorse.

'Vargdenir. Where are you when I need you?!'

He barely kept his emotions in check.

The Bone Maker, who had lain silent since the conflict in the hall of shadows, returned.

"The battle for the soul of our world has begun!" he roared.

***

Gryonae rolled in troubled sleep; the mauve silk sheets were drenched in complete disarray.

"Sharee…" he whispered, turning onto his bruised back, his eyes bolting open, the hilt of Bwanaril in his grasp. Guilt washed over him. "Forgive me," he said hoarsely. He fell back into slumber, only to wake once more as his sword tumbled from the bed and clanged loudly in the chamber. He left the

steel where it was. A *Swar* hooted, from a rail out on the balcony. Gryonae, clad in nothing but a black loincloth, wandered across the polished timber. The great-horned bird spread its wings and flapped away into the moonlight, screeching and hissing, leaving behind the stench of rodent-kill.

'Do you know what it is that truly breaks a man?'

Gryonae watched as his father dragged the thread across his tongue and began to stitch the tear in his tattered shirt. 'It is a loss of hope,' Methorin said.

'You mean when mother died?'

'Yes. That partly. But the belief that all efforts are fruitless. It is a feeling that saps the soul. Men must rise above such things. Responsibility is what makes a man. He must dig deep. Only women can be allowed to be fragile.'

In the darkness, Bone Maker hung his head in his hands and wept.

Do you know, Gryonae, that Tymarian is more warrior born than you?' Methorin chuckled. There was no mockery in the affirmation, just cold, hard facts. 'You take after your mother. She, too, was a dreamer. Though when ruffled, she could explode into a force of nature. You have her personality. I pray that it is strong enough to carry you through this life.'

He wiped his eyes and laughed woefully as the old Saxon poked at his thoughts.

'Let the woman go. You cannot undo what is done. It was you who hired the man to guard Sharee. You misread the louse and murdered him for his crime. Can you blame the girl for seeking the arms of another when you treated her like dung?' Vargdenir had dipped his bread into a bowl of vegetable pottage.

'I cannot let her go,' he had said to the old Saxon.

271

'You must. Are you blind? She was in love with the man. Has she not suffered enough?'

He had pushed his seat away from the table, leaving Vargdenir alone with his meal, and strode out of the Inn into the heat of the apple-shaded sunlight. He had not blamed Vargdenir for his point of view—deep down he had known the man was right.

Pes sind gōd alu,' Vargdenir had said to him in Anglo-Saxon in the Bear Claw Alehouse.

'I don't understand,' he had replied.

'This is good ale!' Vargdenir had said in the Dirakhan vernacular. 'Now. In Novian? Come on! What is it?' The huntmaster had demanded. 'By the gods! How did you survive so long.'

'Ish kar ja oust. Hur tra kalamseetir. Tri-po-larminia. Gra-oo-kir-me-salamor,' The arena champion had reeled off in a blur.

'Is that saying something about the ale,' the old Saxon had remarked, 'or the history of your people over a long period time?'

He had laughed at that. 'That is why we'll use the Dirakhan tongue, master huntsman. Language is about the only thing they created that has any merit.'

Vargdenir had snarled. 'Hæfed hundas!' He threw up his palms. 'Scabby dogs!' The old huntsman had drummed on the table, knocking over his cup of ale. Clicked his finger. 'Landlord! Another two brews!'

The scene faded from Gryonae's mind as a chill night wind brushed his nakedness. He paced back to the warm bed. Wrapped in the sheets, he lay there meditating until morning arrived.

Chapter 27

THE OUIG SKIRMISH
(Kazhelma, West Novia Jorai-Enlyd, Ouig River. 3rd Millennium)

Crouched in the dank cave, the three Grokon captains observed the lone rider galloping across the landscape. Detritus from the wraken's racing hooves sprayed into the wind; the animal sped towards the army, bivouacked by the Ouig River.

"Already our numberzz dwindle from the zzicknezz," bid the goblin. "If they try to crozz the Ouig again, we'll zzlay them on the bankzz," said Drash.

The pot-bellied creature placed its spoon into a bowl of mushrooms and centipedes. Its jaundiced yellow skin carried strange tattoos covering the body. A chunk of red hair was twisted into a cone atop its shaved head, with a lank fringe piling around its muscular neck. The toenails were filed razor-sharp, and white twisted horns protruded from each temple. From the bowl beside him, Drash picked up a morsel of nourishment and chewed on a raw, half-eaten rodent. With an epidermis the shade of dark ferns, he hissed with delight.

"We'll cursh them with the infection," his gravelly voice spat with a growl. "Let them carry that back to their wooden shitty."

"You ish right, Drash," Yakatim said with a laugh. "No fire. Accurshed heat! We'll fill them with disheashe and shend them shkipping back to Novia Jorai.

"Szo be it," said Vunk, the last of the senior commanders. The black goblin, his eyes shimmering like coins of burnished gold, stood and stretched. Bellowing to the subordinates further down the ridge, sitting, biding their time among the rocks, he shouted, "Tell thesze baszeborn we attack when the moon ridesz high!"

***

Umbrella tents, two-poled and made of cotton, dotted the rim of the Ouig River. The green daylight was fading, and the Novian army of weary veterans sat around the campfires, reliving the exploits of the days before. Clad in blue leather

274

armor, the winged helms lay beside them, dented and splashed with green-magenta blood. At the perimeter of the encampment, the lone messenger was challenged by sentinels. Declaring his orders, they pointed to the largest of nine olive-green tents in the distance. The dispatch rider could taste the wafting smoke on his dry tongue and smell the spicy stew the cooks had been preparing. His mouth watered, but his duty would take priority. He saluted and galloped away, winding through the scattered groups of weary men, making for the largest of the dome tents.

In the pavilion, a map was rolled out indicating the nearby river and the lands of Enlyd further to the west. Five commanding officers pored over the elaborate chart. There was a conversation at the tent flap, and the messenger from The Wooden City was ordered to enter. He swept forward, saluted, and handed a sealed scroll to one of the superior officers.

'At last,' he thought. I will be able to eat!

Tennin shook his head, pushing fingers through his long, coal-black hair. "We are to head home," he said. "By order of the new king, Gryonae. The fellow has gall; I'll give him that." An older man, shaven-headed and grey-whiskered, took the scroll and studied it in depth. "Leetzune writes in a bold hand," he told them. "We are to depart immediately and leave these goblins to their plague. Those of us who show symptoms of the sickness are to remain and fight to the last."

One officer, *Numrard*, was of a placid nature—though to doubt his competence as a fully-fledged commanding officer had been the blunder of many a proud egoist—He was fair-minded, yet deadlier than a toxic pool of bubbling sulfur.

275

"How could Leetzune have agreed to such an arrangement with this... pretender?" he said. "Has he lost his mind? I will slice a smile upon this Gryonae's neck, from ear to ear."

The messenger from Medra Tume gave a subtle smile.

"You find something amusing, message-bearer?" asked Numrard; his eyes tightened.

"No, Commander. It's just that the King's nephew said something similar, as he entered the hall to do battle with the Dirakhan's champion."

"Yes? Well? Am I to mind-read?" asked the lithe officer.

"The giant was made an example of. For his lack of respect."

The group cawed with laughter as Numrard's face flushed. "Go eat, message-bearer," he declared. "My patience is beginning to wane."

"What's the meat?" asked the messenger, hitching his blue mount to the long line of restless animals.

The cook said, "Wraken, of course. And don't tether your ride there. Less you want to walk back to Medra Tume."

Figures,' thought the rider.

"I'll take a bowl of stew, some cheese, and red wine."

He tied his wraken to a bush, brushed, watered, and fed the animal, and returned to the field kitchen.

The messenger carried the awkward mixture clumsily, wending his way to the high banks of the Ouig River. There he sat beside a shrub, chewing the tough meat, gazing through the semi-gloom, at the enemy encampment beyond the river.

The goblin multitudes hated naked flame. And beasts of burden. Two things that he, Jinga, could not do without. He ate the cheese. Glugged the red wine. Gripping the bowl of stew with both hands, he poured the remnants into his hungry

276

mouth. The war had taken too many friends. Someday the filth hordes would pay. Maybe the new king would be the man to avenge his fallen companions. Exhausted, he lay down beside the elderberry bush and prayed for a swift, nondramatic return to Medra Tume.

He woke with a start. Behind him were scores of flaming torches as men raced to the banks of the river. A shout went up: "Here they come!"

A mass of arrows hissed through the air, thudding into a dozen flame-bearers; they collapsed lifelessly into the deep foliage. Around them, Novian warriors snatched up the torches to see the impending danger. Most could smell it now. The stench of the foe. A slew of many-colored eyes glowed in the blackness. Snarls and hideous screams drifted on the breeze as the goblin throng clambered up the grassy banks, seeking blood, cutting, slashing at anything that manifested before their shields and scimitars; they charged on.

A wounded warrior, his blue leather protection sliced to shreds, snatched up a burning torch. Thrusting the flame high, its light fell upon the goblin captain Yakatim, who grinned with teeth, the color of his yellow tattooed flesh. One of his white twisted horns had been snapped from his skull, and his lank blue hair was tied back into three ponytails. He screeched at the torchbearer, his double-headed axe severing the exhausted man's arm.

Vunk, his companion captain, golden eyes shining, sprang into the melee, gripping the enemy's tangled hair, he took the screaming warrior's head with a scimitar, tossing it aside like a child might discard a broken toy. "Keep moving!" he growled.

Behind them, the yellow-skinned, tattooed officer, Drash, collapsed, taken by an arrow through the throat.

The hordes swept wide, forcing the defenders back. Each living being—man and goblin alike—endeavored, though all were impaired and ravaged by the incessant disease that plagued their ranks.

As dawn began to appear, the sick and wounded were too weak to press on.

Jinga—the messenger from the city of wood—the only uncontaminated man among them—stood with the last fifty-six combatants from Novia Jorai. All were blood-splattered, panting, and wheezing in the morning air. They had stood their ground nobly, but death had crept among them, with a thousand hands and scythes.

Jinga had not intended to be in the thick of it. He was merely a bearer of tidings! Shwen would curse his misfortune. Trembling, he glanced rearward. The valley was empty, save for the debris of a vanished army. Remnants of cloth rolled and pirouetted on the wind. Carrion birds gathered beneath the green clouds, and the plateau was a vision of betrayal.

Like a slow surf washing over a fist of blue clay, the Grokon hordes swept forward.

When the black tide withdrew, the fist was a flattened glob of blood-red.

The bodies of the dead were buried together in mass graves. The remaining goblin captains—Vunk and Yakatim—forbade the consumption of human flesh due to the plague. The remaining soldiers were commanded to bathe in the river—it was not to their liking—and quarantine to quash the fatal affliction of the plague.

The Ouig River remained part of Enlyd's land, and eventually, army outposts were built along its banks to deter another invasion by its vanquished neighbor.

Chapter 28

HAPPENINGS
(Kazhelma, Novia Jorai, Medra Tume. 3rd Millennium)

A *month later, the returning forces from the borders of Enlyd had*
camped beyond the lake surrounding the wooden city. Gryonae had also
imposed segregation as an added precaution against the epidemic growing
in the southern lands of the enemy. For three weeks, they tarried. Surgeons
clothed in strange garbs and birdlike masks moved among the hordes,
weeding out candidates who showed the slightest symptoms of infection. A

good few were whisked away to the Thoo Hills, never to return. Steadfast, the army prepared to re-arm and replenish rations for the journey back through Palacoumia.

Leetzune, clad in a black morning gown, his greying locks pleated to his shoulders, strode into the palace garden. Betgar waited patiently, a servant refilling his copper cup with spicy tea. The elder chieftain stood and bowed as Leetzune approached.

"Sit down, my friend," he uttered, waving a hand. "If there is anything I tend to agree with concerning your man, Gryonae, it is his dislike for outdated protocol."

He sat opposite the older man with the long white beard, noting how his eyes brimmed with wisdom.

"It is true then?" asked the dethroned ruler.

"Gryonae has ordered that you ride with us back through Palacoumia and beyond to the city of the Dirakhan," Betgar replied.

"For what purpose?"

"He believes that it will bring our people together. It will bond us when the battle begins. So, he says."

Leetzune sighed. "My wife deemed it would be so. She was always cannier than I."

"The armies have returned from Enlyd," the Chieftain told him. "The numbers are filling the plains beyond the great lake and the city of wood. But you will know this."

Leetzune said, "I have spies, of course. What fool wouldn't? Little good they do me."

He noted then the half-dozen leather-armored soldiers loitering below the ripe lemon trees. "I am to be taken by force?" he said with a sneer.

280

"They have their orders. I am hoping you will return with me as a friend. No other man's company would I enjoy more on such a campaign. Together, we may all make a difference. If we stand alone, the world will drown in blood. A sight unseen for millennia. I cannot speak for Gryonae, but I believe he was friends with one called Vargdenir. I have never met a nobler man. We were neighbors, of sorts. There is a belief he was murdered. Gryonae has lost many of his loved ones to the Dirakhan. I think that this was the last straw for Rissak's champion. Our future depends on it. Will you join us, my liege? Gryonae has great faith in you. Shall we right this wrong, once and for all?"

Leetzune was never such a fool that he could be blown over by flattery. But the logic was as clear as the two suns setting each day above the hills.

"Allow me to convince my Queen to return with us. It would sit better with me if she were staying at the palace."

As Leetzune stood, Betgar mirrored his action and bowed. "I have personal reasons for hoping *that* situation would be possible, my Lord. I have a granddaughter. She will need help, should any be offered."

On the morning of the third day of the month of Manindon, the new army was on the move, crossing the bridge spanning the lake. Betgar deemed it wise to leave Suzin at Medra Tume.

'What fool carries a maiden and a newborn babe into a war?' he had told them.

Tennin and Numrard—the two young officers who had served at the Ouig river skirmish—were chosen to take command of the ten thousand-strong cavalry units. In the distance, their dark-yellow gambeson out coats and hoods flapped in the breeze, as they thundered towards the far-flung hills.

The infantry, twenty thousand men, marched behind, each man clad in light blue leather armor, bearing arms, accoutrements, and matching winged helms. Then supply wagons with assortments of food, water, wine, light weapons, and more. Lastly—cocooned within their elite warriors—rode Gryonae, his blood kin, Tymarian, Vargdenir's adopted son, and the brother's two most trusted captains: Drivid and Han-Taglur.

Betgar and Leetzune were transported in a comfortably fitted wagon at the rear, much to their liking. Slowly, they began to surge like a turning tide over the landscape.

Suzin watched. The movement of the vacating army seemed to rumble the very foundations of the high wooden balcony. Plump in her pregnancy and clothed in an expensive gown, she felt desperately alone. The birth of the child might prove to be the only saving grace. She caressed the mound under her velvet robe with a subliminal palm.

"Damn you, outlander!" she spat into the early morning wind.

From the doorway, a slender woman with long black tresses studied the expectant mother with pity. "They are like children," said Queen Urtarn.

Suzin, realizing she was not alone, wiped her nose but kept her gaze forward.

"Men. . ." said Urtarn, clarifying her statement. She moved alongside the girl and forced a smile. "You are not the first, and you will not be the last to be taken advantage of by a persuasive suitor."

"I'm a fool," Suzin told her.

282

"Most men think with their loins. If only they could think with their heads." Urtarn laid a comforting arm upon the younger woman's shoulder. "This world would be a better place."

Suzin broached, "I fear for this child." She swallowed back the taste of fish from that morning's breakfast.

Urtarn sighed. "We were not blessed, Leetzune and I."

"Forgive me, majesty," the maiden said, grasping the blunder. "I did not mean to be impertinent."

The Novian Queen folded her arms across her breast. "Hush now," she uttered. "It is a documented fact."

Suzin turned and bowed her head respectfully. "I will learn my place, majesty."

"This new king, Gryonae, is a man to be reckoned with," Urtarn said. She peered down at the spreading mass, fanning like a bird's tail away from the bridge.

"He scares me," Suzin confessed.

"The Dirakhan would not have made him renowned amongst their race if it were not an intention to be favorable to them. Some people will have a past that would shame a harlot."

Suzin faced out once more into the proliferating green light of morning. "How so? If I am permitted to ask." The pregnant maid bowed respectfully.

"The eating of human flesh, for one," uttered the Queen.

The forest maiden felt a shiver run down her spine. "I was told that in Enlyd, it is practiced by the goblin races there. It's enough to turn the stomach."

Urtarn hung her head, shamefully, "*That* abomination was introduced to them by my ancestors; along with the murder of infants and religious genocide; and of their devouring."

283

The revelation rattled Suzin to the core. Unconsciously, she gripped the life in her womb with the flats of her palms.

"Gryonae," Urtarn stated. "I have seen him with the children of the city. He despises our past. It haunts him deeply."

With sudden understanding, Suzin felt the emotion well up in her eyes. "Which is why he built the school in Medra Tume," she uttered; the words were brimming with perception.

"That would be my guess," the Queen replied.

"Will they return? Could they truly defeat the Dirakhan?"

"Anything is possible. I was no more than the daughter of a wraken trader from a small village far to the east when Leetzune vied for my hand as a minor noble. It's strange the way things can turn."

"I miss him already," Suzin declared sadly.

"Leetzune and I have not spent a day apart in forty years. He can be a stubborn man. But last night, he did something I have never known him to do in all our years together."

Suzin knitted her brows in wonder. "What did he do?"

Urtarn, the taller of them both, took the forest maiden into her embrace and spoke into her ear. "He wept," she said with a whisper. "Now go rest. Maybe a new life for us both has begun this day."

***

Floder no longer rode in a wagon, and as Gryonae's formal executioner, he reveled in *that* position. He trotted among the infantry, astride a saddled wraken. The rag-clothes were gone, replaced by formal black leather armor with a matching cloak and hood. His dog, Droogle, had been trampled to death beneath the wheels of a rolling wagon. He had become

284

attached to the inbred mut, but only as far as any anxious individual living through such troubling times could be. He had utilized the animal's fur to fashion a sheath for a scimitar of one of the dead goblin men whom he had hanged in the forest so many months before. Floder was no stranger to death, but it had troubled him how callous he had been in undertaking the deed. He stroked the wraken's ears, mumbling to himself, a lifelong habit.

"Floder! You hoary bastard!"

The holler nudged the hangman from his reverie. "Sulomé, you toad! You live!" he replied.

Genuine in the greeting of an old friend, he pulled up beside the marching man, whose helm was laced to the shield across his back.

"I thought you left with the stragglers back at the Thoo Hills," the hangman said with a grin of yellow teeth.

"I managed to creep back," Sulomé said. "There'd be no point doing anything else. Everyone from the forests is here." He scratched at his shaved head. "You've come up in the world, I see. Executioner now, is it?"

"Aye," said Floder. "Better meals. And a little more self-respect."

"Well," said the foot soldier, "it took some backbone if it was you who strung up those bastard goblin men in Palacoumia."

"Make no mistake. I strung them up," said Floder. "Ironically, we return now to those woodlands. Back and forth. It feels like we are going round in circles."

Sulomé took a swig of water from the mashak that hung about his shoulder. "I'm damned if I can take it all in," he quipped. "I've never seen a Dirakhan. I will fight bravely. But

I have heard the stories. Frightening. I will have to admit to that."

"They are but men," the hangman pointed out. "They bleed and die. But know this. . ."

Sulomé gazed up once more at the black leather-armored rider.

Floder was grinning. "I'll be there. Every footfall. Right behind you," he said.

The infantryman guffawed. "Of course you will, you insect. That's where you've always been."

Sulomé slung the water sack back over his shoulder. "Stay safe, old friend," he advised the hangman. "There are many here who would lend themselves to the office of executioner should you falter."

"Good advice," said Floder. "I'll bear it in mind."

As the soldier saluted, the hangman pulled at his reins. "Come, Droogle," he said to the renamed wraken.

Chapter 29

LEETZUNE AND BETGAR

The modified wagon moved smoothly. The air was hot after the light rain, and both men lounged on deep pillows, each side of the canvas-topped cart. A hundred riders flanked them. Servants rode close by, obliging the two personalities with refreshments. The Thoo Hills were now a memory, and the weather once more was congenial.

"I should never have agreed to this trip," said Betgar. "I ache like a man who's been roped to a water wheel for a year."

287

He sat up, pushed a knurled finger into his ear, and raked it about.

"At least you had a choice. I presume?" said Leetzune. He had been laying on his back, humming a soft ballad.

"No choice, my Lord. I was dealt the same hand as you: Travel and live or stay and die."

The real king of Medra Tume felt his mood shift. "If we ever ride the storm of this predicament, I would be honored to employ you as my chief advisor. The men I have in my counsel are either fawning toads, lazy, or lacking in common sense."

Betgar gave a wry smile. "A position I *should* be able to fill effortlessly."

"A wise choice, woodsman," said the supplanted King, with rare laughter.

Leetzune barked for bowls of water to wash their faces. "Bring us wine, cheese, and meat. Vegetables… And fruit!"

"What think you of the strange sword the young captain carries?"

"I'm not too familiar with the ancient lore of Novia Jorai, if that is what you're asking," Betgar responded.

"There are more in the scrolls than my chronicles made known." Leetzune guzzled back red wine and nibbled on a rich sliver of orange cheese. "The Galrandir were demigods—the Fallen ones. Many races claim such entities," he said. He coughed violently as a morsel of food went down the wrong pipe. It dislodged, and he spat it out over the side of the wagon. "Most mythologies speak of tangible weapons of enchantment," he rasped. "As my chroniclers declared. If the sword that young Thrydwulf carries *is* such a weapon, it will taint him… and eventually the burden will kill him. Unless…"

Betgar turned and frowned at the displaced monarch. "Unless what?"

288

"Unless…" Leetzune continued, 'he is not of this world."

The old Chieftain scowled. "What are you saying?"

"There are runes. Older than time. Some believe they tell of *one* that will come. A stranger who will yield the weapons of the Galrandir and rid the races of Kazhelma from evil forever." Leetzune paused, choosing his words carefully. "There *is* some mystery surrounding the one you call Thrydwulf? No need to deny it. Suzin has spoken of it to Urtarn." Before the old chieftain could utter a word, Leetzune raised the palms of his hands. "She is my wife, Betgar," he continued to say. "The Queen and I have no secrets."

The Chieftain of Karfilia scratched each side of his head with gnarled hands. "Are you proposing that the boy is this…story dreamed up by ancient stones? Do you realize how absurd that even sounds?"

Leetzune sighed. "I have been known to grasp at straws. I am only a man. So, my wife is always inclined to tell me."

Betgar said, "Gryonae is practically a stranger… though the young man, Thrydwulf, I have met on occasion. A man called Vargdenir reared the boy. You have heard me mention him?"

"I recall," said Leetzune, delving into a bowl of peculiar fruit. He wiped the sticky residue from his hands with a damp orange cloth.

"Vargdenir was in the service of the emperor. Beats me," uttered Betgar with a shrug of his shoulders. "He was so far from the Dirakhan city of Quilaxia that I always felt his position there… meaningless. He must have had his reasons."

"Tell me of the boy, Thrydwulf," the king asked, nonchalantly.

"Vargdenir found him running wild in a forest close to the city. Gryonae would know more. I would not push the matter.

289

I don't know why I say that, but it is a feeling I have. They share something secret. So, I believe."

Leetzune pulled a silver crown from a sack. Tossing the valuable antique onto the ornate cushion beside him.

"Your man, Gryonae, detests this heirloom. He returned it to me. I understand the reasoning. I always found such… pomp ridiculous. It can be tiresome."

Betgar snorted in amusement. "Rissak's arena champion can be a hard-headed fellow."

"It was a noble gesture," said the king. "He could have simply kept it. Or at least left it in Medra Tume."

"Should the need arise, he will ask you to don that crown," Betgar told him.

"So be it. I realize now that he and I share a common goal. I will do all that I can for the survival of my people."

"That too is a noble deed, my Lord," Betgar told him.

A gust of wind flapped the awning overhead.

Birds with deep red wings swooped among the clouds, their caws familiar to the men of the wooden city. Leetzune shielded his eyes and pointed. "We call those blood-wings. They are native only to Novia Jorai. A good omen."

Betgar followed the King's finger with his eyes. He detested all animals, save those prepared for the pot. "I pray it is so," Betgar said, squinting.

The village chieftain caught the old king examining the silver circlet.

The open crown had always been too large. Cumbersome. Much like his reign over Novia Jorai.

The strange light of the afternoon suns glinted on the symbol of authority. At his first acquisition of control, he had donned the anomaly, gazing at his reflection in one of the long mirrors in his bedchamber. The

290

prideful smile sank, noticing more the age in his eyes and the ridiculousness of how he had been chosen and thrust into a position of power. He hadn't even been in line to the throne. The desired pretender had died amid a drunken stupor, falling from a high tower. Leetzune had rushed to the man's aid. The broken body had contorted, with two arms extended, eerily pointing towards him from the wooden steps. Being considered an act of the gods, Leetzune had been selected and crowned. If such a judgement hadn't been fraught with danger for him and Urtarn, he would have laughed at the whimsicality for an eternity. Yet, he felt he had grown into the position. Or at the very least, the position had grown into him.

Betgar felt a gastrocolic reflex and smiled to himself.

'Tell me, Lord Leetzune of Novia Jorai,' he thought with a playful impertinence. 'Have you ever heard the tale of Eckthung the fetor monster...?'

Chapter 30

PALACOUMIA FOREST

Beneath the purple sunset, the crooked trees were ominous.

Light rain swept in from the north, pattering the serrated leaves. The army had encamped before the forest. Prairie grass danced in the blustering winds. Thrydwulf, bone-weary from the ride, slid from his wraken. He watered the beast, wedged a long stick into the mud, securing the animal's reins, and strode away towards Gryonae's pavilion.

"Hail, little brother!" Tymarian called out as Thrydwulf entered the tent. "Join us!"

Considering the weight of their obligation, the small gathering appeared to be in high spirits. Gryonae and Betgar were laughing at some jest. Even Leetzune smiled in his makeshift chair, whilst Han-Taglur and Drivid stood guard at the entrance of the huge tent.

Attendants brought in bowls laden with roasted fowl. Fruits and clay pots filled with red wine sat upon two rudimentary tables.

"Be seated and dine," Gryonae bid them.

To everyone's astonishment, Leetzune broke into song; the tale spoke of unrequited love, stroking across their memories like a sadness. The army's hierarchy raised their cups in appreciation. Each man grabbed a chair, and the company sat randomly within the blue makeshift canvas dwelling.

"On the morrow, our trials begin," Tymarian declared. "Our scouts have combed the forests. It is evident that the Dirakhan now inhabit Palacoumia."

"What of plans?" Betgar asked.

"Guerrilla warfare, of course," Leetzune interjected. He leaned forward, his hands gripping his knees.

"Such tactics are time-consuming," Gryonae told them. "We must reach the city and sack it before winter draws in. We'll destroy them in the greenwood. Punch through. The Dirakhan would have required many bridges to span the deep gorge. When the last of us have crossed, we sever the ropes."

"How do we return?" Betgar quizzed, shaking his head.

"After we lay waste to the city," Tymarian informed him, "we stay."

Betgar and Leetzune pushed themselves to their boots.

"I have a wife to return to!" Snapped the old king.

Betgar erupted. "My Granddaughter needs me! Boy, your plan reeks of treachery!"

Now it was Gryonae who climbed to his war-shoes. "We will establish the city. There will be stragglers of the Dirakhan. They must rebuild the bridges and attempt to head home. There could be many, but eventually they will join us or perish. The way back to Novia Jorai and Palacoumia will be reestablished at the cost of their own endeavors. I intend to free this world, and I swear an oath that you *will* return to your lands once our undertakings have been achieved. If they are not accomplished, there will be no need for homes. None will be left to billet them. We would have failed, and the world will be lost."

"If we are to die in this undertaking," Thrydwulf barged in. "Can we at least not bicker? It's tiresome."

Stern-faced, Betgar and Leetzune slumped back into their seats.

Casting his gaze to the discouraged companions, Tymarian chose his moment, then sprang to his feet.

"Brothers!" he bellowed. "More wine!"

***

General Poya, clad in black leather armor, tied his long white hair into a ponytail. He was slight and peculiar, his features akin to a rodent, but he was renowned for his steadfast determination and deemed by the emperor the only man now qualified to confront the threat against the Dirakhan.

Duty drove him.

A thick early morning fog rolled through the forest, impenetrable by the naked eye.

294

In the eerie silence, from the scattered tree platforms above, shrill horns began to blow.

Poya turned to the captain beside him. "Ready the archers. Be quick about it!"

The surrounding foliage started to tremble. The twang of bowstrings shook the air, and the din of a multitude of wraken hooves began to rumble and thunder through the greenwood.

From out of the semidarkness, a barrage of arrows peppered the undergrowth. Many shafts found their objective, thudding into the Dirakhan bowmen. Screams resounded. Poya took cover behind the bole of a twisted tree. A captain, Fe-lude was his name, raised an arm.

"Let them have it, boys!" he yelled.

The woosh of thousands of fletched reeds echoed about them, the projectiles vanishing into the gloom. The area erupted. Mounted hordes galloped into the fray, causing havoc amongst the Dirakhan. The blue wraken beasts bit at the enemy where they passed. Poya's green gabardine infantry pushed forward as the bowmen sprinted back. Poya sprang away with them to the safety of the fortified barricades. From there, he witnessed the brutal carnage.

The foe's yellow armored coats were splattered with blood.

Poya's keen eyes watched as one of the riders casually removed his winged helm, lashing it to the saddle of his beast.

Instantly, the General's heart clenched.

The man's dark blond hair was thinly plaited and hung to his broad shoulders in several places. Even in the morning mist, the green almond-shaped eyes were notably piercing. A red scar sat upon his cheek.

'So, Shadowgrip,' Poya thought to himself. 'We meet at last.'

295

As if the rider had perceived the General's notion, he gazed directly at the white ponytailed Commander and slipped nimbly from his beast. He drew his serrated sword, hacking into a green-cloaked Dirakhan who sprang before him. Blood spurted. The soldier dropped to his knees. The body, now minus its head, slumped onto a bed of multicolored leaves.

Gryonae turned. The danger, rearward, from a thrusting blade was blocked. Thrydwulf slashed at the culprit's arm. The sword of Galrandion steel sliced through the bone like it was a slab of beef tallow. The Saxon struck again, catching the brawny fellow across the temple. As the man died, Thrydwulf's mind exploded. He saw a woman holding hands with two children. They were weeping at a shrine of pink stones, laying flowers on a crushed, yellowed skull.

Gryonae struck him across the helm. "Focus, little brother!" he raged. "If you do not wish to die here, focus!"

To Thrydwulf's astonishment, Tymarian snatched an arrow from the air, flinging the shaft into a bush. "Brother!" he roared through the fog. "Han-Taglur has fallen!"

"Keep moving!" Gryonae roared. "Less you wish to join him!"

All three, now afoot, charged headlong into the melee, cursing, cutting, and severing flesh like demented demons.

***

"Han, you great lump. Get up!" Drivid sheathed his sword, knelt, and tugged at the giant's helm.

Around them, now, the screams and whimpering of the wounded and dying were rupturing the air, the din like souls being tortured in the catacombs of Hell.

The greenwood was a panorama of twisted figures, all blue leather and blood-drenched green cloaks. "At least you made it home, you oaf," said Drivid, his voice breaking with emotion.

Tennin, one of the youngest captains, paced up and proceeded to examine the giant's body. "There are no wounds, Woodsman," he said.

"His heart gave out," Drivid replied. "I will bury him here. He will not become sport for carrion birds."

"We have orders to keep moving. It will not be wise to loiter," Tennin declared.

"He rests here!" Drivid said with a cold stare. "Tell Gryonae and the others, I will follow along shortly."

Tennin stood and nodded courteously. "As you wish. I will tell them." The young captain surveyed the carnage. "If they still live," he added, grimly. His long, jet-black hair ruffled in the breeze. Donning his winged helm, he stepped over broken bodies and hurried away.

Drivid and four of his brethren woodsmen dug a grave with their swords and hands. The task seemed to take an eternity. They dragged Han-Taglur's body into the shallow hole, covered it with long shields, and piled on the damp earth and foliage.

Ton, one of Drivid's subordinates, spied the rolling wains behind them.

Seated in the first procession of carts, Betgar, ashen-faced, scrutinized the gory glade.

"How many men?" Betgar asked.

"We are still dispatching the fallen enemy and tending to our wounded. There is no count yet. Gryonae has commanded that we keep moving at all costs."

"And the big fellow?" Betgar implored.

297

Drivid swallowed hard, finding it difficult to shape his words. "He lies yonder. He is no more."

Betgar shook his head. "A good man. We will honor his memory in the days to come."

From behind the village chieftain, Leetzune pushed himself up. The King had slipped on the silver crown; his demeanor was calm, his voice proud and authoritative. "You must move the dead. Make a path so that the wagons can get through. Throw aside anything that can be discarded. Place the wounded aboard. Keep any weapons that we can utilize."

Drivid slanted his eyes to Betgar. The old man gave the slightest nod and winked surreptitiously.

"It shall be done, my Lord," uttered the mournful woodsman.

***

By the time Tennin and his Novian comrades had fought their way through the enemy's ranks, Gryonae, Thrydwulf, and Tymarian, battle-scarred and saturated in red, had reclaimed their frantic mounts and were riding exhaustedly through the grape-shaded sunlight.

Shadowgrip had endured a knife blade that pierced his thigh. He had pulled the dagger free with a painful squelch. Tymarian endured two damaged toes from a hammer blow, and Thrydwulf, his gem-studded brand, luminous and magenta, twirled with a speed unmatched. If a fletched shaft came close, the object was effortlessly flicked away. If a sword was swung, the attacker's arm was cleaved. If a hammer was raised, its handle split asunder. The more combatants Thrydwulf slew, the more his head reeled with troubling imagery. Onward he advanced, coughing, spluttering,

298

vomiting, almost to the brink of exhaustion. But the necromantic sword was insatiable. When it cleaved, the blade flashed with a rich magenta pulse. Crimson splattered across his face and helm, and he seemed to physically grow as the battle intensified. He fell from his wraken, sprang to his feet, dispatching five more Dirakhan at full tilt, quicker than his mind could equate the action. He tripped over a rotted branch, smashing his mouth into the wet mud. The dented breastplate squelched, and he was stuck as he tried in vain to himself up from the ferns. A kick to the head almost robbed him of his cognizance. His helm saved the breaking of facial bones. The image of Aeva danced in his thoughts, and he reached his feet. Gryonae was beside him; Bwanaril sang in the air, and three ponytailed enemies screamed and died. "Tymarian!" He bellowed. "To me, brother! TO ME!"

They toiled on each side, like whipped dogs unwilling to surrender a bone. Without warning, the Dirakhan drew back, vanishing into the distant trees, like ghosts being harried by something invisible and terrible.

Those riders who had lost their beasts frantically searched for their wrakens. Remounting, they stood at a halt awaiting the next command from Gryonae.

"They seem to have gone," said Tymarian, shattered and gasping with thirst.

Chapter 31

HALXERIZAN
(Kazhelma, Central Palacoumia Forest. 3rd Millennium)

Lime green light flooded the far clearing. No birds fluttered amid the high branches; the aftermath of battle was everywhere. The smell was potent: the decay of rotting foliage, fecal matter, blood, and much more. Maimed men gasped and groaned, and the dead lay sprawled in grotesque shapes.

Gryonae raised his arm, and his escorts cantered towards the remote glade.

What caught Shadowgrip's eye caused him to flinch. He sheathed his sword, *Bwanaril*, pulling up his mount before a bewildering object.

The soft tissues of the enormous head had decomposed, leaving a semi-white skull. Perched against it was the skeleton of a man, whose clothing was frayed and in tatters. Another bony frame lay close by, clad in a perishing green tunic and hose; in its grasp was a barbed spear.

"Strange indeed," Tymarian uttered, clambering from his wraken.

Both Thrydwulf and Gryonae followed suit.

The Saxon, gripping the hilt of his curious sword, gave the arena warrior an oblique glance.

"Maybe there is more to this than meets the eye," he said astutely.

The statement caught the emperor's champion off guard. He rubbed the wound on his thigh, pulled a water sack from his saddle, and cleaned it best he could. From a pouch, he fished out a crushed bloom, something akin to a yarrow flower, and tended the cut.

"I think I knew this man," he told them. "Or should I say I may have encountered him once?" He crouched and picked up the barbed spear, using it to examine the tattered remnants of clothing. "His name was Brim Thackalton."

"It would appear these fellows met a grizzly end," Tymarian added. Turning askance, he winced, suddenly, at the pain in his toes.

In the distance, the enemy host was marshaling once more.

"There are other pressing matters, brother," he said, drawing his sword.

The mist lifted, as if the forest had suddenly been subjected to a magician's vanishing trick. A bowshot away, was Poya and the hordes of Dirakhan warriors. Within his grasp was a massive silver net that twinkled bafflingly in the sunbeams. Gripping it with both hands, he began to twirl the octagonal mesh slowly about his head. The green-cloaked multitudes stepped back as the netting began to drip beads of phosphorescent silver. Where each drop landed, a fully formed Dirakhan imposter materialized, each clad in the similar garbs of their city born brethren.

Gryonae's bodyguards, to a man, stopped dead in their tracks. Fear gripped them.

"It cannot be!" shrieked Tymarian. "We are doomed!"

Gryonae, the new king, strode on wearily, but Thrydwulf outflanked him. "Be still, Gryonae Kryack!" he commanded.

The champion froze.

The form of the outlander was stretching in size and had grown thrice times its normal dimensions. The voice possessed a deep, imposing, powerful resonance. "Stay here!" it commanded.

Thrydwulf, angst-ridden and bewildered, paced onward, the esoteric sword held high. Poya's diminutive figure shimmered as the developing shape of Thrydwulf drew close. There was a blast of intense light, the general's flesh mushroomed and peeled; claret sprayed like a fountain and a hideous shape slithered from the mashed remains. It took the appearance of something unthinkable and ghastly; the likes of which none born of flesh had ever perceived. Save one: the formidable essence that now occupied the Saxon outworlder.

"Your reign is over, Halxerizan," said Thrydwulf the deity, his voice booming.

The demon's newfangled acolytes thrust forward only to be dispatched by the ancient sword aflame in Thrydwulf's grasp.

302

"You underestimate me, Auknar," the demon spat. "I will cast your soul into oblivion."

Thrydwulf-Auknar stared menacingly, and the Dirakhan host drew back.

"Kubenial," he said, "is God of all wisdom. He will crush you. The eagle, Kraghir, and his mighty talons, will carry your debauched soul beyond paradise back into the pit from whence it came."

The demi-god, Halxerizan, rotated the net once more. Silver grey droplets splashed upon the undergrowth, giving life to another throng of Dirakhan. They stood their ground, awaiting their master's will.

"We are Galrandir, you and I," bellowed Thrydwulf-Auknar. "But you have despoiled our purpose in this world."

"Not so!" said the demon. "I created the Dirakhan to conquer. Kubenial is their god. The eagle is their divine worship."

"They are an abortion," barked the adversary. "A misinterpretation of Kubenial's desires."

The glade fell silent. Only the wind seemed to breathe. Dread hung across the shoulders of each mortal man. The demon's eyes narrowed to slits. "Destroy him!" it screeched.

The Dirakhan stormed forward, determination etched upon each identical face.

Gryonae and Tymarian raised their swords; Drivid and Tennin, now at their side, screamed and staggered. King Leetzune was suddenly riding among them astride a skinny wraken. "Hold!" he roared. "To interfere means madness and certain death! Stay your hands! The Galrandir are at war!"

To Thrydwulf-Auknar, the melee at his rear was no more than insects crawling across a patch of upturned earth, their commotion like an insignificant chorus of crickets attempting song beneath the moon.

Auknar cast up the Galrandion sword. From its tip brilliant shafts of lightning, penetrating the crowns of the trees, bursting boughs aflame, filling the air again with the stench of smoke.

In midair, above the canopies and twisted limbs, a figure began to manifest. A pair of mighty wings formed and flapped. Piercing shrieks echoed as a gigantic eagle glided through the clouds and swooped down. Auknar smite the sword once more against the mint-colored sky. A celestial army of winged beings, armed with spears of polished bone, fluttered down into the forest, and in the blink of an eye, the eagle dissipated on the breeze.

Novian soldiers and woodsmen alike could do naught else but watch as the demon hordes and Auknar's divine host warred within the glades of Palacoumia.

Outside of the magically encased conflict, in a separate scene, Poya's body remained like an animal slaughtered upon the wild grass. The demon, Halxerizan, had evaporated in a puff of grey mist, only to seep away into the mud, carrying with it the enchanted net.

It marred the nearby flowers with a patch of black substance so tainted that nothing again would grow there.

Auknar departed, too, leaving Thrydwulf's body shrunken. He was disoriented, starving for air, and afflicted with a raging thirst. Gasping, he dropped to his knees.

***

Within the enchanted bubble, the Dirakhan moved with one purpose: to maim and kill. They seemed to lack any

304

symptoms of exhaustion and moved, almost as one, in their determined formations. Yet Auknar's divine winged entities matched their resolve.

"Fall back," Leetzune bade his companions from his weary mount. "The sorcery is impassable!"

Gryonae bore Thrydwulf, shoulder-style, from the wall of impenetrable glass, laying him on the deep ferns.

The Saxon would not let go of his sword. As he sheathed it, the purple blade faded to silver, and his cognizance returned.

Tymarian knelt over him, mopping his brow.

"Am I dead?" Thrydwulf asked.

"Not yet. Though it is hard to put into words what just happened."

Thrydwulf moaned as Gryonae hoisted him back onto his shoulder.

"Leetzune is right. We can do no more here," the champion admonished. "We shall return to the wagons. Eat. Rest and regather. And you," he said, slapping Thrydwulf's rump, "keep that brand covered, else it be the death of us all."

***

"How many of us lie slain?" asked Gryonae.

The hierarchy of his commanders sat eating bowls of wraken stew amid the undergrowth.

"Too many to reckon," Drivid told him. "As you know, Han-Taglur fell. Also, Floder…your hangman? Oh, and Numrard. A fine officer. A little deranged but reliable. We were together at Ouig. The river that divides Enlyd from Novia Jorai?"

"Yes. I recall," Gryonae answered tersely. He chewed at a lump of gristle, spitting the vile morsel into the mauve flowers.

305

"The demon has the net," Leetzune uttered. "Our task just grew wings."

"You confessed to knowing little of the Galrandir," Tymarian said.

The old king exhaled. "My sages examined the scrolls further. The net was robbed, so it is written, from the Dirakhan a millennium ago. It seems the Dirakhan were keeping possession of it for the Galrandir. I thought it was no more than a myth."

"I witnessed a creature that bore such a net," said the arena champion. "Maybe it was the same one the demon was wielding."

Gryonae narrated the tale of he and Vargdenir's experience all those long months before.

"We know of such creatures," Betgar added. "They would steal children from outside the village. A bad business. The skull in the wood, yonder, may confirm your story."

Tymarian spoke up. "But what now? Leetzune, you say we cannot aid these celestials against these Dirakhan figurines of flesh. What is the point of marching to the emperor's city if we cannot win?"

"Not all the Dirakhan will be wrought from sorcery," the old king made known. "Those of the city, as far as I believe, *should* be born of women. I know," he said with a groan. "It's a long yarn. But there is still hope to raze Quilaxia to the ground and set the world free."

"Whether we march on Rissak or not may all depend on what happens here," the Saxon ventured. Like an owl spewing wisdom, his words reduced the group to an eerie silence.

Thrydwulf stooped, a childhood habit, when faced with the feeling of impending doom. It floated through his sleeping thoughts like a pike being tugged towards a coracle piled with hooked fish. He was alone, holding aloft a burning brand, wading through deep puddles in a wide limestone cave. He came to a pool where a broken ladder was floating upon the water. Perched next to an ancient stalagmite was a figure, broad and imposing. He smiled, and Thrydwulf felt his anxiety grow wings, readying to flap away into the gloom.

'I am a child of the Galrandir,' said a proud voice in the tongue of the Dirakhan. 'I am here to tell you your work is done. You are heading home?'

'My homeworld is up yonder,' said Thrydwulf. He held the torch high, revealing a shelf thirty feet away. 'I am going to my village.'

'I believe my brother, Halxerizan, the demon, is conquered; I pray it is so. He bears a wound, and it is deep,' said the Galrandir. 'Your purpose was to put an end to him. It was I who brought you here for such a purpose. I could not kill my brother with my own hand, Kubenial would have forbidden it, and sent us both into the void. I am bound by ancient law not to strike him down. My father must now make his decision: cast Halxerizan into the void or let the darkness grow and taint the world and all that dwells there forever. I believe I made Kubenial see the error. Little earthborn, I am in your debt.'

As Auknar stood, the gold bells braced around his ankles jangled, and he laughed, trembling the cavern to its foundations.

Thrydwulf was like a tiny bird at the demigod's feet. But then, to his dismay, shadows, black as obsidian stone, began to creep up the lumpy walls of the cave.

Auknar's cheeks drained to an ashen grey. 'Kubenial is about to show his hand. I must go!'

Thrydwulf stirred in his dream, wrapping himself tighter in his cloak.

Chapter 32

THE STRUGGLE OF LIGHT AND DARK

Vebshiel's pearly skin and blue gown were splattered with blood. The wings on her shoulders were ruffled and stained, yet she clung tightly to the bone spear in her grasp. A spinning axe whooshed through the air, and she launched to the right; the blade thudded into a tree, splintering the scaly bark. Three Dirakhan burst through the bushes, their dark beards cropped, and their black locks tied in ponytails. Speckles of blue blood coated their green woolen cloaks. Instantly, Vebshiel was amongst them, thrusting her javelin, in an attempt to find an eye or throat, shrieking words in a sharp tongue unknown to mortal creatures. To her right, Nurshiel swooped low, carrying off one of the enemy. Deprived of his broken spear, he locked an arm around the Dirakhan's neck. Flapping wildly into the lime green sky, he dropped the abomination from a great height, watching it disappear into the fray below.

He felt the blade enter his sister's body with a shocking jolt. She was no more than a league away. He thrashed his wings earnestly and flew towards the wounded twin.

"We are too late," Vebshiel whispered. "I do not feel the presence of the net or sword." With that declaration, blue blood dribbled over her chin; she winced, trying to retreat from the burning pain in her stomach.

"If the enchanted artifacts are here, we will find them," Nurshiel vowed.

"The fabled Isle is calling," said Vebshiel.

"Stay with me, sister," the angelic warrior pleaded. A blue tear trickled down his cheek, falling upon her black tresses. She emitted a breath as sweet as lilac and was gone.

Nurshiel's cry tore the heavens apart. Cradling her lifeless body in his arms, his rage erupted. "Kraghir!" he roared. "Take her!" From out of the turbulent clouds, the great eagle appeared. Nurshiel rose to meet the golden bird. Gently placing the dead body into its talons, he trashed his wings midair, watching as Kraghir carried her off.

The Celestial's eyes shone with a divine madness. In the glades beneath his white boots, the carnage was everywhere. A phalanx of silver and golden-haired warriors, their exquisite features resolved, collided with a wall of enemy shields. Bone spears snapped only to be replaced by purple blades whirring noisily in the fading light. The shield ranks buckled, and many celestial beings were cut down in mid-flight. Flames licked at the surrounding trees. Smoke billowed. The demon's dark newfangled army and Auknar's angelic warriors fought and died in vast numbers. Emperor Rissak's mortal men had long since perished—suffocating or driven mad within the impassable microcosm.

The conflict, encircled by a huge, ghostly wall of glass now breached the clouds, humming and throbbing, alive with preternatural energy.

The Novian warriors and Palacoumia woodsmen, unable to enter the enchanted battle, could do more than watch and wait.

Thrydwulf woke with a start. The Saxon boy had gone. Only the man remained.

"Easy," Gryonae said. "The hour is late. Most of us are sleeping."

"The sword has prescience," Thrydwulf whispered.

"I do not even know what the word means," Bone Maker replied, fussing with the Saxon's blanket.

"It does not enter the language of my people for long, long years. The sword foretells of things to come. You must take the weapon back!" barked Thrydwulf, distressed.

"You have been chosen by the Galrandir. Such a deed cannot be cast aside. Do you wish to return home, outlander? This weapon may be the only way. I swore to Vargdenir I would aid you where I could. It was an oath. I will die for it even if the whole of Kazhelma should perish. But do not unsheathe that sword again unless your life depends on it. Come," he said. "Let us watch the struggle between light and dark from here. See beyond the mirror of sorcery?" Gryonae pointed with an outstretched finger. "Blood is flowing like a river."

***

"God will not grant them victory," Nurshiel told the Celestial at his side.

Auknar's angel hordes were regrouping. The scene, with the glades now fully ablaze, was more like a perceived hell than a disorientated heaven. Even as Nurshiel pondered an escape from the torment, heavy rain began to fall, dousing the fires. His long golden locks were soon plastered to his head. He raised a wing, squeezing water from its drenched feathers into his mouth.

"Vebshiel's death is a great loss to us all, my friend," said the warrior's comrade. "We may yet have our vengeance. That or we will all meet again at the fabled Isle of Etmoran."

"They are on the march," spat Nurshiel. "Make ready!" he bellowed frantically.

***

Through the night, the conflict raged. The army outside the glass barrier fell into an unnatural slumber. Thrydwulf twisted and turned restlessly. In his dream, his spirit rose from its sleeping flesh.

It wove its way laboriously through the burnt bushes, as if it was wading through water. From behind a charred tree, a figure stepped. Its white skin was covered with bruises and deep lacerations, its pearly gown thick with black blood. The golden hair was matted; the eyes full of sorrow.

'You fought well, child,' Said Thrydwulf-Auknar, the Galrandion demigod of light. 'The dark days may be over. The mystical sword and net will lose their power.'

'The outworlder will return to his people, my Lord?' asked Nurshiel.

311

"It is willed," replied Auknar.

"Then I will presume the work of my brethren is at an end," said the Celestial. "The road ahead is clear. There are now many bridges across the gorge, entering the Dirakhan empire. The outworlder will already know this. For you and he were one. I look forward to the day of your counsel on the Isle of Etmoran, my Lord."

Thrydwulf-Auknar watched as the angelic warrior raised his hands towards the lightning storm. 'Kraghir!' he roared above the thunder, his hair billowing in the wind. 'I am the last. Farewell, Auknar. Your place at the table will be made ready.'

The eagle glided through the tempest: silent, unnerved, purposeful. It snatched the Celestial's extended arms, hauling him towards the clouds.

Auknar observed that the Dirakhan, who were forged from the power of the demon's net, were oozing like piles of sludge upon the forest lawn. Gratified, the demigod drew a shape upon the ether and vanished into thin air.

Chapter 33

BRIDGES

Gryonae and Leetzune's army eased steadily into the glades.

The peculiar wall had disappeared, along with the demon's fabricated fighters and Auknar's winged legions. All that remained were the Dirakhan dead, those born of biological mothers. The butchery made Thrydwulf sick to the stomach. There were no birds, but he knew they would come. This feast of flesh could not be denied. He remembered how Vargdenir had mentioned once that vultures would sometimes follow an

313

army in anticipation of food. The thought caused him to shiver.

The way across the gorge where the bridges were newly fashioned, would not be blocked by Dirakhan. Gryonae asked him how he was so sure. He told the champion of his dream.

'There are many ways to traverse the rocks on foot, but we will need ladders. The wrakens must be herded through the single tunnel—if we are to invade the enemy's lands from the south.'

***

"I'm glad I got to see the village of Karfilia," said Betgar.

He was now driving the furnished wagon that he and the king had been allocated back at Medra Tume. Leetzune rode beside the chieftain on a wraken. He appeared to have aged significantly over the last few months, yet he wore his crown daily, reassuming the regal demeanor he had portrayed in the wooden city.

"I've never seen so much butchery," Betgar remarked with a look of disgust. "And the stench!"

The king, sitting straight in his saddle, said: "Get used to it. There will be more to come."

"What did you make of the spoils left by the enemy?"

"It was probably being guarded by slaves," said Leetzune. "If they have not fled to their freedom, they are probably on their way back to Rissak as we speak."

"Why would they not cut the ropes at the bridges to stop us? Surely that would be the logical thing to do?" asked Betgar.

"For a tactician, that would be so, but these are bondsmen, bred by the Dirakhan to serve," Leetzune went on. "Such

314

decisions are beyond their status. They are bred to obey, not to think."

"We've strayed from what I was hinting at," said Betgar. "I was referring to the barrels of black dust. A strange anomaly."

"Ah," said Leetzune, "the powder kegs. Gryonae has revealed its intent. Years ago, he was selected by Rissak's father to learn from the Quwarshin—the secret order of assassins? He spent time at one of the schools. The powder provokes a flame of fire. He thinks we can use it against the city…to blast our way in. We shall see."

"How could I have missed that council?" said Betgar with a yawn.

"You were sleeping," Leetzune told him.

***

They rode under the creaking branches where Floder the hangman had strung up the nine goblin men; their skeletons were dangling grimly below the sparse autumnal leaves of mauve and crimson. The smell of death was now behind them, though the suspended skeletons of those murdered by Gryonae brought the feeling of mortality seeping back into their bones. They traveled on, arriving at the great lake— *Chilgaron*, Betgar had called it. The water was unpolluted, so the army filled their waterskins, and barrels were loaded onto carts. Wrakens were then permitted to drink at its edge before a considerable number of men were allowed to strip from their robes and leather uniforms and breaststroke out into its depths for brief recreation. They made temporary encampment for two days and nights. A myriad of fires filled the woodlands. Various meats were cooked, canopies were erected, and beasts were tended to and lashed securely in the undergrowth.

315

"We're not too many leagues from the bridges…if the reckoning about the bridges is correct," Gryonae told them.

"If we have to rebuild them ourselves," Tymarian interjected, "more delays. I have sent riders out to scan the gorge. At least we will be prepared, one way or the other."

The hierarchy of the company was bivouacked within an encircling awning, mainly lying sprawled out or sitting cross-legged on thick ground sheets. A handful of foot soldiers stockpiled wood, systematically tossing it into the flames at the center of the group.

The dead hangman's friend, Sulomé, was among the gatherers. He pondered his old ally, Floder. Maybe somewhere along the road, there would be an opportunity to step into his boots. Maybe! Sulomé was snatched from his musing as Gryonae commanded the gatherers to return to their posts.

In a gloomy moment, Thrydwulf pondered upon the two children, whom he was never likely to see. It infused him with sadness and shame. Now a man, rugged and scarred both physically and mentally, he still felt like a child adrift upon a cloud of naivety. The sword of sorcery fueled his brooding with guilt, deep longing, apathy, and utter rage. Reeking of smoke and garlic soup, he closed his eyes, relishing a moment of rest.

'I have something to tell you, Thrydwulf-son-of-Ceolwulf,' said Aeva. Her brown hair shone in the golden sunlight. 'The oaks are whispering secrets to the wind. Do you not hear what they are saying?'

'Your whole family talks in riddles,' Thrydwulf answered. 'Maybe you should ask Immin of horn and bone. He will know the answer. Say it plain,' he snapped in frustration.

'Not yet,' she retorted. 'Wed me first. Maybe then I will tell you what the trees were saying.'

'I know your father—to the annoyance of everyone—enjoys a game of trying to contrive what shade a feather would be if Woden grew it from a thorn bush, but must you adopt his irritating manner?

'Think on what I've said, son-of-Cynwise. I will wait seven moons for an answer. If one is not given, we will not lie together again.'

She rose out of the wood anemones, her blue tunic in disarray, and began the journey home to the village.

Thrydwulf was roused from his slumber.

"But what of your grandchild?" Tymarian argued. "Do you want the girl to be taken into slavery? Or worse! If you and all the chieftains return to their villages, the woodsmen will follow, stripping our army of half its number. If we do not finish this, all the slaughtering will have been in vain. Together, this demon and Rissak, if they are in collaboration, may shape a world the likes of which none of us could ever imagine."

Betgar knew the Novian was right.

"Your grandchild will be safe in Medra Tume, for now," uttered Leetzune. "But if we do not conclude this venture, and split our forces, it will be condemned to failure."

"You fret, old one, as we all do," Gryonae added.

"We stay," Betgar said with a sigh.

"Betgar?" Thrydwulf muttered as he sat up. "I have a confession to make. We need to speak in private. Over there?"

The chieftain of Karfilia village raised the palms of his hands. "We are among friends. We can speak openly."

Before the old man could reach his feet, Gryonae was kneeling at his side, relieving him of sword and knife.

"What is this?" Betgar complained.

"Just a precaution," the champion breathed into his ear.

"Against what?"

"I think he wants to talk to you about something other than bridges."

The chieftain frowned, struggled to his feet, and followed Thrydwulf through the bushes.

***

By mid-morning, the next day, the host was ready to continue. The green suns were shining, and the chattering of birds packed the forest. For three solid hours, the curious mixture of leadership waited as the sea of armor—mainly of butterfly blue—swept through the underwood. Amongst the dense trees, the movement of men, wraken and wagon, was amplified. Thrydwulf, Tymarian, and the two kings mounted their beasts, and Betgar—who had threatened the Saxon with a log of burning wood the night before—slept soundly in his wagon—to everyone's relief.

Many siege ladders were being fashioned, and teams of troops had been assembled. They were learning how to construct arrow bombs employing the black powder that the archers could employ when the time came to attack the city.

Four hundred and fifty leagues further they journeyed, and arrived at the gorge, discovering two dozen wood and rope bridges, stretching across the intense abyss, leading towards the heart of Rissak's realm.

The water rumbled a thousand feet below, and wrakens, tied three abreast, were led across the wide chasm.

Hundreds filed through a winding tunnel, the animals' clopping hooves deafening upon the rocks.

The smooth walls were etched with depictions of stick-like figures engaged in battle; only a few curious men gave the petroglyphs a second glance.

The army set about the task of fixing ladders where they could, so they could scale the granite walls up onto the grassy plateau beyond. The Dirakhan had discarded many fixed climbing ropes, and a myriad of tree stumps and a vast amount of waste wood lay strewn across the landscape.

'The remnants of bridge construction,' Drivid had told them.

***

"It's a week's march to the city," said Tymarian. He wiped the sweat from his brow with a gabardine sleeve, brushed back his dark hair, and patted his blue skittish beast.

"More like two," said Gryonae.

He appeared to be a shadow of the man he had been those months before. Though still determined, a more rational individual had found their way to the surface.

"Do we attack through the mountain pass of Kutrania?" Tymarian asked. "We may be able to enter the city gates there without attempting to storm the walls?"

Leetzune nodded. "The plan has merit," he declared. "What of the boy, Thrydwulf?"

"There is a change in him. Not for the better." Gryonae confessed.

"The sword?" asked the old king.

"I fear it is so," Gryonae replied.

Tymarian shook his head. "Let's make tracks. What are we waiting for?"

Gryonae thrust up his arm, two fingers pointing towards the green clouds. He rolled his wrist. Horns shrilled upon the

319

morning wind, and the drums that had been silent promptly began to beat.

***

Betgar sent word to Thrydwulf that he wanted to talk to the outlander. If any of them survived the madness of the trouble they were embroiled in, he wanted things to be amicable between them. He had thought long and hard about the situation; it was a deed that could not be undone. Acceptance of it seemed the only sensible choice. As Thrydwulf rode up, the old chief beckoned him closer. "Come. Tie the wraken to the cart, boy. Sit beside me," he said.

Thrydwulf was still wary of the old man. His selfish exploit had destroyed Betgar's trust in him. He could sense it. He was remorseful, but in truth, he felt no love for the girl. The act had been nothing more than a lustful indulgence.

"I'm sorry," he said. "The fault is all mine."

The chieftain bit his tongue and scratched his brow. "Why would a world need two suns?" he said. "Sometimes we see two. Sometimes just one. It's an odd curiosity."

'It's to do with orbiting,' thought Thrydwulf.

When Auknar had infused his essence into him to face the demon, he had experienced a million such quandaries simultaneously. But the old chieftain would never have been able to engage in that kind of response.

"Vargdenir had books," Thrydwulf declared. "He was a learned man. There was much he taught me. On many subjects. In Engla land, my homeworld, I couldn't even write a name. We have an oral culture. Vargdenir once told me that it was the very nature of this place that caused his thirst for learning.

320

Where I come from, I would now probably be classed as a scribe. If I returned, my people would never understand my words. The power of the sword, too, was an enlightenment." Thrydwulf knitted his eyebrows. "Would you like to take it as a gift? A token to comfort you from the shame I have laid at you and Suzin's feet?"

Betgar's forehead was pinpricked with cold sweat as he considered the proposal; he brushed the perspiration away with the back of his hand. "Giving me a sword would be like offering a wraken a hammer and a nail." He snorted a laugh. "Complete foolery. I'm afraid *that* curse is all yours, my boy."

"So Gryonae has told me," Said Thrydwulf with a sigh. "May I ask of you a favor?"

'The boy had some nerve!' thought the chief elder from Karfilia.

"You may *ask*," said the old man, exasperated.

"If you should reach Medra Tume, tell Suzin I am deeply sorry that I shamed her."

Betgar was taken aback. "*She* will forgive you, Thrydwulf. It is me she will have a dislike for. I left her *there*, remember? But Leetzune's queen is a good woman—From what I gather. My granddaughter and the child will be in good hands. You love this girl from your homeworld. This...Aeva?"

Thrydwulf confessed that he did.

"Then, no matter what happens, never return to Medra Tume. This day, you are forgiven for your crime. should you carry out another misdeed, I will have my men hunt you down like a dog. There will be no mercy. Do you understand me, boy?"

Thrydwulf nodded sheepishly and climbed into the rear of the wagon, seeking pillows and blankets. "I need to nap. And please, no more chasing me with lumps of burning wood. I'm supposed to be a high-ranking captain in this army."

Betgar snatched up the waterskin beside him, pulled the cork, and tossed it at the impertinent outlander.

Chapter 34

THE WOMAN SHAREE
(Kazhelma, Quilaxia City. 3rd Millennium)

*T*he woman's beryl blue eyes watched intently as she inspected the *kitchen staff. She could never get close enough to Rissak's edible desert plants to poison the prickly pears, mesquite, or agave-like delicacies. She had been granted the position of overseer, and could supervise the dishes, but under no circumstances could she ever be within twenty paces of the food. Not without committing herself to torture and possibly a slow death——another one of the emperor's sick ploys.*

Her once golden hair was unwashed and flecked with premature strands of pewter grey. Though Sharee's body was somewhat emaciated now, her gait and pride still rankled the upper echelons of the emperor's court. Her service to Rissak had not broken her; on the contrary, since her capture, she had bloomed into a flower of silent defiance. A time would come when her child would be free from Rissak's deplorable deviances. She would wait, no matter how long it took, for the blade to fall into the enemy's black heart. Sharee was applying herself to this task. There would be a way to get close enough. And maybe she had already found the key.

"Girl!" she snapped, her voice aloof, "fix a plate and follow me."

Her white smoky gown was wrapped about the middle with a burgundy sash, and her toes placed into black slippers. The smells of the kitchen made her realize how hungry she was, but Sharee paced away into the cool corridor, with the petite maid and a hawk-eyed soldier in tow. They wove through the palace, the movement of their footfalls at a gentle pace. They climbed a sandstone flight of stairs, arriving at a door with an elaborate carving of a great eagle. Sharee tugged at the neck of her gown and knocked upon the door. The adolescent wench standing with a tray of spiced euganta meat lingered as the woman Sharee—following the imposed protocol—stepped away into the shadows.

The middle-aged Vizier who answered the rapping at his door was a handsome fellow. With a grey beard and slate-colored hair, pinned in the distinctive style, and with classic features, he oozed authority.

"Sharee?" he said. Cloaking his discontent, he pulled a hand from the purple gown he was wearing and sighed.

"Food for you, Excellency," said the maid, with a bow.

324

Her white linen, now wrinkled and stained, was unflattering, but Rissak's Vizier noted how pretty the girl *could* have been if she were born into more favorable circumstances.

Sharee emerged from the deep shadows.

"Place the tray on the table," said Yast-Dutan, his tawny eyes fixed upon the woman.

The kitchen maid did as she was ordered. "Will that be all, my Lord?" she asked.

The Vizier clapped his palms together. Knowing her place, she bent low and scurried off.

"You too," said Yast-Dutan, stolidly, to the observant guard. The man hesitated briefly, then marched back to his post by the busy kitchens.

Treading into the passageway, Dutan stared left and right. Squeezing the woman's slender fingers, he led her into the lavish bedchamber.

The vast room was scented with tubuleers *(a fruit akin to oranges.)* Sheets of silk, lavender dyed, embellished the feather-filled mattress, and pillows embroidered with sequins of golden flowers decorated the extravagant spectacle. A satin nightgown, white as a snowflake, was folded upon the bed, and a bathtub of yellow-hued sandstone, full of steaming water, had been filled to the brim behind a pale violet, pleated screen.

"Bathe, Sharee, whilst I eat," the Vizier instructed. "We should talk."

She had given herself to lesser men and in less luxurious surroundings, but the intimate act itself would be no ordeal. On the contrary, she had traded self-respect for self-preservation long ago.

Dutan relieved himself into a copper bedpan, tossing the urine from the balcony to the reeds below.

Sharee watched the act silently. As a streetwalker, she had committed far worse. It was uncouth, but there was more at stake here than a man's lack of good manners. And she knew the role-play. Her grimy garb dropped to the slab floor, and she slid appreciatively into the water laced with bath oils.

Relaxed in their nudity, Dutan lay his head on Sharee's toned stomach.

"We risk death by what we do here," he remarked.

"Everything dies," she said.

"Some lives are worth more than others."

"Only by the Dirakhan. In Rueldumor, *you* would be valued less than a sheo."

"So, I'm a dog?!" the Vizier retorted, "Well, breathe of our meetings in detail to any beyond this boudoir and I promise I will bite you with a fang more deadly than that illiterate culture could comprehend."

"You have my body, Dutan. You will never own my soul."

"I will never need your soul, woman. And there's the irony, I will only ever need *that* which you give so freely, devoid of any pride or dignity."

He distanced himself with an aggressive shove and lay back upon the silk pillows. "What are you offering? I don't need to make pacts with kitchen staff to satisfy my needs. What is it you want?"

"I'm offering you life," she declared stoically.

He laughed, genuinely amused. "You were a harlot shared among the Hirtera for their sport. Have you lost your mind?"

"I ask nothing for myself, only for the life of my child."

To his astonishment, she dropped a curved knife onto the sheets.

Momentarily, he froze, only to claw himself from the bed and stand, chin raised, conveying his Dirakhan pride.

"If you allow my daughter to die," she said, "do you believe that Gryonae will not kill everyone associated with her death? You are the emperor's Vizier. You know he is coming. Even *I* have heard the rumors that come out of the south. Quilaxia will fall. I could convince him to spare your life if you want to live beyond the approaching months. You could kill me now. Or, of course, you could betray me to Rissak and have him slay my child, but rest assured, if he doesn't find her here, he will flay the skin from every Dirakhan alive and burn this city to ashes. He has searched long for me, wishing to destroy that which betrayed him, but rest assured, he knows that his daughter is here... somewhere. She is the motivation. The choice is yours, Dutan. I will plead on your behalf, that is an oath I will swear by on the life of my child."

Of course, Dutan had learned from the dispatches sent by Rissak's slaves back to the empire. But they were chattel. Even he hadn't trusted the news. But what if the reports were true? In that moment, there was a flicker of doubt concerning the supremacy of the Dirakhan nation.

"Tut, tut," he concluded, clapping his hands; his face attempted to conceal the dark thoughts behind his expression.

She dressed quickly back into her grubby clothes. "Excellency..." she uttered, bending her head with a nod.

As she reached the door, the Vizier turned and blenched.

"Sharee," he said softly. "Don't make the mistake of speaking too freely in treacherous company. Check the corridor before you leave. I will think hard on what you've proposed."

327

The woman, Sharee, navigated the gloomy corridor like a ghost; her sandals scuffed where she trod, her blonde hair damp at her shoulders. She could smell the scent of desert lavender on her skin; her mind tripped, and the years fell away.

'Who is that?' Sharee asked the elegant woman at her side.

Her curly grey hair was pushed into a bun, and she was sporting the same black dress she had purchased from the market the day before. The garment was tasteless, and the Dirakhan spice merchant was oblivious to desert city trends. 'That is Kryack,' she replied. 'One of Rissak's gladiatorial monkeys.'

Sharee eyed him approvingly. 'He is quite striking, for a monkey,' she declared, biting her bottom lip.

'He is a peasant,' said Gwyneda. 'You are impressed. I can see.'

'Well, let me put it this way,' said Sharee with a curt laugh. 'I wouldn't climb over him to get to you.'

Gwyneda playfully slapped her friend's arm. 'Go speak to the oaf. I will meet you back here soon. I want to buy another robe, anyway. This one's too tight.'

Sharee watched her weave a path through the crowd, then turned her gaze once more to the stall where the attractive stranger had been bartering for a leather belt. 'Damn!' she vented. She spied his bronde tresses as he paced by a cheap trinket stall and strode off in pursuit.

He was footsure, like a wildcat; his scorched skin wrapped in light clothes. The trousers were yellow, with a loose jacket, worn to trap the breeze and reflect the heat of the suns. Brown leather buskins covered his feet. Sharee lost sight of him and cursed. She turned, and he stood before her with a grin.

'Are you following me, woman?'

His jaw was square, the handsome face nicked with scars, with upturned eyes green as summer leaves. And he carried the aroma of

328

sandalwood, as if the oil was seeping from his pores. He had bathed. A rare event where the men of the desert city were concerned. It was appealing. She stood on tiptoe and glanced over his shoulder.

'I'm looking for my friend,' she said, blushing. 'And who are you that you believe yourself so worthy of anyone's attention?'

'I am Gryonae. Or Shadowgrip. Bone Maker, if it gets me that pretty face and beyond the dress you wear.'

Sharee slid a blade from her sleeve and held it to his throat. 'I can add another smile right here, if grinning like a fool is what motivates a gib-cat like you.'

In a trice, the arena champion had twisted the weapon from her grasp and hurled it over a railing, down onto the street below.

'Don't tell me,' she said with a smirk. 'You've killed men for less.'

'So, you read minds too.' As he brushed past her, she trembled. 'Meet me tomorrow,' he said with a boyish grin.

'Where?!'

'The Bear Claw Alehouse?'

'You jest of course,' she said, making for the stairwell and the sandstone street below.

'Then where?!'

'The Diamond Hope Oasis!'

'That place is nothing but an expensive premises for overblown pea-birds!'

'You should fit right in!' she bellowed.

'Wait! I can't tomorrow!'

Sharee stopped on the stairs and peered, with only her proud head visible, back at the rogue. 'Why?!'

'I have sword play!'

'And?!'

He splayed his hands. 'I might be dead!'

Sharee wondered how different her life might have played out if Bone Maker had not found his way to The Diamond Oasis that night.

329

She reached the level where the emperor's harems were located, hoping to get a fleeting glimpse of Devorra, one Rissak's tortured playthings.

Chapter 35

MT KUTRANIA & SCHUKHULAR
(Kazhelma, Quilaxia. 3rd Millennium)

"I want life spared where possible," Gryonae told Tymarian. "I want the slaying of children made punishable by death. Any perpetrators will be brought to justice. Do you understand? See to it."

Where the army passed, the outer townships were razed and looted. The colored autumn leaves were shedding in the forests. They swept up towards two mountain ranges, divided by a V-shaped pass, whose ridges were now deserted.

"They have been drawn back to defend the city," Leetzune explained to the commanders. He tutored them briefly in the art of war and strategy, as they approached Quilaxia from the south. Three leagues later, the fortified entrance stood before them.

"Do we attempt to blow the iron gateway with black powder? Assault the wall with ladders? What's the plan, brother?" Tymarian asked with a face of stone.

His sibling looked spent. The scar on his cheek a wound too many. Like one who had crawled out of the grave and was commanded to climb an unscalable cliff.

"I would recommend a parley," Leetzune suggested. "If we can get Rissak to this gate, maybe we can force him to surrender without bloodshed."

Gryonae snorted a laugh. "Forgive me, my friend," he said. "I did not mean to mock you, but you do not know this man. He is mad, traitorous, and deceitful. Only by the spilling of his blood shall we win this day."

His leather armor creaked softly as he descended from his wraken. He beckoned Thrydwulf to him with a wave, and soon they stood alone, surrounded by a sea of battle-hardened warriors, mounted and afoot.

Gryonae eyed the outlander from head to foot. The yellow gambeson fitted more tightly, though the once shinny breastplate was thick with mud and dented in places caused by arrow or sword thrust. His brown hair was tied at the nape. A tooth had been chipped from a hammer strike to his helm, but there was a warm glint in his eye.

"Well, brother," said Shadowgrip. "It is time." He scratched his chin; he was almost spent.

"I know," Thrydwulf said with a yawn. "That is why we are here."

"No, brother, it is time for *you*. You must depart."

Thrydwulf stepped back, touching the pommel of the enchanted sword, knowing it was covered and laced with a cloth to deter the very intentions that could manifest within him; he clenched his fists in frustration. "Have you finally lost your mind, Shadowgrip?"

"Nay. I am sound. But they are waiting." The weary champion pointed yonder to where forty warriors were helmed and mounted, joined by wagons laden with supplies—one alone carried a handful of crude ladders. "Drivid is among them. They have their orders."

"What orders?" snapped Thrydwulf. "Say it plain!"

"They are to take you home, outlander. My promise to Vargdenir will be fulfilled. Whether we win or fall here, I will know I kept my word to a friend. Now go. Before my heart breaks. Or do I have to rope you to a wraken and lead you there? Ah. And the sword? It must have been your hand that manifested the demon and the deity. I fear they are gone. I am not sure. But I will not risk your life to prove a point. Take the brand with you. It may be of help."

As the realization struck, Thrydwulf swallowed hard to negate the tears, but still they came. "I will not forget you, King of Medra Tume." The quip was an attempt at levity; Gryonae brushed it aside.

"We fight for *you*, little brother, and all who are worthy of life. I still have a long way to go." He winked with a moist eye. "But I am learning. *Now* I believe my soul is worthy of the chariot ride it will take between the suns. Fairwell, Thrydwulf-son-of-Ceolwulf. Your friends have bid me to say this last goodbye."

They embraced, turned, and parted, neither one glancing back.

They would not meet again under the green suns of Kazhelma.

Tymarian gazed, shielding his eyes with a hand. Thrydwulf and the vetted warriors, along with the carts crammed with cargo, began to move away towards the east. "I pray he makes it," he declared, donning his helm.

"He may yet," said Leetzune. "Well, you talked me out of a kingdom. Let's see if you can talk an emperor out of an empire. Before we drown in blood, grant an old man a last whim; let's see if words can prevail."

***

Yast-Dutan stood on the battlements above the portcullis, sixty feet above the sand.

The arena champion had changed. No longer a sight that could freeze a man in his tracks. It was as if a million moons had sucked the light from his very soul. But he knew without doubt that he could have blinded-folded the Novian snake and still won coinage with a bet on him killing ten men in the blink of an eye.

"Bone Maker!" Dutan bellowed down. "Do you remember me? No? What about these two women? This one, surely?" He pulled Sharee up from the place she had been ordered to crouch.

"Of course I do, you dog!" Gryonae called up, rising in his stirrups. "She is the woman I love."

334

"I have liberated her for you. Surely some gratitude on your part will be forthcoming?" Dutan brushed the demoralized woman aside.

"Where is Rissak?!" Gryonae roared in anger. He unsheathed Bwanaril; it glinted in the sunlight, cruel and hungry for the taste of blood. As he did so, the sching of countless blades being drawn from their scabbards rang out a forbidding chime of resolve.

"I am too old to partake in battle any longer," Leetzune confessed. He galloped away to seek Betgar at a safer distance.

Tymarian trotted up beside his brother, fastening his silver helm in anticipation.

Groups of men carrying curved elongated shields and courageous fellows rolling kegs of gunpowder, wove through the ranks. Teams of ladder bearers joined them.

"Rissak rules from within, Bone Maker! I command from the walls!" Dutan yelled from the rampart.

Alongside Sharee, a damsel took to her slippered feet.

Brown-haired with eyes like walnut shells, she was clad in garments identical to those of the women in the royal harem.

Gryonae, wounded by the vision, gave a raspy cough, noting the outer cloak prettified with ivory beads and colored feathers.

"Behold Devorra!" the vizier hollered over the bulwark. "She possesses your defiance, Bone Maker!"

He dragged the harem prisoner along, a foot or two, piercing the invader with an icy stare. "If it's war you seek, you'll find her dead at the city gates!"

Sharee pondered the pregnancy she had carried from two lovers. Bourfee, the man Gryonae had hired to protect her from the Hinera, and Gryonae himself. Twins had been born, Devorra and Cevile. Both girls.

335

One had died at birth, unknown and forgotten by the world, the other was the arena champion's bastard daughter. What a bloody mess, she thought.

Sharee lunged at the figure of Dutan. Latching hold of his black tunic collar, she dragged them both silently to their deaths. In horror, Devorra leapt to the crenellated wall, gripping the sandstone with desperate fingers.

"FATHER!" she screamed.

Three assaults were carried out against the walls of the city. Three times the invading hordes were repelled. The losses of men were multiplying, and at the rate of death amongst the woodsmen and Novian forces, the taking of Quilaxia began to look impossible. But Gryonae bellowed commands that they should not quit, and the warriors battled on.

***

(Two Days Later)

With no designated heir apparent, the old established succession laws would be put into action. If Rissak died, he had no living blood kin, and that being so, the Imperial Ruling Council would take charge, overseeing affairs.

The elaborate throne stood empty as Dwen, newly appointed head of the council, addressed the gathering of important officials.

The chatter receded as he stood at the bottom step of the dais. Holding up a hand, he hushed them into silence.

"What now?" he said authoritatively. "There is rioting and looting in the marketplaces. A revolt looks imminent."

"And there is other news, honorable Dwen," said a voice from the head councilor's right.

The man stood up from his chair, blue sandaled, clad in a long white robe of linen, his thinning locks tied into the traditional knot—Dwen stared soberly at the figure addressing the group.

"Stragglers returned daily from the charmed woodlands of Palacoumia. Soldier and servant alike. The war was over, even before it had begun."

"Here! Here!" a grating voice from the back piped up.

"What now indeed. There is barely an army left. A host from the south at the gates."

"We have scarcely the numbers to offer more resistance," added the councilor in the white garment. "Quilaxia will fall. If we are not slain, we will surely be taken into slavery."

Squabbling erupted around the throne hall. Once again, Dwen held up his palm. "Send word to the legions in the city. They are to quash any rebellion as we defend the walls. An impossible task, but we are out of options. Even though their numbers fall with each attack. Fate hangs in the balance."

The commotion of men sliding chairs and leaving echoed within the emperor's formal chamber.

Dwen noted the rich red damask tapestries draped from their silver pins. The heads of rulers, intricately carved from hard timbers, black as a bird's wing, were set upon obsidian pedestals and situated against the blue plastered walls. Artwork from ancient battles was fixed below the ornate cornice, and the aroma of crushed lavender flowers filled the wide space. It represented power, but day by day, the empire's strength was waning.

He had been born in Quilaxia, one warm, uneventful night, a thousand years ago—or so it seemed.

Sixty-two summers old, with the libido of a man half his age, he had not considered a wife—the harems fulfilled his lust, and his position of power provided wealth. He contemplated the woman, Sharee. The situation irked him, but he had known of Dutan's exploitation of her. He had always been a jealous man. And this… Gryonae. The arena rat was now raging at the very gates of the empire!

Maybe he, too, could use the girl to his advantage, should surrender become the last alternative.

Chapter 36

THE SILVER NET

Rissak's chamber was quiet as a tomb. He needed rest, yet still he struggled to sleep.

Plush velvet drapes were drawn and tied across the entrance to the balcony, keeping at bay the autumn rain. Two oil lamps, encased in small squares of glass, were attached to brass cords hanging from the ceiling, and the smoke from incense sticks swirled in scrolls, filling the room with a pleasant aroma.

The sentries had been ordered to evacuate the antechamber, and he had bolted the doors against interruptions. Even if the skies were to fall, he promised himself that he would rest before being informed of any catastrophe inflicted by the enemy at the gates. He pondered on Endambia and Eryon—his great aunt and mother—and wondered why his instigation in the deaths of both women had not tortured his mind; it flummoxed him. Patricide, he understood: An obstacle had to be eliminated for him to take the position of authority. Once he had dreamed the darkest dream. After experiencing it, there had been a change in him.

His pursuits of pleasure and power knew no bounds. His soul felt corrupt and tainted. Was he destined for Hell? If so, the halls of Nephthrionigal would have to wait.

Sucking in breath, a tear touched his cheek, and a feeling so potent washed over him, becoming a trial as he choked back the unprecedented emotion.

He lay upon the gold silk sheets, eyes open, conscious. Suddenly, his body was unable to respond to the terror that began to unfold.

Warm yellow light shimmered upon the brass gong across from the bed. A demonic face gradually began to appear. Like a fist slowly pushing through water, the metal remolding itself around it, inching into the very fabric of the room. The brass visage grew eyes of glowing crimson, and its head bore the shape of two horns; a slit manifested for a mouth, to add to the horror, it began to speak.

"Ah. Do you remember now, Rissak?" The voice was almost a squelch, like a man attempting to converse through a mouthful of wet mud. The sickly grin was spreading with the consistency of beeswax. Yet the face did not lose its shape but swelled like baking bread, the shade of yellow copper.

Sweating profusely, Rissak's heart pounded.

340

'For all these years, I believed you were nothing more than a fantasy, come to haunt my dreaming,' thought Rissak.

"You were chosen for a purpose, son of Eryon. It would seem you were not up to the task," Halxerizan declared.

'If you had a plan for me, demon,' Rissak reasoned; he began to hyperventilate, you should have made it known.'

The hideous countenance frowned. "You were created by the Galrandir, fool! Should I have wiped your buttocks too? I positioned your bloodline as the highest order among the Dirakhan. You have induced our downfall." The demon growled, and the bedchamber shuddered. "Because of you, Rissak, emperor of Quilaxia, my sacred children will be vanquished and shamed till the end of mortal time. You set in motion the attempt to slay the outlander chosen by Aukarn. Wounded by the deity's wretched sword, am I. I must shrink and return defeated into the endless void. You should have employed wisdom and subtlety. It seems you possessed neither. You and all my children will fall."

Rissak's mind floated through a sea of abstract thought.

The Casindrian Ocean was dotted with a fleet of countless ships, heading east from out of the west. Several months of gigantic waves pounded the galleys. The suns scorched the top decks, and driving rain drenched the fluttering sails. Reaching the mainland, they hoisted down the rowing boats and hauled their cargo ashore. This was a new world for the Dirakhan race. There would be no return. The ships that survived the journey were set ablaze, and the hordes ventured forth across the vast regions, establishing an empire in a semi-desert, which they called Vuran. The city they named Quilaxia flourished, and domination of the surrounding lands and kingdoms began in earnest.

A thousand years before the vast forests of Palacoumia had been entrenched, the fierce territories of Novia Joria and the country of Enlyd were swiftly subjugated.

In the blink of an eye, Rissak witnessed the rise and ruin of political maneuvering among the races of Kazhelma. The grassy hills shapeshifted, rivers shrank, and desert sands crept towards fertile plains, transforming the landscapes, leaving them arid and eerie. Ridiantee—the man who had fathered Rissak's birth—rode at the head of a cavalry charge, conquering the legions of Abdeoi: tall, dark men, caked in white mud, armed with naught else but long spear and boomerang. In an instant, the many villages were laid waste and swallowed by a blossoming undergrowth of thickets and bushes.

The visions faded, slowly being consumed by an utter blackness.

"Fool! Fool! Fool!"

Halxerizan's words echoed like thunder in the bedchamber, only to dwindle to a menacing whisper.

"Pray to your god, Kubenial. He may hear you. But he'll not come. We will share an eternity of pain in the befouled pits of Nephthrionigal." The demon chuckled gratifyingly. "Now come!" it bellowed.

The room shook to its foundations. The squares of glass upon the oil lamps shattered, and the air became putrid and thick with swarms of blue bloated flies. Trapped within the torment, and way too early, biologically, for the feast, they buzzed with excitement amid the turmoil.

Gold light flared from the lanterns, and all at once, Rissak witnessed the strange octagonal pattern encasing the sleeping quarters. It budged slowly, pulling plaster from the walls and ceiling, cracking and flaking, crumbling the material onto the

342

smooth granite slabs. The sinister net shunted three feet further, toppling the brass gong, dragging the elegant furniture, snagging at several corners of unflushed granite slabs, pulling them loose, their harsh scraping lost amid the mayhem.

Free from the sleep paralysis that had fettered him to the sheets, he reached his knees, shouting for help as the silver web shrank ever inward.

Now buckled and moving, the bed frame stopped suddenly, as if the demon were appropriating some sick whim. It was momentary, and the net began to tighten once more, ripping the lanterns from the ceiling. One clattered to the slabs. The sparks scattered. The other landed upon the velvet pillows, setting the gaudy objects ablaze. Rissak attempted to extinguish the flames, smothering them with silk sheets. It slowed the process, but in his panic, he leaped to the granite floor only to have his bare feet cut by the sliding mesh. Gripping the lethal mesh, he screamed, defecating himself as his fingers were sliced to ribbons.

Across from the flight of steps that led up to Rissak's sleeping quarters, several Imperial Royal Guards were in uproar. In the antechamber, they were thudding upon the thick bolted doors. They could taste the acrid smoke seeping through the tight gaps of varnished wood. Axes resounded, attempting to cleave way through into the emperor's quarters. The task seemed practically impossible.

Grappling hooks and ropes were brought, and three lithe climbers were ordered to enter Rissak's room via the high turrets—a dangerous endeavor, considering the wind and rain—but the task was achieved. Ripping through the drapery with determined swords, to their horror, the guards discovered a macabre scene: The contents of the whole chamber were ensnared within a silver net, perched at the center of the room.

343

All that remained of Rissak were octagonal strips of flesh that had been squeezed and oozed through the corrupt netting. Puddles of blood, innards, broken limbs, and fragments face and skull were mushed together upon the floor, all sprinkled with a multitude of dead flies. A metallic stench mixed with smoke added to the repulsion

'It has begun,' whispered a gruff voice, drenched with malevolence.

Spooked, the men glanced at each other but said nothing. Rushing across the bloodied slabs, they made for the staircase and the doors on the landing below.

There was a flash of fey lightning, the net dissolved, and its contents spread further in a gory mess upon the stones.

Chapter 37

RADAMANTHIR WOOD
(Kazhelma, Quilaxia, Radamanthir Wood.
3rd Millennium)

The trotting of hooves and the rolling wagons were the only din besides the occasional squawking of birds in the forest canopy. Drivid ordered the retinue to halt as Thrydwulf dismounted. The Saxon strolled about with his hands on his hips, kicking the tinged autumn leaves, talking to himself, and cursing in a strange tongue. At one point, he untied the arcane sword, shouting maniacally at the weapon, tossing it into the mud by a shallow stream, only to reclaim it, fasten it around his middle, and remount. Curiously, Gryonae's escorts watched, speechless and fatigued. Drivid raised his hand and let his arm fall. They moved on.

In the late afternoon, they made camp. As night fell, they lit fires, and Thrydwulf sat alone before the flames of a modest blaze, deep in thought.

"Will you accept some company?" came a firm enunciation.

The troubled Saxon peered up. Drivid stood there, clenching two bowls of wraken stew. Surrendering one of the edibles, he perched cross-legged by the younger man.
"A strange day indeed," he continued with a modest lisp. The woodsman had labored most of his lifetime burying the irksome impediment. He smiled, passing over a wooden spoon. "How are you faring?"

"I am sorry that this duty was put upon you," said Thrydwulf.

"If I achieve the task of finding the catacombs below the forest,' Drivid replied, "Gryonae has ordered that our little group ride back to Palacoumia. He declares: *What difference is forty leaves among a forest of thousands?*' You are heading home, too, my friend. Why so gloomy?"

"The time spent here has been an ordeal," Thrydwulf said. "I don't even know if those I left behind in my world still live. It's been years. What if my village has gone? What if the people are gone? What if I get trapped there, alone and unable to return?!"

"It's a predicament. But life is a gamble," said Drivid, philosophically. With a warped spoon, the battler from Karfilia scooped a morsel of meat from his bowl, setting the utensil

346

aside to rest. "But we have done remarkably these long months. I have never dined so well. Han-Taglur and I were in the Gendwood wars, fighting against the Liszom pirates. It was woeful." He brushed fallen leaves from his long silver curls.

"I remember a man from my village," Thrydwulf chimed in, "explaining to my father how the armies of Rome would eat roots and roasted acorns, girdle trees, and munch the bark when they were starving. Animal carcasses were stripped to the bone to reach the marrow; men boiled their sandals to devour the leather. Scitte!"

The stocky woodsman shook his head and began to wolf down his stew.

"Should Gryonae's army fail, I despair of what will become of you all," the Saxon huffed.

"Best not to dwell on such matters, Thrydwulf. You will never know, should you find your way to your homeworld."

A pewter moon hung in the black sky. Curling plumes of irritating smoke and the aroma of cooked wraken flesh were pungent among the trees. Flames crackled and sputtered. A thrilled comrade, discovering a flagon of red wine in one of the carts, burst into song. He traipsed back to the fire, full of glee, laughing. Drivid rose and rambled off. "Captain!" he called over the shoulder of his yellow gambeson. "Join us. The next few days may be our last together. What will it hurt? Drink with us!"

Thrydwulf drooped his head and chuckled. "Fill me a cup!" he chirped with a wide grin.

As they sang, the Saxon danced. All were merry. Thrydwulf told them about the girl called Aeva, and the curious foresters questioned him about his homeworld. Somewhere during the night, a distant horn sounded, intruding on their banter. It was far off, but haunting and unsettling. The men retreated into silence, and Drivid laughed. "We've fought our way through devils and sorcery. You hear a toot on the wind, and you quiver like maidens on a wedding night. Tomorrow, we enter Radamanthir. The search will begin in earnest. Get some rest."

Slippery plant litter, rocks, and roots were hazardous as they rode towards the woodlands. Five cavalrymen had remained with the wagons. The unit began to spread out as they galloped through the trees. The day was overcast and spitting rain, the petrichor an earthy odor, sweet and musky, but these mounted warriors were now steadfast and determined in the execution of their duty—the quicker the matter was resolved, the speedier their return would be to the eldritch forests where they were born.

The group was employing the method of blazing: cutting into the bark of the trees on both sides, to indicate the correct direction when returning to the wagons. On the third day of scouring the vast habitat, Drivid and a serious fellow called Rolfon made a discovery.

"We found this," said Drivid. "The shaft has rotted; this is all that remains."

In awe, Thrydwulf took the iron spearhead into his hands and swallowed hard. "It belonged to my father," he confessed, studying the object with a puzzled frown.

The metal leaf was rusted, the decaying socket crumbling.

"It was atop a hill," said Rolfon. "A miracle," he admitted with a wry smile. "I almost tripped over it."

"You have marked the route?" Thrydwulf asked with a tremor in his voice, his eyes imploring.

"We know the way," Rolfon assured the outlander.

"Show me," Thrydwulf demanded. "And bring the wagons."

Racing determinedly on their trail, the Saxon cantered in close as the warriors reached the hill and dismounted frantically from his saddle. "There is something else…" Drivid said.

The stocky woodsman watched, touched with poignancy as Thrydwulf stepped towards the strange symbol carved into the white bark of a willowy tree.

"*I* made this rune," he confessed, on the brink of tears. "I know now where I am." He grew pale, lifted his yellow gambeson sleeve and pointed to the base of the hill. "The way to my homeworld lies within."

Drivid reached out, grabbing at Thrydwulf's gambeson as he sank pitifully to his knees.

As the moon was waxing, torches had been fashioned and ignited, and ropes and ladders were passed through the gaping entrance into the cave under the hill. Gathering the equipment, Thrydwulf and Drivid led the way, each with a burning brand.

Shadows of men and accoutrements danced in the flickering light upon the cavern walls. Footfalls echoed in the silence, and the whiff of burning wood mingled with the smell of dank earth. They reached a smooth, flat ridge and lowered two short ladders down.

The cave opened into a vast catacomb. Stalactites hung from the ceilings like slender tapering spikes dripping into pools of rippling water, whilst stalagmites rose from the limestone like crooked teeth in a giant's maw.

"This way," said the Saxon, his anxious voice reverberating through the labyrinth. They journeyed north, ankle or knee-deep, splashing or wading through the mineral-enriched puddles. "Far enough," Thrydwulf bellowed. "I need a ladder; lean it against the wall." He bid one of the bearers to set one in a deep pool, placing it against a high ledge of rock. "My friends, it is here we must say goodbye."

The Saxon clasped each forearm of the woodsmen in turn, only to stare forlornly as they began to vanish into the distance, their lights disappearing and wending out of sight. The last remaining warrior was Drivid. He smiled as they gripped arms in the traditional fashion. "I would have liked to have met you sooner, outlander," he announced with a twinkle in his eye. "Han-Taglur spoke true. You are a man of good character. Farewell. May your dreams be many and your troubles few." The woodsman started singing as he strode away. It was a bawdy ballad, cruder than a beggar's fart.

Thrydwulf stood alone. Bracing himself, he plunged chest-deep into the icy water. Fear poked him with an iron finger, and he began to ascend the rickety ladder. Up he climbed, the shaky contraption almost ending his venture with a tumble, but he reached the edge of the rock shelf and sat there. Finally, a whole gamut of emotions swept through him, and he roared, blubbering in his triumph. Pushing the tottering ladder away, it splashed into the pool, clattering on the limestone below. Remembering those years before when he had stood at the tunnel's entrance, the murmuring of language that had been unreal and challenging, he knew it now; it was Dirakhanian, spoken by the demigod Auknar of the Galrandir.

'Throw down the sword!' the deity had been imploring. 'Return it! Take it from this world at your peril!'

350

Chapter 38

GATEWAY FROM KAZHELMA
(Britain, Southern England. 5ᵗʰ Century AD)

Thrydwulf eased himself further back from the ledge of rock and placed the burning flame at his feet. Unbuckling the sword belt from around his middle, he laid it on the mud beside him. Lifting the cloth away from the stitched leather hilt, he gripped it tight—The lightheadedness was immediate, and his mind began to flood with prophetic imagery.

He witnessed formations of shields cocooning men spinning kegs of black powder. They rolled them to the rusted iron gate. Boiling water, granite boulders, and projectiles poured down, but still the barrels blew, and the portcullis twisted and snapped. Like blue ants, Leetzune and Betgar's people charged through into Quilaxia. Thrydwulf's visual globes shut tight, but his third eye bore witness. He observed as Gryonae and Tymarian stormed the battlements. Side by side, they hacked through the Dirakhan ranks. An arrow caught the prisoner of Rothshim through the shoulder. Regardless, he thrust at the bowman who tripped from the bulwark, his head splattering like a melon on the sandstone steps further down. Gryonae rescued a young woman clad in fine robes. Bruised and battered she clung to the arena champion like a limpet to a rock. He hauled her from the fray, carrying her beyond the city walls. Tymarian and a myriad of devoted warriors raged through the imperial palace. Rissak was nowhere to be found. The emperor's council were tracked down, hiding themselves in the throne room. They were put to the sword, regardless of Gryonae's order to spare life. The battle was brutal. The city burned. Dirakhan militias were organized to surrender their weapons. Building huge piles in the market squares, the instruments of war were set ablaze. Prisoners rallied into lines and marched beyond the walls of the metropolis into makeshift camps that were basic and crudely constructed. Winter came and went, and the drama shed its cloak.

There, on an imperial throne carved from obsidian glass, sat the emperor Gryonae. He was laughing, chatting to a maiden with long brown curly hair; she was dressed in a lavish golden gown. She peeked from behind a fan of feathers, all silver and aquamarine. Gryonae pouted and tossed his extravagant headdress at her suntanned feet. He took her hand, and they wandered down into the palace gardens. At an extravagant memorial the couple stopped. Chiseled into the stone was the name Sharee. The woman knelt and wept as the grey-haired emperor, Gryonae, looked on.

Thrydwulf flinched and scene shifted its focus. He recognized Tymarian sitting astride a huge euganta. The dark hairy beast was trotting along. The warrior had cut his hair short, and the black locks were now grey as washed slates. Seated behind the ghost of Rothshim, with arms around his waist, was a slender woman with charcoal locks flecked with strands of silver; she was stunning and possessed sage green almond eyes. Allina! He had found her?!

A journey that should have taken them several weeks was a fleeting moment. They galloped into Medra Tume, straight to the school that Gryonae had been so adamant about building. They were clothed in Novian gowns of academic regalia—were they teachers?!

Then more ambiguity fluttered into vision. Betgar and Leetzune rolled into the City of Wood on a wagon, pointing and poking each other like quarrelsome siblings. The old men climbed clumsily from the cart, pushed at one another, and promptly parted ways—An age-old routine between the visiting neighbors—The king ambled en route to the castle, and the woodsman plodded back towards the city gates.

Time oozed away like fruit butter being squeezed through burly fingers.
Urtarn fell to the chamber floor, clutching her chest.

Suzin blossomed into queenhood; she sat upon an elaborate throne of burnished wood. A young man with mousy hair sat perched beside her satin-covered knees. His child?! Unable to bear more of the confusion, he opened his eyes.

'Throw down the sword! You were to find it and take it to Palacoumia! The evil would have seen through the plot of others in the world, never of those beyond it! Many have been chosen! He cannot read the thoughts of those born beyond this reality! You fulfilled the prophecy! Your deed is done!' The sound of Auknar's voice shook the cavern.

Thrydwulf, with all the strength he could muster, launched the weapon of incantation back into the world of Kazhelma.

As it struck the water with a loud splash, Auknar's arcane portal began to close; filling with wet earth, it stuck together, squelching like clay on a potter's wheel. Snatching the burning torch, Thrydwulf dived through the aperture; it exploded with a charge of electric energy, and he crawled through the mud.

Smoke began to fill the claustrophobic tunnel. Reaching a blockage of earth, he laid the dwindling torch aside and frantically dug with his fingers. Thrydwulf wheezed and coughed as a gust of cold air whipped through a finger-sized hole of dirt. Up on his knees, he wriggled out into Engla land.

The Saxon, endeavoring to gather what was left of his sanity, almost collapsed, but girded himself. Reclaiming the torch from the passage between the worlds, he clambered down the leaf-spattered bank.

The stream was freezing, but he thanked Woden for the added glow of moonlight, guiding his way.

He rested against a mighty oak, shivering, then strove on.

Blobs of red holly berries caught his eye. There was the scream of a fox. Was it mating season? The frigid wind stung his face and tensed his muscles till there, yonder, beyond all those years of hope, stood the village. Light spilled through the cracks of the huts. Tossing aside the dead torch, he lumbered through the darkness, pushing his way into an empty shack.

Gone were the dogs, the sick mother, the slight maiden who had carried his child. The hut was damp, cold, mildewed, with a musty odor. It almost broke him. He sped to the adjoining shelter and lunged in out of the night.

Thrydwulf's eyebrows knotted as he gazed upon the two occupants within the hut. The woman, with brown hair braided, strong cheekbones, and hazel eyes, stood stunned, slowly rising to her feet.

"Thrydwulf?" she muttered in disbelief. Wiping her hands on her green shawl, she gestured forward, but froze, like wary prey before a mouth of gnashing teeth. She was uncertain, as she gathered her thoughts.

Sunn found her voice. "Where have you been?"

The child, Leax, dumbstruck, nestled nervously behind his mother and stared with a fitful gaze.

Algar's father! Could this truly be him?

Thrydwulf's blue leather leggings and yellow gambeson were caked in mud. He wore a bushy beard, long hair, and scars marred his anxious face. He was monstrous to behold.

"And where is Oeric?" She almost demanded, filled with trepidation.

The stray returnee's shoulders slumped at those brittle words.

"He died," the man answered stoically.

The room fell silent—all the more eerie for the crackling of the burning fire.

"Where is Aeva, and Cynwise?" asked Thrydwulf.

A pang of sorrow washed over the woman, as she said softly: "Cynwise sleeps beside your father Ceolwulf, on the mountain."

It took Gryonae's captain all he could muster to hold his composure. "And Aeva?"

"Many have passed on," Sunn told him. She gazed at the man's cicatrices, sensing the controlled anger. The woman knew she could not stall indefinitely.

"She married again. A man called Kim. Kimball-son-of-Brant, from the village of Ciselhyrst. You have a son. Algar, he is called. They promised to return and visit, but in truth, she was banished. She never doubted her love for you, Thrydwulf. That was another two winters ago."

"Algar is my brother!" Leax blurted from the safety of his mother's shoulder.

Thrydwulf's stern pose thawed, and a smile brushed his lips.

"He chose well in his friendship," replied the warrior in a peculiar Germanic phrase.

"My husband Feran is away hunting. Sit by the fire. I will make some food."

Thrydwulf perched at the table as the smoke wafted around him. "Tell me of my mother."

"All in good time," Sunn replied. "We must talk. I wish to know it all."

"Yes. Everything," echoed Leax, his fear melting. He slid next to the mud-encrusted stranger, full of excitement."

"Seaver is Chief of the village now. Caelin's son," Sunn told him. What can you do?"

Thrydwulf blew into his hands and held them towards the fire. "I will talk with Seaver-son-of-Caelin. I need to fetch my family back home to the village."

"He is dangerous. Disliked. Fickle," Sunn proclaimed.

Thrydwulf spat at the charred logs in the fire. "I know. I felt the same way about my own father."

Chapter 39

SEAVER
(Britain, Southern England. 5ᵗʰ Century AD)

Word reached Seaver of the return of Ceolwulf's son.

He sat in the village hall in the carved chair surrounded by his thegns and serving maids. He twitched, spilling half of a horn of ale, roared in anger, and flung the vessel, leaving it sizzling upon the glowing embers of a dying fire.

The door at the end of the dwelling creaked open, and the long-lost vagabond, Thrydwulf, marched in.

Seaver noted the strange attire and the attempt for it to have been brushed clean. The designs were none he knew: Blue trousers of... leather? The padded shirt, dirty buttercup-tinted, was also a curious anomaly.

The wayfarer bore battle scars: Nicks about the hairline and across the fingers and at his throat. He carried a spear. This weapon was Saxon-fashioned—belonging to Feran, Sunn's traitorous husband. Seaver, at that moment, wished he had exiled them all. This was no boy. It was a warrior. And his movements were calculated. Maybe too his intentions!

"Hail! Seaver-son-of-Caelin!" said Thrydwulf, feigning respect.

Six thegns stood behind the returnee; all but one was a stranger. Thrydwulf could not recall the name, but they had wrestled over pale blue thrush eggs when they were children.

Seaver coughed, "So, you come out of the bushes at last. What do you seek after all this time?"

Thrydwulf gripped his spear with both hands. "I seek Aeva, daughter of Hunwald and Hilda, who was banished, along with my child."

"Hunwald's daughter is gone. She is now the wife of Kimball-son-of-Brant. The boy, too. They reside at Ciselhyrst."

Before the thegns could respond, Thrydwulf lunged forward, jerking his spear point towards the chieftain's throat.

"You want to be dead, Seaver-son-of-Caelin?" snarled Thrydwulf.

As his guards advanced, Seaver twitched and fearlessly pushed the javelin tip aside.

"If that were the case," said the chieftain, "I would have drunk a barrel of ale and lain upon a pallet in my hut until my warriors had deemed it time to bear me away and bury me below the hill—where the best of us already lie sleeping.

For the memory of your father, Ceolwulf, I will grant you life. On one condition. You leave this village never to return. None of you. Agree, and it shall be granted. Refuse, and I will slay you here, and even should your woman and child return to Caelinford, with or without you, their lives will be forfeit. This is my last word on the matter. You are a blight on the name of your people. Oath-say now or never leave this hall alive!"

Thrydwulf threw a stare that pierced into the very soul of Seaver. "I should not *want* to return to this place. Know this also. Should any man attempt to bar my way, I will carry him and a host of you scittes to the very gates of Valhalla!"

Seaver leaned forward in his chair. "Then, Thrydwulf, Ceolwulf's son, it would appear we have reached an agreement. Throw this Canis out of my hall. Let him go on his way. We owe his father that much."

Seaver sneezed, spat, and cussed as Thrydwulf was escorted from the social hall of Caelinford village.

***

The following dawn, Sunn—and the man who had wandered the lands of Kazhelma—sat before the glowing embers of a fire in the anxious woman's hut.

"Maybe you and the boy should come with me," Thrydwulf said, pondering and biting his bottom lip. "It is dangerous for you here." He stared across to where Leax was sleeping on a bed of ruffled hides.

359

"Seaver has no trouble with me," the woman stated. "And I have a husband. Feran should return soon. But I have a gift. He will curse me for parting with it, but it will serve you on your journey to Ciselhyrst." She rose, pulling her cloak about her shoulders as she opened the door and strode out into the morning mist. A few minutes later, the muffled thump of a horse's hooves sounded on the grass outside. Thrydwulf reached the threshold of the hut and threw up his hands in refusal. "*Na!*" he said. "That I cannot do."

"You can and you must!" Sunn responded. "He is saddled and ready to travel."

Thrydwulf stepped forward, patting the animal's mane. "I could promise to bring him home, but it would be a lie," he confessed."

Sunn said, "I told you. It is a gift."

"I cannot return to Caelinford. Seaver has forbidden it. Under pain of death… For me, Aeva and my son."

"I pray to *Frig* that they are safe. Don't be so hard on Kim. He possessed many fine qualities. She was forced into that marriage by that stuttering fool, Seaver. She never gave up hope until the last. She had to think of Algar."

They embraced tenderly, as the warrior thanked her.

"You remember the way to Ciselhyrst? It's been a long time." She said and pointed. "Take the road hence. Three-or four-days travel at the most. Wait! I almost forgot." The godsend hurried into the hut and returned with a hemp sack full of edibles, along with Feran's spear, handing them over. Thrydwulf shook his head and proffered a subtle smile. "Woman, you are written on my heart. Maybe in a few winters, I will chance a sneak back and see if things have changed here. · Give my regards to your boy. Thank him for me. What is the name of the horse?"

360

"Leax calls him *Hasufel*."

"Grey hide," said Thrydwulf, with a nod and a grin. "It is fitting. May Woden watch over you, Sunn. I am in your debt. I pray we meet again under better circumstances."

She waved and watched him ride away into the mist.

Chapter 40

CISELHYRST
(Britain, Southern England. 5th Century AD)

The Saxon's grey mount galloped along the woodland path; the way had been eroded by the traffic of horse and human feet. Pigeons flapped from their flimsy nests atop the dense oak trees. A red deer drifted across the path behind him, and its grace filled him with the wonder of bygone days lived in his childhood. Squirrels scurried, and a pair of wild boars dashed through the white wood anemones, a vision that filled his head with images of Vargdenir.

'Fill the pipe, boy. The suns are sinking.'

With those bittersweet thoughts, he clopped his way through the chilly forest with another borrowed article from Aeva's childhood friend—much to his eternal shame—a brown woolen cloak that was wrapped tightly around him.

His hair was long and braided at each ear, his beard unkempt, his attention honed. The path rose, and *Hasufel* trotted up the slope leading through a host of gaunt silver birches. There, on the far-flung hill, stood Ciselhyrst, grouped with wattle and daubed huts, bedecked with thatched roofs.

Livestock roamed on the common land, and wheat and barley fields had been sown by the indwellers.

At the edge of woodland, Thrydwulf spied a sparkling stream and wove the horse down through the delicate bluebell flowers to drink.

The man from Kazhelma perched silently in his saddle, plunged his spear into the mud, and folded his arms.

A boy was kneeling by the gurgling water, filling two buckets to haul back to the settlement. He pulled from his pocket an object and washed it.

"What is it you have there?" the rider asked, startling the youth. He dropped the piece of metal from his grasp into the cold brook. Plunging his naked arm into the water, he rescued the cherished item and cursed. "Do you always creep up on people like that?"

"I seek Ciselhyrst," said the rider. "This is the village?"

The warrior from Kazhema already knew the answer.

"Everyone knows *that* around these parts," the youth retorted. "Are you *dysig*?"

"There have been some who have claimed it was so," the man said with some amusement.

"Who are you? And what do you want?" asked the boy, slipping the lump of melted brass back into his pocket.

His hair was curly brown, his skin pale, his tunic and trousers green, and his face was molded into a petulant frown.

"I carry a message," Thrydwulf told the sapling.

"For whom?"

"For Kim-son-of-Brant. You know such a man?"

The youth's face blenched, and he took a step back, dragging a knife from a sheath upon his belt.

"He was my father. He died last winter."

Those words struck Thrydwulf like a hammer blow. His eyebrows knitted, and he fought to rein in the tense emotion.

That Thimbleful of time stood still.

The rider's wraken whinnied, dismantling the awkwardness.

"He was not your father, Algar," the stranger exclaimed, his voice almost splintering.

Algar frowned, lifting one of the spilt buckets for added protection. "How do you know my name?" he snarled.

"Go fetch Aeva," the man from Kazhelma demanded.

"Tell her your father waits for her at the edge of the stream."

With all the strength he could muster, Algar charged.

Thrydwulf met the attack full on, lifting the boy, holding tight, nuzzling him unyieldingly.

"Forgive me, child," the warrior whispered. "The fault was not my own. I did not mean to leave you."

Algar clung to the stranger like a crab to a rock.

As the midday sun pushed through the grey clouds, his young muscles relaxed, and the tears cascaded down his face.

"I don't want you to wait here," the boy sobbed.

He delved into his pocket and pulled free the melted lump of bronze. "It's your raven-winged chape," said Algar, between weeping. "I found it by Cula's Ford!"

"Tell me about that day," his father uttered softly.

***

Aeva stood on the threshold of her lodging. Smoke whiffled from the reeded roof. She caught sight of Algar astride a grey horse; frantically, he waved to her as the animal moved effortlessly across the autumn turf. Behind the beast, a man was carrying two buckets of water. Seeing her, his face lit up, and he beamed from ear to ear.

Was she dreaming?! She called out a name in disbelief, slumping, suddenly, down upon the damp, yellowed grass.

The man—Thrydwulf-son-of-Coelwulf—came to the woman's side and lifted her gently to her feet, dragging her into his arms.

"I am back," he told the widow as she wept. "I have a tale of woe that begins with Oeric." He breathed deep, drooping his head in sorrow.

Aeva held him tight, lest he vanish upon the wind. Taking his hand, she led him into the warm fusty shelter at the edge of Ciselhyrst village.

"It was snowing that night…" Thrydwulf said softly. "Do you remember…?"

THE END

Fryn Hawkweaver is the pen name of
Lee Mitchell, author of
Gateway to Kazhelma.
He is also a singer/songwriter,
published music composer, and
poet.

He originally came from London, England, and now resides
in Montana, USA.

Please leave an honest review on Amazon.
Much appreciated.
Lee Mitchell.

367

JUST A FEW DEDICATIONS.
To people and their families:
Too many other fine folks to mention!

BILLY & NATASHA SMITH
CATHY MATTINGLY
CHRIS PARRY
CHRISTY MITCHELL
DAN BRANHAM
DAVE LEE
DEBBIE & STEVE ONEY
DEBBIE LAWRENCE
DOM (& the girls)
DOROTHY & LONNIE
LAWSON
EDDIE GREENWELL
HOWARD BRADEEN
JACKIE & RICK
JEANETTE & IVAN
WOLLERSHEIM
JESSE CULLINAN
JOHN PODVIN
KARAN & LEE MEECHAN
KELLY JO MITCHELL

KENTON HALL
KIKA WILLIAMS
KIM MITCHELL
MARCELLA SCOTSON
MARK & TAMSIN MITCHELL
MAUREEN ANN CADELL
MICHAEL ZARUTA
MY RAY (R.I.P.))
NUALA GARVEY
PARAMJIT DHILLON
PAT BUTLER
PAULINE MARIE CONWAY
SANDRA MCGUINESS
SARAH MITCHELL
SLETTEN CANCER
INSTITUTE
TERRY MCGUINESS
TONY MCGUINESS
VICTORIA SCOTT

Printed in Dunstable, United Kingdom